COR

A NOVEL OF THE
OREGON® FILES

BERKLEY BOOKS   NEW YORK

2

> "When the going gets tough, I read Clive Cussler,
> for no one can spin a yarn that's so thoroughly
> spellbinding and entertaining as he can."
> —Harold Coyle

> "Cussler is a master at building suspense and tension."
> —*Richmond Times-Dispatch*

CORSAIR

For five novels, Clive Cussler has brought readers into the world of the *Oregon*, a seemingly dilapidated ship packed with cutting-edge technology and captained by the daring Juan Cabrillo. Now the *Oregon* and its crew face their biggest challenge yet—with a danger torn from today's headlines . . .

The U.S. Secretary of State's plane has crashed en route to a summit in Libya. The CIA, distrusting the Libyans, hires Juan Cabrillo to search for her—and their misgivings are well founded. The crew locates the plane, but the diplomat has vanished, thanks to a deceitful Libyan minister with his own plans.

Plans Cabrillo cannot let happen.

But what does it all have to do with a two-centuries-old naval battle, and the even older Islamic scrolls the Libyans are so determined to find? The answers will lead Cabrillo and crew into the mists of history, and into a pitched battle against modern-day corsairs—with the fate of nations being decided on the high seas.

THE *NEW YORK TIMES* BESTSELLING NOVELS OF
THE *OREGON* FILES

PLAGUE SHIP • *SKELETON COAST* • *DARK WATCH* •
SACRED STONE • *GOLDEN BUDDHA*

"Readers will burn up the pages."   —*Publishers Weekly*

SAIR

CLIVE CUSSLER

with Jack Du Brul

THE BERKLEY PUBLISHING GROUP
Published by the Penguin Group
Penguin Group (USA) Inc.
375 Hudson Street, New York, New York 10014, USA
Penguin Group (Canada), 90 Eglinton Avenue East, Suite 700, Toronto, Ontario M4P 2Y3, Canada
(a division of Pearson Penguin Canada Inc.)
Penguin Books Ltd., 80 Strand, London WC2R 0RL, England
Penguin Group Ireland, 25 St. Stephen's Green, Dublin 2, Ireland (a division of Penguin Books Ltd.)
Penguin Group (Australia), 250 Camberwell Road, Camberwell, Victoria 3124, Australia
(a division of Pearson Australia Group Pty. Ltd.)
Penguin Books India Pvt. Ltd., 11 Community Centre, Panchsheel Park, New Delhi—110 017, India
Penguin Group (NZ), 67 Apollo Drive, Rosedale, North Shore 0632, New Zealand
(a division of Pearson New Zealand Ltd.)
Penguin Books (South Africa) (Pty.) Ltd., 24 Sturdee Avenue, Rosebank, Johannesburg 2196,
South Africa

Penguin Books Ltd., Registered Offices: 80 Strand, London WC2R 0RL, England

This is a work of fiction. Names, characters, places, and incidents either are the product of the authors'
imagination or are used fictitiously, and any resemblance to actual persons, living or dead, business
establishments, events, or locales is entirely coincidental. The publisher does not have any control
over and does not assume any responsibility for author or third-party websites or their content.

CORSAIR

A Berkley Book / published by arrangement with Sandecker, RLLLP

PRINTING HISTORY
G. P. Putnam's Sons hardcover edition / March 2009
Berkley international edition / March 2010

Copyright © 2009 by Sandecker, RLLLP.
Cover illustration copyright © 2009 by Craig White. Typographic styling by Lawrence Ratzkin.

ISBN: 978-0-425-23581-2

BERKLEY®
Berkley Books are published by The Berkley Publishing Group,
a division of Penguin Group (USA) Inc.,
375 Hudson Street, New York, New York 10014.
BERKLEY® is a registered trademark of Penguin Group (USA) Inc.
The "B" design is a trademark of Penguin Group (USA) Inc.

PRINTED IN THE UNITED STATES OF AMERICA

10 9 8 7 6 5 4 3 2 1

CORSAIR

". . . that it is founded on the Laws of their Prophet, that it is written in their Koran, that all nations who should not have acknowledged their authority were sinners, that it is their right and duty to make war upon them wherever they could be found, and to make slaves of all they could take as Prisoners, and that every Musselman who should be slain in Battle are sure to go to Paradisc."

—*Thomas Jefferson's testimony to the Continental Congress explaining the justification given to him by the Barbary ambassador to England, Sidi Haji Abdul Rahman Adja, concerning their preying on Christian ships, 1786*

"We ought not to fight them at all unless we determine to fight them forever."

—*John Adams on the Barbary pirates, 1787*

THE BAY OF TRIPOLI
FEBRUARY 1803

N O SOONER HAD THE SQUADRON SIGHTED THE FOR-
tified walls of the Barbary capital than a storm struck
suddenly, forcing the ketch *Intrepid* and the larger brig *Siren*
back out into the Mediterranean. Through his spyglass, Lieutenant Henry Lafayette, the *Siren*'s First Officer, had just by
chance spotted the towering masts of the USS *Philadelphia*,
the reason the two American warships had ventured so close
to the pirates' lair.

Six months earlier, the forty-four-gun *Philadelphia* had
chased a Barbary corsair too close to Tripoli's notoriously
treacherous harbor and grounded in the shallow shoals. At
the time, the frigate's captain, William Baimbridge, had done
all he could to save his ship, including heaving her cannons
over the side, but she was hard aground, and high tide was
hours away. Under threat of a dozen enemy gunboats, Baimbridge had no choice but to strike the colors and surrender the
massive warship to the Bashaw of Tripoli. Letters from the
Dutch Consul residing in the city reported that Baimbridge

and his senior officers were being treated well, but the fate of the *Philadelphia*'s crew, like that of most others who fell to the Barbary pirates, was slavery.

It was decided among the American commanders of the Mediterranean fleet that there was no hope of recapturing the *Philadelphia* and sailing her out of the harbor, so they determined she would burn instead. As to the fate of her crew, through intermediaries it was learned that Tripoli's head of state was amenable to releasing them for a cash settlement, totaling some half a million dollars.

For centuries, the pirates of the Barbary Coast had raided all along Europe's coastline, rampaging as far north as Ireland and Iceland. They had pillaged entire towns and carried captives back to North Africa, where the innocents languished as galley slaves, laborers, and, in the case of the more attractive women, as concubines in the various rulers' harems. The wealthiest captives were given the chance to be ransomed by their friends and family, but the poor faced a lifetime of drudgery and anguish.

In order to protect their merchant fleets, the great naval powers of England, Spain, France, and Holland paid exorbitant tributes to the three principal cities of the Barbary Coast—Tangiers, Tunis, and Tripoli—so the raiders would not attack their vessels. The fledgling United States, having been under the protection of the Union Jack until independence, also paid a tribute of nearly one-tenth her tax revenue to the potentates. That all changed when Thomas Jefferson took office as the third President, and he vowed that the practice would cease immediately.

The Barbary States, sensing a bluff by the young democracy, declared war.

Jefferson replied by dispatching an armada of American ships.

The very sight of the frigate *Constitution* convinced the Emperor of Tangiers to release all American sailors in his custody and renounce his demand for tribute. In return, Commodore Edward Preble returned to him the two Barbary merchant ships he'd already captured.

The Bashaw of Tripoli wasn't so impressed, especially

when his sailors captured the USS *Philadelphia* and renamed her *Gift of Allah*. Having taken one of America's capital ships, the Bashaw felt emboldened by his success and rebuffed any attempt at negotiation, save the immediate payment of his tribute. There was little concern on the Americans' part that the Barbary pirates would be able to sail the square-rigged ship and use her as a corsair, but the thought of a foreign flag hanging from her jack staff was enough to gall even the most novice seaman.

For five days after the Americans espied the *Philadelphia*, protected by the one hundred and fifty guns of Tripoli's inner harbor, the skies and seas raged in a battle as fierce as any aboard the two warships had seen. Despite the best efforts of their captains, the squadron became separated and drifted far to the east.

As bad as it was aboard the *Siren*, First Officer Lafayette couldn't imagine what the crew of the *Intrepid* faced during the tempest. Not only was the ketch much smaller than his ship, coming in at a mere sixty-four tons, but until the previous Christmas the *Intrepid* had been a slave ship called *Mastico*. She'd been captured by the *Constitution*, and when her holds were inspected the Americans discovered forty-two black Africans chained below. They were to be a gift of tribute to the Sultan in Istanbul from Tripoli's Bashaw.

No amount of lye could mask the stench of the human misery.

The storm finally abated on February twelfth, but it wasn't until the fifteenth that the two ships rendezvoused at sea and made their way back to Tripoli. That night, Captain Stephen Decatur, the squadron commander, convened a war council aboard the plucky little *Intrepid*. Henry Lafayette, along with eight heavily armed seamen, rowed over to join him.

"So you get to wait out the storm in comfort and now come aboard looking for glory, eh?" Decatur teased, reaching out to give Lafayette a hand over the low gunwale. He was a handsome, broad-shouldered man, with thick dark hair and captivating brown eyes, who wore the mantle of command easily.

"Wouldn't miss it for the world, sir," Lafayette replied.

Though the two men shared the same rank, were the same age, and had been friends since their midshipmen days, Lafayette deferred to Decatur as the squadron commander and captain of the *Intrepid*.

Henry was as tall as Decatur but had the slender build of a master fencer. His eyes were so dark they appeared black, and in the native garb he had donned as a disguise he cut as dashing a figure as the legendary pirate they hoped to one day face, Suleiman Al-Jama. Born in Quebec, Lafayette had crossed into Vermont as soon as he turned sixteen. He wanted to be part of America's experiment in democracy. He already spoke passable English, so he anglicized his first name from Henri and became an American citizen. He joined the Navy after a decade working the timber schooners of Lake Champlain.

There were eighty men crammed onto the sixty-foot ketch, though only a few wore disguises. The rest were to hide behind her gunwale or wait in the hold when the *Intrepid* sailed past the stone breakwater and into Tripoli's principal anchorage.

"Henry, I'd like you to meet Salvador Catalano. He's going to be our pilot once we near the harbor."

Catalano was thickset and swarthy, with a massive bush of a beard that spread across his chest. His head was covered with a filthy linen turban, and in his belt was stuck a wickedly curved knife with a red semiprecious stone set into its pommel.

"I assume he didn't volunteer," Lafayette whispered to Decatur as he moved to shake the pilot's hand.

"Cost us a king's ransom, he did," Decatur retorted.

"Pleased to meet you, Mr. Catalano," Henry said, grasping the Maltese's greasy palm. "And on behalf of the crew of the USS *Siren*, I want to thank you for your brave service."

Catalano threw a wide, gap-toothed grin. "The Bashaw's corsairs have raided my ships enough times that I thought this is fitting revenge."

"Good to have you with us," Lafayette replied absently. His attention was already on his new, temporary home.

The *Intrepid*'s two masts stood tall, but several of her stays sagged, and the sails she presented to the wind were salt-crusted and oft-patched. Though her deck had been scrubbed with both lye and stones, a fetid miasma rose from the oak timbers. Henry's eyes swam with the stench.

She was armed with only four small carronades, a type of naval cannon that slid on tracks mounted to the deck rather than rolling backward on wheels when fired. The men of the raiding party lay sprawled where they could find space on the deck, each with a musket and sword within easy reach. Most still looked like they were suffering the aftereffects of the five-day storm.

Henry grinned at Decatur. "Hell of a command you have here, sir."

"Aye, but she's mine. To the best of my knowledge, Mr. Lafayette, no one has yet called you captain in all your years of service."

"True enough"—Lafayette threw a smart salute—"Captain."

Another night would pass before the winds picked up enough for the *Intrepid* to make her approach on Tripoli. Through a brass telescope, Decatur and Lafayette watched the walled city slowly emerge from the vast, trackless desert. Spread along the high defensive wall and sprouting from the ramparts of the Bashaw's castle were more than a hundred and fifty guns. Because of the seawall, called the mole, which stretched across the anchorage, they could see only the tops of the *Philadelphia*'s three masts.

"What do you think?" Decatur asked Henry, whom he had appointed his First Officer for the attack. They stood shoulder to shoulder behind the Maltese pilot.

Henry looked up at the *Intrepid*'s spread of canvas and at the wake trailing behind the little ketch. He judged their speed to be four knots. "I think if we don't slow down we are going to enter the harbor long before sunset."

"Should I order the topsail and jib reefed, Captain?" asked Salvador Catalano.

"It's best we do. The moon's going to be bright enough later on."

Shadows lengthened until they began to merge, and the last

of the sun's rays set over the western horizon. The ketch entered
Tripoli Bay and began closing in on the imposing walls of the
Barbary city. The rising crescent moon made the stones of
the mole, fortress, and the Bashaw's castle gleam eerily, while
the black gun emplacements dotting the fortifications exuded
an air of menace. Peeking over the wall was the thin silhouette of a minaret, from which the men on the *Intrepid* had just
heard the call to prayer moments before sundown.

And at anchor directly below the castle lay the USS *Philadelphia*. She appeared in good shape, and the Americans
could see that her once-discarded cannons had been salvaged
and refitted in her gunports.

The sight of her sent conflicting emotions through Henry
Lafayette. He was stirred by her beautiful lines and sheer
size, while his anger boiled at the thought of the Tripolian
flag hanging over her stern and the knowledge that her three-
hundred-and-seven-man crew were hostages in the Bashaw's
prison. He would like nothing more than for Decatur to order
his men to swarm the castle and free the prisoners, but he
knew that command would never come to pass. Commodore
Preble, the commander of the entire Mediterranean squadron,
had made it clear that he wouldn't risk the Barbary pirates
getting more American prisoners than they already had.

Clustered around the harbor and tied along the breakwater
were dozens of other ships, lateen-rigged merchantmen and
rakish pirate craft bristling with cannons. Lafayette stopped
counting after twenty.

A new emotion tightened his chest. Fear.

If things didn't go as planned, the *Intrepid* would never
make it back out of the harbor, and every man aboard her
would be dead—or, worse, a prisoner destined for slavery.

Henry's mouth was suddenly dry, and the countless hours
he'd trained with his cutlass seemed not nearly enough.
The pair of mismatched .58-caliber flintlock pistols tucked
into the sash he'd wound around his waist felt puny. Then
he glanced down at the sailors hiding behind the *Intrepid*'s
gunwales. Armed with axes, pikes, swords, and daggers,
they looked to be as bloodthirsty as any Arab pirate. They

were the finest men in the world, volunteers all, and he knew they would carry the day. A midshipman was moving among them, making certain the squad leaders had their lamps lit and their lengths of whale-oil fuse ready.

He again looked to the *Philadelphia*. They were close enough now to see a trio of guards standing at her rail, their curved scimitars plainly visible. But with the wind so light, it took a further two hours before they were in comfortable hailing distance.

Catalano called out in Arabic, "Ahoy, there."

"What do you want?" one shouted back.

"I am Salvador Catalano," the Maltese pilot said, keeping to the script Decatur and Lafayette had worked out. "This is the ship *Mastico*. We are here to buy livestock for the British base on Malta but were caught in a storm. Our anchor was torn off so we cannot moor. I would like to tie up to your magnificent ship for the night. In the morning, we will dock properly and effect repairs."

"This is it," Decatur whispered to Henry. "If they don't go for it, we're going to be in trouble."

"They will. Look at us from their perspective. Would you be concerned about this little ketch?"

"No. Probably not."

The guard captain scratched his beard, eyeing the *Intrepid* warily, before finally shouting back, "You may tie up, but you must leave at dawn."

"Thank you. Allah has a special place in His heart for you," Catalano called out, then switched to English and whispered to the two officers. "They have agreed."

Lafayette stood at Decatur's shoulder as the light breeze slowly pushed the *Intrepid* closer and closer to the side of the *Philadelphia*. The big frigate's cannons were run out and the protective tampions removed from the barrels. The nearer they drew, the more the muzzles seemed to grow in size. If the pirates became suspicious, a broadside at this range would turn the ketch into kindling and rip the eighty men aboard to shreds.

Drawing nearer still, the pirates lining the rail were a good fifteen feet above the *Intrepid*'s deck. They began muttering among themselves and pointing as they made out the shapes of men cowering behind the ketch's gunwales.

Ten feet still separated the ships when one pirate shouted, *"Americanos!"*

"Tell your men to attack," Catalano wailed.

"No order to be obeyed but that of the commanding officer," Decatur said evenly.

Above them, the Barbary pirates were drawing their swords, and one fumbled with the blunderbuss strapped across his back. A cry went up just as the oak hulls came together, and Decatur shouted, "Board her!"

Henry Lafayette touched the Bible he kept on him at all times and leapt for an open gunport, hooking one hand around the wooden edge and clasping the warm bronze cannon with the other. He kicked his legs through the gap between the gun and the side of the ship and came up on his feet, his blade keening as he drew it from its scabbard. By the light of a single lamp hanging from the low ceiling, he saw two pirates wheeling back from another gunport as more men scrambled aboard. One of the pirates turned and saw him. The pirate's broad scimitar was suddenly in his hand as his bare feet pounded the decking. He shrieked as he charged, a technique most appropriate when confronting unarmed and untrained merchant sailors.

Henry wasn't fazed. The fear he had been sure would paralyze him had turned to cold rage.

He let the man come, and as the pirate began a hip-high cutting stroke that would have sliced Henry in half Henry stepped forward lightly and sank his blade into the other man's chest. The force of the pirate's charge ran the steel through his ribs and out his back. The heavy scimitar clattered to the deck as the corsair slumped against Lafayette. He had to use his knee as leverage to pull his blade from the pirate's chest. Henry whirled at a moving shadow and ducked under the swinging arc of an ax aimed at his shoulder. He countercut back with his sword, the edge slicing through cloth, skin, and muscle. He hadn't had the angle to eviscerate his foe, but the amount of blood that gushed from the wound told him the pirate was out of the fight.

The gun deck was a scene out of hell. Dark figures hacked and slashed at one another with abandon. The crash of steel on steel was punctuated by screams of pain when blade met skin. The air was charged with the smell of gunpowder, but above it Henry could detect the coppery scent of blood.

He waded into the fray. With its low ceilings, the gun deck wasn't an ideal field to battle with a sword or pike, but the Americans fought doggedly. One of them went down when he was struck from behind. Henry saw that the corsair who had hit him towered over everyone else. His turban almost brushed the support beams. He swung his scimitar at Henry, and, when Henry parried, the power of the blow made his entire arm go numb. The Arab swung again, and it took every ounce of strength for Lafayette to raise his blade enough to deflect the flashing sword.

He staggered back, and the pirate pressed his advantage, swinging wildly, keeping Henry on his back foot and always on the defensive. Decatur had been adamant during their planning that the raid was to be as silent as possible because of the massive pirate armada lying at anchor in the harbor. With his strength quickly waning, Lafayette had no choice but to yank his pistol from the sash around his waist. He pulled the trigger even before he had acquired his target. The small measure of powder in the pan flashed, and as the gun came up the main charge blew with a sharp report. The .58-caliber ball smashed into the pirate's chest.

The shot would have dropped a normal man to the deck before he had time to blink, but the giant kept coming. Henry had just an instant to raise his sword as the scimitar swiped at him again. His blade saved him from having his arm cut off, but the stunning momentum tossed him bodily across the gun deck. He fell against one of the *Philadelphia*'s eighteen-pounders. With Decatur's orders about silence still ringing in his ears, Lafayette fumbled for the lit oil lamp slung in a pouch around his waist and held the flame to the bronze cannon's touchhole. He could smell the powder charge burning, although the sizzle barely registered above the sounds of the fight still raging across the ship. He kept his body between the great gun and his attacker, trusting that with his years of experience manning naval cannons his timing would be perfect.

The pirate must have sensed his opponent was spent by the way Lafayette just stood there, as if accepting the inevitable. The pirate raised his Saracen sword and started to swing, his body anticipating the resistance of the blade cutting through flesh and bone. Then the American leapt aside. The Arab was too committed to check his swing or to notice the smoke coiling from the back of the cannon. It roared an instant later in a gush of sulfurous smoke.

There were thick hemp lines designed to retard the force of the recoil and keep the gun from careening across the deck, but they still let the cannon rocket back several feet. The butt of the gun hit the pirate square in the groin, shattering his pelvis, crushing his hip joints, and splintering both thighbones. His limp body was flung against a beam, and he collapsed to the deck, folded in half—backward.

Henry took a second to peer out the gunport. The eighteen-pound cannonball had smashed into the fortress across the harbor, and an avalanche of rubble tumbled from the gaping hole.

"Two with one shot. Not bad, *mon ami* Henri, not bad at all." It was John Jackson, the big bosun.

"If Captain Decatur asks, it was one of these rotters who fired the gun, eh?"

"That's what I saw, Mr. Lafayette."

The cannon going off had acted like a starter's pistol at the beginning of a race. The Arab pirates abandoned their defense and began rushing for the gunports, leaping and falling into the calm waters of the harbor. Those scrambling up the ladders for the main deck would doubtless run into Decatur and his men.

"Let's get to work."

The men returned to the starboard side of the ship where crewmates aboard the *Intrepid* were standing by, ready to start passing combustibles up to the raiding party. Followed by Jackson and six others burdened with kegs of black powder, Henry Lafayette descended a ladder, passing crews' quarters where hammocks still hung from the rafters but all other gear had been scavenged. They dropped lower still, to the orlop deck, the lowest on the frigate, and entered one of the ship's holds. Most of the naval stores had been taken, but enough remained for the men to start burning the frigate.

They worked quickly. Henry decided where they would lay their fuses, and when they were set he lit them with his oil lamp. The flames grew quickly, much quicker than any of them had anticipated. In an instant, the hold filled with reeking smoke. They started back up, holding their sleeves over their mouths so they could breathe. The ceiling above them suddenly burst into flames with a roar like a cannon blast. John Jackson was knocked off his feet and would have been crushed by a burning timber if Henry hadn't grabbed one of his legs and dragged him across the rough planking. He helped the bosun up, and they started running, their team at their heels. They had to leap and duck as chunks of flaming wood continued to crash down from above.

They reached a ladder, and Henry turned, urging his men upward. "Go, go, go, damn you, or we're going to die down here."

He followed Jackson's ponderous rump as a jet of fire raced down the corridor. Henry rammed his shoulder into Jackson's backside and heaved with everything he had. The two emerged from the hatch, rolling to the side, as a volcanic eruption of flame bellowed up from the hold, hit the ceiling, and spread like an unholy canopy.

They were in a sea of fire. The walls, deck, and ceiling were sheathed in flames, while the smoke was so thick that tears streamed from Henry's eyes. Running blindly, he and Jackson found the next ladder and emerged on the gun deck. Smoke streamed out the ports, but enough fresh air reached them that for the first time in five minutes they could fill their lungs without coughing.

A small explosion shook the *Philadelphia*, knocking Henry into John Jackson.

"Let's go, lad."

They clambered out one of the ports. Men on the *Intrepid* were there to help them settle in on the small ketch. Crewmen slapped Henry's back several times. He thought they were congratulating him on a job well done, but in fact they were putting out the smoldering cloth of his native shirt.

Above them on the rail, Stephen Decatur stood with one boot up on the bulwark.

"Captain," Lafayette shouted, "lower decks are clear."

"Very good, Lieutenant." He waited for a couple of his men to climb down ropes and then descended to his ship.

The *Philadelphia* was engulfed in fire. Flames shot from her gunports and were starting to climb her rigging. Soon, the heat would be intense enough to cook off the powder charges in her cannons, eight of which were aimed directly at the *Intrepid*.

The forward line holding the ketch to the frigate was cast off easily enough, but the stern line jammed. Henry pushed men aside and drew his sword. The rope was nearly an inch thick, and his blade, dulled by combat, still sliced it clean with one blow.

With the fire consuming so much air, the ketch couldn't fill her sails, and the jib was dangerously close to tangling with the *Philadelphia*'s burning rigging. The men used oars to try to force their vessel away from the floating pyre, but as soon as they pushed free the conflagration drew them back in again.

Bits of burning sail from the frigate's mainmast fell like confetti. One sailor's hair caught fire.

"Henry," Decatur bellowed, "unship the boat and tow us free."

"Aye, aye."

Henry, Jackson, and four others lowered the dinghy. With a line secured to the *Intrepid*'s bow, they pulled away from the ketch. When the rope came taut, they heaved against the oars, straining to gain inches. When they pulled the paddles from the water for another stroke, half the distance they had gained was lost to the fire-born wind.

"Pull, you sons of dogs," Henry shouted. "Pull!"

And they did. Heaving against the sixty-four deadweight

tons of their ship and the powerful suction of the fire, they fought stubbornly. The men hauled on the oars until the vertebrae crackled in their backs and veins bulged from their necks. They pulled their ship and crew away from the *Philadelphia* until Decatur could get sails up her mainmast and fill them with the slight breeze now blowing in from the desert.

There was a sudden bloom of light high up on the castle wall. A moment later came the concussive roar of a cannon. The shot landed well beyond the ketch and rowboat, but it was followed by a dozen more. The water came alive with tiny dimples—small-arms fire from lookouts and guards running along the breakwater.

Aboard the *Intrepid*, men manned the oars, rowing for everything they were worth, while behind them the *Philadelphia* suddenly flared as the remainder of her canvas caught fire.

For twenty tense minutes, the men pulled while, around them, shot after shot hit the water. One ball passed through the *Intrepid*'s topgallant sail, but other than that the ship wasn't struck. The small-arms fire died away first, and then they were beyond the reach of the Bashaw's cannons. The exhausted men collapsed into each other, laughing and singing. In their wake, the walls of the fortress were lit with the wavering glow of the burning ship.

Henry brought the dinghy about and slipped it under the davits.

"Well done, my friend." Decatur was smiling, his face reflecting the ethereal glimmer behind them.

Too exhausted to do anything but pant, Henry threw Decatur a weak salute.

All eyes suddenly turned toward the harbor as the raging towers that were the *Philadelphia*'s masts slowly collapsed across her port side in an explosion of sparks. And then, as a final salute, her guns cooked off, an echoing cannonade that sent some balls across the water and others into the castle walls.

The men roared at her act of defiance against the Barbary pirates.

"What now, Captain?" Lafayette asked.

Decatur stared across the sea, not looking at Henry when he spoke. "This won't end tonight. I recognized one of the corsairs in the harbor. It was Suleiman Al-Jama's. She's called the *Saqr*. It means 'falcon.' You can bet your last penny that he's making ready to sail against us this very moment. The Bashaw won't take vengeance on our captured sailors for what we did tonight—they are too valuable to him—but Al-Jama will want revenge."

"He was once a holy man, right?"

"Up until a few years ago," Decatur agreed. "He was what the Muslims called an Imam. Kind of like a priest. Such was his hate for Christendom that he decided preaching wasn't enough, and he took up arms against any and all ships not flying a Muslim flag."

"I heard tell that he takes no prisoners."

"I've heard the same. The Bashaw can't be too happy about that since prisoners can be ransomed, but he holds little sway over Al-Jama. The Bashaw made a deal with the devil when he let Al-Jama occasionally stage out of Tripoli. I've also heard he has no end of volunteers to join him when he goes raiding. His men are suicidal in their devotion to him.

"Your rank-and-file Barbary pirate sees what he is doing as a profession, a way to make a living. It is something they've been doing for generations. You saw tonight how most of them fled the *Philadelphia* as soon as we boarded. They weren't going to get themselves killed in a fight they couldn't win.

"But Al-Jama's followers are a different breed altogether. This is a holy calling for them. They even have a word for it: jihad. They will fight to the death if it means they can take one more infidel with them."

Henry thought about the big pirate who had come at him relentlessly, battling on even after he'd been shot. He wondered if he was one of Al-Jama's followers. He hadn't gotten a look at the man's eyes, but he'd sensed a berserker insanity to the pirate, that somehow killing an American was more important to him than preventing the *Philadelphia* from being burned.

"Why do you think they hate us?" he asked.

Decatur looked at him sharply. "Lieutenant Lafayette, I have never heard a more irrelevant question in my life." He took a breath. "But I'll tell you what I think. They hate us because we exist. They hate us because we are different from them. But, most important, they hate us because they think they have the right to hate us."

Henry remained silent for a minute, trying to digest Decatur's answer, but such a belief system was so far beyond him he couldn't get his mind around it. He had killed a man tonight and yet he hadn't hated him. He was just doing what he'd been ordered to do. Period. It hadn't been personal and he couldn't fathom how anyone could make it so.

"What are your orders, Captain?" he finally asked.

"The *Intrepid*'s no match for the *Saqr*, especially as overcrowded as we are. We'll link up with the *Siren* as we planned, but rather than return to Malta in convoy I want you and the *Siren* to stay out here and teach Suleiman Al-Jama that the American Navy isn't afraid of him or his ilk. Tell Captain Stewart that he is not to fail."

Henry couldn't keep the smile off his face. For two years, they had seen little action, with the exception of capturing the *Intrepid* and now burning the *Philadelphia*. He was excited to take the fight to the corsairs directly.

"If we can capture or kill him," he said, "it will do wonders for our morale."

"And severely weaken theirs."

• • •

AN HOUR AFTER DAWN, the lookout high atop the *Siren*'s mainmast called down, "Sail! Sail ho! Five points off the starboard beam."

Henry Lafayette and Lieutenant Charles Stewart, the ship's captain, had been waiting for this since sunup.

"About damned time," Stewart said.

At just twenty-five years of age, Stewart had received his commission a month before the Navy was officially established by Congress. He had grown up with Stephen Decatur, and, like him, Stewart was a rising star in the Navy. Shipboard scuttlebutt had it that he would receive a promotion to captain before the fleet returned to the United States. He had a slender build, and a long face with wide-apart, deep-set eyes. He was a firm but fair disciplinarian, and whatever ship he served on was consistently considered lucky by its crew.

Sand in the hourglass drizzled down for ten minutes before the lookout shouted again. "She's running parallel to the coast."

Stewart grunted. "Bugger must suspect we're out here, number one. He's trying to end around us and then tack after the *Intrepid*." He then addressed Bosun Jackson, who was the ship's sailing master. "Let go all sails."

Jackson bellowed the order up to the men hanging in the rigging, and in a perfectly choreographed flurry of activity a dozen sails unfurled off the yards and blossomed with the freshening breeze. The foremast and mainmast creaked with the strain as the two-hundred-and-forty-ton ship started carving through the Mediterranean.

Stewart glanced over the side at the white water streaming along the ship's oak hull. He estimated their speed at ten knots, and knew they would do another five in this weather.

"She's spotted us," the lookout shouted. "She's piling on more sail."

"There isn't a lateen-rigged ship in these waters that's faster than us," Henry said.

"Aye, but he draws half the water we do. If he wants, he can stay in close to shore and beyond the range of our guns."

"When I spoke with Captain Decatur, I had the impression this Suleiman Al-Jama isn't afraid of a fight."

"You think he'll come out to meet us?"

"Decatur thinks so."

"Good."

For the next fourteen hours, the *Siren* doggedly pursued the *Saqr*. With a greater spread of canvas, the American brig was several knots faster than Al-Jama's raider, but the Arab captain knew these waters better than anyone. Time and again he would lure the *Siren* dangerously close to shoals and force her to tack off the chase in search of deeper water. The *Saqr* also managed to find stronger winds close to the shore, winds driven off the searing desert beyond the cliffs that towered over the coastline in unending ramparts.

The gap between the ships noticeably shrank when the sun started to set and the inshore breeze slowed.

"We'll have him within the hour," Stewart said, accepting a glass of tepid water from his cabin steward.

He surveyed the open gun deck. Crews were standing by their cannons, the keen edge of expectation in their eyes. Shot and powder charges were laid in and at the ready, though not too much in case a gun took a direct hit. Powder monkeys—boys as young as ten—were ready to scamper back and forth to the magazine to keep the weapons fed. Men were aloft in the rigging, ready to alter sail as the battle dictated. And pairs of Marine marksmen were making their way to the fighting tops on the foremast and mainmast. Two were brothers from Appalachia, and while no one on the crew could understand them when they spoke they both could load and shoot four times a minute and score bull's-eyes with all four shots.

Two white plumes suddenly obscured the *Saqr*'s fantail, and a moment later came the boom of the shots. One ball landed fifty yards off the *Intrepid*'s port bow while the other landed well astern.

Stewart and Lafayette looked at each other. Henry gave voice to their mutual concern. "Her stern chasers are long guns. Double our range at the very least."

"Mr. Jackson, come about to port ten degrees," Stewart ordered, to throw off the *Saqr*'s gunners. "Standing order for a similar maneuver with every shot fired. Turn toward where the closest ball falls."

"And your orders if we're hit?" the big bosun asked before he could stop himself.

Stewart could have had Jackson lashed for such an insolent comment; instead, he said, "Dock yourself a day's pay, and hope we have more ship than you have salary."

The wind close to shore suddenly died. The *Saqr*'s large triangular sails lost tension and flapped uselessly while those aboard the *Intrepid* remained taut. They came in astern of the pirate ship at a slight angle, so as to avoid her aft guns. At a hundred and fifty yards, three of the *Saqr*'s cannons fired, blowing a wall of smoke over the corsair's flank that completely hid her from view. Two rounds went high, while the third struck the *Siren*'s hull but didn't penetrate.

Stewart remained silent, closing the distance, increasing his chances of a hit with each foot gained. He saw they weren't yet targeted by any of the other guns, so he waited until the Arab crew was running out the weapons they had just cleaned and reloaded.

"Fire as you bear!"

Four carronades went off with one throaty roar that beat in on Henry's chest as if he'd been kicked. The bow was enveloped in smoke that whipped along the length of the *Intrepid*'s hull as she charged the *Saqr*. On the fighting tops, the Marines were busy with their muskets, picking off pirates on the *Saqr*'s deck who thought they were invisible behind the ship's railings.

Two more cannons roared before anyone could see if their first salvo scored. The *Saqr* responded with a raking broadside that had been perfectly aimed. One ball smashed a carronade with a lit fuse, knocking the weapon on its side as it fired. That ball hit the adjacent gun crew, killing two men and maiming another. Bags of powder burned like incandescent flares. Another of the *Saqr*'s shots smashed the *Intrepid*'s mainmast, though not enough to topple it, while others ripped needle-sharp splinters from the bulwarks with enough velocity to run a man through.

"Mr. Jackson," Stewart shouted over the sounds of battle, "take some sail off the mainmast before we lose it entirely. Mr. Lafayette, take charge up on the bow. Get those fires out and the carronades sorted."

"Aye, aye, sir." Henry threw a quick salute and raced for the bow as musket fire from the *Saqr* raked the decks.

He looked over to see a fire raging on the Barbary ship. The *Intrepid* was giving as good as she got. He could see one figure shouting orders, not in a panicked way but with a calm that belied the situation. He wore clean white robes and had a contrasting dark beard shot through with two lines of white whiskers falling from the corners of his mouth. His nose was large and so heavily hooked it could almost touch his upper lip.

Suleiman Al-Jama must have felt the scrutiny, because he chose that moment to look across at the American ship. At a hundred yards, Henry could feel the hatred radiating off the man. A fresh blast from the guns obscured the pirate captain for a moment, and Henry had to duck as the railing behind him burst apart. When he looked again, Al-Jama was still staring.

Henry looked away.

He reached the bow and quickly organized a bucket brigade to douse the flames. The one carronade that had been hit was destroyed, but the gun next to it was in good order. Henry took command of it himself. The teenage midshipman who had been in charge of this section of guns was burned beyond recognition.

He aimed the loaded gun and touched the fuse with a length of smoldering slow match. The gun bellowed, sliding back on its guide rails in the blink of an eye. Lafayette had men swabbing the barrel before he checked the *Saqr* for damage. Their ball had hit next to one of the gunports, and through the hole it had blown into the wood he could see that men were down, writhing in agony.

"Reload!"

At nearly point-blank range the two ships pounded on each other like prizefighters who don't know when to quit. It was getting darker now, but they were so close that the crews could aim using the glow of the fires that flashed and ebbed.

The weight of shot from the *Saqr* began to die down. The Americans were destroying her cannons one by one. And when no return fire came from the Tripolian vessel for nearly a minute, Stewart ordered the *Siren* in tighter.

"Boarding parties at the ready."

Sailors took up grappling hooks to bind the two ships fast, while others passed out pikes, axes, and swords. Henry checked the priming pans of the two pistols tucked into his belt and drew his cutlass.

Pushing a swell of white water off her bow, the *Siren*

charged the *Saqr* like a bull, and when the ships were a dozen feet apart the hooks were thrown. The instant the hulls smashed into each other, Henry leapt across to the other ship.

No sooner had his feet touched the deck than a series of blistering explosions raced along the length of the pirate vessel. Her cannons hadn't been silenced at all. They had pretended to be unarmed to lure the *Siren* in close. Twelve guns poured their shot into the American brig, raking the line of men at her rail. Stewart had to veer off sharply. Sailors hacked at the grappling ropes in a desperate bid to get free.

Seeing his shipmates cut down like that pained Henry as if it were his own flesh torn apart. But he didn't have time to jump back aboard before his ship had put twenty feet between herself and the pirate vessel. He was trapped on the *Saqr*. Musket balls from the Marines whined over his head.

The Arabs manning the *Saqr*'s guns hadn't noticed him leap. The only course open to Henry was to jump into the sea and pray he was a strong enough swimmer to reach the distant shore. He started creeping for the far rail and had almost made it when a figure suddenly loomed above him.

He instinctively went on the charge before the man could fully comprehend what he was seeing. Henry pulled one of his pistols with his left hand and fired an instant before his shoulder collided with the man's chest.

As they tumbled over the railing, he recognized the distinctive white streaks in the other man's beard: Suleiman Al-Jama.

They hit the bath-warm water tangled together. Henry broke the surface to find Al-Jama next to him, gasping to fill his lungs. He was thrashing wildly, but oddly, too. It was then that Henry noticed the dark stain on the otherwise white robe. The ball from his pistol had hit the captain at the shoulder joint, and he couldn't lift that arm.

Looking quickly, he saw the *Saqr* was already fifty feet away and was again trading broadsides with the *Siren*. There was no way anyone on either ship could hear Henry shouting, so he didn't bother.

Al-Jama's efforts to keep his head above water were growing weaker. He still couldn't get his lungs to reinflate, and his heavy robes were dragging him under. Henry had been a strong swimmer his entire life, but it was clear the Arab was not. His head vanished below the surface for a moment, and he came up sputtering. But not once did he cry out for help.

He went under again, longer this time, and when he returned to the surface he could barely keep his lips out of the water. Henry kicked off his heavy boots and used his dirk to slice open Al-Jama's robe. The clothing floated free, but Al-Jama wouldn't last another minute.

The coastline was at least three miles distant, and Henry Lafayette wasn't sure if he could make it at all let alone while towing the pirate, but Suleiman Al-Jama's life was in his hands now and he had the responsibility to do everything in his power to save him.

He reached around Al-Jama's bare chest. The captain thrashed to push him off.

Henry said, "The moment we fell off the ship, you stopped being my enemy, but I swear to God that if you fight me I'll let you drown."

"I would rather," Suleiman replied in heavily accented English.

"Have it your way, then." With that, Henry pulled his second pistol and smashed it into Al-Jama's temple. Grabbing the unconscious man under one arm, he started paddling for shore.

ONE

S T. JULIAN PERLMUTTER SHIFTED HIS CONSIDERABLE bulk in the backseat of his 1955 Rolls-Royce Silver Dawn. He plucked a tulip flute of vintage champagne off the fold-down table in front of him, took a delicate sip, and continued reading. Stacked next to the champagne and a plate of canapés were photocopies of letters sent to Admiral Charles Stewart over the length of his incredible career. Stewart had served every President from John Adams to Abraham Lincoln, and had been awarded more commands than any officer in American history. The original letters were safely tucked away in the Rolls's trunk.

As perhaps the leading naval historian in the world, Perlmutter deplored the fact that some philistine had subjected the letters to the ravages of a photocopier—light damages paper and fades ink—but he wasn't above taking advantage of the gaffe, and he started reading the copies as soon as he had settled in for the drive back from Cherry Hill, New Jersey.

He'd been after this collection for years, and it had taken his considerable charm, and a rather large check, to see that it wasn't given to the government and archived in some out-of-the-way location. If the letters turned out to be uninteresting, he planned to keep the copies for reference and donate the originals for the tax benefit.

He glanced out the window. The traffic into the nation's capital was murder, as usual, but Hugo Mulholland, his long-time chauffeur and assistant, seemed to be handling it well. The Rolls glided down I-95 as if it were the only car on the road.

The collection had passed through numerous generations of the Stewart family, but the branch that held them now was dying out. The only child of Mary Stewart Kilpatrick, whose row house Perlmutter had just left, had no interest in it, and her only grandchild was severely autistic. St. Julian really didn't begrudge the price he'd paid, knowing the money would help support the boy.

The letter he was reading was to the Secretary of War, Joel Roberts Poinsett, and had been written during Stewart's first command of the Philadelphia Navy Yard between 1838 and 1841. The letter's contents were rather dry: lists of supplies needed, progress on the repairs of a frigate, remarks about the quality of sails they had received. Though competent at his job, it was clear in the writing that Stewart would much rather captain a ship again than oversee the facility.

Perlmutter set it aside, popped a canapé in his mouth, and washed it down with another sip of champagne. He leafed through a couple more letters, settling on one written to Stewart by a bosun who had served under his command during the Barbary Wars. The writing was barely legible, and the author, one John Jackson, appeared to have had limited schooling. He reminisced about being a part of the raid to burn the USS *Philadelphia* and the subsequent gun battle with a pirate ship called the *Saqr*.

St. Julian was well aware of these exploits. He'd read Captain Decatur's firsthand account of the burning of the American frigate, although there wasn't much material on the fight with the *Saqr* other than Stewart's own report to the War Department.

Reading the letter, St. Julian could almost smell the gun smoke and hear the screams as the *Saqr* lured the *Siren* in close, then let loose with a surprise broadside.

In the letter, Jackson asked the admiral about the fate of the brig's second-in-command, Henry Lafayette. Perlmutter recalled that the young lieutenant had leapt aboard the Tripolian ship a moment before her cannons fired, and he presumably had been killed since no ransom had ever been asked for his return.

He read on, piqued as he realized he had it wrong. Jackson had seen Lafayette fighting the *Saqr*'s captain, and both had gone over the port rail together. "The lad fell into the sea with that fiend (spelled *feinde*) Suleiman Al-Jama."

The name jolted Perlmutter. It wasn't the historical context that surprised him—he dimly recalled the *Saqr*'s captain's name. Rather, it was the present-day incarnation of the name that tripped him up: Suleiman Al-Jama was the nom de guerre of a terrorist only slightly less wanted than Osama bin Laden.

The *modern* Al-Jama had starred in several beheading videos and was the spiritual inspiration for countless suicide bombers throughout the Middle East, Pakistan, and Afghanistan. His crowning achievement had been leading an assault on a remote Pakistani Army outpost that left more than a hundred soldiers dead.

St. Julian searched through the letters to see if Stewart had responded and kept a copy, as had been his practice. Sure enough, the next letter in the stack was addressed to John Jackson. He read it once, rushing through it in astonishment, then read it again more slowly. He sat back so the leather seat creaked under his weight. He wondered if there were any contemporary implications to what he had just read and decided there probably weren't.

He was about to start perusing another letter when he reconsidered. What if the government could use this information? What would it gain them? Most likely nothing, but he didn't think it was his call to make.

Normally, when he came across something interesting in his research, he would pass it along to his good friend Dirk Pitt, the Director of the National Underwater and Marine Agency, but he wasn't sure if this fell under NUMA's sphere of influence quite yet. Perlmutter was an old Washington hand and had contacts throughout the city. He knew just who to call.

The car's telephone had a Bakelite handset and rotary dial. Perlmutter detested cell phones and never carried one. His thick finger barely fit in the telephone dial's little holes, but he managed.

"Hello," a woman answered.

St. Julian had called her direct line, thus avoiding an army of assistants.

"Hi, Christie, it's St. Julian Perlmutter."

"St. Julian!" Christie Valero cried. "It's been ages. How have you been?"

Perlmutter rubbed his bulging stomach. "You know me. I'm wasting away to nothing."

"I'm sure that's the case." She laughed. "Have you made my mother's Coquilles St.-Jacques since you cajoled her secret recipe out of me?"

Apart from his vast knowledge of ships and shipping, Perlmutter was a legendary gourmand and bon vivant.

"It's now part of my regular repertoire," he assured her. "Whenever you'd like, give me a call and I'll make it for you."

"I'll take you up on that. You know I can't follow cooking instructions more sophisticated than 'Pierce outer wrapper to vent and place on microwave-safe dish.' So is this a social call or is there something on your mind? I'm a little swamped here. The conference is still months away, but the dragon lady is running us ragged."

"That is no way to refer to her," he admonished mildly.

"Are you kidding? Fiona loves it."

"I'll take your word for it."

"So what's up?"

"I've just now come across something rather interesting and I thought you might like first crack at it." He relayed what he'd read in Charles Stewart's letter to his former shipmate.

When he finished, Christie Valero had just one question. "How soon can you be in my office?"

"Hugo," St. Julian said when he replaced the telephone on its cradle, "change of plans. We're going to Foggy Bottom. Our Undersecretary of State for Mideast Affairs would like to have a chat."

TWO

THE INDIAN OCEAN WAS A SHIMMERING JEWEL, PER-
fectly clear and blue. But on its surface was a flaw in
the shape of a five-hundred-and-sixty-foot freighter. The ship
was barely making headway, though her single stack belched
copious amounts of noxious black smoke. It was clear the
vessel was plying the sea-lanes far beyond her intended life
span.

She was so low in the water that she had been forced on a
circuitous route from Mumbai to avoid any storms because
seas much above four feet would wash across her deck. Her
port side would ship water in smaller swells because she
had a slight list to that side. The hull was painted a scabrous
green, with patches of other colors where the crew had run
out of the primary shade. Tongues of scaly rust ran from her
scuppers, and large metal plates had been welded to her sides
to shore up structural deficiencies.

The tramp freighter's superstructure was just aft of amidships, giving her three cargo holds on her foredeck and two
aft. The three cranes towering over the decks were heavily

rusted and their cables frayed. The decks themselves were littered with leaky barrels, broken machinery, and clutter. Where pieces of her railing had rusted away, the crew had hung lengths of chain.

To the men studying her from a nearby fishing boat, the freighter didn't appear promising, but they were in no position to ignore the opportunity she presented.

The Somali captain was a wiry, hatchet-faced man missing a tooth in the center of his mouth. The other teeth around the gap were badly rotted, and his gums were black with decay. He conferred with the three other men on the crowded bridge before plucking a hand mic from the two-way transceiver and thumbing the button. "Ahoy, nearby freighter." His English was heavily accented but passable.

A moment later a voice burst over the tinny speaker. "Is this the fishing boat off my port beam?"

"Yes. We are in need of doctor," the captain said. "Four of my men are very sick. Do you have?"

"One of our crew was a Navy medic. What are their symptoms?"

"I do not know this word *sim-toms*."

"How are they sick?" the radio operator on the freighter asked.

"They throw up bad for days. Bad food, I think."

"Okay. I think we can handle that. Come abeam of us just ahead of the superstructure. We will slow as much as we can, but we won't be able to stop completely. Do you understand?"

"Yes, yes. I understand. You no stop. Is okay." He shot a wolfish grin at his comrades, saying in his native tongue, "They believe me. They're not going to stop, probably because the engines wouldn't refire, but that isn't a problem. Abdi, take the helm. Put us alongside near the superstructure and match their speed."

"Yes, Hakeem."

"Let's get on deck," the captain said to the other two.

They met up with four men who had been in the cabin below the wheelhouse. These men had ragged blankets draped over their thin shoulders and moved as if crippled with cramps.

The freighter dwarfed the sixty-foot fishing boat, though with her so low in the water the ship's rail wasn't that far above their own. Crewmen had hung truck tires for fenders and retracted a section of railing near the superstructure to make it easier to transfer the stricken men aboard. Hakeem counted four of them. One, a short Asian man, wore a uniform shirt with black epaulettes. Another was a large African or Caribbean islander, and the other two he wasn't sure.

"Are you the captain?" Hakeem called to the officer.

"Yes. Captain Kwan."

"Thank you for doing this. My men are very sick, but we must stay at sea to catch fish."

"It is my duty," Kwan said rather haughtily. "Your boat will have to stay close by while we treat your men. We're headed to the Suez Canal and can't detour to take them ashore."

"That is not a problem," Hakeem said with an oily smile as he handed up a line. The African crewman secured it to a rail stanchion.

"Okay, let's have them," Kwan said.

Hakeem helped one of his men step onto their boat's railing. The gap between the two vessels was less than a foot, and in these calm seas there was little chance of his slipping. The two of them stepped up and across to the freighter's deck and moved aside for two more at their heels.

It was when the fourth jumped nimbly onto his ship that Captain Kwan became wary.

As he opened his mouth to question the seriousness of their condition, the four men with the blankets let them drop away. Concealed underneath were AK-47s with the wooden butts crudely cut off. Aziz and Malik, the two other crewmen from the fishing boat, grabbed matching weapons from a wooden chest and rushed aboard.

"Pirates!" Kwan yelled, and had the muzzle of one weapon rammed into his stomach.

He dropped to his knees, clutching his abdomen. Hakeem

pulled an automatic pistol from behind his back while the other armed men hustled the freighter's crew away from the rail and out of sight of anyone who may have been on the bridge wing high overhead.

The Somali leader dragged the captain to his feet, pressing the barrel of his pistol into Kwan's neck. "Do as you are told and no one will be hurt."

There was a momentary spark of defiance behind Kwan's eyes, something he couldn't suppress, but it was fleeting, and the pirate hadn't noticed. He nodded awkwardly.

"You will take us to the radio room," Hakeem continued. "You will make an announcement to your crew that they are to go to the mess hall. Everyone must be there. If we find anyone walking around the ship, he will be killed."

While he was talking, his men were cuffing the stunned crew with plastic zip ties. They used three on the muscle-bound black man, just in case.

While Aziz and Malik took charge of the other crewmen, Kwan led Hakeem and the four "sick" pirates into the superstructure, a pistol pressed to his spine. The interior of the ship was only a few degrees cooler than outside, thanks to a barely functioning air-conditioning system. The halls and passageways looked as if they hadn't been cleaned since the freighter had slipped down the ways. The linoleum flooring was cracked and peeling, and dust bunnies the size of jack-rabbits lurked in every corner.

It took less than a minute to climb up to the bridge, where a helmsman stood behind the large wooden wheel and another officer was hunched over a chart table littered with plates of congealing food and a chart so old and faded it could have depicted the coastline of Pangaea. The windows were nearly opaque with rimed salt.

"How'd it go with the fishermen?" the officer asked without looking up. His voice had an odd British inflection that wasn't quite right. He lifted his head and blanched. His big, innocent eyes went wide. The four pirates had the entire room covered with their assault rifles, and the captain's head was bent sideways with the pressure of the pistol jammed into his neck.

"No heroics," Kwan said. "They promised not to harm anyone if we just follow their orders. Open a shipwide channel please, Mr. Maryweather."

"Aye, Captain." Moving deliberately, the young officer, Duane Maryweather, reached for the intercom button located next to the ship's radio. He handed the microphone to his captain.

Hakeem screwed the pistol deeper into Kwan's neck. "If you give any warning, I will kill you now, and my men will slaughter your crew."

"You have my word," Kwan said tightly. He keyed the mic, and his voice echoed from loudspeakers placed all over the vessel. "This is the captain speaking. There is a mandatory meeting in the mess hall for all crew members immediately. On-duty engineering staff are not exempt."

"That is enough," Hakeem snapped, and took away the microphone. "Abdul, take the wheel." He waved his pistol at Maryweather and the helmsman. "You two, over next to the captain."

"You can't leave just one man at the helm," Kwan protested.

"This is not the first ship we have taken."

"No. I suppose it isn't."

With no discernible government, Somalia was ruled by rival warlords, some of whom had turned to piracy to fund their armies. The waters of this Horn of Africa country were some of the most dangerous in the world. Ships were attacked on an almost daily basis, and while the United States and other nations maintained a naval presence in the region, the seas were simply too vast to protect every ship that steamed along the coast. Pirates usually used fast speedboats and mostly robbed the ships of any cash or valuables, but what started out as simple larceny had expanded. Now entire ships were being hijacked, their cargoes sold on the black market and their crews either abandoned in lifeboats, held for ransom to the vessel's owners, or killed outright.

So, too, had the sizes of the targeted ships increased along with the savagery of the attacks. Where once only small coastal freighters were the primary targets, the pirates now preyed on tankers and containerships, and had once raked a cruise liner with automatic fire for fifteen minutes. Recently, a new warlord had started putting a stranglehold on other pirates along the north coast, consolidating his power base until every pirate in the region was loyal to him alone.

His name was Mohammad Didi, and he'd been a fighter in the capital, Mogadishu, during the chaotic days of the mid-1990s, when the United Nations was trying to stave off epidemic starvation in the drought-ridden country. He had secured a name for himself plundering trucks loaded with emergency food and supplies, but it was during the Black Hawk Down incident that he cemented his reputation. He had led the charge against an American position and destroyed a Humvee with an RPG. He had then dragged the bodies from the burning wreckage and hacked them to pieces with a machete.

After the inglorious withdrawal of the U.S. Marine Corps, Didi continued to build his power base until he was one of only a handful of warlords controlling the country. Then, in 1998, he had been linked to the Al-Qaeda bombings of the American embassies in Kenya and Tanzania. He had given the bombers safe haven for the weeks leading up to the attack, as well as several men to act as lookouts. With an indictment at the World Court in The Hague and a half-million-dollar price on his head, Didi knew it was only a matter of time before one of his rivals would try to collect on the bounty. He moved his operation out of Mogadishu and into an area of coastal swamps three hundred miles to the north.

Before his arrival, most victims of piracy were set free immediately. It was Didi who had initiated the ransom demands. And if they were not met, or the negotiations seemed to be faltering, he unceremoniously had the crews killed. It was rumored that he wore a necklace of teeth with gold fillings extracted from the men he had personally murdered. It was to Didi that the pirates taking control of the old freighter had pledged their oath.

Hakeem and one of his men forced Captain Kwan to take them to his office, while the other pirates escorted the bridge staff to the mess hall. Kwan's office was attached to his cabin one deck below the pilothouse. The rooms were spartan but clean, with just a couple of tacky velvet clown paintings on the otherwise bare metal walls. There was a framed photograph of Kwan and a woman, most likely his wife, on the empty desk.

Brassy light blazed through the single porthole.

"Show me crew manifest," Hakeem demanded.

There was a small safe bolted to the deck in the corner of the office behind Kwan's desk. The captain stooped over it and began to work the combination.

"You will step back when you open the door," the pirate ordered.

Kwan glanced over his shoulder. "I assure you we have no weapons." But he did as he was told. He swung open the door and took a step back from the safe.

With his assistant covering Kwan with his AK, Hakeem bent over the safe, pulling out files and folders and dumping everything on the captain's desk. He made a sound when he opened one particularly thick envelope and discovered bundles of cash in several currencies. He fanned a wad of hundred-dollar bills under his beaky nose, inhaling as if testing a fine wine.

"How much you have?"

"Twelve thousand dollars, maybe a bit less."

Hakeem stuffed the envelope into his shirt. He rifled through the papers until he found the crew's manifest. He couldn't read his native Somali, let alone English, but he recognized the various passports. There were twenty-two in all. He checked them, pulling out Kwan's, Duane Maryweather's, and that of the helmsman. He also found the passports belonging to the three men who had been on deck when they had boarded the ship. He was pleased. They had already accounted for a quarter of the crew.

"Now, take us to the mess hall."

When they arrived, the brightly lit room was packed with men. A few smoked cigarettes, so the air was as thick as smog, but it masked the stench of nervous sweat. They were a mix of races, and even without the weapons pointing at them they were a dour lot. These were down-on-their-luck men who could find no better employment than aboard a broken-down old tramp freighter. They had maintained her well beyond her years for the simple reason that they would never find another after she was gone.

One of Kwan's people held a bloody rag to the back of his head. He had obviously said or done something to set off one of the hijackers.

"What's going on, Captain?" asked the chief engineer. His jumpsuit was streaked with grease.

"What does it look like? We've been boarded by pirates."

"Silence," Hakeem roared.

He went through the stacks of passports he'd brought from Kwan's office, comparing the photographs to the men seated around the mess until he was certain every member of the crew was accounted for. He had once made the mistake of trusting a captain about his ship's complement, only to find that there had been two others who had beaten one of Hakeem's men to death and almost managed to radio a Mayday before they were discovered.

"Very good. No one is playing hero." He set aside the passports and looked around the room. He was an excellent judge of fear and liked what he saw. He sent one of his men out to the deck to cast off their fishing boat with orders for Abdi to make for their base as quickly as he could with the news they had captured the freighter. "My name is Hakeem, and this ship is now mine. If you follow my orders, you will not be killed. Any attempt to escape and you will be shot and your body fed to the sharks. Those are the two things you must remember at all times."

"My men will follow orders," Kwan said resignedly. "We'll do whatever you say. We all want to see our families again."

"That is very wise, Captain. With your help, I will contact the ship's owners to negotiate your release."

"Bastards won't spring for a gallon of paint," the engineer muttered to a table companion. "Fat luck they'll pay to save our hides."

Two of the gunmen had been in the kitchen gathering up anything that could be used as a weapon. They emerged dragging a linen bag full of forks, steak knives, kitchen knives, and cleavers. One gunman remained in the mess while the other continued to haul the bag out into the hallway, where it would most likely be thrown over the side.

"These guys know what they're doing," Duane whispered to the ship's radio operator. "I would have gone for a knife as soon as their guard was down."

Maryweather hadn't realized one of the pirates was directly behind him. The Kalashnikov crashed down on the back of his neck hard enough to drive his face into the Formica-topped table. When he straightened, blood dripped from a nostril.

"Talk again and you will die," Hakeem said, and from the tone of his voice it was clearly the last warning. "I see there is a bathroom attached to the mess hall, so you will all remain here. There is only one way in or out of this room, and it will be barred from the outside and guarded at all times." He switched to Somali and said to his men, "Let's go see what they are carrying for cargo."

They filed out of the mess and secured the door with heavy-duty wire wrapped around the handle and tied to a handrail on the opposite wall of the passageway. Hakeem ordered one of his men to stay outside the door while he and the others systematically searched the vessel.

Given the ship's large external dimensions, the interior spaces were remarkably cramped, and the holds smaller than expected. The aft holds were blocked by rows of shipping containers so tightly packed that not even the skinniest pirate could squeeze by. They would have to wait until they reached harbor and the containers were unloaded before they would know what was inside them. What they discovered in the forward three holds made whatever was in the containers superfluous. Amid the crates of machine parts, Indian-made car engines, and table-sized slabs of steel plate, they found six pickup trucks. When mounted with machine guns, the vehicles were known as technicals and were a favored weapons platform across Africa. There was another, larger truck, but it looked so dilapidated it probably didn't run. The ship was also carrying pallets of wheat in bags stenciled with the name of a world charity, but the greatest prize were hundreds of drums of ammonium nitrate. Used primarily as a potent fertilizer, the nitrate compound, when mixed with diesel fuel, became a powerful explosive. There was enough in the hold to level half of Mogadishu, if that was what Mohammad Didi wanted to do with it.

Hakeem knew that Didi's exile into the swamps wasn't permanent. He always talked about returning to the capital and taking on the other warlords in a final confrontation. This massive amount of explosives would surely give him the edge over the others. In a month or less, Hakeem was sure Didi would be the ruler of all of Somalia, and he was just as sure that his reward for taking the freighter would be greater than anything he could imagine.

He now wished he hadn't sent Abdi ahead so quickly, but there was nothing he could do about it. Their little radio couldn't pick up anything beyond a couple of miles, and the fishing boat was already out of range.

He returned to the bridge to enjoy the Cuban cigar he had pilfered from the captain's cabin. The sun was sinking fast over the horizon, turning the great ocean into a sheet of burnished bronze. Dusk's beauty was lost on men like Hakeem and his band of pirates. They existed on an ugly, cruel level where everything was judged based on what it could do for them. Some would argue that they were the product of their war-ravished country, that they never stood a chance against the brutality of their upbringing. The truth was that the vast majority of Somalia's population had never fired a gun in their lives, and the men who aligned themselves with a warlord like Didi did it because they enjoyed the power it gave them over others, like the crew of this ship.

He liked seeing the captain's head bowed in defeat. He liked the fear he saw in the sailors' eyes. He had found a picture of the captain and a woman in the office, the captain's wife, he assumed. Hakeem had the power to make that woman a widow. For him, there was no greater rush in the world.

Aziz and Malik entered the bridge. They had helped themselves to some new clothes from the officers' quarters. Aziz, only twenty-five but a veteran of a dozen hijackings, was so slender that he'd had to cut extra holes in the belt to keep his new jeans up around his waist. Malik was in his forties, and had fought at Mohammad Didi's side against the United Nations and the Americans. Shrapnel from a street fight with a rival gang had left the right side of his face in ruin, and the blow had affected his mind. He rarely spoke, and, when he did, little of what he said made sense. But he followed orders to the letter, which was all Hakeem demanded of him.

"Go get the captain. I want to talk to him about the company that owns this ship. I want to know how much he thinks they will be willing to pay." He studied Aziz's eyes. "And lay off the bang." He used the African nickname for marijuana.

The two pirates descended the stairs to the main deck. With the sun setting, the interior of the ship was gloomy. There were only a few functioning lamps, so shadows clung to the ceilings and walls like moss. Aziz nodded to the guard to untie the wire. He and Malik had their weapons at the ready when the door creaked inward. All three men gaped.

The mess hall was empty.

THREE

MALIK AND AZIZ HAD JUST STEPPED INTO THE empty mess hall when the guard felt a presence down the hall. He peered into the gloom, raising his rifle. Had he not been so spooked by the crew vanishing, he would have calmly explored the passageway. But every nerve in his body tingled with electricity as if a mild current had been applied to his skin. His finger curled around the trigger, and he unleashed a wild, ten-round burst. The juddering flame from the barrel of his AK-47 revealed the hall was deserted, while the bullets did nothing more than scrape more paint off the dingy walls.

"What is it?" Aziz demanded.

"I thought I saw someone," the guard stammered.

Aziz made his decision quickly. "Malik, go with him and search this deck. I will tell Hakeem what has happened."

The pirate leader had heard the gunfire and met up with Aziz halfway down from the bridge. He was holding his pistol like he had seen in music videos, arched at arm's length and turned flat on its side, and his eyes were bright with anger.

"Who was shooting, and why?" He didn't slow his pace when they met, forcing Aziz to double back quickly.

"The mess hall is empty, and Ahmed thought he saw someone. He and Malik are searching now."

Hakeem wasn't sure what he was hearing. "What do you mean the mess hall is empty?"

"The crew is all gone. The wire was still on the door and Ahmed was awake, but somehow they are gone."

The mess door was barely ajar when they arrived, so Hakeem kicked it open with all his strength. It crashed against the doorstop with a booming echo. Just as they had left the crew hours earlier, all twenty-two members were still seated around the tables. They all had tense, anxious expressions.

"What was that gunfire?" Captain Kwan asked.

Hakeem gave Aziz a murderous look. "A rat."

He grabbed the younger man by the arm and pushed him from the room. As soon as the door was closed behind Hakeem, he slapped Aziz across the face and backhanded him in a perfect follow-through. "You fool. You're so stoned right now, you don't know which is your dung hand."

"No, Hakeem. I swear it. We all saw—"

"Enough! I catch you smoking bang during one of my operations again, I will shoot you where you stand. Got it?" Aziz's eyes were cast down, and he said nothing. Hakeem grabbed Aziz's jaw so their eyes met. "Got it?" he repeated.

"Yes, Hakeem."

"Retie this door, and find Malik and Ahmed before they shoot up more of the ship."

Aziz did as he was ordered while Hakeem lingered. Hakeem pressed his ear to the door but couldn't hear anything through the thick metal. He glanced around the empty corridor. There was nothing out of the ordinary, but he had the sudden sense that someone was watching him. The sensation tingled at the base of his skull and raced down his back so that he visibly quivered. *Damn fools will have me chasing shadows next.*

• • •

TWO DECKS BELOW THE MESS, in a section of the ship
the pirates couldn't dream existed, Juan Rodriguez Cabrillo
watched the Somali shiver. A slight smile played at the corners of his mouth.

"Boo," he said at the image on the large, flat-panel display
that dominated the front of the room known as the Operations Center.

The op center was the high-tech brains of the vessel, a low-
ceilinged space that glowed faintly blue from the countless
computer screens. The floors were covered in antiskid, anti-
static rubber, and the consoles were done in smoky grays and
black. The effect, as was the intention, was a darker version
of the bridge of television's starship *Enterprise*. The two seats
directly in front of the main display panel were the ship's helm
and weapons-control station. Ringing the room were worksta-
tions for radio, radar, sonar, engineering, and damage control.

In the middle sat what was known as the Kirk Chair. From
it, Cabrillo had an unobstructed view of everything taking
place around him, and from the computer built into the arm
of the well-padded seat he could take control of any function
aboard his ship.

"You shouldn't have let them do that," admonished Max
Hanley, the president of the Corporation. Cabrillo held the
title of chairman. "What if Mohammad Didi's boys came
back when the secret door was open?"

"Max, you worry like my grandmother. We would have
retaken the *Oregon* from them and gone to plan B."

"Which is?"

"I'd tell you as soon as I came up with it." Juan stood and
stretched his arms over his head.

He was solidly built, topping out near six feet, with a
strong, weathered face and startlingly blue eyes. He kept his
hair in a long crew cut. An upbringing on the beaches of
southern California and a lifetime of swimming had bleached
it white blond. Though he was on the other side of forty, it
was still thick and stiff.

There was a compelling aura about Cabrillo that people picked up almost immediately but could never really put their fingers on. He didn't have the polish of a corporate heavy hitter or the rigidity of a career soldier. It was more a sense that he knew what he wanted out of life and made certain he got it every day. That, and he possessed a wellspring of confidence that knew no bottom—a confidence earned over a lifetime of achievement.

Max Hanley, on the other hand, was in his early sixties and a veteran of two tours in Vietnam. He was shorter than Cabrillo, with a bright, florid face and a halo of ginger curls in the shape of a horseshoe around his balding head. He could stand to lose a few pounds, something Juan delighted in teasing him about, but Max was rock solid in every sense of the word.

The Corporation had been Cabrillo's brainchild, but it was Max's steady hand that made it such a success. He managed the day-to-day affairs of the multimillion-dollar company and also acted as the *Oregon*'s chief engineer. If any man loved the ship more than Juan, it was Max Hanley.

Despite the seven heavily armed pirates roaming the vessel and the twenty-two crew members held "captive" in the mess hall, there was no concern in the op center, especially on Cabrillo's part.

This operation had been planned with meticulous attention to detail. When the pirates had first come aboard—arguably, the most critical moment, because no one knew how they were going to treat the crew—snipers positioned in the bows had held all seven Somalis in their sights. Also, the deck crew wore micro-thin body armor, which was still under development in Germany for NATO.

There were pinhole cameras and listening devices secreted in every hallway and room in the "public" parts of the ship, so the gunmen were observed at all times. Wherever they went, at least two members of the Corporation shadowed them from inside the *Oregon*'s hidden compartments, ready to react to any situation.

The old freighter was really two ships in one. On the outside, she was little more than a derelict trying to stay one step

ahead of the breaker's yard. However, that was all a façade to
deflect her true nature from customs inspectors, harbor pilots,
and anyone else who happened to find themselves aboard her.
Her state of dilapidation was meant to make anyone seeing
the *Oregon* immediately forget her.

The rust streaks were painted on, the debris cluttering
her deck was placed there intentionally. The wheelhouse and
cabins in the superstructure were nothing more than stage
sets. The pirate currently manning the helm had zero control
over the ship. The helmsman in the Operations Center was
fed data from the wheel through the computer system, and he
made the appropriate course corrections.

All this was a shell over perhaps the most sophisticated
intelligence-gathering ship in the world. She bristled with
hidden weapons, and had an electronics suite to rival any
Aegis-class destroyer. Her hull was armored enough to repel
most low-tech weapons used by terrorists, such as rocket-
propelled grenades. She carried two minisubs that could be
deployed through special doors along her keel, and a McDonnell Douglas MD-520N helicopter in her rear hold, hidden by
a wall made to look like stacked containers.

As for the crew's accommodations, they rivaled the grand-
est rooms on a luxury cruise ship. The men and women of the
Corporation risked their lives every day, so Juan wanted to
ensure they were as comfortable as possible.

"Where's our guest?" Max asked.

"Chatting up Julia again."

"Think it's the fact she's a doctor or a looker?"

"Colonel Giuseppe Farina, as his name implies, is Italian. And I happen to know he considers himself the best, so
he is after her because she is female. Linda Ross and all the
other women have blown him off enough since he first came
aboard. Our good Dr. Huxley is the last one left, and since
she can't leave medical in case there's an emergency, Colonel
Farina has a captive audience."

"Damned waste to have an observer with us in the first
place," Max said.

"You go with the deal you've got, not the one you want,"
Juan pontificated. "The powers that be don't want anything

to go wrong during the trial once they get their hands on Didi. Farina's here to make sure we follow by the engagement parameters they set out for us."

A sour look crossed Max's pug face. "Fighting terrorists using the Marquess of Queensberry rules? Ridiculous."

"It isn't so bad. I've known 'Seppe for fifteen years. He's all right. With no way to extradite Didi through legal channels, because Somalia doesn't have a functioning court system—"

"Or anything else."

Juan ignored the interruption. "We offered an alternative. The price we pay is 'Seppe's presence until we get Didi into international waters and the U.S. Navy takes him off our hands. All Didi has to do is set foot on this ship and we've got this in the bag."

Max nodded reluctantly. "And we've loaded what looks like enough explosives aboard so he'll want to see it for himself."

"Exactly. The right bait for the right vermin."

The Corporation had taken on what was an unusual job for them. They typically worked for the government, tackling operations deemed too risky for American soldiers or members of the intelligence community, on a strictly cash-only basis. This time they were working through the CIA to help the World Court bring Mohammad Didi to justice. U.S. authorities wanted Didi sent straight to Guantánamo, but a deal was hashed out with America's allies that he be tried in Europe, provided he could be captured in a manner that didn't include rendition.

Langston Overholt, the Corporation's primary contact in the CIA, had approached his protégé, Juan Cabrillo, with the difficult task of grabbing Didi in such a way that it couldn't be construed as kidnapping. True to form, Cabrillo and his people had come up with their plan within twenty-four hours while everyone else involved had been scratching their heads for months.

Juan glanced at the chronometer set in one corner of the main view screen. He checked the ship's speed and heading and calculated they wouldn't reach the coast until dawn. "Care to join me for dinner? Lobster Thermidor, I think."

Max patted his belly. "Hux has me scheduled on the Stair-Master for thirty minutes."

"Battle of the Bulge redux," Juan quipped.

"I want to see *your* waistline in twenty years, my friend."

● ● ●

THE SHIP REACHED the coastline a little after dawn. Here, mangrove swamps stretched the entire width of the horizon. Hakeem took the wheel himself because he was most familiar with the secret deepwater channels that would allow them access to their hidden base. While this was the largest vessel they had ever taken, he was confident he could reach their encampment without grounding, or at least get close enough so they wouldn't have much trouble unloading their cargo.

The air was hazy and heavy with humidity, and the moment the sun peeked over the horizon the temperature seemed to spike.

As the big freighter eased deeper into the swamp, her wake turned muddy brown from the silt her engines churned up. Hakeem had no idea how to read the fathometer mounted on a bulkhead at the helm, but only eight feet of water separated the ship's bottom from the muck. The trees grew denser still, hemming in the ship, until their branches almost met overhead.

The channel was barely wide enough for him to maneuver. He didn't remember it being so small, but then again he had never seen it from the wheelhouse of such a large vessel. The bow plowed into a submerged log that would have holed his fishing boat, but to the freighter it was a mere annoyance scraping along the hull. There was one more turn before they reached their base, but it was the tightest one yet. The opposite bank looked closer than the length of the ship.

"Do you think you can do it?" Aziz asked.

Hakeem didn't look at him. He was still angry about the incident the night before. "We're less than a kilometer from camp. Even if I don't, we can unload the ship and ferry everything back."

He tightened his grip on the wheel, bracing his feet a little farther apart. The prow eased into the corner, and he waited until the last second to start cranking the wheel. The ship didn't respond as quickly as he had hoped and continued to drive toward the far bank.

Then, ever so slowly, the bows started to come about, but it was a little too late. They were going to hit. Hakeem slammed the engine telegraph to full reverse in hopes of lessening the impact.

Several decks below, Cabrillo sat in his customary seat in the op center. Eric Stone was by far the *Oregon*'s best ship handler; however, he was currently locked in the mess hall pretending to be Duane Maryweather. In this instance, Cabrillo wouldn't have had him at the conn anyway. For waters this tight, Juan trusted no one but himself in control of his ship.

Though Hakeem had called for full reverse, Cabrillo ignored his command and hit the bow thruster instead. He also turned the nozzles of the directional pump jets that powered the ship as far as they would go.

Back on the bridge, it had to have seemed that a miracle wind had come up suddenly, although none of the trees moved. The bow swung sharply around as if pushed by an invisible hand. Hakeem and Aziz exchanged a startled look. They couldn't believe the freighter could turn so quickly, and neither realized the vessel had also righted itself in the channel after coming out of the turn. Hakeem uselessly turned the wheel anyway, still believing he had control.

"Allah has surely blessed this mission from the start," Aziz said, although neither man was particularly religious.

"Or maybe I know what I am doing," Hakeem said sharply.

The pirate camp lay on the right-hand bank, where it rose until it was almost level with the freighter's deck. The high ground protected the area from tides and spring flooding. There was a hundred-foot-long wooden dock built along the shore, accessible from the bank by several flights of steel stairs dug into the hard soil. The stairs had been taken from one of the first ships they had hijacked. Hakeem's boat was tied to the jetty along with two other small fishing vessels.

Beyond the bank lay the camp, a sprawl of haphazardly placed buildings made of whatever could be salvaged. There were tents once meant for refugees and traditional mud huts, plus structures built of native timber and sheathed in corrugated metal. It was home to more than eight hundred people, three hundred of them children. The perimeter was defined by four watchtowers made of lengths of pipe and weather-worn planks. The grounds were littered with trash and human waste. Half-feral dogs roamed in lean, mangy packs.

Throngs of cheering people lined the riverbank and crowded the dock to the point there was a real danger of its collapsing. There were half-naked kids, women in dusty dresses with infants strapped to their backs, and hundreds of men carrying their assault rifles. Many were firing into the air, the concussive noise so common here that the babies slept right through it. Standing in the center of the dock, and surrounded by his most trusted aides, was Mohammad Didi.

Despite his fearsome reputation, Didi wasn't a physically imposing man. He stood barely five feet six, and his self-styled uniform hung off his thin body like a scarecrow's rags. The lower half of his face was covered in a patchy beard that was shot through with whorls of gray. His eyes were rheumy and ringed in pink, while the whites were heavily veined with red lines. Didi was so slender that the big pistol hanging from his waist made his hips cock as if he suffered from scoliosis.

There was no trace of a smile, or any other expression, on his face. That was another of his trademarks. He never showed emotion—not when killing a man, not when holding one of his countless children for the first time—never.

Around his throat was a necklace made of irregular white beads that on closer inspection revealed themselves to be human teeth fitted with gold fillings.

It took Hakeem fifteen frustrating minutes to maneuver the big freighter to the dock, once approaching so fast that the people standing on it fled back to the riverbank. It would have taken longer, but Cabrillo finally had enough of the Somali's pathetic attempts and docked the ship himself.

Pirates on the rail threw ropes down to the crowd below, and the ship was made fast against the pier.

The thick smoke that had poured from the funnel trickled off to a wisp. Hakeem gave a blast on the horn, and the crowd redoubled their cheers. He sent Aziz to find help lowering the boarding stairs so Mohammad Didi could see for himself what they had captured.

• • •

IN THE OP CENTER, Giuseppe Farina pointed at the monitor. "There's our man right in the center."

"The one with the chicken feathers growing off his face?" Max Hanley asked.

"*Sí*. He is not much to look at, but he is a hardened killer." Farina wore Italian Army fatigues, and black boots so shiny they looked like patent leather. He was handsome, with dark eyes and hair, olive skin, and a sculpted face. The laugh lines at the corners of his mouth and across his forehead were earned from having a well-developed sense of fun and mischief. When Juan had been in the CIA working a Russian contact in Rome, he and 'Seppe had torn up the town on more than one occasion.

"Just so our orders are clear, we have to wait until Didi boards the *Oregon*, right?" Juan asked. Farina nodded, so he added, "Then what?"

"Then you capture him any way you want. This is a flagged vessel, and therefore the sovereign property of . . . Where is this ship registered?"

"Iran."

"You joke."

"Nope," Juan said with a lazy smile. "Can you think of a better country to deflect suspicion of us being an American-backed espionage ship?"

"No," Giuseppe conceded with a nervous frown, "but that might raise eyebrows in The Hague."

"Relax, 'Seppe. We also carry papers listing the *Oregon* as the *Grandam Phoenix*, registered in Panama."

"Odd name."

"It was a ship in a book I read years ago. Kinda liked it. There won't be any problems once you get Didi to the World Court."

"*Sí.* As soon as he steps foot on your ship, he is no longer in Somalia. So he is, ah, fair game."

"How are you guys going to explain in court that an Italian colonel happened to be on a freighter hijacked by a guy who's got a half-million-dollar bounty on his head and a standing indictment?"

"We don't," Farina said. "Your involvement will never be known. I have brought a drug with me that will wipe out his memories of the past twenty-four hours. He will awake with the worst hangover in history, but there is no permanent harm. We have a captured fishing boat standing by beyond Somalia's twelve-mile territorial limit. You transfer Didi to it in international waters, and then the American cruiser, performing interdiction duties, boards her and finds the prize. Slick and simple, and no rendition."

"Madness," Max grumbled.

"Chairman," Mark Murphy said to get Juan's attention. Murph was the ship's defenses operator. From his workstation next to the helm, he could unleash the awesome array of weapons built into the former lumber carrier. He could launch torpedoes, surface-to-surface and surface-to-air missiles, fire any number of .30-caliber machine guns hidden aboard as well as the radar-guided 20mm Vulcan cannons, the 40mm Orlikon, and the big 120mm gun in its bow redoubt.

Cabrillo looked past Murphy and saw on the screen that the boarding stairs were down and Mohammad Didi was moving toward them.

"'Come into my web,' said the spider to the fly."

FOUR

BAHIRET EL BIBANE,
TUNISIA

ALANA DIDN'T MIND THE SAND OR THE TREMENDOUS heat that blasted out of the desert in unending waves. What got to her were the flies. No matter how much cream she slathered onto her skin or how often she checked her tent's mosquito netting at night, there seemed to be no relief from the winged devils. After nearly two months on the dig, she couldn't tell where one welt ended and its neighbor began. To her dismay, the local workers didn't seem to even notice the biting insects. To make herself feel a little better, she'd tried to think up some discomfort in her native Arizona that these people couldn't handle but couldn't come up with anything worse than traffic congestion.

There were eleven Americans and nearly fifty hired laborers on the archaeological dig, all under the leadership of Professor William Galt. Six of the eleven were postdocs like Alana Shepard. The other five were still in grad school at the University of Arizona. Men outnumbered women eight to three, but so far that hadn't become an issue.

Ostensibly, they were here digging at a Roman site a half

mile inland from the Mediterranean. Long believed to be a summer retreat for Claudius Sabinus, the regional governor, the complex of crumbling buildings was turning out to be far more interesting. There appeared to be a large temple of some kind completely unknown before. The buzz around the camp among the archaeologists was that Sabinus was the head of a sect, and, given the time he ruled the area, there was speculation he might have become a Christian.

Professor Bill, as Galt liked to be called, frowned on conjecture, but he couldn't stop his people from discussing it around meals.

But that was just for cover. Alana and her small team of three were here for something quite different. And while it had an archaeological component, their mission wasn't about discovering the past but rather saving the future.

So far, things were not going well. Seven weeks of searching had turned up nothing, and she and the others were beginning to think they had been sent on a fool's errand.

She recalled being excited about the project when she'd first been approached by Christie Valero from the State Department, but the desert had burned away any remaining enthusiasm long ago.

Standing just five feet four, Alana Shepard was often confused for one of her students though she was a year shy of her fortieth birthday. Twice divorced—the first was a big mistake she made when she was eighteen, the second an even bigger mistake she made in her late twenties—she had one son, Josh, who stayed with her mother when Alana was in the field.

Because it was easier to maintain short hair in the desert, her dark bangs were cut across her forehead, and the hair at the back of her head barely covered the nape of her neck. She wasn't particularly beautiful, but Alana was so petite that she was universally considered cute—a term she professed to hate but secretly loved. She had a double doctorate from the University of Arizona in geology and archaeology, which made her particularly suited to the job, but no number of sheepskins hanging on her office wall in Phoenix would help her find something that wasn't even there.

She and her team had combed the dried-up riverbed for miles inland without seeing any sort of anomaly. The sandstone canyon carved by the river millions of years ago was as featureless as a utility corridor until it reached what once had been a waterfall.

There had been no need to search farther upstream than that. When the river was flowing two hundred years ago, the falls would have been an insurmountable obstacle.

The sound of a rock drill broke Alana from her reverie. The machine was mounted on the back of a truck and positioned horizontally so it could bore into the cliff face. The diamond-tipped bit chewed through the friable sandstone with ease. Mike Duncan, a geologist from Texas with oil-field experience, manned the controls at the rear corner of the rig. They used the cutter head to probe old landslides to see if they hid any sort of cavern or cave. After more than a hundred such holes, they had nothing to show but a half dozen worn-out bits.

She watched for several minutes, pausing to wipe perspiration from her throat. When forty feet of the drill had been rammed into the ground, Mike killed the diesel engine. Its roar faded until Alana could hear the wind again.

"Nothing," he spat.

"I still say we should have shot a few more holes in that rock slide about a mile downstream." This from Greg Chaffee. He was their government minder. Alana suspected CIA but didn't want to know if she was right. Chaffee had no academic or professional qualifications to be with them, so his opinion was generally ignored. At least he did his share of whatever job she set out for him, and he spoke Arabic like a native.

Emile Bumford was the fourth member of the little group. Bumford was an expert on the Ottoman Empire, with a particular focus on the Barbary States. He was a prissy lout, in Alana's estimation. He refused to leave the camp set up near the Roman ruins, saying that his expertise wasn't needed until they actually found something.

This was true, but back in Washington, D.C., when they had met Undersecretary Valero, he had boasted of vast field experience, saying he "loved the feel of dirt under his finger-nails." So far, he hadn't lifted one of those manicured nails to do anything other than constantly straighten the safari jacket he wore as an affectation.

"Another one of your feelings?" Mike asked Chaffee. They shared a common interest in horse racing and trusted their guts with the ponies as much as the information they read in the racing forms.

"Can't hurt." Chaffee shrugged.

"Won't help either," Alana said, a little harsher than she intended. She lowered herself to the ground in the truck's shadow. "Sorry, that sounded worse than I wanted it to. But the cliffs are too tall and steep there. It wouldn't have been possible to lead camels down to unload a ship."

"Are we sure this is even the right old riverbed?" Mike asked. "You don't find too many large caverns in sandstone. It's too soft. The roof would collapse before erosion could make it large enough to hide a boat."

Alana had thought the same thing. They should be look-ing for limestone, which was perfect for caverns because it was soft enough to erode but tough enough to withstand the aeons. The problem was they hadn't found anything other than the sandstone and a few basalt outcroppings.

"The Charles Stewart letter was pretty clear as to the loca-tion of Al-Jama's secret base," she said. "Remember, Henry Lafayette stayed there for two years before the old pirate's death. Satellite imagery shows this to be the only possible riverbed within a hundred miles of where Lafayette said they lived."

"Hey, at least it's on this side of the Libyan border," Greg added. His blond hair and fair skin made him especially sus-ceptible to the sun, so he wore long sleeves and a big straw hat. His shirts were always stained at the collar and under the arms and had to be washed out every night. "Despite the upcoming summit in Tripoli, I don't think old Muammar Qaddafi would like us digging around in his backyard."

Mike said, "My father worked the Libyan oil fields before Qaddafi nationalized them." He was taller and leaner than Greg, hardened by a lifetime of working outdoors so the wrinkles around his blue eyes never vanished. His hands were callused like the bark of an oak tree, and the corner of his mouth bulged with a wad of tobacco the size of a golf ball. "He told me the Libyan people are about the nicest in the world."

"People, yes. Government, not so much." Alana took a swig from her canteen. It was as warm as bathwater. "Even with them hosting the peace thing, I don't see them really changing their tune." She looked at Greg Chaffee, asking pointedly, "Doesn't the CIA believe they once sheltered Suleiman Al-Jama, the terrorist who took his name from the pirate we're looking for?"

He didn't rise to the bait. "What I read in the papers is that Al-Jama tried to enter the country but wasn't allowed in."

"We've been up and down this wash for weeks. There's nothing here," Mike said disgustedly. "This mission is a complete waste of time."

"The nabobs in the know don't seem to think so," Alana answered, but with reservations.

She thought back to her meeting in Washington with Christie Valero. In the Foggy Bottom office with Undersecretary Valero had been one of the largest men Alana had ever seen. He had the unforgettable name of St. Julian Perlmutter, and he reminded her of Sydney Greenstreet, except while the old actor had always seemed sinister Perlmutter was the quintessential jovial fat man. His eyes were as bright blue as Alana's were green. Valero was a trim, pretty blonde a few years older than Alana. The walls of her office were decorated with photographs of the places she'd been stationed in her twenty-year career, all in the Middle East.

She had risen from her desk when Alana had been shown into the room, but Perlmutter remained on the sofa and shook her hand sitting down.

"Thank you for agreeing to meet with us," Christie said.

"It's not every day I get an offer to meet with an Undersecretary."

"They're a dime a dozen in this town." Perlmutter chuckled. "Turn on a light at a party and they scurry like cockroaches."

"Another crack like that," Christie said, "and I'll have you blacklisted from all the embassy dinners."

"That's hitting below the belt," St. Julian said quickly, then laughed. "Actually, that's hitting the belt line precisely."

"Dr. Shepard—"

"Alana. Please."

"Alana, we have a particularly interesting challenge that's suited to your talents. A few weeks ago, St. Julian came across a letter written by an admiral named Charles Stewart in the 1820s. In it, he describes a rather incredible tale of survival by a sailor lost during the Barbary Coast War of 1803. His name was Henry Lafayette."

Christie Valero outlined Lafayette's role in the burning of the *Philadelphia* and how he was presumably lost at sea following the attack on the *Saqr*. St. Julian picked it up from there.

"Lafayette and Suleiman Al-Jama made it to shore, and Henry removed the pistol ball with his bare fingers and packed the wound with salt he scraped from rocks. The pirate captain was delirious for three days, but then his fever broke and he made a full recovery. Fortunately for them, Henry managed to gather rainwater to drink, and he was skilled at foraging for food along the shore.

"Now, you must understand that Al-Jama was a pirate not because of the financial reward. He did it because of his hate for the infidel. The man was the Osama bin Laden of his day."

"Is this where Suleiman Al-Jama gets his name?" Alana asked, referencing the modern-day terrorist.

"Yes, it is."

"I had no idea his name had a historical context."

"He chose it very carefully. To many in the radicalized side of Islam, the original Al-Jama is a hero and a spiritual guide. Before turning to piracy he was an Imam. Most of his writings survive to this day, and are closely studied because they give so many justifications for attacking nonbelievers."

"There was a painting done of him before his first sea voyage," Undersecretary Valero said. "We often find pictures of it in places of honor whenever there's a raid on a terrorist stronghold. He is an inspiration to terrorists throughout the Muslim world. To them, he's the original jihadist, the first to take the fight to the West."

Alana was confused, and said, "I'm sorry, but what does any of this have to do with me? I'm an archaeologist."

"I'm getting to that," St. Julian replied. His stomach grumbled, so he gave it an affectionate rub. "And I'll make it brief.

"Now, Lafayette and Al-Jama couldn't have been more different if one of them had been from Mars. But they shared a rather strange bond. You see, Henry had saved Suleiman's life not once but twice. First by towing him to shore, then by nursing him back from the bullet wound. It was a debt the Muslim simply couldn't ignore. Also, Henry, who was French Canadian, looked exactly like Al-Jama's long-dead son.

"They were stranded in the desert at least a hundred miles from Tripoli. Suleiman knew that if he returned Henry there, the Bashaw would imprison him with the crew from the *Philadelphia*, or, worse, try him for burning the ship and execute him.

"However, there was an alternative. You see, apart from using the city, Al-Jama also had a secret base in the desert far to the west. It was from there he staged many of his raids, allowing him to avoid any naval blockade. He assumed that his ship would defeat the *Siren* and that his men would meet him at their *lair*."

A natural storyteller, Perlmutter put extra emphasis on the last word to bolster the drama.

"So they headed west, walking along the shore whenever they could, but they were oftentimes forced to trek inland. Henry didn't know how many days it took them. Four weeks was a rough estimate, and it must have been utter hell. Water was always scarce, and on more than one occasion both thought they were going to die from thirst. 'Water, water, every where, / Nor any drop to drink.' Coleridge had it right. They were saved by the occasional rain squall and the juice of clams they found.

"A funny thing happened, too. The two men began to

become friends. Al-Jama spoke some English, and because Henry was already bilingual he was able to pick up Arabic very quickly. I can't imagine what they discussed, but talk they did. By the time they reached the hideout, Al-Jama wasn't keeping Henry alive because of an obligation. He did it because he genuinely liked the young man. Later, he would call Henry 'son,' and Henry referred to him as 'father.'

"At the secret base, they discovered the *Saqr*, but the men, who had thought their captain dead, had returned to their homes along the Barbary Coast. In his report to the Navy Department, Charles Stewart stated the *Saqr* was burning heavily and sinking after they broke off the engagement, but obviously it survived.

"By Henry's account, the hideout was well provisioned, and there was an elderly servant to attend to their needs. Every few months, a camel caravan would come by to barter for food in exchange for some of the plunder Al-Jama had hoarded, though he made them promise not to tell his men he was alive."

"Plunder?" Alana asked.

"Henry's exact words were 'a mountain of gold,'" Perlmutter replied. "Then there's the belief that Al-Jama was in possession of the Jewel of Jerusalem."

Alana looked to Undersecretary Valero. "Do you want to send me on some sort of treasure hunt?"

Christie nodded. "In a manner of speaking, but we're not interested in gold or some mythical gemstone. What do you know about fatwas?"

"Isn't that some kind of proclamation for Muslims? There was one issued to kill Salman Rushdie for writing *The Satanic Verses*."

"Exactly. Depending on who issues them, they carry tremendous influence in the Muslim world. Ayatollah Khomeini issued one during Iran's war with Iraq, giving permission for soldiers to blow themselves up in suicide attacks. You must be aware that suicide is expressly forbidden in the Koran, but Khomeini's forces were being routed by Saddam's, and he was desperate. So he said it was okay to blow yourself up if you're taking your enemies with you. His strategy worked—maybe too well, from our perspective. The Iranians pushed back Iraq's Army and eventually came to a cease-fire, but his fatwa remained in place, and is still used as the justification for suicide bombers from Indonesia to Israel. If it could somehow be countered by an equally respected cleric, then we might see a drop in suicide bombings all over the world."

Alana was beginning to understand. "Suleiman Al-Jama?"

St. Julian leaned forward, the couch's leather creaking. "According to what Henry told Charles Stewart after his return to the United States, Al-Jama did a complete reversal of his earlier position concerning Christians. He had never even spoken to one until Henry rescued him. Henry read to him from the Bible he carried, and Al-Jama began to focus on the similarities between faiths rather than the differences. In the two years before he died in the hideout, he studied the Koran like never before, and wrote extensively on how Christianity and Islam should coexist in peace. That is why I believe he didn't want his sailors to know he had survived the attack, because they would want to go raiding again and he did not."

Christie Valero interrupted. "If those documents exist, they could be a powerful tool in the war on terrorism because it would cut the underpinnings of many of the most fanatical terrorists. The killers who so blindly follow Al-Jama's early edicts on murdering Christians would be honor-bound to at least consider what the old pirate had written later in his life.

"I don't know if you are aware," she continued, "that there is a peace conference in Tripoli, Libya, in a couple of months. This is going to be the largest gathering of its kind in history, and perhaps our greatest shot at ending the fighting once and for all. All sides are talking serious concessions, and the oil states are willing to pledge billions in economic aid. I would love for the Secretary of State to have the opportunity to read something Al-Jama wrote about reconciliation. I think it would tip the scales in favor of peace."

Alana made a face. "Wouldn't that be, I don't know, largely symbolic?"

"Yes, it would," St. Julian answered. "But so much of diplomacy is symbolism. The parties want reconciliation. Hearing about it from a revered Imam, a powerful inspiration for violence who changed his mind, would be a diplomatic coup, and the very thing these talks need to be a success."

Alana recalled feeling excited about helping to bring stability to the Middle East following her meeting with Valero and Perlmutter, but now, after weeks searching vainly for Al-Jama's secret base, she felt nothing but tired, hot, and dirty. She pushed herself to her feet. Their break was over.

"Come on, guys. We have another hour or so before we have to head back to the Roman ruins and check in with the dig supervisor." As part of their deal for tagging along with that other expedition, Alana and her team had to return to camp every night. It was an onerous burden, but the Tunisian authorities insisted that no one spend a night alone in the desert. "Might as well check where Greg's gut is telling him our discovery awaits, 'cause the geology isn't telling me squat."

FIVE

CABRILLO'S PLAN TO CAPTURE MOHAMMAD DIDI was simple. As soon as he and his entourage entered the superstructure, armed teams would surround them with overwhelming force. The surprise alone should ensure the capture went down smooth and easy. Once they had him, they would back away from the pier and make their way out into the open ocean. None of the fishing boats had a chance at catching the disguised freighter, and Juan hadn't seen any signs the rebels had a helicopter.

He was so confident that he wasn't bothering to participate. Eddie Seng, who had pretended to be Captain Kwan, would lead the team. Eddie was another CIA veteran, like Cabrillo, and was one of the most proficient fighters on the *Oregon*. Backing him, as always, would be Franklin Lincoln. The big former SEAL had been on deck when the pirates came aboard, and they had wrongly assumed he was African. Linc was a Detroit native and about the most unflappable man Cabrillo knew.

But as Cabrillo watched the view screen, he saw his plans fly out the window.

The camera was mounted high atop one of the ship's gantry cranes and had an unobstructed view of the dock. Moments before Didi was to step onto the boarding stairs, he paused, spoke a few words to his followers, and moved aside. Dozens of Somalis raced up the gangplank, shouting and whooping like banshees.

"Chairman!" Mark Murphy cried as the multitude swarmed the ship.

"I see it."

"What are you going to do?" Giuseppe Farina asked.

"Give me a second." Juan couldn't tear his eyes away from the screen. He keyed a mic button built into his chair. "Eddie, you copying this?"

"I'm watching it on a monitor down here. Looks like plan A is out. What do you suggest?"

"Stay in the staging area and out of sight until I think of something."

Mohammad Didi finally started to climb the gangway, but already there were at least a hundred natives aboard the old ship and more were trickling up behind their leader.

Juan thought through and discarded his options. The *Oregon* and her crew carried enough firepower to kill every last Somali, but that was one option he didn't even consider. The Corporation was a mercenary outfit, a for-profit security and surveillance company, but there were lines they would never cross. Indiscriminately targeting civilians was something he would never condone. Taking out the guys brandishing AKs wouldn't weigh on Juan's conscience too much, but there were women and children mixed with the crowd.

Eric Stone raced into the Operations Center from an entrance at its rear. He was still dressed as Duane Maryweather. "Sorry I'm late. Looks like the party's bigger than we intended."

He took his seat at the navigation station, tapping knuckles with Murph. The two were best friends. Stone had never gotten over being a shy, studious high school geek, despite his four years at Annapolis and six in the Navy. He dressed mostly in chinos and button-down shirts, and wore glasses rather than bother with contact lenses.

Murph, on the other hand, cultivated a surfer-punk persona that he couldn't quite pull off. A certified genius, he had been a weapons designer for the military, which was where he'd met Eric. Both were in their late twenties. Mark usually wore black, and kept his hair a dark, shaggy mess. He was in his second month of trying to grow a goatee, and it wasn't going well.

Polar opposites in so many ways, they still managed to work as one of the best teams on the ship, and they could anticipate Cabrillo as if able to read his mind.

"Depress the—" Cabrillo started.

"—water-suppression cannons," Murph finished. "Already on it."

"Don't fire until I give the order."

"Righto."

Juan looked over to Linda Ross. She was the Corporation's vice president of operations. Another Navy squab, Linda had done stints on an Aegis cruiser and had worked as an assistant to the Joint Chiefs, making her equally skilled at naval combat and staff duties. She had an elfin face, with bright almond eyes and a dash of freckles across her cheeks and nose. Her hair, which changed routinely, was currently strawberry blond and cut in what she called the "Posh." She also had a high, almost girlish voice that was incongruous with belting out combat orders. But she was as fine an officer as any of her male shipmates.

"Linda," Cabrillo said, "I want you to monitor Didi. Don't lose him on the internal cameras, and tell me the minute he enters the hold."

"You got it."

"'Seppe, are you satisfied that Didi came onto this ship of his own free will?"

"He's all yours."

Juan keyed the microphone again. "Eddie, Linc, meet me down in the Magic Shop, double time."

Juan slipped a portable radio into a pocket and fitted headphones over his ears so he could stay on the communications

grid. As he ran from the room, he asked over his shoulder
for Hali Kasim to patch him in to Kevin Nixon, the head
magician of the Magic Shop. Launching himself down teak-
paneled stairwells rather than wait for one of the elevators,
Cabrillo told the former Hollywood makeup artist what he
had in mind. After that, he got in touch with Max Hanley
and gave him his orders. Max grumbled about what Juan
wanted to do, knowing it would make for a maintenance
headache for his engineers later on, but he admitted it was
a good idea.

Cabrillo reached the Magic Shop on Eddie and Linc's
heels. The room looked like a cross between a salon and a
storage shed. There was a makeup counter and mirror along
one wall, while the rest of the space was given over to racks
of clothing, special-effects gear, and all manner of props.

The two gundogs, as Max called them, wore black combat uniforms festooned with pouches for extra ammunition,
combat knives, and other gear. They also carried Barrett
REC7 assault rifles, a possible successor to the M16 family
of weapons.

"Lose the hardware," Cabrillo said brusquely.

Kevin bustled into the Magic Shop from one of the large
storerooms where he kept disguises. In his arms were gar-
ments called *dishdashas*, the long nightshirt-type clothes
commonly worn in this part of the world. The cotton had
once been white but had been artfully stained to appear old
and worn out. He gave one to each man, and they shrugged
them over their clothes. Linc looked like he was stuffed into
a sausage casing, but the shirt covered everything but his
combat boots.

Nixon also gave them headscarves, and as they started
winding them around their skulls he applied makeup to
darken Eddie's and Juan's skin. A perfectionist, Kevin
detested doing anything slipshod, but Cabrillo's impatience
radiated off of him in waves.

"It doesn't have to be perfect," Juan said. "People see what
they expect to see. That's the number one rule in disguise."

Linda's voice came over Juan's microphone. "Didi is
about two minutes from the main hold."

"Too soon. We're not ready. Is there anyone on the bridge?"

"A couple of kids are playing with the ship's wheel."

"Hit the foghorn and pipe it down to the hold through the speakers."

"Why?"

"Trust me," was all Juan said.

The horn bellowed across the mangrove swamp, startling birds to flight and sending the mongrel camp dogs cowering with their tails tucked between their legs. Inside the corridor where Mohammad Didi and his retainers were walking toward their prize, the sound was a physical assault on the senses. Clamping their hands to their heads did little to mitigate the effect.

"Good call," Linda told the Chairman. "Didi has stopped to send one of his men back to the wheelhouse. Those kids are in for it when he gets there."

"What's going on everywhere else?"

"The horn hasn't stopped people from looting. I see two women carrying the mattresses out of the captain's cabin. Another pair are taking those hideous clown pictures. And don't ask me why he's bothering, but a guy is working on pulling up the toilet."

"A throne by any other name," Juan quipped.

Kevin had finished with their makeup by the time Didi's lieutenant arrived on the bridge and cuffed the two boys behind the ears. Linda disengaged the horn when the pirate reached for the controls, though he looked at the panel oddly because he hadn't actually hit any button. He shrugged and hurried back to be with the warlord.

An armorer had arrived in the Magic Shop and handed over three Kalashnikov AK-47s. The weapons looked as battle worn as the ones the pirates carried, but like every facet of the *Oregon* this was a ruse. These rifles were in perfect working order. He also gave them filter masks that they tucked into the pockets of their dishdashas.

"You got us down here," Linc said, "and got you boys looking like a couple of imitation homeys, but I don't know the plan."

"We couldn't waltz up to Didi dressed like a bunch of ninjas with so many armed rebels roaming the ship. We need to get close to him without raising an alarm."

"Hence the mufti," Eddie surmised.

"In all the excitement," Juan explained, "we'll blend in and wait for our moment."

"If Didi decides to open the drums of ammonium nitrate and discovers they're filled with seawater, he's going to sense a trap and hightail it off the *Oregon*."

"Why do you think I'm rushing, big man? Kevin?"

Nixon stepped back and looked at his handiwork. He rummaged in a desk drawer and handed Juan and Eddie aviator-style sunglasses. Their skin tone was right, but without latex appliances there wasn't much he could do about their features. Given enough time, he could make either of them a twin of Didi, but the addition of the shades made him satisfied. He gave a nod, and was going to pronounce his work complete, but Juan was already leading the others out of the room.

"Linda, where is Didi now?" Cabrillo asked over the radio.

"They're just outside the hold. There are probably twelve men with him. All of them are armed to the teeth. Speaking of which, our pirate leader, Hakeem, is grinning ear to ear."

"I bet he is," Juan replied. "But not for long."

He led Linc and Eddie to an unmarked door on one of the *Oregon*'s elegant corridors. He opened a peephole on a two-way mirror, and when he saw the room beyond was dark he swung open the door and the three men stepped through. A pull on an overhead fixture revealed they were in a utility closet, with a mop sink, buckets, and shelves loaded with cleaning supplies. This was one of the many secret passages between the *Oregon*'s two sections.

It was only when Juan put his hand on the knob to open the door to the public part of the ship that he thought about the fact he was potentially entering a combat situation. A jolt of adrenaline hit him like a narcotic. The old feelings were there—fear, anxiety, and a dose of excitement, too—but the more times he faced danger, the longer it took to quell those feelings and empty his mind of distraction.

This was the moment none of the Corporation operators

ever discussed or acknowledged in any way. He could imagine Linc's and Eddie's horror if he turned to them and asked if they were as scared as he was. This was the essence of any good soldier, the ability to admit he is afraid while having the discipline to channel it into something useful in combat.

Juan didn't pause. He pushed open the door and stepped into the public part of the ship. Two Somali women hustled by carrying rolled-up carpet they must have pulled from one of the cabins. They didn't give Cabrillo's party a second glance.

The three men rushed aft until they found a stairwell leading them deeper into the freighter. There was an armed guard stationed at the foot of the stairs, and when Juan tried to pass he grabbed for his arm, saying something in Somali that Cabrillo didn't understand.

"I need to speak with Lord Didi," Juan said in Arabic, hoping the man knew the language.

"No. He is not to be disturbed," the guard replied haltingly.

"Have it your way," Juan muttered in English, and cold-cocked the man with a haymaker that lifted the slightly built Somali off his feet.

Cabrillo shook out his wrist while Linc and Eddie dragged the guard under the metal scissor stairs.

"Make sure we don't forget that guy when this is over," Juan said, and started off toward the hold. According to Linda Ross, Mohammad Didi had been in there for three minutes so far and was still inspecting the trucks.

"What's his mood?"

"Like a kid in a candy store."

"Okay, I think it's time. Tell Max to start pumping out the smoke and to get ready on those water cannons. Remember, I want people getting off, not rushing aboard to grab anything else."

"Roger."

Perhaps the *Oregon*'s single greatest hidden feature was the fact she wasn't powered by traditional marine diesels. Instead, she employed something called magnetohydrodynamics. Magnets cooled by liquid helium stripped free electrons out of the seawater and gave the ship a near-limitless supply of electricity. This was used to power four jet pumps that shot water through a pair of directional drive tubes deep in the hull. The revolutionary propulsion system could move her eleven thousand tons through the waves at unimaginable speeds. But to maintain the illusion that she was a derelict vessel, she had smudge generators that could belch smoke from her stack to simulate poorly maintained engines.

It was this smoke that Max was redirecting into the ventilation system in the parts of the ship the Somali pirates thought they controlled.

Approaching the open door to the number three cargo hold, Juan noted soot boiling out of the ventilation grilles set into the low ceiling. It would take no more than fifteen minutes to fill the ship with the noxious gas. They could hear voices echoing from inside the hold.

"Ready?" Juan asked. Linc and Eddie nodded.

They rushed into the hold, Juan screaming, "Fire! Fire!"

Didi and his dozen-strong entourage looked over from where they were examining one of the heavy-duty pickups. "What's all this?"

"There is a fire. Smoke," Juan said, knowing he spoke Arabic with a Saudi accent that must sound strange to the Somali. "It is coming from everywhere."

Didi glanced at the drums of ammonium nitrate. Juan wasn't sure if he was thinking about taking them before flames engulfed the ship or if he was concerned they could detonate. They could smell the smoke now in the unventilated hold. A pall of it hung near the entry door. Juan looked over at Hakeem. The pirate sensed he was being studied and looked back. He had no idea what was going on behind the sunglasses Cabrillo wore, and would have drawn his pistol and fired if he knew the depths of hatred Juan had for pirates.

Linda's voice came over the headset hidden under his turban. "Just so you know, the women and young children are making for the gangplank, but not many of the soldiers seemed concerned."

"Have you seen the flames yourself?" asked Mohammad Didi.

"Er, no, sir."

A wary look flashed behind the strongman's eyes. "I do not know you. What is your name?"

"Farouq, sir."

"Where are you from?"

Juan couldn't believe it. There was a potential fire raging on the ship, Didi had seen the smoke, and he wanted a life history.

"Sir, there isn't time."

"Oh, all right. Let's see what has you so spooked. Someone probably just burned food in the galley."

Juan motioned for Eddie to lead them back down the corridor to the stairwell. Didi walked slowly and stayed in the middle of his group, despite Juan's urging him to rush. Eddie looked back just before stepping over the coaming of a watertight door. Cabrillo nodded.

The instant Mohammad Didi, preceded by Juan and Linc, stepped over the threshold, a steel panel concealed in the ceiling came down under hydraulic force. It happened so fast that the men trapped on the other side didn't have time to react. One second the path was open and the next a metal barrier barred them from leaving the corridor.

The trapdoor had cut the number of guards in half, but it was still too many to take on in such close quarters.

"What's going on?" Didi asked no one in particular.

Hakeem remembered Malik's and Aziz's wild story about the mess hall being empty. He looked around with superstitious dread. There was something not right with this ship, and his heightened desire to get off had nothing to do with the possibility of a fire.

Two pirates tried unsuccessfully to lift the slab of steel, while their comrades pounded on the metal from the other side. The smoke was growing thicker.

"Leave them," Didi shouted, also feeling that things were not what they seemed.

He led the charge up the stairs, not noticing that the guard he had posted earlier wasn't there. What started as a fast walk turned into a jog and then an outright sprint.

This guy has the instincts of a rat, Juan thought. He slowed his pace so he could talk to the op center without attracting attention. "Linda, are you tracking us?"

"I've got you."

"I can't grab Didi with all these guards. When we break out onto the deck I want you to hit us. Got it?"

"Got it."

They climbed up past the corridor with the nearest secret entrance and emerged on the main deck by the gangplank. The moment they set foot outside the superstructure and into the burning sun, a lance of water from a fire-suppression cannon hit Didi square in the chest. The blast sent him back into his men, dropping three of them. Linc wrapped his big arms around two who had managed to stay on their feet and crashed their heads together with a dull knock. Had he wanted to, he could have cracked their skulls, but he was satisfied when they dropped to the deck.

Hakeem ignored the torrent sloshing across his feet and stared at Juan in disbelief. The gush of seawater had scoured the makeup from his face and torn away the sunglasses to reveal his piercing blue eyes. His shout of alarm rose above the wail of women doused by the blast. He was swinging his AK to his hip when Juan slammed into him with his shoulder, driving the pirate into the ship's rail. The impact was enough to curl the pirate's finger around the trigger.

A juddering blast of autofire ripped from the gun. Fortunately, it passed harmlessly over the heads of the milling women and children, but it turned what had been an orderly exodus into a stampede and caught the attention of other armed men.

Juan vented his rage into the Somali by ramming an elbow into his stomach. Hakeem's Kalashnikov clattered to the deck. As the pirate's eyes goggled and his mouth worked to suck air into his deflated lungs, Cabrillo hit him again on the point of the jaw hard enough to fling him over the rail. Juan glanced over to see Hakeem had the bad luck of landing not in the narrow band of water separating the ship from the dock but on the transom of the fishing boat he'd first used in his attack on the *Oregon*. By the way Hakeem's neck was twisted, Juan knew it was broken and the pirate was dead.

He couldn't be more pleased.

He pushed through the panicked throng of Somalis. Water continued to fountain from the fire cannon, splattering against the ship, so it was like running through a cyclone. No one seemed to notice his white skin until a boy of maybe six carrying a stack of sheets and towels saw him and opened his mouth to shout a warning. Juan pinched his arm in the hopes of making the kid start crying, a sound coming from dozens of wailing children trying to get off the ship with their mothers. Instead, the boy dropped to the deck and wrapped his arms around Juan's leg. Cabrillo tried to pull away, but the boy hung on with the tenacity of a moray eel. Then he made the mistake of trying to bite Cabrillo's calf. Having never seen or even heard of a dentist, the boy clamped down as hard as he could and managed to snap off four of his baby teeth. He started to bawl as blood dripped from his blubbering lips.

Cabrillo shook the kid loose and reached his teammates. "Come on, guys."

Mohammad Didi was almost on his feet. The water had torn away his shirt, revealing a chest riddled with shrapnel scars, while water dripped from his beard. Looking like a drowned rat, he was more determined than ever to get off the *Oregon*. He lunged forward and ran into the proverbial immovable object.

Franklin Lincoln towered over the Somali warlord.

"Not so fast, my friend," the big man said, and grabbed Didi around the upper arm while at the same time pulling the pirate's pistol from its holster.

"Help me!" Didi shouted to his men.

The powerful jet of water and the spatter it kicked up when it hit the deck made it impossible to see what was happening just ten feet away, but the yell galvanized Didi's men. They started forward, shielding their eyes from the spray, their rifles held one-handed. Fingers were an ounce of pressure away from loosening a barrage.

"Let's go!" Juan helped drag Didi deeper into the super-structure, with Eddie covering their rear.

The pirates broke through the waterfall-like cascade, and

as soon as their eyes adjusted to the dim interior they realized that their leader was in trouble. One of them triggered off a half dozen rounds, ignoring the danger to Didi.

Juan felt the heat of the bullets singe his neck before they hit the ceiling and ricocheted down the passageway.

Running backward, Eddie put the gunman down with a double tap from his AK, then thumbed the selector to automatic and fired a wild volley of his own. The three remaining pirates dove flat, giving the team time to round a corner.

Juan took point position, listening to Linda in his ear for warnings about other pirates still on board. He paused at a corner when she told him there was an armed Somali a few feet from him. He peeked around the junction, saw the man's back was to him, and gave him a rap on the back of the head with the AK's butt.

Either he had miscalculated or the pirate had the hardest skull in the world, because the man turned on Juan and rammed his gun into Juan's stomach, shoving him far away enough so he could take a shot.

Juan kicked out with his left foot as the gun swung toward him, pinning the barrel against the wall. The gunman tried to yank it free but couldn't. Cabrillo swung his AK like a baseball bat and hit the pirate in the head a second time. The blow opened a gash on his cheek and sent him sprawling.

Linda's next warning came the instant Juan looked farther up the corridor. Two more pirates emerged from the mess hall, their guns blazing. Juan took a bullet just above his right ankle, the impact making him stagger. He lost his balance and was falling when Eddie grabbed his arm and yanked him back around the corner.

"You okay?" Seng asked.

Juan flexed his knee. "Peg leg seems all right." Below the knee, Juan Cabrillo had a prosthetic leg thanks to a hit from an artillery shell from a Chinese destroyer during a mission for the National Underwater and Marine Agency. It is what the boy on deck broke his teeth on.

Cabrillo adjusted his headset, which had come loose. "Talk to me, Linda."

"The two who just fired are taking cover positions at the mess-hall door and you've got a half dozen more coming up from behind."

"Eddie, watch our back."

Juan ran across the hall to one of the cabins. The door was locked, and there hadn't been enough time for the Somalis to force it open and strip the cabin bare. Juan rammed a master key into the handle and threw the door open. The cabin was supposed to be for the ship's chief engineer, so it was smaller than the captain's cabin Eddie had used earlier. The furniture was still cheap to maintain the ruse that the *Oregon* was little more than a scow, and the décor consisted of Spanish bullfighting posters and models of sailing ships in bottles. He strode through the cabin and into the small head. Above the porcelain sink was a mirror affixed to the bulkhead with glue. He jabbed the barrel of his AK into the glass and smashed it to fragments. He plucked one the size of a playing card off the linoleum floor and raced out of the room.

He edged up to the corner again and eased the fragment of mirror out into the hallway so he could see the two gunmen. They were crouched at the mess door as Linda had said, one hunched down and the other standing over him. Both had their weapons trained on the corner, but in the uneven light couldn't see the mirror.

As slowly as a cobra lulling its prey, Cabrillo inched the barrel of his assault rifle around the corner, so only a tiny bit was showing.

Some call it the sixth sense—the body's ability to know its position relative to its surroundings, its orientation in space. Cabrillo's sixth sense was so honed that even looking at a mirror reflection, crouched on the floor, and with six terrorists gunning for them, he could feel the precise angle he had to raise the Kalashnikov's barrel. He brought it up a fraction of an inch and fired.

The stream of bullets smashed into the wall next to the mess hall door and ricocheted off with enough force to impact the door and slam it into the protruding barrels of the pirates' guns. Cabrillo was moving even as the door was swinging closed, using his fusillade as cover fire. The pirates made no attempt to withdraw their weapons or open the door with rounds pounding it from the outside, which allowed Juan enough time to reach it without being seen. He jammed the barrel of his gun into the crack between the door and frame and fired off another burst at point-blank range. Blood sizzled on the hot barrel when he pulled his weapon clear. He looked through the opening and saw both gunmen were down, their bodies riddled with bullet holes.

He waved to his men, and they charged after him, Linc nearly lifting the Somali warlord off his feet to keep him moving.

"They're coming," Linda warned.

Juan knew she meant the six tangos she'd mentioned earlier. He dropped the magazine from the AK's receiver and slapped home a fresh one. There was a round still in the chamber—no matter how hot things got in combat, Cabrillo knew to never let his gun empty completely—so he didn't need to cock it. As soon as he saw the flicker of shadow moving around the corner they had just used for cover, he opened up, firing past his men in a desperate bid to buy them the time they needed to reach cover.

The sound was deafening in the enclosed space, and the combination of smoke pumping through the ventilators and the pall left from so much gunfire made it impossible to breathe or see that well.

A blast of light from the end of the hall was a burst of return fire. Eddie Seng went sprawling, as if suddenly shoved from behind. Unable to stop his fall with his hands, he crashed to the deck and slid into the Chairman. One-handed, Juan grabbed him by the collar and dragged him into the mess, all the while firing with his left.

Didi continued to struggle in Linc's powerful grip as he was manhandled into the mess hall. All the furniture was gone, and, unbelievably, a pair of men was wrestling the stove out the kitchen door despite the gun battle raging just outside. When the pair realized the men who had rushed into the room weren't their friends, they dropped their burden and reached for the weapons they'd left lying across the burners.

Juan fired fast and from the hip but still managed amazing accuracy. Both men's chests erupted in a gush of blood and torn meat.

A secret door seamlessly built into a bulkhead clicked open. Linda had been watching them with the hidden camera and had men standing by to help. A pair of operatives rushed into the room, and ten seconds later Mohammad Didi had FlexiCuffs around his wrists. They hustled him back through the door and closed it behind them. Eddie was groaning and trying to get to his feet. Juan gently lifted him up and helped him through the door. Once through, Juan fell back on the wall with his hands on his knees, dripping water onto the plush carpet. It took him a moment to catch his breath.

"That could have gone better," he panted.

"You can say that again," Eddie agreed.

"You okay?"

"The bullet grazed a plate in my flak jacket. Hurts like hell, but I'm good to go. Just give me a minute."

Giuseppe Farina approached with Dr. Huxley. Hux wore her de rigueur white lab coat over a pair of surgical scrubs and had a leather medical bag gripped in her right hand. She was in her early forties, with dark hair pulled back in a ponytail, and a no-nonsense look in her eyes.

"Not being too cowboy for you, are we?" Juan grinned at the Italian observer.

Farina cast a murderous look at Didi, and said, "I had hoped, maybe, for a little more."

"Who are you people?" Didi demanded in accented English. "You cannot take me. I am a Somali citizen. I have rights."

"Not once you set foot on this ship before it had cleared customs," Juan informed him. "You're on my territory now." It took all his willpower not to rip the grisly necklace from around Didi's neck and cram it down his throat.

Julia set her bag on the deck, rummaged through it, and stood holding a syringe and a pair of surgical scissors. With Didi firmly in Linc's grip, she cut away part of his sleeve and swabbed his skin with alcohol.

"What are you doing?" Didi's eyes had gone wide. He

tried to wiggle free, but Linc's arms were like iron bands around his body. "This is torture."

Juan was in front of the warlord before anyone knew he was moving. He pulled Didi from Linc's grip. With one hand around Didi's throat, Juan used the leverage of the corridor wall to lift the Somali off his feet so they were eye to eye. Didi began to gag, but no one made a move to help him. Even their European observer was spellbound by the utter rage that puffed up the Chairman's face and turned his skin red.

"You want to see torture? I will show you torture, you murderous piece of filth." He used the thumb and index finger of his other hand and pinched a nerve bundle in Didi's shoulder. Didi must have felt as if he'd been seared with a hot poker, because he let out a wail that echoed down the corridor. Juan dug in deeper, changing the pitch of the pirate's scream as if he were playing a musical instrument.

"That's enough, Juan," Dr. Huxley said.

Cabrillo released his grip and let Didi, who clutched at his throat and shoulder, fall to the floor. He was weeping, and a silver string of saliva oozed out of the corner of his mouth.

"Like I figured," Juan said as if the outburst had not occurred, "in the heart of every bully lies a coward. I wish your men could see you now."

Hux bent over the prostrate killer and slid the needle home. A moment later, Didi's eyes fluttered and rolled back into his skull so only the whites showed. Hux bent over him a second time and thumbed down the lids.

"Congratulations, Juan." 'Seppe extended his hand. "Mission accomplished."

"Not until we're clear of Somali waters and that scumbag is off my boat." He tapped his radio. "Linda, tell Max to cut the smoke and give me a sit rep."

"The pirates who were chasing you are milling around the mess hall. One is checking on the guys you took down, but those boys aren't in any condition to tell them much. On deck, the water cannons are having the desired effect. People are scrambling off the ship as fast as they can."

"How many do you estimate are still aboard?"

"Forty-three precisely. And that includes the rebels you

trapped down near the hold. The guard you left unconscious under the stairs has already been taken care of. He came awake the moment he was tossed into the water."

"Tell Eric to make ready to pull away from the dock."

"What do we do with the pirates still roaming around the superstructure?" Linda asked.

"Lock it down, and get the armorer up here with tranq guns and NVGs."

In the op center, Linda relayed Juan's orders. On the big monitor she watched as a group of kids was trying to dodge the powerful spray from one of the water cannons, turning it into a game of dare. From her seat in the middle of the room, she hit a toggle to take command of that particular cannon and cut the flow of water. The kids stopped dashing around, looking like their favorite toy had been taken away. Linda adjusted the aim and electronically opened the valve again. The blast caught the boys at the knees, knocking all six flat and tumbling them like flotsam toward the boarding stairs. They didn't stop rolling until they landed on the dock in a sodden tangle of limbs. The boys quickly got to their feet and fled into the village.

"Locking down now," Mark Murphy said after typing at his workstation for a moment. He made the last keystroke, and all over the ship hidden steel shutters slammed closed over every door, hatch, and window, effectively sealing the entire superstructure.

A cat might have been able to maneuver in such darkness, but a man without night vision goggles was as good as blind.

Linda switched the internal cameras to thermal imaging and scanned the feeds until she had checked every compartment and hallway. There were still thirteen people locked inside the ship. When she switched the cameras to low-light mode, she made out that they were all armed men. Over the speakers, she could hear them calling out to one another, but no one dared move from where he stood.

Just as Linda finished her sweep, Juan came over the radio. "How do we look?"

"We've got thirteen. The pirates who were in the mess are

out in the hallway now with the others you tangled with, so I'd say you're clear."

"Good enough for me."

"Happy hunting."

Two decks above, Juan doused the lights in the hallway and slid a pair of third-generation night vision goggles over his eyes. In his hand he carried a sleek-looking pistol with walnut grips and an especially long barrel. Powered by compressed gas, the tranquilizer gun could fire ten needles laced with a sedative so potent it would drop an average-sized man in ten seconds. While that may sound like a short amount of time, it could give a gunman ample opportunity to loosen an entire magazine from an automatic weapon—hence the darkness.

Eddie and Linc were similarly armed.

Cabrillo opened the secret door again. Through the goggles, the world had gone an eerie shade of green. Reflective surfaces shone a bright white that could be distracting had Juan and his people not been so used to NVGs. When the hatch closed behind them, they padded forward until they were pressed to the mess-hall door. The air still smelled sharply of smoke.

"There are three of them to your right," Linda said over the tactical net. "Ten feet down the corridor and moving away from you."

Using hand signals, Juan relayed the information to his men and like wraiths out of a nightmare they slid out the mess and took aim simultaneously. The tranquilizer guns gave a soft whisper, and even before the darts found their marks Cabrillo and the others were back in the mess.

The barbs hit the men in their shoulders, the ultrafine needles having no trouble piercing clothing and lodging in flesh. The sharp sting made all three whirl around, and one opened fire in panic. The muzzle flash revealed an empty corridor, and for the second time in twelve hours Malik and Aziz were chasing ghosts.

"This ship is crewed by evil djinns," Aziz managed to wail before he was overtaken by the drug. Malik, who was a larger man, swayed for a moment before he, too, tumbled flat, landing on the unconscious third rebel.

"Ten to go," Linda said. "But we've got another problem."

"Talk to me," Juan said tersely.

"The pirates onshore are getting organized. There's some guy rallying them to reboard the *Oregon*. He has maybe twenty-five or thirty looking like they're going to try it."

"Am I on the speakers?"

"Affirmative."

"Mark, pop open one of the deck .30s and scatter that crowd. Eric, pull us away."

Eric Stone and Mark Murphy shot each other a grin and made to carry out Cabrillo's order. Murphy keyed in the command to one of the .30-caliber machine guns hidden in an oil barrel on deck.

The barrel's lid hinged open and the weapon emerged in a vertical position before its gimbal it until the barrel was pointed at the earthen embankment behind the dock. On Murphy's computer, a camera slaved to the M60 gave him a sight picture, including an aiming reticle.

He loosened a volley over the heads of the crowd, the gun barking and a string of empty shell casings falling to the deck in a metal rain. The armed pirates either dropped flat or vanished over the embankment. A few lying prone returned fire, raking the area where the remotely operated gun still smoked. Their 7.62mm rounds were as effective as hitting a rhino with a spitball.

Next to Murphy, Eric Stone dialed up the power from the magnetohydrodynamic engines. The water this deep into the swamp was brackish from having mixed with fresh, but it maintained enough salinity for him to ramp the ship up to eighty percent capacity. He engaged reverse thrust. The power of the massive hydro pumps boiled the water at the *Oregon*'s bow, and the great ship began to back away from the wooden dock.

The ropes the pirates had used to secure the vessel lost their slack, then went as taut as bowstrings before the old hemp broke. Eric eased the ship back from the dock a good fifty feet and then engaged the dynamic positioning system to keep the *Oregon* at those exact GPS coordinates.

There was no way he would attempt to maneuver the ship out of the swamp without the Chairman on deck to lend a hand if he got into trouble.

But then his mind was changed for him.

Like a barrage from a group of archers, a flurry of rocket-propelled grenades came sizzling over the embankment. The smoke they trailed seemed to fill the sky from horizon to horizon.

SIX

Eric slammed his fist on the collision alarm button. The electronic cry would carry to every deck and compartment on the ship. It was a sound the crew knew well.

At this close range there wasn't enough time to deploy the 20mm Gatling close-in defense system; however, Mark Murphy was getting it ready for the second salvo he was sure would follow.

A few of the rockets went radically off course, corkscrewing into the water or into the mangroves to detonate harmlessly. Even with the bow facing the attack, the *Oregon* was still a large enough target to make it difficult to miss. RPGs slammed into her prow, blowing off her fore railing and tearing a fluke off one of her anchors. Others skimmed over the bow and exploded against the superstructure below the closed-off bridge windows.

Had this been any other ship, the onslaught would have turned the vessel into scrap. But the *Oregon*'s armor held. A few craters had been cored into the steel, and paint had been burned off all over the superstructure, but none of the rocket grenades had penetrated. There remained vulnerable areas, however. The ship wasn't entirely impervious to a rocket attack. The smokestack shielded the ship's sophisticated radar dish, and a lucky shot could easily destroy it.

"Incoming," Juan heard over the radio earbud an instant before the first RPG homed in on his ship.

The blasts at the bow gave him and his team enough warning to clamp their hands over their ears and leave their mouths open to prevent unequal pressure in their sinuses that would blow out their eardrums.

The superstructure rang as though it were a giant bell. Each explosion sent the men reeling back, though they were nowhere near the sections getting pummeled. In those compartments, the staggering concussions were lethal. One pirate, who had been leaning against a wall that took one of the rocket strikes, had his insides jellied by the blast, while the two men with him permanently lost their hearing.

"Tell Eric to get us the hell out of here," Juan shouted into his microphone. He could barely hear his own voice, while Linda's was an unintelligible squeal.

As soon as Eric had mashed the collision alarm, he disengaged the GPS and reconfigured the view on the main screen so half of it showed a camera shot over the *Oregon*'s fantail while the other monitored the pirate lair. There was neither time nor room to turn the five-hundred-foot ship.

He moved the throttles once again into reverse.

The channel looked so narrow he felt like he was going to thread a needle while wearing oven mitts. At least the first mile was straight, so he added more power, backing the big freighter as carefully as he possibly could. It didn't help that a breeze had picked up, and the hull and superstructure were acting like a sail.

A pair of RPGs was launched from the dock. This time, Mark had the redoubt opened for the six-barreled Gatling gun, and it spooled up to nearly a thousand rpms.

The Vulcan shrieked and the Russian-made rocket-propelled grenades ran into the solid curtain of the 20mm rounds it had spewed. Both warheads detonated over the water, while the embankment beyond was chewed apart by the slugs that over-shot. Mark saw that pirates were getting ready to follow the *Oregon* in their fishing boats. They wouldn't be an issue once they reached thc sea, but until Eric maneuvered them through the mangroves the fishing boats had the edge.

Mark aimed low along the hull of the first boat and unleashed a one-second burst. The shells ripped open the water immediately adjacent to the boat, dousing the rebels and, more important, warning them. They dove off the boat and were halfway down the dock when Murph unleashed the autocannon again.

The small trawler disintegrated in a mushrooming cloud of shredded wood, splintered glass, and torn metal. When the gas tank erupted, the blast knocked the pirates flat, as greasy smoke rose into the air.

The men on the second boat had pulled away from the dock before they realized they were next. Mark almost chuckled at how comically they leapt from the doomed boat, giving little thought to their comrades. When it was clear of men, he fired. The pilothouse was blown away like a garden shed caught in a tornado. So much of the bow was destroyed that, with the throttles open, water poured into the hull until the boat vanished entirely. It reminded him of a submarine sinking beneath the waves, only this craft was never surfac-ing again.

Up in the superstructure, Juan and his two teammates took up the chase again. Still unable to hear Linda because his ears continued to ring, Cabrillo relied on his hunter's instincts. They moved slowly and methodically, checking and clearing the area room by room. When they discovered the grisly chamber where one of the rockets had hit, they darted the two deafened pirates. The third man looked like a rag doll with half its stuffing removed.

The explosions, and the fact that they could feel the ship under way, sent the rebels into near panic. They screamed for one another in the blackness, and the ones who found a sealed door clawed at the metal with their bare hands. They had no idea they were being stalked until a dart shot out of nowhere.

Had these men not preyed on unsuspecting ships off the coast, Juan could almost dredge up some pity for them. But he had a mariner's special loathing for pirates and piracy, so he felt nothing when he fired the final time and sent the last of them into dreamland.

"Okay, Linda, that's it," Juan reported. "Unseal the superstructure and get some support in here. Tell Hux to treat the wounded as best she can, but I want this scum off the ship in thirty minutes."

Cabrillo stripped off the cumbersome night vision goggles when the plates over the exterior doors and ports lifted and the fluorescent lights flickered to life. His wiped the sweat from his forehead with his sleeve. It came away soaked, and he knew that the temperature was only partially responsible for the perspiration. His limbs trembled with the aftereffects of the adrenaline high.

A few moments later, the superstructure was crawling with personnel to deal with the unconscious gunmen. Giuseppe appeared at Juan's side and handed him a water bottle glistening with dew. He walked with Juan as the Chairman headed for the op center. The Italian had to lengthen his stride to keep pace.

"I was thinking, *amico*, it might be wise to take a few of these men with us when we put Didi on the fishing boat we have."

Cabrillo drank deeply, then said, "Better cover story than Didi out on his own sunset cruise?"

"*Sí.*"

"Did you have enough of that amnesia drug?"

"I have enough for two more, I should think."

"Fine by me," Juan said casually as they entered the ship's nerve center.

With one sweep of his eyes, Cabrillo took in the operational situation. They were far enough from the rebel compound that they were no longer under threat of attack from the RPGs, and since he didn't see any boats in pursuit he assumed Murph had taken care of them. Eric had backed up the *Oregon* until she was almost in the tight turn.

"How are you doing, Mr. Stone?" he asked.

"It's like pushing string, sir. Between the incoming tide, rising wind, and shoaling bottom, I don't see how you got us into this jam in the first place."

"Want me to take over?"

"I'd like to give it a try myself first."

"Incoming!" Murph suddenly shouted.

Unknown to the crew, there was a causeway running alongside the channel that the rebels had cleared to make a road. While the ship was slowly backing out of the swamp, armed rebels had boarded several trucks and raced after the lumbering freighter. When it paused in the tight confines of the turn, they opened fire with more RPGs.

Murph still had the Gatling port opened, but he had let the gun barrels stop rotating. He spun it up with the press of a button and opened fire. He was too slow for the first two rockets, which hit the hull and detonated harmlessly, but he managed to swat two more out of the air.

"I have the conn," Cabrillo said.

"Roger," Eric replied instantly.

Where Eric was approaching the tricky turn slowly and methodically, Juan ramped up the engines and engaged the bow thruster, remembering that they were in reverse so he had to call on the opposite side.

The Vulcan sounded like an industrial saw when it screamed again. On the causeway, one of the technicals had its front axle torn off. The vehicle catapulted over its truncated front end, scattering men, weapons, and a cascade of broken glass. It landed on its roof and dug a deep furrow into the rocky soil, its rear wheels spinning.

A second pickup was hit broadside. The kinetic energy of the tungsten shells flipped the two-ton truck onto its side and the gas tank exploded. It erupted in a blooming rose of flame and smoke. Mark had a bead on the third when it vanished behind a thick tangle of vegetation. He waited for it to reemerge on the other side of the copse of trees, but seconds trickled by with no firm sighting.

Watching the undergrowth through the zoom camera lens, he thought he saw movement yet still held his fire. With the ship accelerating down the channel, the angle continued to shift. In a moment, he would have to switch from the Vulcan mounted along the *Oregon*'s flank near the bow to the second gun located at the stern. Mark activated the hydraulics that would open the fantail doors. The plates slid aside to reveal the multibarrel weapon, but it would take a moment for it to be run out and the camera switched on his monitor. The jungle he'd been watching erupted in blinding flashes that came in a continuous blur. A second later, 20mm rounds from a truck-mounted antiaircraft cannon raked the *Oregon*. Unlike the RPGs, the cannon's hardened rounds tore into the ship's armor, gouging divots into the steel, and when two hit the same spot they bored through and began to wreak havoc on the interior spaces.

The only saving grace was that the ship's ballast tanks were full to make her look heavily laden, so only one of her secret decks was exposed. One round penetrated the executive boardroom and blew through a pair of leather-backed chairs before embedding itself in the far wall. Another entered the pantry and tore apart a pallet of flour so the air became a solid-white curtain of dust. A third exploded into the cabin of an off-duty engineer. He'd been sitting at his desk, watching the battle on the ship's closed-circuit television system, which saved his legs from the blast of shrapnel, but his back and neck were shredded as though he'd been mauled.

This all happened in the blink of an eye. Mark watched helplessly. He was impotent until the computer told him the second gun was ready.

"Wepps, what the hell?" Juan growled without taking his attention off the delicate maneuver of turning the big ship.

"One more sec . . ."

Murphy's board turned green, and he unleashed the weapon. The jungle where the technical lay hidden was swept away by the onslaught. Trees up to a foot thick were mowed down like wheat before a combine. One trunk plummeted to the earth, a halo of wood chips choking the area. It smashed into the technical's bed, silencing its twin cannons, but Mark kept up the remorseless torrent of rounds until the trees were gone and all that remained of the truck and crew was a smoldering ruin of torn metal and rended flesh.

The *Oregon* was halfway through the turn. Cabrillo had judged it precisely. He backed his ship with the expertise of a truck driver parallel-parking a big rig. The stern came mere inches from the muddy bank. They were so close that someone standing near the jack staff could have plucked leaves from the trees. Then she swung around, almost pivoting on a dime, so her fantail was pointed eastward toward the open ocean.

Eric gave Cabrillo a look of respect bordering on hero worship. He never would have dared maneuver the ship so fast through such a tight channel.

"Think you can take it from here?" the Chairman asked his helmsman.

"I got her, boss man." The ship automatically recorded its position using the constellation of GPS satellites. All Stone had to do now that the trickiest corner had been negotiated was run a reverse course through the nava-computer and the ship would steer herself around the tricky swamps and shifting shoals. He already had the coordinates where the derelict fishing boat awaiting Mohammad Didi had been pre-positioned.

Juan got up from his command chair and turned to Giuseppe Farina. "Let's figure out who you want to keep and who's going over the side. I want the pirates off the ship before we clear the mangroves."

He led the Italian observer down several decks to the *Oregon*'s boat garage. Here, near the waterline, was a large door that could be opened to the sea. There was a ramp built into the ship, covered in Teflon to make it slick. From it, the crew could launch Zodiacs, Jet Skis, or her RHIB—rigid-hull inflatable boat. That particular craft was built for the Navy SEALs, with a bladder of air around its hull to give it buoyancy in any conditions and a pair of powerful outboards that could shoot it across the waves at better than fifty knots. The lighting was white fluorescents, but red battle lamps could be lit for night operations.

The crew had already inflated a large black raft, and the unconscious forms of the pirates had been loosely bound to it. Once they awoke, they would be able to free one another and paddle the raft back to shore. Hux still had the wounded in the medical bay, while the dead would be given burials at sea.

"We'll take this one and this one and that guy on the far side," Farina said, pointing to Malik and Aziz. "When they took the ship, they appeared to have some leadership role. Who knows? They might prove to be an intelligence asset."

"The younger one probably isn't worth it. Guy smokes more dope than a hippie at a Grateful Dead concert."

"They no longer tour, you know," 'Seppe teased.

"You know what I mean."

"We'll use him anyway. A little forced detoxification might do him some good."

Thirty minutes later, Hux arrived in the boat garage with a couple of crewmen acting as orderlies. They wheeled down several gurneys for the injured pirates.

"How are they?" Juan asked.

"We have a casualty," Hux told him.

"What? Why wasn't I told?"

"No sense informing you until I had him stable."

"Who is it? What happened?"

"One of those triple-A rounds penetrated Sam Pryor's cabin. He took some shrapnel to his back. I pulled out about twenty small fragments. He lost a good amount of blood, and there's some torn muscle, but he's going to be fine."

"Thank God," Juan breathed, thinking about the reprimand Mark Murphy had coming. He should have had the stern Gatling online much sooner. "So what about these guys?"

"Two have hearing loss," Dr. Huxley replied in a no-nonsense tone. "I don't know if it's permanent, and there isn't much I could do either way. Couple more have superficial wounds. I dug out the shrapnel, cleaned and dressed them, and pumped them with as much antibiotic as I dared. If they get infected, they're in for a rough time of it, considering the conditions they live in."

The two Somalis who'd been shot had been given a nylon satchel. Cabrillo guessed they contained additional medication and written instructions on how to use it. He also guessed the men wouldn't take the drugs and they would end up on Somalia's booming black market.

The wounded were set on the raft and the outer door was cranked open. Juan called up to the op center for Eric to bring the ship to a stop. At the leisurely speed they were doing, it took only a few minutes for the pump jets to slow the ship until she was wallowing in the gentle waves like an old sow. Water lapped just below the bottom edge of the ramp. Beyond, Cabrillo could see they were just about to break out of the mangroves. With the tide coming in, the raft would drift westward until it became entangled in the swamp. The men would wake in about an hour, so other than mild dehydration they would be fine.

He helped push the raft until it was sliding down the ramp. It hit the water without a splash, and its momentum carried it a few yards from the ship.

Juan tapped the intercom button again. "Okay, Eric, take us away nice and easy, and when they're a quarter mile astern open her up and get us to the fishing boat."

"Roger that."

A half hour later, Juan and 'Seppe Farina were outside, standing on the wing bridge. Crewmen were at work repairing the cosmetic damage caused by the RPG attacks. Railings were being replaced and scorch marks covered in thick marine paint. Men were slung over the side on bosuns' chairs welding patches to the hull where the antiaircraft rounds had pierced the armor. Other men were inside, restoring the cabins with mattresses and furniture from the ship's stores. Max Hanley was compiling a list of everything they would need to buy in order to put the old freighter back to her former "glory."

The *Oregon* plowed through the calm waves at better than thirty knots, far from her maximum speed, when Linda Ross's already high-pitched voice squeaked from the tinny speaker. "Chairman, we have a radar contact four miles dead ahead."

Juan swung a pair of binoculars to his eyes and a moment

later saw a speck on the otherwise deserted ocean. It took a few more minutes for it to resolve itself into a fishing boat much like the one that had initially attacked.

"When is the American destroyer going to be in this area?" Juan asked his friend.

"Dawn tomorrow. More than enough time for us to steal off into the night. Didi and the others probably won't be awake yet, and, if they are, they will be so nauseated by the drug they'll be as docile as lambs. And do not worry—the boat has no radio or fuel, and the chance someone will happen across it before your Navy is absolutely zero."

Eric brought the *Oregon* alongside the old fishing vessel so that men in the boat garage could simply leap aboard her with lines to secure it to the freighter. Cabrillo and Farina personally carried Mohammad Didi onto the stinking boat. They lugged him into the cabin below the pilothouse, and when they tossed him on an unmade bunk they might accidentally have thrown him too hard. His head hit the frame with a satisfying clunk.

Cabrillo looked down on the warlord with utter contempt. "We should've had your ass Gitmo'd for all the suffering you've caused, but that wasn't my call. The worst cell in the worst jail in the world is too good for you. Imprisonment in Europe will probably feel like a vacation after living like you have, so all that I can hope is that when they hand down that life sentence you have the decency to die on the spot."

Back on deck he couldn't help but chuckle. Linc and Eddie had tied Aziz to a chair with a fishing rod in one hand and a bottle of beer taped in the other.

No sooner had the ropes been cast away than Hali Kasim, the *Oregon*'s communications specialist, came over the intercom. "Chairman, you have an urgent call from Langston Overholt."

"Pipe it down here." Juan waited a beat, and said, "Lang, it's Juan. Just so you know, you're on speakerphone. With me is our Italian liaison."

"I'll cut the pleasantries for now," Overholt said from his Langley office. "How soon can you be in Tripoli?"

"Depending on traffic through the Suez Canal, maybe four days. Why?"

"The Secretary of State was on her way there for some preliminary talks. We just lost communication with her plane. We fear it crashed."

"We'll be there in three."

SEVEN

OVER THE SAHARA DESERT

WHEN HER FINGER SLIPPED OFF THE STRING, FIONA cursed. She looked up quickly to make sure no one heard, even though she was alone in the private bedchamber in the rear of the aircraft. Her mother had been a strong believer in using soap in the mouth to discourage profanity, so her reaction was automatic even forty years later.

The violin was her refuge from the world. With bow in hand she could empty her mind of all distractions and concentrate solely on the music. There was no other activity or hobby that could quiet her thoughts so thoroughly. She often credited it with keeping her sane, especially since accepting the appointment to head the State Department.

Fiona Katamora was one of those rare creatures who come along once in a generation. By her sixth birthday, she was giving violin concerts as a soloist. Her parents, who had been interned during World War II because both had been born in Japan, had taught her Japanese while she taught herself Arabic, Mandarin, and Russian. She entered Harvard when she was fifteen and law school when she was eighteen.

Before taking the bar exam, she took time off to sharpen her fencing skills, and would have gone on to the Olympics had she not torn a ligament in her knee a week before the opening ceremony.

She did all this and much more and made it look effortless. Fiona Katamora possessed a near-photographic memory, and required only four hours of sleep a night. Apart from her athletic, academic, and musical talents, she was charming, gracious, and possessed an infectious smile that could brighten any room.

Fiona had more than a hundred job offers to consider when she passed the bar, including a teaching position at her alma mater, but she wanted to dedicate herself to serving the public trust. She joined a Washington think tank specializing in energy matters, and quickly made a name for herself with her ability to see causalities others simply couldn't. After five years, one of her papers was submitted as a doctoral thesis, and she was awarded a Ph.D.

Her reputation within the Beltway grew to the point that she was a regular consultant at the White House for Presidents of both parties. It was only a matter of time before she was tapped for a cabinet post.

Still unmarried at forty-six, Fiona Katamora remained a stunning beauty, with raven hair as glossy as obsidian and a smooth, unlined face. She was trim and, at five feet six, tall for her ancestry. In interviews, she said she was simply too busy for a family of her own, and while gossip magazines had tried to link her to various men of wealth and power, she almost never dated.

In her two years as Secretary of State, she had worked wonders around the globe, restoring America's reputation as peacemaker and impartial arbiter. She had helped broker the longest cease-fire to date between the government of Sri Lanka and Tamil Tiger separatists, and had used her skills to settle a disputed election in Serbia that had threatened to become violent.

Fiona had shaken things up within the corridors of the State Department as well. She had garnered the nickname "dragon lady" because she had swept house at Foggy Bottom, cutting out layer upon layer of redundant staff, until State was the model of efficiency for the rest of the government.

And now she was headed for what could be the crowning moment of a remarkable career. The preliminary talks were meant to establish the framework for what was to be called the Tripoli Accords. If anyone could bring peace to the Middle East after ten presidential administrations failed, it would be Fiona Katamora.

She finished playing the Brahms piece she'd been practicing and set the violin and bow aside. She wiped her fingers on a monogrammed handkerchief and did some exercises to work out the mild cramping. She feared that arthritis was starting to make inroads.

There was a knock on the cabin door.

"Come in," she said.

Her personal assistant, Grace Walsh, popped her head around the jamb. Grace had been with Fiona for more than a decade, following her boss from plum job to plum job.

"You wanted me to tell you when it was four."

"Thanks, Gracie. What's our ETA?"

"Knew you'd ask, so I spoke with the pilot. We're about forty-five minutes out. We'll be over Libyan territory shortly. Can I get you anything?"

"A bottle of water would be great. Thanks."

Fiona buried herself in the stack of papers spread out on the bed. They were dossiers on all the major players expected at the upcoming summit, including brief biographies and photographs. She'd gone over them all before, committing most to memory, but she wanted to make sure she had everything just right. She quizzed herself on which ministers were related to their country's rulers, names of wives and children, educational backgrounds, anything to make this as personal as possible.

She was most intrigued by Libya's dynamic new Foreign Minister, Ali Ghami. His was by far the smallest dossier. Reportedly, Ghami had been a low-level civil servant until he'd come to the attention of Libya's President Muammar Qaddafi. Within days of a meeting between the two men, Ghami had been elevated to Foreign Minister. In the six months since, he had been on a whirlwind tour throughout the region, drumming up support for the peace conference. His reception in various Middle Eastern capitals had been cool at first, but his dynamic personality and utter charm had slowly started to change minds. In many ways, he was like Fiona, and maybe that was why she couldn't get her mind around what bothered her about him.

Grace knocked again and stepped into the bedroom. She set a bottle of Dasani on the nightstand and turned to go.

"Hold on a sec," Fiona said, and showed her the photograph of Ghami. "What does your woman's intuition tell you about him?"

Grace took the picture and held it close to one of the Boeing 737's windows. In the official photograph, Ghami wore a Western-style suit cut perfectly for his physique. He had thick salt-and-pepper hair and a matching mustache.

Gracie gave her the picture back. "I'm the wrong person to ask. I fell in love with Omar Sharif when I saw *Doctor Zhivago* as a teenager, and this guy has that same vibe."

"Handsome, yes, but look at his eyes."

"What about them?" Gracie asked.

"I can't put my finger on it. There's something there, or something missing. I don't know."

"Could just be a bad picture."

"Maybe it's that I just don't like going into this knowing virtually nothing about our host."

"You can't have crib notes on everybody," Grace teased gently. "Remember when you did a background check on that cute lawyer you wanted to—"

A loud, jarring crash cut Grace off in midsentence. The two women looked at each other, eyes wide. Both had spent countless hours in the air over the years and knew whatever that sound was, it wasn't good.

They waited a beat to see if anything else was happening. After a few seconds, they simultaneously released a held breath and shared a nervous chuckle.

Fiona got to her feet to ask the pilot if anything was wrong. She was halfway to the door when the aircraft shuddered violently and started to fall from the sky. Grace screamed when the wild descent pressed her up against the ceiling. Fiona managed to keep on her feet by pushing her hands against the molded plastic overhead.

In the forward section of the executive jet, she could hear other staffers screaming as they fought the effects of temporary weightlessness.

"I don't know what happened," the pilot, an Air Force colonel, said over the intercom, "but everyone get yourselves strapped in as quickly as you can." He left the intercom on while he and his copilot tried to regain control of the hurtling aircraft, so Fiona and the others could hear the tension in his voice. "What do you mean you can't reach anyone? We were talking with Tripoli two minutes ago."

"I can't explain it," the copilot replied. "The radio's just dead."

"Don't worry about it now. Help me—damn, the port engine just kicked out. Try to restart it." The intercom suddenly clicked off.

"Are we going to crash?" Grace asked. She had regained her feet, and she and Fiona clutched each other like little girls in a haunted house.

"I don't know," Fiona said more calmly than she felt. Her insides fluttered, and her palms had gone greasy.

"What happened?"

"I don't know. Something mechanical, I guess." That answer didn't satisfy her at all. There was no reason the plane should have plummeted like that with both engines functioning. It could even fly on one engine. Something else had to have caused their sudden drop. And what was that loud bang? Her first and only thought was that they had been hit by a missile, one meant to cripple the plane, not destroy it.

The gut-wrenching descent slowly started to even out. The pilots had managed to regain enough control so they were no longer in free fall, but they were still plunging toward earth at breakneck speed.

Fiona and Grace groped their way into the main cabin and strapped themselves into the big leather chairs. Secretary Katamora said a few reassuring words to her people, wishing she could do more to alleviate the fear she saw etched on their faces. The truth was that she was barely in control of her own emotions. She feared that if she spoke more her terror would rise to the surface and bubble over, like lava erupting from a volcano.

"Ladies and gentlemen"—it was the copilot—"we don't know what just happened. One of our engines is down and the other is barely producing thrust. We're going to have to land in the desert. I don't want anyone to worry. Colonel Markham has actually done this before in an F-16 during the first Gulf War. When I give the signal, I want everyone to assume the crash positions. Tuck your head between your knees and wrap your arms around them. As soon as the plane comes to a stop, I want the steward to open the cabin door as quickly as possible. Secretary Katamora's Secret Service detail is to get her off the plane first."

There was only one agent on board. The rest of Fiona's detail, plus a number of her staff, had been in Libya for nearly a week preparing for her arrival.

The agent, Frank Maguire, unbuckled his seat belt, paused until the aircraft stopped buffeting for a second, and switched seats so he was between Fiona and the door. He quickly strapped himself in as the Boeing lurched violently. When the time came, he could grab her and have her out of the door in seconds.

Holding Grace's hand, Fiona started to do something she hadn't in years: pray. But it wasn't for their lives. She prayed that if the worst did happen and they died in the crash, the momentous opportunity of the summit wouldn't be lost forever. Unselfish to the end, Fiona Katamora cared more about the cause of peace than her own life.

She chanced looking out the window. The terrain not far below the aircraft was rough desert punctuated by jagged hills. Not a pilot herself, she still knew the odds were long despite the crew's assurance.

"Okay, folks," the copilot announced, "this is it. Please assume the crash positions and hang on tight."

The passengers heard the pilot ask, "Do you see th—" before the intercom went silent again. They had no idea what he had seen, and would be better off not knowing anyway.

EIGHT

ALANA SAT IN THE DRILL TRUCK'S PASSENGER'S SEAT while Mike Duncan drove. The old riverbed was littered with rounded boulders. Some could be steered around, others they had to muscle over. Her backside was a sea of bruises after so many weeks traversing the same terrain.

At camp the night before, they had pleaded their case to the Tunisian representative, who believed they were searching for a Roman mill and waterwheel, that returning to the old ruins every night was an unnecessary precaution. They begged to be allowed to stay out for a few days, pointing out that Greg Chaffee had a satellite phone, so they would never really be out of contact with the main archaeological team.

While the legitimate members of the archaeological dig were making tremendous strides in excavating the Roman ruins, Alana's team still had nothing to show for their weeks of effort. It was hoped that if they could remain out in the desert longer, and thus roam wider, they might pick up the trail of the old Barbary corsair, Suleiman Al-Jama.

The only thing keeping her going now was her nightly

e-mail chat with her son back in Phoenix. She marveled at the advance in technology. Her first dig as an undergrad, at a site in the Arizona desert less than two hundred miles from school, had been more isolated than this godforsaken dust bowl, thanks to modern satellite communications.

The Tunisian government minder continued to refuse their request until Greg took him aside for about two minutes. When they had returned to the dining tent, the official beamed at Alana and granted them permission, provided they checked in every day and returned within seventy-two hours.

"Baksheesh," Greg had replied to her inquiring look.

Alana had paled. "What if he refused the money and reported you?"

"This is the Middle East. We would have been in trouble if he hadn't."

"But . . ." Alana didn't know what to say.

She had always lived her life by one simple dictum: Obey the rules. She had never cheated on a test, reported every penny on her tax return, and set her car's cruise control at the posted speed limit. For her, the world was very black-and-white, and this made things simple in one sense and incredibly difficult in another. She could always feel comfortable with the moral choices she made, but she was forced to live in a society that spent most of its time searching for the gray areas so it could avoid responsibility.

It wasn't that she was naïve to the way the world worked, she just couldn't allow its petty corruptions into her life. It never would have occurred to her to bribe the representative from Tunisia's archaeological ministry because it was wrong.

On the other hand, she certainly wouldn't turn down the opportunity Greg's actions presented. So they were driving again, with the intention of finding a way past the waterfall in the vain hope that Suleiman Al-Jama's secret base was somewhere in the desert wastes beyond.

The truck was loaded with enough water and food to last the party three days. They had brought only one tent, but Alana felt comfortable enough with her companions that it wouldn't be a problem. They also carried a fifty-gallon drum of fuel strapped in the bed, with enough diesel to extend their range a farther three hundred miles, depending on how much they used up running the drill.

No one was optimistic about their chances. The waterfall was simply too tall for a sailing ship to navigate. However, they were desperate. The Tripoli Accords were fast approaching. Alana was aware that the Secretary of State was flying in to Libya this very day for a brief round of preliminary talks, so she felt the added pressure.

"Do you have to hit every pothole and rock?" Greg asked from the rear bench seat of the open-topped truck.

"As a matter of fact, I do," Mike deadpanned.

Greg shifted to the right so he was behind Alana. "Then hit them with the left-side tires, will ya?"

It was another sparkling-clear day, which meant the temperature hit one hundred and eight degrees when they stopped for lunch. Alana handed out chilled bottles of water from the cooler and gave each man a sandwich the camp staff had prepared. According to the odometer, they had come seventy miles, and if she remembered correctly the falls were a further thirty.

"What do you think about over there?" Mike asked with his mouth full of food. He used his sandwich like a pointer to indicate the far bank of the old river. Where usually they were hemmed in by steep cliffs, here, in a curve in the watercourse, erosion had carved into the bank so it was a ramp up to the desert floor.

"Looks to be a sixty percent grade, or steeper," Greg said.

"If we can find something on top to secure the winch, we should be able to pull ourselves up, no problem."

Alana nodded. "I like it."

As soon as they finished their meal, something the heat made unappealing to them all, Mike drove the truck to the base of the riverbank. Seen up close, the gradient appeared steeper than they had originally estimated, and the height a good thirty feet more. He forced the truck up the bank until the rear wheels lost traction and began to throw off plumes of dust. Alana and Greg leapt from the vehicle. She began to unspool the braided-steel cable from the winch mounted to the front bumper, while Greg Chaffee, the fittest of the bunch, threw himself into the task of climbing the slope. His boots kicked up small avalanches of loose dirt and pebbles with each step, and he was quickly forced to scramble up the hill using his hands and arms as well as his legs. He cursed when his big straw hat went flying away, rolling down the hill behind him. With no choice, he clipped the hook to the back of his belt and kept going, scraping his fingers raw on the rough stone.

It took Greg nearly ten minutes to reach the summit, and, when he did, the back of his shirt was soaked through with perspiration, and he could feel the bald spot on the crown of his head parboiling. He vanished from sight for a moment, dragging the wire behind him.

When he reemerged, he shouted down to the other two, "I looped the wire around an outcropping of rock. Give it a try, and pick up my hat on the way up."

The winch could be controlled from inside the truck's cab, so Alana fetched the hat before it blew away and hopped back into her seat. Mike jammed the transmission into first, fed the engine some gas, and engaged the winch's toggle. While not especially powerful, the winch's motor ran through enough gears to give it the torque it needed. The truck started a slow, stately ascent up the bank. Alana and Mike exchanged grins, while above them Greg gave a triumphant shout.

The flick of a shadow crossing her face drew Alana's attention. She glanced skyward, expecting to see a hawk or vulture.

A large twin-engine jet was passing overhead at less than a thousand feet. Incongruously, Alana could barely hear the roar of its exhaust. It was as if the engines were shut down and the jet was gliding. She knew of no landing fields in the area, at least on this side of the Libyan border, and guessed correctly that the plane was in trouble.

She noticed two details as the jet banked slightly away. One was a jagged hole near the tail that was stained with what she guessed was hydraulic fluid. The other thing she saw were words written along the aircraft's fuselage: UNITED STATES OF AMERICA.

Greg had stopped whooping. He placed his hand above his eyes, shading them from the sun, and he turned in place, tracking the path of the crippled government jet.

Alana gasped aloud when she realized what plane that was and who was on it.

Concentrating on getting the truck up the hill, Mike Duncan hadn't seen a thing, so when Alana sucked in a lungful of air he thought something was happening with the tow cable, and asked, "What is it?"

"Get to the top of the hill as fast as you can."

"I'm working on it. What's the rush?"

"The Secretary of State's plane is about to crash."

Of course, there was nothing Mike could do. They were at the mercy of the slowly turning winch.

Alana shouted up to Greg, "Can you see anything?"

"No," he replied over the rig's snarling engine. "The plane flew over some hills a couple miles from here. I don't see any smoke or anything. Maybe the pilot was able to set it down safely."

For eight agonizing minutes, the truck climbed up the hill like a fly crawling over a crust of bread. Greg kept reporting that he saw no smoke, which was a tremendous relief.

They finally emerged from the dry riverbed. Greg unsnapped the tow hook from the cable and unwound it from a sandstone projectile the size of a locomotive. The cable had cut deeply into the soft stone, and he had to brace his foot against the rock to pull it free.

"It could have come down in Libya," Mike muttered.

"What was that?" Alana asked.

"I said the plane could have come down across the border in Libya." He spoke loudly enough for Greg to hear as well.

Alana was the team leader but she looked to Chaffee for validation, her suspicions that he was from the CIA making him the expert in this type of situation.

"We could be the only people for fifty or more miles," Greg said. "If they managed to land, there could be injuries, and we have the only vehicle out here."

"Who do you really work for?" asked Alana.

"We're wasting time."

"Greg, this is important. If we have to cross into Libya, I need to know who you work for."

"I'm with the Agency, all right. The CIA. My job is to keep an eye on you three. Well, the two of you, since the good Dr. Bumford hasn't left camp since we arrived. You recognized the plane, didn't you?" Alana nodded. "So you know who's on board?"

"Yes."

"Are you willing to let her die out here because you're afraid we might run into a Libyan patrol? Hell, they invited her. They aren't going to do anything to us if we're trying to rescue her, for God's sake."

Alana looked over at Mike Duncan. The rangy oilman's face was a blank mask. They could be discussing the weather, for all the concern he showed. "What do you think?" she asked.

"I'm no hero, but I think we should probably check it out."

"Then let's go," Alana replied.

They started off across the open desert. It was like driving on the surface of the moon. There was no hint of human habitation, no inkling they were on the same planet even. From the river to the string of hills Greg mentioned was nothing but a boulder-strewn plain devoid of life. This deep in the desert, only a few insects and lizards could survive, and they had the good sense to remain in their burrows during the torturous afternoons.

As they drove, Greg tried unsuccessfully to reach his superiors on his satellite phone. His had a dedicated government communications system, the same one used by the military, so there was no reason he shouldn't get through but he couldn't. He replaced the chargeable battery with another he carried in a knapsack.

"This piece of junk," he spat. "Thirty-billion-a-year budget and they send me out with a five-year-old phone that doesn't work. I should have known. Listen, you guys, you ought to know that this wasn't really a priority mission. If we found Al-Jama's papers, great. But if not, the conference was going ahead anyway."

"But Christie Valero said—"

"Anything to get you to agree to come. Hey, Mike and I both know from playing the ponies that long shots sometimes pay, too, but this has been a farce since day one. For me, this mission is punishment for a screwup I made in Baghdad a few months ago. For you guys . . . I have no idea, but they sent me out here with crap equipment, so you figure it out."

After Greg's revealing outburst, the team drove on in silence, the mood in the truck somber. Alana was torn between thinking about what Greg had said and what they would find when they came across Secretary Katamora's plane. Both options were grim. She had never met Fiona Katamora, but she admired her tremendously. She was the kind of role model America needed. To think of her dead in a plane crash was just too horrible to contemplate.

But to consider Greg's words was painful, too, so she decided he was simply wrong. Who knew what baggage he carried that made him so jaded. Christie Valero and St. Julian Perlmutter had laid out a convincing case. Being able to undercut the justifications Islamic radicals used to validate their murderous actions would be perhaps the greatest stride yet in the war on terror. More than ever, she was certain that this mission, while admittedly a long shot, was critical to the upcoming peace talks, and she didn't care what Greg said about it.

Mike steered them into a canyon between the hills, shaded and much cooler than the open desert. It snaked through the low mountains for a half mile before they emerged on the other side. There still wasn't any evidence that the Secretary's plane had crashed, no column of black smoke rising up into the sky. Considering how low the plane had been flying, it had to be on the ground by now, so Alana let herself hope it had landed safely.

They continued on for another hour, knowing that they had passed the unmarked border at some point and were now in Libyan territory illegally. Her only solace was Greg's fluency in Arabic. If they ran into a patrol, it would be up to him to talk their way out of trouble.

The desert rose and fell in unending dunes of gravel and dirt that sent off shimmering curtains of heat. It made the distant horizon look fluid. The truck crested another anonymous hill, and Mike was about to take them down the far side when he braked suddenly. He rammed the gearbox into reverse and twisted in his seat to look behind them.

"What is it?" Alana cried as the vehicle plunged back down the hill they had climbed moments earlier.

Her answer came not from Mike but from Greg. "Patrol!"

Alana looked ahead as a military vehicle came over the hill, a soldier propped up in a hatch in the truck's roof. He was hanging on to a wicked-looking machine gun. With its tall suspension, balloon tires, and boxy cab, the truck looked perfectly suited for the desert.

"Forget it, Mike," Greg shouted over the keening engine. "Running from them is only going to make it worse."

Mike Duncan looked undecided for a moment, then nodded. He knew Chaffee was right. He eased off the gas and applied the brake. When the truck came to a stop, he killed the engine and left his hands on the wheel.

The Libyan patrol vehicle stopped twenty yards away, giving the roof gunner an optimal position to cover the trio. Back doors were thrown open and four soldiers dressed in desert fatigues rushed out, their AKs at the ready.

Alana had never been so frightened in her life. It was the suddenness of it all. One second they had been alone and the next they were looking down the barrel of a gun. Multiple guns, in fact.

The Libyan soldiers were shouting and gesturing with their weapons for them to get out of the truck. Greg Chaffee was trying to speak to them in Arabic, but his efforts had no effect. One soldier stepped back a pace and raked the ground with automatic fire, the bullets kicking up geysers of sand that blew away on the wind.

The sound was staggering, and Alana screamed.

Mike, Greg, and Alana threw their hands over their heads

in the universal signal of surrender. A soldier grabbed Alana's wrist and yanked her from the open cab. Mike made a move to protest the rough treatment and had the butt of an AK slammed into his shoulder hard enough to numb his arm to the fingertips.

Alana sprawled in the dirt, her pride injured more than her body. Greg jumped from the rear seat, keeping his arms pointed skyward.

"Please," he said in Arabic, "we didn't know we had traveled into Libya."

"Tell them about the plane," Alana said, getting to her feet and dusting off her backside.

"Oh, right." Chaffee addressed the soldiers again. "We saw an aircraft that looked like it was about to crash. We were trying to see if it had."

Though none were wearing insignia on their uniforms, one of the soldiers was clearly their leader. He asked, "Where did you see this?"

Greg was relieved he had opened a dialogue. "We are part of an archaeological expedition working just across the border in Tunisia. The plane flew over where we were working at no more than a thousand feet—ah, three hundred meters."

"Did you see the plane crash?" the unshaved soldier asked.

"No. We didn't. We think it might have actually found someplace to land in the desert, because we haven't seen any smoke."

"That is good news for you," was his non sequitur reply.

"What's that supposed to mean?" Greg asked.

The Libyan ignored the question and stepped back to his patrol vehicle. He came back a moment later with something in his hands. None of the Americans could tell what he had until he handed them over to one of his men. Handcuffs.

"What are you doing?" Alana demanded in English when one of the soldiers grabbed her shoulders from behind. "We haven't done anything wrong."

When the warm steel snapped around her wrist, she turned and spat in the face of her captor. The man backhanded her hard enough to send her sprawling.

Mike pushed aside a soldier, getting ready to cuff him, and had taken two strides toward where Alana lay semiconscious, when the group's leader reacted to the aggressive move. He drew a pistol from a holster at his hip and calmly put a bullet between the oilman's eyes.

Mike Duncan's head snapped back, and his body toppled a couple of feet from Alana. Dazed by the blow, she could do nothing but stare at the obscene third eye in Mike's forehead. A trickle of dark fluid oozed from it.

She felt herself lifted to her feet but could do nothing to either resist or assist when she was manhandled into the back of the patrol truck. Greg Chaffee, too, seemed to be in shock as he was placed on a bench seat next to her. The interior was hot, hotter than even the open desert, and it was made worse when a soldier threw a dark cloth bag over her head.

The material absorbed Alana Shepard's tears as soon as they leaked from her eyes.

NINE

CORINTHIA BAB AFRICA HOTEL,
TRIPOLI, LIBYA

Ambassador Charles Moon stood from behind his desk as soon as his secretary opened his office door and stepped aside. In a show of respect, Moon met his guest halfway across the carpeted room.

"Minister Ghami, I appreciate you taking the time out of your busy schedule to come see me in person." Moon's tone was grave.

"At a time like this, President Qaddafi wishes he could have expressed our government's concern in person, but affairs of state wait for no man. Please accept my humble presence as a sign that we share your anxiety at this disastrous event." He held out his hand to be shaken.

The U.S. Ambassador took his hand and motioned to the sofas under the glass wall overlooking the sparkling waters of the Mediterranean. Near the horizon, a tanker was plowing westward. The two men sat.

Where Moon was short in stature and wore his suit like a gunnysack, the Libyan Foreign Minister stood a solid six feet, with a handsome face and perfectly coiffed hair. His suit had the distinctive tailoring of Savile Row, and his shoes were shined to a mirror gloss. His English was nearly flawless, with just a trace of an accent that added to his urbane sophistication. He crossed his legs, plucking at his suit pants so the fabric draped properly.

"My government wants to assure you that we have scrambled search-and-rescue teams to the area, as well as aircraft. We will not stop until we are certain what happened to Secretary Katamora's plane."

"We deeply appreciate that, Minister Ghami," Charles Moon replied formally. A career diplomat, Moon knew that the tone and timbre of their conversation was as important as the words. "Your government's response to this crisis is everything we could wish for. Your visit alone tells me how serious you feel toward what could turn out to be a terrible tragedy."

"I know the cooperative relationship between our two nations is in its infancy." Ghami made a sweeping gesture with his hand to encompass the room. "You don't even have a formal embassy building yet and must work out of a hotel suite, but I want this in no way to jeopardize what has been a successful rapport."

Moon nodded. "Since May of 2006, when we formalized relations once again, we have enjoyed nothing but support from your government, and at this time don't believe anything, ah, *deliberate* has occurred." He emphasized the word, and drove the point home further by adding, "Unless new information comes to light, we view this as a tragic accident."

It was Ghami's turn to nod. Message received. "A tragic accident indeed."

"Is there anything my government can do to help?" Moon asked, though he already knew the answer. "The aircraft carrier *Abraham Lincoln* is currently in Naples, Italy, and could aid in the search in a day or two."

"I would like nothing more than to take you up on your kind offer, Ambassador. However, we believe that our own military and civilian search units are more than up for the task. I would hate to think of the diplomatic consequences if another aviation accident occurred. Further, the people of Libya have not forgotten the last time American warplanes were flying in our skies."

He was referring to the air strikes carried out by Air Force FB-111s and carrier aircraft on April 14, 1986, that leveled several military barracks and severely crippled Libya's air defense network. The strikes were in response to a spate of terrorist bombings in Europe that the U.S. had linked to a Libyan-backed group. Libya denied they had been involved, but history notes that there were no further such bombings until Al-Qaeda emerged a decade later.

Ghami gave a little smile. "Of course, we accept that you have most likely retasked some of your spy satellites to over-fly our nation. If you happen to spot the plane, well, we would understand the source of that information should you choose to share it." Moon made to protest, but the Libyan cut him off with a gesture. "Please, Mr. Ambassador, you need not comment."

Moon smiled for the first time since the transponder on Fiona Katamora's plane went silent twelve hours earlier. "I was just going to say that we would doubtlessly share such information."

"There is one more thing we need to discuss," Ghami said. "At this time, and with your approval, I see no reason to cancel or even delay the upcoming peace conference."

"I spoke with the President this morning," Moon informed him, "and he expressed the same sentiment. If, God forbid, the worst has happened, it would do Secretary Katamora's memory a disservice by canceling what she believed was the greatest opportunity to achieve regional stability. She more than anyone, I believe, would want us to proceed."

"In the event that, well, as you say, the worst has occurred, do you know who would represent your government at the conference?"

"Frankly, no. The President refused to even speculate."

"I understand completely," Ghami said.

"He and Secretary Katamora were particularly close."

"I can well imagine. From what I've read and seen on the news, she was a remarkable woman. Forgive me, *is* a remarkable woman." Ghami stood, clearly irritated at his gaffe. "Mr. Ambassador, I won't take up any more of your day. I simply wanted to express our concern in person, and you have my word that as soon as I hear anything I will call you regardless of the time."

"I appreciate that."

"On a personal note, Charles"—Ghami used his Christian name deliberately—"if this is Allah's will, I certainly don't understand it."

Moon recognized that only the most heartfelt sentiment would cause Ghami to even suggest that he was questioning the will of his God. "Thank you."

The United States Ambassador led the Libyan Foreign Minister to the bank of elevators. Almost as an afterthought, Moon asked Ghami, "I wonder, if there is wreckage, how we should proceed."

"I don't understand."

"If the plane crashed, my government would most likely request that a team of American examiners inspect the remains in situ. People from the National Transportation Safety Board are experts at determining exactly what forces were in play to cause an airplane to crash."

"I see, yes." Ghami rubbed his jaw. "We have specialists who perform a similar function here. I can't see it as a problem. However, I'll need to consult with the President."

"Very well. Thank you."

A minute after Moon returned to his office, there was a knock on the door. "Come in."

"What do you think?" asked Jim Kublicki, the CIA station chief at the American Embassy. A former college football star, Kublicki had been with the Agency for fifteen years. He was nearly as tall as the doorframe, which meant he would never be a covert operative because he stood out in any crowd, but he was a competent administrator, and the four agents assigned to the embassy liked and respected him.

"If they're involved in some way, Ali Ghami's out of the loop," Moon replied.

"From what I've heard, Ghami is Qaddafi's fair-haired boy. If they intentionally shot down that plane, he'd know."

"Then my gut tells me the Libyans didn't do anything and whatever has happened was an accident."

"We won't know for certain until they find the wreckage and get a team to examine it."

"Obviously."

"Did you ask him if we can bring over folks from the NTSB?"

"I did. Ghami agreed, but he wants to talk it over with Qaddafi. I think Ghami wasn't prepared for the question and wants a little time to figure out how to accept without admitting our people are better than his. They can't afford a diplomatic flap by refusing."

"If they do, that would surely tell us something," Kublicki said with a spook's inherent paranoia. "So, what's he like in person—Ghami, I mean?"

"I'd met him before, of course, but this time I got a better sense of the man behind the diplomatic niceties. He's charming and gracious, even in these circumstances. I could tell he was truly disturbed by what's happened. He's poured a lot of his own reputation into this conference, only to see it marred before it starts. He's really upset. It's hard to believe a regime like this could produce someone like that."

"Qaddafi saw the writing on the wall when we took down Saddam Hussein. How long after we pulled him out of the spider hole did Libya agree to abandon its nuke program and disavow terrorism?"

"A matter of days, I believe."

"There you go. A leopard can change his spots once he sees the consequences of jerking around the good old U.S. of A."

The corners of Moon's mouth turned downward. He wasn't much for jingoism, and had been dead set against the Iraq invasion, though he acknowledged that without it the upcoming peace summit might never have been proposed. He shrugged. Who really knew? Events had unfolded the way they had and there was no use revisiting past actions. "Have you heard anything?" he asked Kublicki.

"NRO has shifted one of their spy birds from the Gulf to

cover Libya's western desert. The imaging specialists have the first pictures now. If that plane's out there, they'll find it."

"We're talking thousands and thousands of square miles," Moon reminded. "And some of that is pretty mountainous."

Kublicki was undeterred. "Those satellites can read a license plate from a thousand miles up."

Moon was too upset about the situation to point out that being able to see details of a specific target had no relation to searching an area the size of New England. "Do you have anything else for me?"

Realizing he was being dismissed, Kublicki got to his feet. "No, sir. It's pretty much a wait-and-see kind of thing now."

"Okay, thanks. Could you ask my secretary to get me some aspirin?"

"Sure thing." The agent lumbered out of the office.

Charles Moon pressed his thumbs against his temples. Since hearing about the plane's disappearance, he had managed to keep his emotions in check, but exhaustion was cracking his professional façade. He knew without a doubt that if Fiona Katamora was dead, the Tripoli Accords didn't stand a chance in hell. He had lied to Ali Ghami during their meeting. He and the President had discussed who would represent the United States. The President had told him that he would send the VP because an Undersecretary simply didn't carry enough clout. The problem was, the Vice President was a young, good-looking congressman who'd been put on the ticket to balance it out. He had no diplomatic experience and, everyone agreed, no brain either.

The VP had once met with Kurdish representatives at a White House function and wouldn't stop joking about bean curds. At a state dinner for the Chinese President, he'd held out his plate to the man and asked, "What do you call china in China?" Then there was the video clip, an Internet favorite for months, of him staring at an actress's cleavage and actually licking his lips.

Not one for praying, Charles Moon had the sudden urge to get on his knees and beg God for Fiona's life. And he wanted to pray for the untold hundreds and thousands who would keep dying in the seemingly unending cycle of violence if she was gone.

"Your aspirin, Mr. Ambassador," his secretary said.

He looked up at her. "Leave the bottle, Karen. I'm going to need it."

TEN

A S SOON AS THE POLISHED-BRASS ELEVATOR DOORS
opened on the *Oregon*'s lowest deck, Juan Cabrillo felt
the pulsing beat against his chest. It wasn't the ship's revolutionary engines producing the throbbing presence in the carpeted corridor but rather what had to be the most expensive
stereo system afloat. To him, the music blaring from the only
cabin in this section of the freighter sounded like a continuous explosion with a voice-over track that seemed to mimic
a dozen cats fighting in a burlap bag. The wailing rose and
fell in no relation to the beat, and every few seconds feedback
from the musicians' amplifiers would shriek.

Mark Murphy's taste in music, if this could be called
music, was the reason there were no other cabins in this part
of the *Oregon*.

Cabrillo paused at the open door. Members of the Corporation had been given generous stipends to decorate their cabins any way they saw fit. His own was done in various types
of exotic woods and resembled an English manor house more
than a nautical suite. Franklin Lincoln, who had had nothing

growing up on the streets of Detroit, and who had spent twenty years in the Navy sleeping wherever they told him to, furnished his cabin with a cot, a footlocker, and a pressed-metal wardrobe. The rest of his money went into a customized Harley. Max's cabin was a mishmash of unmatched furniture that looked like it had come from Goodwill.

And then there was Mark and his partner in crime, Eric Stone. Eric's room was a geek's fantasy, with every conceivable video-game console and controller. The walls were adorned with pinup girls and gaming posters. The floor was a static-dampening rubber that was crisscrossed with a couple thousand feet of cables. His bed was an unmade pile of sheets and blankets tucked into one corner.

Mark had gone for a minimalist vibe. The walls of his cabin were painted a matte gray, with a matching carpet. One wall was a video display system nearly eighteen feet across and composed of dozens of individual flat screens. There were two overstuffed leather chairs, a queen-sized bed, and a stark chest of drawers. The room's dominant feature was the speakers. The four of them stood seven feet tall and resembled Frank Gehry's Guggenheim Museum in Bilbao, Spain. Murph claimed that sharp angles in a speaker system affected the sound. Considering the garbage he listened to, Juan wasn't sure how his young weapons specialist could tell.

Murph and Stone were standing in front of the video display, looking at satellite imagery provided by Langston Overholt. With the *Oregon* driving hard for Libya, Cabrillo had finalized a contract with Lang to act as a covert search-and-rescue group and had gotten his people thinking about what they would find once they reached their destination. He had also asked for the raw satellite imagery that he was certain the National Reconnaissance Office had obtained within a few hours of Secretary Katamora's disappearance.

Mark and Eric had altered some basic pattern-recognition software to help them search the imagery for a downed aircraft. The NRO had a dedicated staff of dozens doing the same thing, with hardware and software more sophisticated than what was at his people's disposal, but Juan was confident they would find the downed 737 first.

Juan flipped the light switch to get their attention.

Murph pointed a remote at the stereo rack and muted the system.

"Thank you," Juan said. "Just so I don't buy the CD by mistake, who was that?"

"The Puking Muses," Mark replied as though Cabrillo should have known.

"Yeah, no way I'd make that mistake."

Mark was wearing ripped jeans, and a shirt that said PEDRO FOR PRESIDENT. His hair was a tangled dark mane, and to Juan's surprise he had shaved off the scraggly whiskers he called a beard. Eric was in his customary buttondown shirt and chinos.

Cabrillo touched his chin and said, "About time you got rid of the dead bird on your face."

"This girl I'm chatting up on the Net said I'd look better without it." Mark's cockiness had returned following the Chairman's rebuke over his mistake in Somalia. Sam Pryor, the wounded engineer, said he harbored no ill feelings but was going to make Murph his personal valet once he got out of Medical.

"Smart woman. Marry her. So what have you got so far? Wait. Before you answer, what is that?"

He pointed to the map on the screen where the Sahara Desert met the Mediterranean, about fifty miles west of the recognizable urban sprawl of Tripoli and its suburbs. Where the coastline usually ran in a fairly even stroke, there was an area where the sea pushed inland in a perfectly shaped rectangle. It was obviously a man-made feature, and, from the scale on the monitors, enormous.

"A new kind of tidal power station," Eric said. "Just came online a month ago."

"I didn't think the Med has high enough tides," Juan mused.

"It doesn't, but this power station doesn't rely on the ebb and flow of the tides. The place they built the plant had been a narrow-mouthed bay that was much deeper than normal for the region. They built a seawall across its mouth and pumped it dry. They then expanded the dried-out bay so it was wider and deeper than it was originally. There is a series of sluice gates running along the seawall near its summit and sloping downward. During high tide, water pours through the gates, down pipes, and turns turbines to produce electricity."

"That doesn't make any sense. Eventually, the old bay will fill with water. I don't care how big they made it."

"You're forgetting the location." Eric had a little smirk on his face. When he'd first read about the project, he had intuitively grasped the facility's secret. When Juan stared back blankly, he added, "The desert."

The Chairman suddenly understood. "Evaporation. Brilliant."

"The reservoir had to be wide and broad but not necessarily deep. They calculated typical evaporation rates to get the right size for the amount of electricity they wanted to produce. By the time the sun goes down in the evening, the artificial lake is virtually empty. Then the tide rises, water pours in through the powerhouse, and the cycle is repeated."

"What about the . . ."

"Excess salt? It's trucked away at night, and sold to European municipalities as a deicing agent for roads. Completely renewable, clean energy, with the bonus of a few million dollars a year in road salt."

"There is a potential problem," Mark said. "Over time, the excess evaporation could change weather patterns downwind from the site."

"The report I read said it would be negligible," Eric said, defending the project from Mark's natural paranoia.

"That report was written by the Italian company that developed the plant in the first place. Of course they're going to say it's negligible, but they don't really know."

"Not our problem," Cabrillo said before Mark could ramp up one of his conspiracy theories. "Finding the Secretary's plane is. What have you got so far?"

Murph chugged half a can of Red Bull before answering. "Okay, we've got a couple of scenarios. Number one is the plane exploded in midair, either the result of a catastrophic failure, like TWA 800 over Long Island south shore, or a missile strike, also like TWA 800, depending on who you believe. If that's the case, then we would have wreckage strewn over a hundred square miles when we factor in the plane's speed and altitude."

"It would be nearly impossible to spot any of it without knowing approximately where the event occurred," Eric said, wiping his glasses on the tail of his shirt.

"We know when their transponder and communications died," Mark pointed out. "A quick extrapolation of their course, speed, and estimated time of arrival at Tripoli International would have put the event just on Tunisia's side of the border with the wreckage landing on Libya's."

"Is that what you have there?" Juan asked, pointing to the desert imagery on the multipanel display.

Murph shook his shaggy head. "No, we already checked it out, and nada. We saw an abandoned truck and a lot of tire tracks left by what we assume are border patrols, but no plane."

"That's good news, then," Juan said. "Her aircraft didn't suffer a midair explosion."

"Good and bad," Eric replied. "Since we don't know the nature of the event, it becomes much more difficult to figure out. Did the oxygen system fail and kill the crew, so the plane just kept flying until it ran out of fuel? If that's the case, it could have struck five hundred miles or more to the east of Tripoli, possibly even in the Med. Or there could have been an engine failure. If that happened, the plane would have glided for miles before impact."

"But that wouldn't explain the radio silence," the Chairman pointed out. "The crew would have radioed an emergency."

"We know that," Mark said a little defensively. "Still, we have to investigate every possible theory to winnow—good word, eh?—to winnow down our target area. It's unlikely the radios would die the same moment as the engines, but stranger things have happened. Hey, that reminds me, have the feds talked to the ground people who serviced that plane last? You know, it could have been sabotaged."

"Lang said the FBI is conducting interviews as we speak."

"They should check out the flight crew, too. One of them could be Al-Qaeda or something."

"The crew's all Air Force personnel," Juan replied. "I doubt they are a security threat."

"The CIA said the same thing about Aldridge Ames, and I'm sure the FBI had vetted Robert Hanssen." Despite his genius intellect, or maybe because of it, Murph delighted in pointing out the mistakes of others. "There's no reason some Air Force guy couldn't be bought. He could have flown the plane to some remote Libyan base, where they're torturing the Secretary of State right at this moment." He looked to Eric, his eyes a little glassy with inspiration. "What do you bet they're waterboarding her? Good enough for the guys we have at Gitmo, right? Or they've attached electrodes to her—"

"Gentlemen, let's not get ahead of ourselves," Juan interrupted before they started coming up with more lurid torture techniques.

"Oh sure, sorry," Eric muttered, even though he had remained silent during Mark's excited outburst. "Um, well, if both engines failed, we factored speed, altitude, and estimated a fifteen-hundred-foot-per-minute descent rate. That gives us a target area of roughly eighty nautical miles."

"So that's what you have on the screen?" Cabrillo asked.

"Not exactly," Eric said.

Mark overrode his friend's next words, "Yes, we had to consider the engine failure–radio dying scenario, but we discounted it pretty quickly and came up with something better."

Juan was losing patience with his brain trust, but he kept it to himself. He knew Murph and Eric delighted at showing off their intellect, and he wouldn't rob them of their fun.

"So what's the answer?"

"The plane's tail came off."

"Or at least part of it," Eric amended.

"A structural failure in the tail could very likely damage the radio antennas, which would explain the blackout," Mark said. "It could also knock out the plane's transponder at the same time."

"Depending on the extent of the damage," Eric went on, "the aircraft could still fly for some distance. It would be highly unstable, and the pilot would have minimal control. He could only steer the plane by alternating thrust to each of its engines."

"The danger comes from the fact the 737 doesn't have fuel-dump capabilities. He would have had to fly in circles to burn off avgas or risk coming in too heavy." Juan made to ask a question, but Mark anticipated him. "They refueled in London when they stopped for a quick meeting with England's Foreign Secretary. By my calculations, they had enough to keep going for at least an hour after the plane went dark."

Cabrillo nodded. "Even throttled back, she could have cruised for a couple hundred miles."

"But they didn't," Eric said, "or they would have tried an emergency landing in Tripoli."

"Good point. So where the hell are they?"

"We combined two of our scenarios. Engine failure and the tail coming apart," Mark said proudly. "It's plausible. Highly unlikely, but it could happen. That narrowed our area to about a hundred square miles. We found one potential spot, but it turned out to be a vaguely airplane-shaped geologic formation." He pointed to the center screen. "And there, we found that."

Juan stepped forward. The screen showed a mountainous area, nearly inaccessible to anything other than a chopper or a serious four-wheel drive. Mark hit a button on the panel's control and the shot zoomed in. "There it is," the Chairman whispered.

Near the top of one of the mountains was the plane. Or what was left of it. The wreckage stretched for a half mile or more up the slope. He could see marks on the ground where it first impacted, rose up again, and then belly flopped, tearing itself apart as it decelerated. Fire had scorched the ground about halfway between the second impact and the main debris site. The fuselage, at least the two-thirds of it that had stayed together, was a charred tube surrounded by the shredded remains of the wings. One engine lay a hundred feet from the aircraft. Juan couldn't spot the second.

"Any signs there were survivors?" he asked, knowing the answer.

"Sorry, boss man," Eric said. "If there were, they haven't done anything to signal for help. Mr. Overholt said we should be getting another set of satellite images in about ten hours. We'll compare the two and see if anything at the site has changed. But look for yourself. It doesn't appear likely that anyone could have survived a crash like that, not with the fire and all."

"You're right. I know. I just don't like it. Fiona Katamora was one of the good ones. It's a damned shame for her to die like this. Especially on the eve of the Tripoli Accords." The certainty that she was dead was like a heavy stone in the pit of Cabrillo's stomach. "Listen, guys, good work finding the wreckage. Zap a quick note to my computer with the exact coordinates so I can pass them on. No sense wasting the government's imaging specialists' time searching if we've already found her. I'm sure Lang's going to want us to investigate the site before reporting it to the Libyans. By the way, where are they searching?"

"They're off by a few hundred miles," Mark said. "If you want my opinion, I think they're just going through the motions. They know we've got the satellites, so they're fumbling around until our government tells them where to look."

"Probably right," Juan agreed. "Anyway, we've got to be able to get up there and we can't use our chopper covertly, so map a route in for the Pig."

"Max doesn't like when you call it that," Eric reminded.

"He gave it the ridiculous name Powered Investigator Ground, so we'd call it the Pig. He just grumbles about the nickname because he likes to grumble." Juan tried to say this lightly, but his thoughts were on the victims of the plane crash.

If he closed his eyes, he could imagine the terror they must have all felt as the plane was about to barrel into the side of the mountain. He wondered what Fiona Katamora's last thoughts were.

An hour later, he was alone in his cabin, sitting with his feet propped up on his desk, a Cuban cigar between his index and middle fingers. He watched the smoke pool lazily along the coffered ceiling. Everything was set for their arrival in Tripoli the following night. He had gotten hold of a shadowy facilitator in Nicosia, Cyprus, who went by the name *L'Enfant*, the Baby, a man Juan had never met but who had contacts all over the Mediterranean. For a fee, the Baby had made all the customs arrangements for unloading the Pig. He had also gotten together the proper visas for the team Cabrillo would take with him into the mountains. Langston had been adamant that they verify that the Secretary of State was dead.

Juan didn't relish combing the wreckage, but he knew they had to be certain.

He again glanced at the hard copy of the satellite image sitting on his blotter. Something about the wreckage pattern bothered him, but he couldn't say what. He'd pulled up pictures of plane crashes from the Internet and saw no obvious discrepancies. Not that any two crashes were identical, and there was nothing glaringly out of place. Still, there was something.

With Cabrillo's fluency in Arabic, it was no surprise he had spent time in Libya during his years with the CIA. The two missions he'd been assigned hadn't been that dramatic. One had been helping a general and his family to defect. The other had been a secret meeting with a scientist who claimed he worked on Qaddafi's nuclear weapons program. It turned out the guy had virtually no useful information, so nothing came of it. Juan had liked the people he'd met and sensed that they weren't too keen on their government but were too frightened to do anything about it. Such was life in a police state.

He wondered if that had changed. Was Libya really opening up to the West or did they still see us as enemies? For all he knew, both factions coexisted within the halls of power.

He made a decision anyway. He wasn't going to trust that what happened to Katamora's plane was an accident until he heard the flight voice recorder for himself. And he wasn't going to believe she was dead until he saw the DNA result from the samples Langston wanted them to gather.

He had been a success as a CIA agent because he had good instincts and knew to trust them. He'd done even better with the Corporation for the same reasons.

Something wasn't right, and he was determined to find out what.

ELEVEN

IT TURNED OUT THAT THE HARBOR PILOT ASSIGNED to take the *Oregon* into the Port of Tripoli was their contact. He was an affable man of medium height, with thick curly hair just beginning to gray. His eyebrows stretched across his forehead in an unbroken line, and one of his incisors was badly chipped. He worried at the tooth with his tongue whenever he wasn't talking, which led Juan to think it was a recent break. There was a little bruising at the corner of the man's mouth to bolster Cabrillo's assumption.

The man explained that he did what he did because he needed the extra money to take care of his extended family. His brother-in-law had recently lost his construction job in Dubai, so his family had moved into the man's house. His parents were both alive, blessings to Allah, but they ate him out of house and home. And he had two upcoming weddings to pay for. On top of that, he claimed he made regular contributions to an assortment of aunts, uncles, and cousins.

All this information had come in the time it took them to walk from the boarding ladder to Juan's topside cabin.

"You are indeed an honorable man, Mr. Assad," Juan said with a straight face. He didn't believe a word of it. He suspected that the proceeds from Assad's corruption went to maintaining a mistress, and either she or the wife had recently hit him hard enough to crack the tooth.

The pilot waved a dismissive hand, the cigarette clutched between his fingers moving like a meteorite in the dim cabin. The sun was well beyond the horizon, and the *Oregon* was far enough from the harbor that little light from the city filtered through the salt-rimed porthole. Juan had only turned on the anemic desk lamp. Although he had disguised himself a bit—a dark wig, glasses, and gauze in his cheeks to puff up his face—he didn't want Assad getting a good look at him, though he knew from experience that men like Assad didn't want to take a good look anyway.

"We do what we must to get by," Assad pontificated. He laid a well-used leather briefcase on Cabrillo's desk and popped the lid. "Our mutual friend in Cyprus said you wished to off-load a truck and needed visas and passport stamps for three men and a woman." He withdrew a handful of papers as well as a customs stamp. Juan knew the routine and gave him four passports. They had come from Kevin Nixon's Magic Shop and with the exception of the photographs bore no accurate information about the crew accompanying Cabrillo into the desert.

It took the harbor pilot a few minutes to record names, numbers, and other information before he stamped a fresh page in each of the passports and handed them back.

He then gave Juan some more papers. "Give these to the customs inspectors for your truck. And these"—he pulled out a pair of license plates and set them on the desk—"will make it much easier traveling in my country."

That saved Cabrillo the hassle of stealing a set from a vehicle in town. "Very thoughtful. Thank you."

The Libyan smiled. "All business is customer service, yes?"

"True enough," Juan agreed.

"How good are you at remembering numbers?"

"I beg your pardon?"

"Numbers. I want to give you a cell phone number, but I do not want you to write it down."

"Oh. Fine. Go ahead."

Assad rattled off a string of digits. "Give the person who answers a number where you can be reached, and I will call it within the hour." Assad chuckled. "Provided I am not with my wife, eh?"

Juan smiled dutifully at the joke. "I'm sure we won't need your services, but, again, thank you."

Assad's bonhomie suddenly faded and his eyes narrowed under his unibrow. "I don't see how three men and a woman in a truck can be any great danger to my country, but if I become suspicious about anything I hear in the news I will not hesitate to contact the authorities. I have ways that keep me out of it, understand?"

Juan wasn't angry at the warning. He'd been expecting it and had heard it from dozens of such men over the years. Some might actually have had the juice to back it up. Assad could be one of them. He had that look. And Juan knew that next on the agenda, if Assad held true to form, would be a little fishing expedition.

"The American government must be very upset about the death of their Secretary of State," Assad remarked.

How Juan loved a cliché. "I'm sure they are. But, as you saw from my passport, I am a Canadian citizen. I have no control over what happens with our neighbor to the south."

"Still, they must be anxious to locate the wreckage."

"I'm sure they are." Cabrillo was as stone-faced as a professional poker player.

"Where exactly are you from?" Assad asked suddenly.

"Saint John's."

"That is in Nova Scotia."

"Newfoundland."

"Ah, part of the Gaspé."

"It's an island."

Assad nodded. Test administered and passed. Perhaps the captain really was Canadian.

"Maybe your government is willing to help their southern friends in this matter," he probed.

Juan understood that Assad needed reassuring they were here about the plane crash and not something else. It was the only logical assumption Assad could make, given the timing of their arrival, and the Chairman saw no reason not to give the Libyan some peace of mind. "I am sure they would be more than willing to lend any assistance they could."

Assad's smile returned. "Foreign Minister Ghami was on television last night, calling for people with information about the crash to come forward immediately. It is in everyone's best interest the plane be found, yes?"

"I guess so," Juan replied. He was growing tired of Assad's questions. He opened a desk drawer. Assad leaned forward as Cabrillo pulled out a bulging envelope. "I think this takes care of our transaction."

He handed it across. Assad stuffed it into his briefcase without opening it. "Our mutual friend in Cyprus told me that you are an honorable man. I will take his word and not count the money."

It took all of Juan's self-control not to smirk. He knew full well that before Assad brought the *Oregon* into its berth, he would have counted the cash at least twice. "You said earlier that business is all about customer service. I will add, it's also about reputation."

"Too true." Both men got to their feet and shook hands. "Now, Captain, if you will kindly lead me to your bridge I will not delay you further."

"My pleasure."

● ● ●

CABRILLO HAD ALWAYS HELD the belief that organized crime had begun on the docks and quaysides of the ancient Phoenician seafarers when a couple of stevedores pilfered an amphora of wine. He imagined they had given a cup or two to the guards for looking the other way, and he also thought that someone saw them and extorted them to steal more. In that one simple act were the three things necessary for a crime racket—thieves, corrupt guards, and a boss demanding tribute. And the only thing that had changed in the thousands of years since was the scale of the theft. Ports were worlds unto themselves, and no matter how authoritarian the local rule they maintained levels of autonomy that only the corrupt could fully exploit.

He had seen it over and over in his years at sea, and had used the ingrained corruption of harbors as an entrée into the criminal underground in several cities during his tenure with the CIA. With so many goods entering and leaving, harbors were ripe for the picking. It was little wonder the Mafia was so heavily invested with the Teamsters Union back in its heyday.

Containerization of general cargo had temporarily quelled petty thievery because the goods were locked up in bonded boxes. But soon the bosses figured they might as well just steal entire containers.

Juan was standing on the wing bridge, overlooking the dock, with Max Hanley at his side. Fragrant smoke curled from Max's pipe and helped mask the smell of bunker fuel and rotting fish that permeated the port. Across from their berth, a mobile crane on crawler treads was swinging a container from a coastal freighter. There were no lights on the crane, and the overhead gantry lamps were shut off. The tractor trailer waiting to take the load didn't even have its headlights on. Only a single flashlight carried by a crewman standing near the container gave the scene any illumination. Mr. Assad had gone straight from the *Oregon* to oversee the unloading. Cabrillo could just make out his silhouette, standing with the ship's captain, on the dock. It was too dark to see the envelope exchange, but Eric had reported the act after watching with the *Oregon*'s low-light camera.

"Looks like *L'Enfant* knows his men," Max said. "Our Mr. Assad is a busy boy."

"What was it Claude Rains said in *Casablanca*, 'I am only a poor corrupt official'?"

Cabrillo's walkie-talkie squawked. "Chairman, we have the hatch cover off. We're ready."

"Roger that, Eddie. Assad said we can use our own crane to unload the Pig, so get it fired up and ready."

"You got it."

Like the mysterious ship tied to the opposite dock, the *Oregon* was completely dark. On the other side of the harbor, tall cranes mounted on rails were off-loading a massive containership under the brutal glare of sodium-vapor lights. Beyond it stretched a field of stacked containers, and past that was a security fence and a series of warehouses and towering oil-storage tanks.

One of the *Oregon*'s only working deck cranes started swinging across the horizon, cable paying off the crane's drum as the crane's arm was positioned over the open hatch. The braided-steel cable vanished into the hold for five minutes before being drawn back up through the tackle. The boom took the weight easily.

Although he couldn't see details in the darkness, Juan recognized the shape of the Pig. The Powered Investigator Ground was Max's brainchild. From the outside, the Pig looked like a nondescript cargo truck emblazoned with the logo of a fictitious oil-exploration company, but under its rough exterior was a Mercedes Unimog chassis, the only unmodified part on the vehicle. Its turbo-diesel engine had been bored, stroked, and tuned to produce nearly eight hundred horsepower, and, with a nitrous oxide boost, could push past a thousand. The heavily lugged, self-sealing tires were on an articulating suspension that could raise the vehicle up and give it almost two feet of ground clearance, six inches more than the Army's storied Humvee. The four-person cab squatting over the front tires was armored enough to take rifle fire at point-blank range. The boxy body was similarly protected.

When Eric and Mark first heard Max's plans for the Pig, they had called him Q, in honor of the armorer from the James Bond franchise. A .30-caliber machine gun was hidden beneath the front bumper. It was also fitted with guided rockets that launched from hidden racks that swung down from the truck's side, and a smoke generator could lay down a dense screen in its wake. From a seamless hatch on the roof, the Pig could fire mortar barrages, and could be mounted with another .30-cal or an automatic grenade launcher as well. The cargo area could be reconfigured to meet mission parameters—

anything from a mobile surgical suite to a covert radar station to a troop carrier for ten fully kitted soldiers.

And yet, other than the larger than normal tires, not one aspect of the Pig gave away her true nature. She was the land-based version of the *Oregon* herself. If an inspector opened the rear doors, he would be confronted with the curved sides of six fifty-five-gallon drums stacked floor to ceiling. And if the inspector were really curious, the first row could be removed to reveal a second. The first ones were actually spare fuel tanks that gave the Pig an eight-hundred-mile range. The second row was a façade to shield the interior of the truck, so they played the odds that no one would ever ask to remove it.

"Well, Max old boy, I guess we get to see if this contraption of yours was worth the effort."

"Ye of little faith," Max replied dourly.

Cabrillo turned serious. "You're set on what to do?"

"As soon as you get clear of Tripoli, I'm leaving the harbor and steaming west. We'll take up a position in international waters due north of the crash site, with the chopper on ten-minute alert."

"I know you'll be at the helo's maximum range, but it's good to have a little insurance just in case. If things go as planned, you shadow us offshore when we make our escape into Tunisia."

"And if things don't go as planned?"

Juan gave him a look of mock horror. "When was the last time things didn't go as expected?"

"A couple days ago in Somalia, a few months ago in Greece, last year in the Congo, before that in—"

"Yeah, yeah yeah . . ."

A burst of static erupted from the speaker in the wheel-house. Juan strode in, plucked the microphone off the wall, and said, "Cabrillo."

"Chairman, the Pig's on the dock and we're good to go. Latest intel puts the Libyan search-and-rescue a good three hundred miles from the crash site."

"Okay, Linda, thanks. I'll meet you at the gangway in five." He went back out onto the flying bridge.

Max tapped his pipe against the rail, unleashing a shower of sparks that tumbled down the side of the ship and winked out one by one. "See you in a couple of days."

"You got it." Rarely would they wish each other luck before a mission.

● ● ●

JUAN DROVE, WITH MARK MURPHY riding shotgun and Linda Ross and Franklin Lincoln occupying the rear bench seat. All four wore khaki jumpsuits, the ubiquitous uniform of oil workers all over North Africa and the Middle East. Linda had trimmed her hair and tucked it under a baseball cap. With her slender build, she could easily pass for a young man on his first overseas job.

It was still dark by the time the lights of Tripoli faded in the rearview mirror. Traffic on the coast road was nearly nonexistent, and after an hour they had yet to come upon any roadblocks. A police cruiser had slashed by, its dome lights flashing and its siren keening, but it passed the truck without incident and vanished into the distance.

Cabrillo was confident in their fake papers, but he preferred to remain anonymous as long as possible. He wasn't as worried about a legitimate stop by the authorities. What concerned him were corrupt cops setting up roadblocks to shake down motorists. He had cash on hand for such a situation; however, he knew things could spiral out of control quickly.

Mark had keyed in way points on the Pig's integrated navigation system to get them to the downed airliner, and it was just their luck that there was a roadblock less than a hundred feet from where they were supposed to leave the highway and begin their trek into the desert. Two police cars were parked so that they cut the two-lane road down to one. A cop wearing a reflective vest was leaning into a car headed in the opposite direction, his flashlight bathing the interior of the sedan. Juan could make out two more men in one of the cars. He suspected there was a fourth keeping himself out of view.

As he slowed, Juan asked, "Murph, can we pass through and turn farther down the road?"

The young weapons expert shook his head. "I mapped our route exactly from the satellite pictures. If we don't turn here, we come up against some pretty steep cliffs. You can't see it in the darkness, but there's a switchback trail just to our left that will get us to the top."

"So it's here or never, eh?"

"'Fraid so."

Cabrillo braked the big truck far enough from the make-shift roadblock so the car could pass him once the cops were satisfied. In a concealed pocket to the right of his seat he could feel the butt of his preferred handgun, the Fabrique Nationale (FN) Five-seveN. The military-grade SS190 rounds had unbelievable penetrating power, and, because of their small size, twenty could be loaded into a comfortable grip magazine. He left it for the moment.

At this distance, Juan could see it was a family in the car. The wife's head was covered in a scarf, so her face was a pale oval in the flashlight's glow. She held a baby over her shoulder and was bouncing it gently. He could hear its crying over the wind. A second child was standing in the backseat. Though he couldn't understand the words, he could hear the tension in the voices as the father argued with the cop.

"Is this stop legit or a case of *mordida*?" Linc asked, using the Spanish word for bite and the Mexican euphemism for bribery.

Juan was opening his mouth to reply when suddenly the cop pulled back from the open car window and yanked a pistol from his holster. The woman's startled scream echoed across the night, pitched even higher than the infant wailing in her lap. The husband in the driver's seat threw up his hands in supplication.

Car doors were flung open as the other two police officers jumped from their vehicles, both going for the automatics on their hips. One strode toward the passenger's side of the sedan while the other raced toward Cabrillo and his team, his pistol leveled at the cab.

Juan's wary apprehension turned into instant fury because he knew they were going to be too late.

Mark Murphy yanked open the glove compartment and a tray automatically slid out and opened to reveal a flat-panel display and a keyboard with a small joystick. As he fumbled to activate the forward-mounted machine gun, the cop who had been leaning into the car fired.

The hapless driver's head exploded in a red spray that coated the inside of the windshield with blood and gore. It obscured Cabrillo's view of the gunman firing twice more. The woman and her baby's cries were cut off mid-keen. A fourth shot, and Juan was certain the kid in the backseat was dead in what he now knew was a shakedown gone bad.

Instinct took over. Cabrillo jammed the transmission into gear and hit the pedal. Acceleration wasn't the Pig's strong suit, but it lurched from a standstill like a snarling animal. The cop running for them stopped and opened fire. His bullets gouged harmless craters into the safety glass or ricocheted off the truck's armored plate.

"Got it," Mark yelled.

Juan glanced over for a second. The video screen showed a camera mounted beneath the secreted machine gun that gave Mark an aiming reference. The gun had lowered itself so the barrel peeked from under the bumper.

"Do it!" Juan snapped.

Mark keyed the weapon, and a juddering vibration rattled the truck while a plume of fire erupted under the cab. Bullets tore into the road in a line aimed straight for the nearest gunman. The corrupt cop turned to run to his left but made his move too early. He gave Murph ample time to adjust his aim. The rounds took the cop in the calf, and then walked up his body, punching holes into him at a rate of four hundred rounds a minute. The kinetic force drove him to the asphalt and rolled him once so he lay faceup. His torso looked as if he'd been mauled by a lion.

The cop who had gunned down the family lunged for his car while the third retreated back to his. Mark lifted the trigger as soon as the first one was down and swiveled the barrel to take on the third killer. Rounds pummeled the car, blowing out its windshield and side windows and shredding the bodywork. Both tires deflated, and the vehicle settled closer to the road. The gunman found temporary cover behind the partially closed door but must have understood his position was untenable. He scrambled across the seat, threw open the far door, and fell to the ground on the opposite side of his cruiser. He hunkered behind the front tire and kept low as autofire raked the vehicle.

For the moment, he was neutralized, so Juan cranked the wheel over and steered for the other car. The triggerman was halfway into his seat when the Pig's powerful halogen lights swept across the car and then centered on him. He raised his pistol and fired as fast as the gun would allow. His rounds had no more effect than his partner's on the truck bearing down on him.

Cabrillo felt nothing but cold rage as he drove straight for the murderer.

"Brace yourselves," he said needlessly an instant before the Pig barreled into the cruiser.

There was a terrific crunch of metal as the door slammed into the gunman's body, cutting off one leg at the ankle, one arm at the wrist, and his head. The impact skidded the police cruiser until its tires hooked on the macadam and the car flipped on its roof.

"First car! First car!" Linda cried from the backseat.

Juan looked over to see the driver was reaching into the cruiser. No doubt going for his radio, he thought. He had no time to turn the ponderous truck to line up the .30-caliber, so he pulled the FN Five-seveN from its hiding place and tossed it back to Linda. She caught it one-handed while the other hand was cranking down her bulletproof window.

She thumbed off the safety and opened fire as soon as she had the room to stick the gun out the window. Linc reached over to keep cranking it down to give her a better field of fire.

Linda's angle was all wrong to hit the gunman, so as the window lowered she thrust her upper body out of the truck, bracing herself by gripping the big side mirror with her left hand. She then fired. She was cycling the trigger so fast the distinctive whip-crack of the Five-seveN sounded like a string of firecrackers.

Cabrillo was about to caution Linda that he suspected there was a fourth shooter manning the checkpoint when the crooked cop emerged from behind a dune near the shoulder of the road and opened up with a machine pistol. The weapon was woefully inaccurate at this range, and at five hundred rounds a minute it took only four seconds to unload its long magazine. Rounds whipped around the Pig, flying off when they struck the armor and starring the glass when they hit the windshield. One round flew through the open window over Linda's hunched backside and struck the doorframe an inch from Linc's head. The impact gouged a sliver of metal off the frame that sliced into the ex-SEAL's neck. Had the angle been just a few tenths of a degree different, the shrapnel would have sliced his jugular.

Pressing one hand to his bleeding neck, Linc had the wherewithal to grab Linda's ankles when Juan spun the wheel to put the armored side of the Pig between them and the shooter. He barely kept her from tumbling to the road.

"You're hit," she said when she saw the blood oozing through his fingers.

"I've cut myself worse shaving in the morning," Linc deadpanned. However, he didn't demur when Linda unclipped a first-aid kit stored under her side of the bench seat.

Cabrillo had spun the Pig in a tight turn to line up the underslung .30-caliber for another go. Linda's actions had bought them the few seconds they had needed. Her cover fire had pinned the gunman behind the cruiser once again, and only now was he reaching back in to work the radio.

Mark opened fire as soon as he had a shot. He wasn't aiming for the driver's compartment. The shooter was too well protected. Instead, Mark riddled the rear of the vehicle until gasoline gushed from the perforated tank. Because every seventh round was a magnesium-tipped tracer, it took only a second-long burst to ignite the growing lake. Flame blossomed from under the car in a concussive whoosh that was strong enough to lift the car's rear end off the asphalt. The Libyan started running for the desert but wasn't fast enough.

The mixture of fuel and air in the tank exploded spectacularly, flipping the car into the air, its undercarriage burning like a meteor as it cartwheeled. It crashed into the dirt a few feet from the fleeing gunman and kicked up a flaming spray of dust that engulfed the man. When it cleared, his clothes were burning, flaring like a torch. He dropped to the ground, trying to smother the flames, but he was soaked in gasoline and the fire refused to die.

Murph sent another burst from the machine gun into him. It was a mercy shot.

"Where's the last guy?" Juan shouted.

"I think he took off into the desert," Linc said. Linda had a gauze pad taped to his neck and was cleaning the blood from her hands.

Cabrillo cursed.

It was only a matter of time before another vehicle came along. But he had no choice. They couldn't afford to leave any witnesses behind. He heaved the wheel over and left the road.

The Pig's rugged suspension handled the soft sand with ease, and soon they were barreling along at forty miles per hour. The gunman's tracks were clearly visible in the beam of the halogen lamps, widely spaced divots that told him their guy was running with everything he had.

It took only another minute to spot the corrupt police officer sprinting like a startled hare. Even with the big truck bearing down on him, he made no effort to surrender. He just kept running. Juan brought the Pig up right on his heels so he would feel the engine heat burning into his back.

"What are we going to do with him?" Mark asked. There was genuine concern in his voice.

Juan didn't answer for a second. He'd seen and caused death in a hundred forms but hated killing in cold blood. He'd done it before, more times than he cared to think about, but he knew every time he did he lost a little more of his soul. He wished the Libyan would turn and fire at them, but Juan could see the man had abandoned his weapon back at the checkpoint. The smart thing would be to run him over and be done with it.

Cabrillo's ankle flexed to gun the engine and then relaxed

again. There had to be another way. The gunman suddenly
tried to dodge out of the way of the Pig. He lost his footing in
the soft sand and went down. Juan slammed the brakes and
turned the wheel sharply, skidding the truck in a desperate
bid to avoid running the guy over. All four of them in the cab
felt the impact.

Before the Pig had settled on its suspension, Juan had his
door open and was jumping to the ground. He bent over the
body. A quick glance told him everything he needed to know.
He climbed back into the truck, his mouth a tight, fixed line.

Cabrillo focused his mind on the image of the man firing at the Pig, of Linda hanging out the window, of the flesh
wound in Linc's neck, but nothing he knew would make
him feel better about what had just happened. When they
regained the road, he drove for the civilian vehicle. The one
police cruiser was still burning.

Juan took back his pistol from Linda, rammed home a fresh
magazine, and racked the slide. He jumped down from the cab,
keeping the weapon pointed in a two-handed combat grip,
swinging from one mangled police car to the next. He reached
into the first one and yanked the radio microphone from its
attachment point and tossed it into the desert, in case a Good
Samaritan came along and wanted to call the authorities. The
second would be a melted puddle of plastic, so he ignored it.

He approached the family sedan, taking a deep breath as
he leaned in the window. The smell of blood was a coppery
film that coated the back of his throat. The husband and wife,
as well as their two children, were dead. The only solace he
could find was the bullet wounds had been instantly fatal.
That did nothing to lessen his anger at the senseless slaughter. He noticed a slim wallet sitting on the father's lap. Ignoring the blood splatter, he grabbed it. The driver's name was
Abdul Mohammad. He had lived in Tripoli, and, according
to his ID card, had been a high school teacher. Also in the
wallet Juan found just a couple of dinar.

He didn't feel so bad about running down the fourth
gunman.

The young family had died because they were too poor
to pay a bribe.

TWELVE

Seven monotonous hours passed as the team traveled across the desert. Linc slept most of the time, his big body swaying to the rhythms of the Pig churning over the rough terrain. Linda had offered to drive for a while, but Cabrillo declined. He needed to keep focused and out of his head. Every time the image of the slaughtered family crept to the forefront of his mind, his knuckles would blanch as he gripped the steering wheel.

Mark and Eric Stone had done a fantastic job mapping their route through the mountains using the satellite photos, and the truck had delivered more than Max had promised. The engine barely strained going up the steepest inclines, and her brakes were more than ample to keep the Pig under control during the descents. Max Hanley had even rigged chains that could be lowered behind the rear tires like long mud flaps. The chains dragged across the ground and obliterated any sign of the vehicle's passage.

There was little fear they would be tracked from the checkpoint. However, there was a palpable sense of urgency.

It wouldn't take the Libyan authorities long to figure out what had happened on the highway, and they would want to catch the people who killed the cops, corrupt or not.

Juan received regular updates from Max aboard the *Oregon*. The Navy was rotating a squadron of E-2C Hawkeyes thirty miles off the coast. The propeller-driven, early-warning aircraft were keeping an eye on Libya's search-and-rescue efforts. These reports were shared with Cabrillo, so as the dawn flared and aircraft of the Libyan SAR teams once again took to the skies he knew if any were getting close to their location.

So far they had been in the clear. Once again the Libyans were concentrating their efforts more than a hundred miles from the crash site.

"GPS puts us two klicks from the wreckage," Mark said. "Stoney and I spotted a good place to hide the Pig near here."

Cabrillo looked around. They were in a shallow valley up in the mountains at an elevation of four thousand feet. Nothing grew on the bare, rocky slopes, and only sparse vegetation clung to the valley floor. This was a true wasteland.

"Turn left and go another five hundred yards," Murph ordered.

Juan followed his directions and they approached another rise in the elevation, but before they started climbing he spotted what his guys had seen on the satellite pictures. There was a narrow cleft in the rock, just wide enough and deep enough to hide the Pig from any observation except from directly overhead.

"Perfect," he muttered, and drove into the tight crevice. He killed the engine, noting they still had two-thirds of their fuel supply. The Pig got better cross-country mileage than Max had anticipated.

They sat for a moment, letting their hearing adjust to the lack of the growling diesel.

"Are we there yet?" Linc asked dreamily.

"Near enough, big man. Wakey, wakey."

Linc yawned, and stretched as much as he could. Linda reached behind them and toggled a hidden switch. The rear wall of the cab slid down to reveal the cargo hold. Because of the nature of this mission, they had brought a minimal amount of gear. Apart from a small arsenal of submachine guns and rocket-propelled grenade launchers, there were four knapsacks that had been prepacked with equipment aboard the *Oregon*. She reached in and started passing them back. As soon as she handed Cabrillo his, he jumped from the truck, knuckling kinks out of his spine.

Even in the sheltered fissure, the air was hot and dry and tasted of dust. He couldn't imagine how anyone could live out here, but he knew the Sahara had been inhabited for millennia. He considered it a testament to mankind's adaptability and ingenuity.

A moment later, the others joined him. Mark consulted the handheld GPS device he carried and pointed north.

They had been mostly silent during the drive, and no one felt the need to talk now. Juan took point as they started climbing another nameless hill. A pair of wraparound sunglasses protected his eyes, but he could feel the heat rising on his neck. He plucked a handkerchief from his hip pocket and tied it loosely around his throat. It felt good to be walking after so many hours cooped up in the Pig.

Fifteen minutes later, they moved around a sharp rise in the topography and came across the first bit of wreckage. It was a mangled piece of aluminum the size of a trash-can lid—a section of a wing, perhaps. An aviation expert would have identified it as part of the hatch that covered the 737's front gear assembly.

Juan looked up the slope and saw it was littered with debris. In the distance, three-quarters of the way to the hill's summit, lay the largest section of the aircraft's fuselage. It looked to him like the aftermath of a tornado, where bits of some poor family's house lay scattered in no discernible order.

There was no denying the savagery of the impact. Apart from the fifty-foot length of charred fuselage, most of the chunks of metal and plastic were no bigger than the first they had come across. The ground had been torn up by the crash, leaving huge scars in the earth. The explosion of aviation kerosene had scorched most of the area as if a forest fire had passed by, only here there were no trees.

During their approach, the wind had been at their back, so they couldn't smell the stench of fuel. Now it lay heavy in the air, making breathing difficult. All four tied cloth around their noses and mouths in an effort to filter the worst of it.

They fanned out as they searched the scene. Mark was taking digital photographs of some of the larger pieces, focusing in on where the metal had torn. He took several of the sheared-off bolts that had once secured a row of seats to the cabin floor. He had already looked around in vain for the tail section, the part he and Eric Stone had suspected had come apart and caused the crash. If they were right, it would be miles from here.

"Chairman," Linda called. She was off to the left near the mangled remains of one of the plane's CFM International engines.

He was at her side in a moment. She pointed silently at the ground.

Juan looked closer. Half buried in the dirt was a severely burned human hand. It was little more than a twisted claw, but judging by the size it was male. Cabrillo snapped on a pair of latex gloves and bent over the severed member. From his knapsack, he took out a plastic tube. He popped open one end and extended a swab. He took a sample of blood from the ragged tear along the wrist and resealed the evidence-collection tube. He then slipped off the wedding band from the third finger and examined the inscription inside.

He handed it to Linda. She took it and read the inscription aloud. "FXM and JCF 5/15/88." She gave him a steady gaze. "Francis Xavier Maguire and Jennifer Catherine Foster. Married May fifteenth, 1988. I studied the crew and passenger manifest. He was on Katamora's Secret Service detail."

Any hope Juan had harbored that Secretary Katamora was still alive evaporated. It wasn't that he had seen anything suspicious in the satellite photographs. It was his own desire to see something that had tricked him into believing. As final confirmation, Linc approached, his expression dark.

"I found a partial identification tag on the port engine.

The serial number checks out. This was their plane." He laid a meaty hand on Cabrillo's shoulder. "Sorry."

Juan felt as though he'd been kicked in the gut. He was well aware of the global implications of her death. He also knew that until a team of experts arrived they would never know the cause of the crash. The evidence was so badly damaged that he considered calling off their search. Their very presence here could contaminate the site for the group from the NTSB. But he had a contract to fulfill with Langston Overholt, and Cabrillo wasn't one to leave a job half finished no matter how futile.

"Okay," he finally said. "We'll keep getting samples. But be very careful."

He looked down at his feet. All of them wore shoes with no tread on the soles. They were leaving no footprints. He replaced the wedding band on the amputated hand and made sure it was in the exact position in which they'd found it.

Mark had already gone ahead to the large section of fuselage, so the three of them followed suit. The length of cabin ran from just aft of the cockpit and included half of the area where the wings attached to the aircraft. On the port side, where there would normally be a row of windows, the fuselage was torn open, so the aluminum bent inward like a long, obscene, lipless mouth. Severed wires and hydraulic lines dangled from the aircraft, and fluid had leaked from some of them to stain the rocky soil.

Beyond it, farther up the hill, were the shattered remains of the cockpit. The nose of the aircraft was punched in for a good eight feet, so the metal skin resembled the accordion joint of a tandem bus.

Juan climbed up into the fuselage. What once had been an opulent cabin befitting a cabinet secretary was now nothing but ruin. Puddles of melted plastic pooled all along the floor. Seats were identifiable only because of their metal frames.

He did a quick count and totaled up eleven corpses. Like the Secret Service agent's hand, they were burned beyond recognition. They were just genderless piles of charred flesh. No clothing remained, and because of the violence of the crash they lay scattered haphazardly. The stench of cooked meat and putrefaction was strong enough to overpower the smell of aviation fuel. The drone of flies rose and fell as they scattered and resettled when Juan moved from body to body.

The sudden jet of nausea-induced saliva forced him to swallow hard.

Mark Murphy was on his hands and knees peering under one of the burned-up club chairs with a miniature flashlight clamped between his teeth. Despite the grisly surroundings— or maybe because of them—he was humming to himself.

"Mr. Murphy," Juan said, "if you don't mind . . ."

The Chairman's voice startled Mark up from where he was working. He pulled the flashlight from his mouth. "This has got to be the best con job I have ever seen."

"Beg pardon?"

"The crash site is bogus, Juan. Someone's been here before us and tampered with the evidence."

"Are you sure? It looks about how I'd expect."

"Oh, the crash is legit, all right. This is Fiona Katamora's plane, but someone has been fooling around with it."

Juan settled down on his haunches so he was eye level with Murphy. "Convince me."

Instead of addressing the Chairman, Mark called over to Linc. "You notice it yet?"

"What are you talking about?" Linc replied. "I notice a seriously messed-up airplane and some bodies that I'll be seeing in my nightmares for the rest of my life."

Mark said, "Take that rag off your face and sniff."

"No way, man."

"Do it."

"You are one squirrelly dude," Linc said, but lowered his bandanna and took a tentative breath. Detecting something, he breathed in deeper. A spark of recognition widened his eyes. "I'll be damned. You're right."

"What is it?" Juan asked.

"You wouldn't recognize it because I doubt very much you ever came across it during your CIA days, and neither would Linda because the Navy doesn't use it."

"Use what?"

"Jellied gasoline."

"Huh?"

"Like napalm," Linc said.

Mark nodded at the former SEAL. "Most likely, a good old-fashioned flamethrower. Here's the scenario as I see it. They somehow forced the plane to land somewhere inside Libyan territory and took the Secretary off. Then they flew it here and intentionally crashed it into this mountain, using either a retrofitted remote-controlled system or, more likely, a suicide pilot.

"When they came up here to make sure everything was okay and remove any trace of said pilot, they discovered the cabin hadn't burned as much as they'd like, so they squirted it with a flamethrower. If we hadn't come along the smell would have dissipated and would have been undetectable. The anomaly would only have shown up when the guys from the NTSB analyzed their samples under a gas chromatograph and discovered traces other than aviation fuel."

"You're both sure?" Juan asked, looking from one man to the other.

Linc nodded. "It's like the perfume of your first girlfriend."

"She must have been something," Linda quipped.

"Nah, it's one of those smells you never forget."

Juan felt like he was being given a second chance. His earlier pessimism sloughed off, and he felt a charge of energy surging through his body. And then he had another thought, and his mood soured. "Wait a second. What evidence do you have that the plane landed before the crash?"

"That should be in the landing gear. Follow me."

As a group, they climbed down out of the fuselage and clambered into the dim cargo area below the passenger cabin. It reeked of burned fuel, but they didn't have to contend with the smell of what a couple days in the desert did to the bodies. Mark went unerringly to an access panel set into the floor. He popped the toggles and heaved the hatch open on its long piano hinge. Below lay the large tires and truck of the 737's port-side landing strut. Everything looked remarkably well, considering.

Murph jumped down into the well and played his flashlight beam on one of the tires. He crawled all the way around it, his eyes inches from the rubber.

"Nothing," he muttered, and hunkered even lower to check the other wheel.

He popped up a minute later, holding up a small piece of rock as if it were the Hope Diamond. "Here's your proof."

"A stone?" Linda queried.

"A piece of sandstone wedged into the tread. And there's sand on the bottom of the lower hatch." When he saw the look of confusion on the faces peering down at him, he added, "This plane supposedly took off from Andrews Air Force Base, flew to London, and then crashed, right? Where in the heck could it have picked up a lump of sandstone that looks exactly like every lump of rock for a thousand miles around us?"

"It landed in the desert," Juan said. "Murph, you did it. That *is* the proof."

Juan slipped the stone into his breast pocket. "In case the NTSB guys miss it, this needs to be analyzed to be certain, but I'd call it a smoking gun."

The sound came out of nowhere, and all four ducked instinctively as a large helicopter roared directly overhead. It was so low that its rotor wash kicked up a maelstrom of dust.

It had come in from the northeast, most likely a Libyan military base outside of Tripoli, and had to have flown nap-of-the-earth to avoid detection by the Navy's AWACS planes. That was why no one had called in a warning. As it began to slow into a landing hover, they could see it was a big Russian-built Mi-8 cargo chopper, capable of carrying nearly five tons. Its turbines changed pitch as it neared the top of the hill about five hundred yards from the truncated fuselage.

"You want further proof they know about this crash site?" Mark asked, and pointed at the khaki-painted helo. "That sucker knew right where he was headed."

"Come on." Juan started toward the rear of the cargo hold. "Let's find cover before the dust settles around their chopper."

They crawled through the fuselage and jumped to the ground on the far side. There was little natural cover near the remnants of the aircraft, so they ran down the slope until they came across a narrow dry wash that had served to drain rainwater off the mountain aeons ago. When everyone was settled, Juan buried them under a thin layer of sand and heaped as much onto himself as possible. Their view wasn't the best, but they were far enough away he doubted anyone from the chopper would wander by.

"What do you think's going on?" Mark asked in a whisper.

"I haven't the foggiest," Juan replied. "Linda? Linc?"

"No clue," Linc rumbled.

"Maybe someone realized their little stage setting isn't as good as they thought," Linda said, "and they've come back to tweak it."

Up at the summit, the turbines spooled into silence and the big rotor began to slow. In moments it was beating the air no harder than a ceiling fan. The large clamshell doors under the tail boom split open and men began to emerge. They wore matching desert-camouflage uniforms, and their heads were covered in red-and-white kaffiyehs, the wraparound scarves favored by Islamic militants throughout the Middle East.

"Regular army or guerrillas?" Linc asked.

Juan watched for nearly a minute before answering. "Judging by how they're milling around, I'd say irregulars. Real soldiers would have been ordered into a parade formation by now. Just don't ask me what they're doing in a chopper with Libyan military markings."

To add more confusion to the situation, two men backed out of the helicopter, drawing on the reins of a camel. The dromedary fought them on shaky legs, growling at the men and spitting. Then it vomited onto one of its handlers, a copious display of what it thought of the flight. Laughter drifted down to the Corporation team.

"What the hell are they doing with that thing?" Mark asked. "It looks half dead."

Juan was no judge of camels, though he'd ridden them a few times, and while he preferred horses, he hadn't found the experiences too bad. He did have to agree. Even at this distance, the animal didn't look healthy. Its coat was uneven and dull, and its hump was half of what it should be.

He had a suspicion about what was taking place but held his tongue and watched the events unfold.

After a few more minutes, the twenty or so men descended on the debris field. The two with the camel led it aimlessly over the area, tracking back and forth, laying fresh tracks over old so it would appear there had been more than one animal. It wasn't until Cabrillo realized that some of the men wore leather sandals that he was certain what was going on.

"Linda's right. They don't think the crash site will stand up under a thorough forensic review. They're contaminating it by pretending to be a group of nomads who wandered by."

They watched for nearly an hour as the men systematically trashed everything they could lay their hands on. They beat on the debris with sledgehammers, yanked out hundreds of yards of charred wiring, and moved chunks of the aircraft so nothing lay in proper relation to the rest. They got at the plane's big tires by prying open the landing gear doors and shot them flat with pistols. They also hauled parts of the plane up to the helicopter. When the helicopter was full, it flew off with a couple of the men and then returned twenty minutes later. Juan assumed they had dumped the detritus farther into the desert.

What had been a confusing jumble of aluminum, plastic, and steel but would have been recognizable to crash experts was now completely ruined. They went so far as to dismember and then bury the bodies in several unmarked graves, and make a couple of cooking fires as though nomads had camped here for a few days. When they were finished with the camel, one of the men shot it between the eyes.

Finally, it looked as though they were about finished up. Several men scattered in different directions, presumably to find some privacy to relieve themselves before their return flight back to their base.

Juan turned to his team. "Here's what I want you to do. Get back to the Pig and make for the Tunisian border, but don't head for the coast right away. Wait for me to make contact through Max on the *Oregon*. Tell him what we've discovered and make sure he tracks me."

All Corporation operatives had tracking chips surgically implanted in their legs. The chip used the body's own energy as a power source, though it required an occasional transdermal recharge. Utilizing GPS technology, the chips could be localized to within a couple dozen yards.

"What are you doing?" Linda asked.

"I'm going with them."

"We don't even know who they are."

"Exactly why I'm going."

One of the masked men was coming to within a hundred yards of where they crouched. He was roughly the same height and build as Cabrillo, which had given him the idea. Juan's normally blond hair had been dyed dark, and he wore brown contacts. With his fluency in Arabic and the kaffiyeh covering his features, he might just pull off the switch.

He tossed the Pig's keys to Linc and had started to slide back from their concealed position when Linda grabbed his arm. "What do we do with the guy?"

"Leave him. I have a feeling the Libyan government is going to announce they've located the crash site within the next twenty-four hours. Pretty soon, this place will be crawling with people. Let him explain what the hell he's doing here."

With that, Cabrillo slipped away. Crawling on his elbows, he covered the distance to the unsuspecting man in under a minute. It helped that the distant helicopter's turbines were beginning to turn over with a whine keen enough to set his teeth on edge.

Screened from the others behind a hillock, Juan waited for the man to finish his business before rushing the last few yards. The man's back was turned, and just as he started to stand upright and reach to pull up his trousers, Cabrillo struck him in the back of the head with a fist-sized stone. He recalled the Somali he'd struck in a similar fashion less than a week earlier and put enough behind the blow to collapse the Libyan in the dust.

Juan nodded to himself when he felt a pulse at the man's

throat and started stripping off his clothes. Fortunately, the man was one of the few wearing boots. They would hide the shining titanium struts of his artificial leg. Removing the kaffiyeh revealed an average-looking guy in his late twenties or early thirties. There was nothing about his features to make Juan think he wasn't Libyan, though he couldn't be positive. There was no wallet in his uniform pockets or any other means of identification. The clothes didn't even have labels.

Cabrillo dragged the unconscious man farther from the crash site, and made certain his own satellite phone was secure behind his back. Without it, he never would have considered what he was doing. Then he waited, though not for long. Someone began shouting, bellowing over the roar of the chopper's engines.

"Mohammad! Mohammad! Come on!"

Now Juan knew the name of the man he was to impersonate. He tucked his scarf a little tighter around his face and emerged from behind the hill. The soldier they earlier identified as the leader of the twenty-man team stood fifty feet from the chopper. He waved Juan in. Cabrillo acknowledged him and started jogging.

"Another minute and we would have left you out here with the scorpions," Juan was told when they came abreast.

"Sorry, sir," Cabrillo said. "Something I ate earlier."

"Not to worry." The team leader slapped him on the shoulder, and together they climbed up into the chopper. Inside its rear cargo compartment, fold-down seats lined both walls. Juan slouched into one a little ways off from the others, making sure his pant cuff covered his metal ankle. He was pleased to note that not everyone had lowered their kaffiyehs, so he laid his head against the warm aluminum hull and closed his eyes.

He had no idea if he was in the middle of a regular Army platoon or surrounded by fanatical terrorists. In the end, if they discovered him, he decided it probably wouldn't matter. Dead was dead.

A moment later, they were airborne.

THIRTEEN

THE MUSIC CAME IN EVER-RISING WAVES AS IT neared its crescendo. The orchestra had never played better, never had more passion. The conductor's face glistened with sweat, and his baton whirled and flared. The audience beyond the bright spotlights was held rapt by the performance, knowing they were experiencing something magical. The rhythmic pounding from the percussion section sounded like an artillery barrage, but even that couldn't drown out the swelling notes from the violins and woodwinds.

Then came an off-key sound.

The musicians staggered in their play but somehow managed to find their place again.

The dull thud came again followed by a sharp click, and the music stopped entirely.

Fiona Katamora returned from the performance she had been playing in her head, her right hand poised with an imaginary bow, her left curled for her fingers to rest on the strings.

Practicing music in her mind had been the only way to keep herself sane since her capture.

Her cell was a featureless metal box with a single door and a chamber pot that was infrequently emptied. A low-wattage bulb protected by a wire cage gave the only illumination. They had taken her watch, so there was no way for her to know how long she'd been their prisoner. She guessed four days.

Moments before their aircraft made its emergency landing in the open desert, their pilot had come over the intercom to explain that they had spotted an old airfield. He managed to eke a few more miles out of their descent and set the aircraft down. The landing on the dirt strip was rough, but he had gotten them down in one piece. The cheer that went up when the wheels finally stopped rolling had been deafening. Everyone was up at once, hugging, laughing, and wiping at their joyous tears.

When the pilot and copilot stepped from the cockpit, their backs were slapped black-and-blue, and their hands shaken until they were probably ready to fall off. Frank Maguire had opened the main door, and a warm desert breeze had blown the stink of fear from the cabin.

And then his head had exploded, spraying blood and tissue onto the stewardess standing behind him.

A swarm of men emerged from along the length of the runway, where they had been hiding in foxholes covered with tarps and sand. They wore khaki uniforms, their heads swaddled in scarves. Several had ladders, and before anyone could think to reseal the cabin, one of the ladders was set against the bottom sill. The pilot rushed to push it back, like a knight defending a castle wall. He was hit in the shoulder by the same sniper that killed Maguire. He went down clutching at the wound. An instant later, three men brandishing AK-47s had reached the cabin.

Fiona's assistant, Grace Walsh, screamed so shrilly that Fiona later recalled being annoyed with her at the same time she feared for her life.

It all happened so fast. They were herded back away from the open door to allow more men to enter the plane. The terrorists kept repeating in Arabic, "Down. Everybody get down."

Fiona somehow had managed to find her voice. "We will do whatever you say. There is no need for violence." And she had gotten down on her knees.

Seeing her take the lead, the crew and staff sank to the cabin floor.

One of the men yanked Fiona to her feet and pushed her toward the exit at the same time that another man was climbing the ladder. Unlike the others, he wore dark slacks and a white short-sleeved oxford shirt.

Fiona knew the moment she saw him she would never forget his face. It was angelic, with smooth coffee-colored skin and long curling lashes behind wire-framed glasses. He was no more than twenty years old, slender, and almost bookish. She had no idea how he related to the gun-wielding savages shouting at her people. Then she noted he had something in his hands. A set of Arab worry beads and a copy of the Koran.

He smiled shyly as he passed her and was led into the cockpit.

She looked back to see her people being handcuffed to their seats, understanding telescoping in on her so the horror hit like a physical blow.

"Please don't do this," she begged the man grasping her arm.

He shoved her even harder toward the ladder. Fiona went wild, clawing at his face with her fingernails and trying to ram her knee into his groin. She managed to rip off his kaffiyeh and saw he didn't have the classic Semitic features of a typical Libyan. She guessed he was Pakistani or Afghani. He balled up his fist and punched her hard enough that she momentarily lost consciousness. One second, she was scratching and kicking, and the next she was lying on the carpet, the left side of her face pulsing with pain. Men standing outside on the ladder started dragging her off the plane.

Fiona caught Grace's eye just before she was hauled away. She had somehow managed to stifle her tears. Grace, too, realized what was about to happen.

God bless you, Grace mouthed.

"You, too," Fiona replied silently, and then she was outside, being manhandled down to the ground.

They took her about a hundred feet from the aircraft and forced her to her knees, her wrists cuffed behind her back. Through the small cockpit window she could see the young man fiddling with the controls. She also saw that there was a hole in the plane's tail section. It looked like a missile had struck the plane but hadn't exploded. Which, she assumed, was the point. They wanted her but wanted the world to think she was dead.

The last of the terrorists finished securing the people left aboard. The suicide pilot stepped from the cockpit and hugged the last gunman at the door's threshold. He paused there, waving to the others, who cheered him riotously. When the gunman was on the ground and the ladder hauled away, the pilot closed the hatch and retook his place in the cockpit.

Tears were running down Fiona's cheeks. She could see faces pressed to the aircraft's windows. Those were her people—men and women she had worked with for years. For them, she would show no weakness, and she willed herself to stop crying.

The working engine fired up, its howl building until it hurt her ears. There had been vehicles hidden along the dirt strip under camouflage tarps, one of which was a small utility tractor like those seen at airports the world over. It approached the big plane's front landing gear, and the driver attached a tow hook.

It took several minutes for him to position the plane at the foot of the compacted-earth airstrip. Another moment passed before the engine beat changed and the Boeing started accelerating down the runway.

Fiona prayed that the damage done by the missile strike was severe enough to prevent the aircraft from reaching its takeoff speed, but with so little fuel in the tanks and so few passengers on board she could see it gaining speed rapidly. It flashed by her, its exhaust like a reeking hot breath. The terrorists were firing their AKs into the air, cheering as the plane's nosewheel slowly lifted from the ground. It hung awkwardly for a long moment and then the tail struck the gravel strip, a result of the damage and the inexperience of the pilot.

The nose started to fall back to earth, and Fiona was sure her prayers had been answered. They were running out of graded runway. He wouldn't be able to take off.

And then the plane rose majestically into the air at a slight tilt. The cheering redoubled, and the amount of ammunition pumped into the sky was staggering.

Fiona bit her lip as the jetliner slowly gained altitude. She had no idea how far they were going to take it. For all she knew, they were headed for Tripoli, to crash it into the conference hall where the peace summit was to be staged. Yet none of the terrorists acted as though they were ready to leave. They all looked skyward as the aircraft shrank into the distance. She couldn't bear to watch but couldn't tear her eyes from it.

The plane started to wing over, its nose now pointed at a hill some distance away. The pilot made an effort to regain control, and for a moment the aircraft leveled. Then in one violent maneuver it flipped completely onto its back. It slammed into a hill with enough force to shake the ground. Chunks of it went spinning away. The wings separated from the fuselage before bursting into flame. One of the engines tore free of the conflagration and somersaulted up the hill, kicking up gouts of earth. Dust blown up by the impact obscured the scene for many moments before slowly dissipating. The wings burned on while the white tube of the fuselage rolled safely out of the fire's reach.

Fiona gasped while the men around her roared with approval.

Even from this distance, she knew no one had survived. Though they had been spared the horror of burning alive, no one could have lived through such a violent crash. Off to her side, just out of earshot, several of the terrorists began speaking in low, earnest tones. She could tell by their body language that they were disappointed that the plane hadn't burned more thoroughly, and were probably deciding how best to proceed.

Across the runway, a tarp was pulled off a large earthmoving machine. Its engine bellowed, and soon it began erasing the evidence of the landing by systematically tearing up the strip they had graded to lure Fiona's pilots into landing there. At the pace they were going, in just a few hours no trace of their presence would remain.

The meeting ended abruptly. The person Fiona assumed was the group's leader issued orders to the others. She missed most of it, but did hear, "Make sure to remove any trace that the plane was hit by a missile, and don't forget the handcuffs." He finally approached her where she knelt on the stony ground.

"Why have you done this?" she asked in Arabic.

He leaned in close. All she could see were his eyes, dark pools of insanity. "Because Allah willed it to happen." He called to one of his men. "Bring her. Suleiman Al-Jama will want to inspect his prize."

A hood was tossed over her head, and she was manhandled into the back of a truck. The next time she was allowed to see, she was here in this cell, covered in a kind of burqa she recognized as the Afghani *chadri*. Her entire body was covered except for her eyes, which were shielded by a fine mesh of lace.

The noise she had heard that ended the concert in her head was a key being rammed into the lock and the bolt thrown. The door squealed open. She had yet to see any of her captors' faces, other than the suicide pilot and the man she'd grappled with on the plane. The two men who filled the doorway were no different. They wore matching khaki uniforms without insignia and traditional headscarves.

One of them actually snarled when he saw she had managed to tear herself free of the burqa despite her cuffed hands. Averting his eyes so as not to look her in the face, he recovered it from where she'd been using it as a pillow and quickly draped it over her head and body.

"You will show respect," he said.

"I recognize your accent," Fiona replied. "You're from Cairo. The Imbaba slums, if I'm not mistaken."

He raised a hand to strike her but stopped himself. "Next time, my fist flies if you dare speak again."

The guards took her from her cell and led her outside the prison building. She was actually grateful for the lace mesh, which protected her eyes from the brutal glare of the sun pounding against the desert floor. She could tell by its angle that it was late morning, but the heat wasn't as bad as it should have been. They were higher in the mountains, she decided.

Keeping track of details like that and playing classical music in her head helped Fiona keep from dwelling on her predicament and the fate of her friends and staffers.

The terrorist camp looked like the hundreds she'd seen in surveillance pictures. There were a few wind-battered tents tucked up against a cliff that was pockmarked with countless caves. The largest, she knew, would be their last redoubt if the camp were ever attacked, and she had no doubt it was rigged with enough explosives to take down half the mountain.

A drill instructor was leading a batch of men through calisthenics on a parade ground. Judging by the crispness of their movements, they were nearing the end of their training cycle. A little ways off, in the lee of the mountain looming over the camp, another group was gathered to live fire AK-47s. The targets were too far away for Fiona to judge their accuracy, but with the amount of money funneled into terrorist groups such as Al-Jama's they could afford to waste rounds training even the worst recruit.

Beyond the shooting range she could see a half mile into a shallow valley, with an even larger massif of mountains on the far side. There was excavation work under way at the bottom of the valley, and a rail line. She could see several boxcars on a siding next to a row of dilapidated wooden buildings. On the far side of the structures hulked a monstrous diesel locomotive that dwarfed a smaller engine that was configured much like the truck used to bring her here. The burqa's mesh face screen made seeing details impossible.

Again, she had no intelligence on this place. A terrorist

camp near a railhead had never been mentioned in any of the reports she read ad nauseam from the CIA, NSA, and FBI. This many years into the war on terror and they were still playing catch-up.

The guards led her into a cave a short way off from the main cavern. There were electric wires strung from the ceiling and bare lightbulbs every thirty or so feet. The air was noticeably colder and had that clammy feeling like an old basement in a long-disused building. They came to a wooden barrier built across the cave with an inset door. The guard who'd threatened to strike her knocked and waited until he was summoned.

He opened the door. They were at the very back of the cave. The room was ringed on three sides with rough stone. Thick Persian carpets were laid four or five deep on the floor, and a charcoal brazier smoldered in a corner, connected to the outside through a chimney tube that followed along next to the wires.

A man sat cross-legged in the middle of the room. He wore crisp white robes and a black-and-white kaffiyeh around his head. He was studying a book by the dim light— the Koran, she suspected. He didn't look up or acknowledge their presence.

If ever there was a posed scene, this was it, Fiona thought. Had this been her office, she would have been at her desk, bent over an important-looking document with a pen in hand. She'd kept people waiting for up to thirty seconds, but this man didn't look up for a full minute. His tactic of dominance was wasted on her.

"Do you know who I am?" he asked, closing the Koran with reverence.

"Ali Baba?" she said to goad him.

"Are you to be my Scheherazade?"

"Over my dead body."

"That isn't my particular predilection, but I'm sure it can be arranged."

Fiona had no desire to let him pretend to be anything other than the monster he was. "No one knows your real name, but you go by Suleiman Al-Jama. Your stated goals are the destruction of Israel and the United States and the formation of an Islamic State stretching from Afghanistan to Morocco, with you as . . . Sultan?"

"I'm not sure what title I'll take," Al-Jama said. "Sultan works, but it has decadent connotations, don't you think? Harems, palace intrigues, and all that."

He rose to his feet in a quick, fluid motion and got tea from a brass urn placed near the brazier. His motions were graceful but predatory in their swiftness. He poured himself a glass but didn't offer any to Fiona.

Now that he was standing, she could see he was nearly six feet tall, with broad shoulders and, judging by the thickness of his bare wrists, strongly built. She couldn't see his features, and in the wavering light and through the burqa's lace she could discern little of his eyes, other than the impression that they were deep-set and dark.

"Your Jesus said, 'Blessed are the peacemakers.' Did you know he is a prophet in Islam? Not the last one, of course. That is Muhammad, peace be upon Him. But your 'Savior' is recognized as a great teacher."

"We both worship the God of Isaac and Abraham," Fiona said.

"But you do not believe in His final pronouncements to His last chosen Prophet, the holy words written through Muhammad and laid into the Koran."

"My faith begins and ends with a death and resurrection."

Al-Jama said nothing, but she could tell he had a stinging retort. He finally uttered, "Back to the quote. Do you think you are blessed?"

"If I can bring about the end of violence, I think the work itself is what is blessed, not those who participate."

He nodded. "Well said. But why? Why do you desire peace?"

"How can you ask that?" Despite her earlier reservations, she felt herself drawn into the conversation. She had expected a tirade on the evils of the West, not an intellectual Q-and-A session. It was obvious the self-styled Suleiman Al-Jama was well educated, so she was curious how he would justify his brand of mass murder. She'd listened to tapes of Bin Laden's ramblings, read transcripts of detainees at Guantánamo, and watched dozens of martyrdom videos. She wanted to know how he differed, although she already knew that the difference, if any, had no meaning at all.

Al-Jama said, "Peace equals stagnation, my esteemed Secretary. When man is at peace, his soul atrophies and his creative spirit is snuffed. It is only through conflict that we are truly the beings that Allah intended. War brings out bravery and sacrifice. What does peace bring us? Nothing."

"Peace brings us prosperity and happiness."

"Those are things of the flesh, not of the spirit. Your peace is about owning a better television set and fancier car."

"While your war brings suffering and despair," Fiona countered.

"Then you *do* understand. For these are things of the spirit, not the body. These are the things we are meant to feel. Not the comfort of a grand home but the experience of shared hardship. This is what brings us closer to Allah. Not your democracy, not your rock music, not your pornographic movies. They distract us from our true reason for existence. We serve no other purpose on earth than to subjugate ourselves to Allah's will."

"Who knows what His will is?" she asked. "Who decided you know His intentions more than anyone else? The Koran forbids suicide and yet you sent a young man to intentionally crash a planeload of people into a mountainside."

"He died a martyr."

"No," she said sharply. "You convinced some poor boy that he was dying a martyr and he would have his seventy-seven virgins in heaven, but don't tell me for one instant you believe it. You are nothing more than a cheap thug trying to wrest power from others and exploiting the blind faith of a few to obtain your goals."

Suleiman Al-Jama clapped his hands together and gave a delighted laugh. He switched to English. "Bravo, Secretary Katamora. Bravo."

Though he couldn't see it because of the burqa, a surprised look crossed Fiona's face. The sudden shift in language and the conversation's intensity momentarily confused her.

"You seem to recognize that this has always been about power on the world stage. Centuries ago, England gained it using her superior Navy. The United States has it now because of her wealth and nuclear arsenal. What do the nations of the Middle East have but the willingness of some of their citizens to blow themselves up? A crude weapon, yes. But let me ask how much your country has spent on Homeland Security since a handful of men with hardware-store knives took down two of your largest buildings? A hundred billion? Five hundred billion?"

The number was closer to a trillion, but Fiona said nothing. This wasn't going as she had expected at all. She had thought Al-Jama would spout a bunch of corrupted passages from the Koran to explain why he'd done what he had, not expose himself as a man bent on dominance.

"Before the attacks on the World Trade Center, one in five hundred thousand Muslims was willing to martyr himself. Since then, the number has doubled. That's ten thousand men and women ready to blow themselves up in the jihad against the West. Do you really think you can stop ten thousand attacks once they are unleashed? People like that boy who flew the plane and Bin Laden in his cave in Pakistan may believe in the cause of jihad, Madame Secretary, but they are mere pawns, tools to be exploited and discarded. We have a near-unlimited pool of willing martyrs now, and soon we will begin to use them in coordinated attacks that will see the world's boundaries redrawn in the way I have always envisioned."

He spoke not as a zealot but almost like a corporate president outlining growth projections for his company.

"You don't need to do this." Fiona found herself pleading.

"It's too late to stop." He pulled the kaffiyeh from down below his chin. Fiona had to will herself not to faint when she saw his face. "And your death will be the first strike."

fan since you went dark."

the mudflat. Are you

FOURTEEN

No sooner had Linc gotten behind the wheel of the Pig and fired the engine than Mark Murphy opened the truck's voice-activated communications system.

"Call Max."

The ringing of a telephone sounded inside the off-road vehicle. The Pig was so well built, they could barely hear the engine as Linc guided the truck out of its hiding place and pointed its blunt snout toward the Tunisian border.

A voice no one recognized answered the call. "Max's Pizza. Is this for pickup or delivery?"

"Be something if they would deliver," Linc said. "I could go for a slice."

"Sorry. Wrong number." Mark cut the connection and tried again. "Call Max Hanley."

This time Max's voice muttered hello when the phone was answered.

"Max, it's Mark Murphy. I'm in the Pig with Linda and Linc."

"Glad you finally called," Max said. "The stuff's hit the fan since you went dark."

"I can imagine. Are you in the op center?"

"Yeah."

"Have someone pull up the screen for the bio-tracking chips."

"Just a second." There was a moment's pause. While they waited, Mark used the Pig's computer to jack into the *Oregon*'s closed-circuit television system so the image of the futuristic control room popped up on his screen. Max was standing next to the communications station, watching over the duty officer's shoulder.

"That's interesting," Hanley muttered. "I have the three of you heading west at forty miles per hour, presumably in the Powered Investigator Ground, while the Chairman is going northeast at a hundred miles an hour. What happened, you guys get into an argument?"

"Funny. Make sure you stay on him. We're on our way to the Tunisian border. Juan's with the people we're certain brought down the Secretary's plane. We don't believe she's dead."

"Did you say the plane was brought down?"

"I did, and I don't think Fiona Katamora was on it when it crashed."

"How the hell did they pull that off? Tell me in a second. You'd better hightail it out of there. Twenty minutes ago, the Libyans announced that they've located the wreckage, and their government has given permission for a team from our NTSB to examine it. They had been prestaged in Cairo and will be in Tripoli by noon, but I'm sure the Libyans will be swarming that area sooner."

"They're not going to find anything," Mark told him. "A team of men came in on a chopper to demolish the site and ruin any chance of a reconstruction. They moved wreckage around, took some away, and smashed up just about everything they could lay their hands on. They even brought a lame camel to lay tracks all over the place."

"A lame camel?"

"To make it look like nomads had done the damage," Mark explained.

"Someone's thinking a couple of steps ahead," Max grunted.

"Is the NTSB coming to Libya general knowledge?" Linda asked.

"No. Langston told me it was cleared at the highest levels and kept under wraps."

"That means the tangos have a source in the government if they knew to come back and mess with the wreckage."

"Or they're government sponsored," Max countered. "Mark, you said you don't think Secretary Katamora was on the plane."

"There's pretty convincing evidence that the plane landed in the desert before the crash."

"You think they took her off?"

"Why else would they land it, take off again, and slam it into a mountaintop? They want the world to think she's dead."

"What do they gain by that?"

"Come on, Max," Linda said. "She's the damned Secretary of State. She's either an intelligence coup for these people or the best bargaining chip in history. Remember, she was the last President's National Security Advisor. If we think she's dead, we aren't going to be looking for her. They could extract information from now until doomsday and we'd never be the wiser."

There was a pause in the conversation as all of them digested the implications of Linda's theory. The terrorists getting their hands on Fiona Katamora was probably more damaging than if they had kidnapped the President. As a politician only in his first year of office, he was kept away from the operational minutiae that went into fighting the war on terror. Because of the positions she'd held over the years, and the insatiable ability of her mind to absorb details, Fiona knew more about America's ongoing operations and the nation's plans for the future than the Chief Executive.

"We have to get her back," Max said.

There was no need to respond to such an obvious statement.

"Is there anything else going on that we need to be aware of?" Mark asked.

"Yeah. Langston forwarded information about a mission on behalf of the State Department being carried out in Tunisia very close to the Libyan border."

"State's running ops now?" Linc asked.

"It was cleared through Langley, and they sent a minder along with the team. It was given medium priority because there wasn't much of a chance for success."

"What are they doing in Tunisia?"

Max explained about the letter that first came to light through St. Julian Perlmutter and how it related to the historic pirate Suleiman Al-Jama during the Barbary Wars. He told them of the belief that the old corsair might have left writings in a hidden cave someplace along a dried-up river course that expounded on ways Islam and Christendom could coexist peacefully.

"Does sound like a long shot," Linda said when he finished. "Is this connected to the plane crash?"

"It's kind of coincidental that these two events happened around the same time and near the same place, but there's no hard evidence of a link. The Secretary wasn't even aware of the expedition. It was handled by an Undersecretary named Christie Valero. Apparently, she thought it was worth trying for. And for whatever it's worth, so do I. Pronouncements from influential clerics carry a tremendous amount of weight in the region. It was Ayatollah Khomeini who declared that anyone who—"

"'—commits an act of suicide while engaged with the enemy shall be considered a martyr,'" Linda finished for him. "We know our history, Max. And I'm willing to bet you just learned that little factoid when you spoke with Overholt."

Hanley didn't deny it. "Anyway, three of the four people State sent to Tunisia are now considered missing. They had been given permission by the local government chaperone to stay away from the camp for seventy-two hours, but their truck's overdue."

"The supposition at Langley is that this is connected to Fiona's abduction, right?" Mark asked doubtfully.

"They're not supposing anything," Max replied with a tone that said he didn't give a whit for Mark's skepticism. "But Lang wants us to check it out anyway."

Linda said, "I don't think that's a good idea. We just saw Juan fly off with either a group of terrorists or members of Libya's Special Forces, but either way they're involved in the crash. We shouldn't be traipsing across the desert searching for lost archaeologists when he could need us at a moment's notice."

"Hold on a second," Murph interrupted, a hint of excitement in his voice. "Where's Stoney?"

"He's not on duty right now so he's probably in his cabin."

"Max, pipe this call down to him, and we'll be right back." Max made the switch. Eric Stone came up on a webcam a moment later, slurping from an energy drink. "Hey, how is it playing Lawrence of Arabia?" he said in greeting.

"Are you bogarting my Red Bull?" Murph accused.

Eric quickly pulled the can out of camera range. "Nope."

"Jerk. Listen, when we were checking the satellite pictures we spotted an abandoned truck out in the open desert not too far from our flight path estimates."

"I remember."

"Flash me a close-up and give me the GPS coordinates."

"Hold on." Eric glanced down from the webcam and started typing at his computer. Over his shoulder, an online gaming avatar that looked like a toad in medieval armor had been set by a macroprogram to grind out points by repeatedly arranging a basket of flowers.

"Looks like a real badass game you're playing, Eric," Linc remarked when he glanced over at the computer screen in front of Murph. "Let me guess, Sir Ribbet and the Bouquet of Death?"

Stone looked over his shoulder, saw that he could never explain what he was doing to a warrior like Linc, and killed that computer screen with a remote control. "Okay, I've e-mailed the GPS numbers and a zoom shot of the truck. I'm now looking at your tracking information. You're only about a hundred miles from it. Shouldn't take more than a couple of hours."

"As the crow flies, Stoney, not as the Pig crawls, but thanks. Would you also send that picture to the main screen in the op center and route this call back to Max?"

"On its way."

"Talk to you later."

"Is that their truck?" Mark asked Hanley as soon as he'd reestablished contact.

"Overholt said it had some kind of drill rig on the back, so I'd say it is. How did you know where to find a picture of it?"

"I'm a genius, Max," Murph replied without a trace of irony. "You know that."

"Okay, genius, you just bought yourself a detour. I want you guys to check out the truck, and then I need you to interview the fourth member of the search team, a Dr. Emile Bumford. He's still at the Roman archaeological site that the State Department team was using as cover. He's already spoken with the Undersecretary at State, who set this up. From what Lang told me Bumford's useless, but a face-to-face might get us something."

"What about the Chairman?" Linda persisted. "I feel like we're abandoning him."

"Sweetie," Max soothed, "this is Juan Cabrillo we're talking about. With his luck that chopper's headed to some five-star seaside resort, and ten minutes after they land he'll have a drink in one hand and a woman in the other."

• • •

IT TOOK THE BETTER part of eight hard hours to cross the desert to where Eric and Mark had spotted the abandoned drill truck on the satellite pictures. The landscape was a fractured plane of endless hillocks and riverbeds that rattled their organs until they felt their bodies were nothing more than liquid held in check by their skin.

Mark and Linda had switched places so she rode shotgun

next to Linc. He drove in a loose-armed, relaxed pose, as if the rough terrain were no more bothersome than an occasional pothole on an interstate highway. As the sun hovered over the distant horizon, they were approaching the GPS coordinates Eric Stone had provided. The Pig was still performing as advertised, and their remaining fuel was just enough to get them across the border into Tunisia. There they would need to find diesel. Linc was hoping they could buy a supply at the archaeological site, but most likely it would need to be choppered in from the *Oregon*. He would have to call Max about making the arrangements so they could sling a bladder of diesel under the Corporation's new McDonnell Douglas MD-520N. With its hook-lifting capacity of a ton, George Adams, their pilot, could more than handle the fuel needed to fill the Pig's many tanks.

Something sticking up from the otherwise barren desert caught Linc's attention. It was less than a quarter mile off to their left. He wasn't sure what it was. From a distance and in the uncertain light, it appeared to be pulsating. He pointed it out to Linda and Mark. Neither knew what to make of it. They were a mile from the abandoned truck, but Linc felt it was worth a look, so he parked the Pig behind a low dune and killed the engine.

"Mark, grab me my REC7, will you?" Linc asked. Next to him, Linda drew a Glock 19, the compact version of the 17, one of the most popular combat pistols in the world.

Mark opened the door to the rear compartment and handed Linc his assault rifle. Not as proficient with small arms as he was with the *Oregon*'s state-of-the-art arsenal, Murph tucked an antique Model 1911 .45-caliber pistol into the small of his back when he unlimbered his lanky frame from the truck.

The three of them kept in a crouch and used natural cover to approach the unknown object thrust up from the ground. When they were fifty yards off, they heard an obscene crying sound, something that wasn't human but still reminded them all of an infant's scream.

"What the hell is that thing?" Mark asked with superstitious dread.

Linc was just ahead of the other two, his rifle tucked high

against his shoulder, as he peered intently, trying to understand what he was seeing. The object looked like an inverted cross, but there were two dark shapes moving on either side of the cross, shuffling around in an ungainly motion.

Then one of the shapes spread a pair of wide black wings, and Linc knew immediately what he was seeing. A man had been crucified with his head pointed toward the ground, and a pair of bald-necked vultures was sitting on the crux of his underarms. The feathers around their heads were matted with gore as they feasted upon the corpse. One had torn off a strip of flesh that now hung in its beak. It jerked its head back and forth to force the meat down its gullet.

Linc knew from an experience in central Africa when he was with the SEALs that no warning shot in the world would chase the repugnant birds from their favored carrion. He fired for effect, putting two rounds downrange, and the vultures were blown off their unholy perch. A couple of feathers drifted lazily on the slight breeze and settled a few feet away from their bodies.

"Oh, God . . . Oh, God . . . Oh, God," Mark Murphy kept repeating, but, to his credit, he stayed with Linc and Linda as they drew nearer.

The birds had inflicted unspeakable wounds to the body. They'd had days to tear and rip into the man's flesh, but there was enough recognizable to see he was Caucasian and he'd died from a single bullet to the head. Because of the blood that had soaked into the ground below the crucifix, it was impossible to tell if he'd been shot before or after he'd been strung up. Being only a mile from the drill truck, it wasn't a leap in logic to assume that this was what remained of one of the State Department people.

In Linc's mind he could concede that the terrorists might have felt that killing the man had been an operational necessity. But the desecration of his body in an intentional perversion of Christ's death had been done merely for the fun of it.

Without a word, Linc started back to the Pig to get a shovel.

The grisly task took twenty minutes in the soft soil, and when he was finished only a thin sheen of sweat greased his torso and shaved head. While he worked, Linda and Mark cast ahead for the truck only to discover it had been moved since the satellite flyby. They found clearly defined tire tracks leading off to the west. They also saw a second set of tracks from a vehicle lighter than the drill truck. Between the two sets of tracks was a single brass shell casing that still smelled of gunpowder, and a red-black stain in the earth that was being painstakingly cleared away one sand grain at a time by columns of ants.

When they told Linc what they'd seen, all agreed that the State Department team had inadvertently crossed the border into Libya, where they had been discovered by a patrol. For some reason, one of their party had been shot in the head and the others taken prisoner. The body had been driven a short distance and crucified.

"It's possible they saw Katamora's plane fly overhead," Mark suggested. "Realizing it was in trouble, they might have decided to investigate."

"And they just happened to run into a border patrol?" Linda's comment was more a dubious statement than a question.

"Not a border patrol," Linc countered, sensing where Linda was heading. "The terrorists sent out teams along the projected flight path to eliminate anyone who saw the plane."

"Judging from where the ambush took place, the State people were well south of their own base camp," Mark pointed out. "They were in the right place, only it was the wrong time."

"What do you want us to do?" Linc asked Linda Ross.

As the Corporation's vice president of operations, she was the ranking member on the team. She considered calling Max and leaving the decision up to him, but Hanley hadn't seen the condition of the body, couldn't feel what she'd felt at that moment when she realized what it was. When it came to tactical matters, Linda rarely allowed her emotions to interfere with her decisions. No good commander does. However, this time, looking at her companions, she knew the right call was to go after the butchers who did this. With luck, they would take one alive. It was doubtful a foot soldier would know the overall plans these people had for the Secretary of State, but any intelligence was better than nothing.

"They've got a hell of a head start," she said, her jaw barely moving because of her anger.

"Don't matter to me," Linc said.

"If it makes it easier," Mark said, "there's a fifty-fifty chance the two other Americans were taken prisoner when the Libyans took their truck."

Linda hadn't thought of that, and it was the last piece of information to cement her decision. "Mount up."

Tracking the drill truck's tire tracks across the desert was as easy as following the dotted lines on a country road. The vehicle was heavy enough that the marks hadn't yet succumbed to the constant scouring of the wind. And when the sun sank over some distant mountains, Mark activated the Pig's FLIR system. Designed for attack helicopters, the Forward Looking Infrared system could detect ambient heat sources and would give them a warning many miles off if they approached the warm engine of the truck.

Linc strapped a pair of night vision goggles over his head. Using both passive and active near-infrared illuminators, he could drive comfortably in total darkness if necessary. However, the quarter moon rising behind them gave the third-generation system more than enough light.

No one spoke as they drove across the wasteland. There was no need. All three of them shared the same thoughts, the same concerns, and also the same desire to avenge the dead man. None of them cared about the bumps and ruts that the powerful truck bulled through. What the massive shock absorbers couldn't take, their bodies would.

"How far are we from the Tunisian border?" Linda asked after a couple of hours.

Mark checked their position on his computer. "About eight miles."

"Keep sharp. I doubt they'll cross it."

The ghostly shadows cast by the risen moon suddenly winked out as a curtain of clouds crossed in front of it. Linc's

NVGs didn't have enough light to process, so he keyed the active illuminators, sending out wavelengths in the near-infrared spectrum that were undetectable to human vision but which showed clearly in his goggles.

They drove like that for another mile. Mark Murphy was well aware that the active signal from Linc's goggles could be seen by anyone else equipped with a night vision device, so he never took his eyes off the FLIR. So far, the desert ahead remained completely dark on the thermal scans.

And then a tiny blip showed itself. It was too small to be a man, he thought, and he dismissed it as some nocturnal animal when suddenly a burst of light exploded in the truck's cabin across nearly every wavelength.

The hot exhaust from an RPG showed like a streak of white lightning on Mark's screen while Linc's NVGs were nearly overwhelmed by the blast of the rocket motor. They had stumbled into a perfectly laid ambush, and had the man with the grenade launcher fired a moment sooner they would have been blown apart in the opening salvo.

FIFTEEN

The Pig was at the crest of a hill, so they commanded the high ground, but without cover it did them no good. Their forward momentum didn't give Linc enough time to jam the transmission into reverse, so he took the only option open to him. As the rocket came at them on its unguided, flat trajectory, the former SEAL mashed the accelerator and charged down the slope. He pressed a button on the dash to activate the hydraulic suspension, lowering the vehicle's center of gravity by pushing the wheels out well beyond the fenders.

Murph no longer had the ground clearance to engage the .30-caliber machine gun mounted under the front bumper, but Linc's move had given the truck enough stability to race across the face of the dune without tipping. Linc hit another switch to lower the curtain of chains behind the rear tires to cover their tracks. At the speeds he was hitting, the heavy lengths of chain hurled up a dense cloud of billowing dust, something their FLIR could see through but which the grenadier's NVGs could not.

The rocket-propelled grenade impacted the earth where the Pig had been seconds before, blasting a harmless fountain of dirt and debris into the air. Tracer fire began to knife out of the darkness, converging on the rampaging truck like fire hoses.

"Linda—" Linc started to say, but she cut him off.

"I'm on it."

She opened the door to the rear cargo area and launched herself through feetfirst. She went immediately for the switch that opened the top hatch, and the instant it was opened she pushed the secondary machine gun up and onto its roof mounts. The hatch covers gave her protection from the sides, so she aimed for the gunmen firing at them straight ahead. The .30-caliber roared in her hands, and spent brass arced away from the breach in a shimmering blur. She poured rounds into one particularly dense area of fire. In the darkness, she couldn't tell what was happening a hundred yards away, but the stream of tracers racing for the Pig withered away to nothing.

She swung the gun to counter Linc's erratic driving, ravaging another foxhole. There must have been a grenadier with the men firing assault rifles because the position was blown apart by an explosion that sent shattered bodies high into the sky.

Another RPG blasted out of the night, but the aim was so far off that Linc could afford to ignore it. He pointed the Pig at a long mound of sand that was giving several attackers perfect cover. He went up its face at an angle, and when he reached the top he threw the heavy truck into a four-wheel drift so that when they reached the bottom on the far side Linda had the entire row of gunmen in her sight's crosshairs. She walked her rounds up the defile, tearing apart the defensive positions in a fury of destruction.

"I've got a massive thermal image here," Mark said, staring at his computer.

"Range?"

"Five hundred yards. It's partially obscured by the topography, but there is something big out there, and it's getting hotter."

"Missiles," Linc ordered.

Even bouncing over the rough ground, Mark didn't miss a keystroke as he worked his computer. Hydraulically operated panels opened along the Pig's sides just enough to reveal the blunt nose cones of four FGM-148 Javelin antitank missiles. Normally a shoulder-fired weapon, the Javelin carried a seventeen-pound warhead, and had proved capable of defeating any armored vehicle it had ever engaged.

The Javelin was an infrared-guided fire-and-forget weapon, so as soon as Mark locked his computer's targeting reticle on the unknown heat signature, the missile was ready.

"Fire in the hole," he shouted for Linda's benefit, and launched the rocket.

It came out of its tube in a gush of hot exhaust and streaked across the desert. Linc turned the wheel so Linda could engage another machine-gun nest that was peppering the Pig's flank with a steady barrage of fire. It seemed the only active enemy still willing to engage them.

The Javelin homed in on the heat source with single-minded determination, ignoring the battle raging around it and the futile attempts of a couple of men to shoot it down as it roared into a secret desert base. Fifty feet from its target, its seeker head suddenly lost the signal, though it picked up a cooler, and closer, contact. Still, it ignored the bait and maintained its original course.

What the missile didn't know was that a fuel truck had passed between it and its target, the cooler thermal image being its engine. The rocket slammed into the tank just behind the cab. The driver died in an instant as the fuel-air mixture detonated in a blossoming fireball that seemed to lick the heavens. A cluster of nearby tents was torn to shreds by the blast, their guy ropes turned to ribbons, and the poles reduced to split wood. Cargo netting strung up from date palms to hide the compound from satellite photography flared like tinder. Pieces of metal blown from the truck scythed down the ground crew that had been working at the base, but the shrapnel did nothing to the machine the crew had been servicing.

In the towering flames of the destroyed truck, Linc, Mark, and Linda saw two things at the same time. One was that the drill truck belonging to the State Department team had been blown onto its side by the explosion and its undercarriage was aflame. The second was what the perimeter guards had been protecting.

Nestled in a sandbag bunker was a Russian-built Mi-24 helicopter gunship, perhaps the most feared battlefield chopper in history. The heat from its twin Isotov turbines spooling up was what Mark had detected on the FLIR. The rotors were a blur as the pilot readied the flying tank killer for takeoff.

"Holy crap!" Murph cried. "If he gets that thing off the ground, we're toast."

Even as he said it, the chopper, code-named Hind, hauled itself into the sky. The pilot rotated the helo on its axis while still partially covered by the walls of sandbags. Mounted under the nose of the Hind was a four-barreled Gatling gun, and when it cleared the top of the walls it erupted.

Linda just managed to duck through her hatch when the desert around the Pig came alive with hundreds of .50-caliber rounds. Bullets pounded into the armored windshield with enough force to star the glass, and if the onslaught continued for even a few seconds more the glass would disintegrate.

Linc dropped a gear and hit the gas, throwing a rooster tail of sand in their wake. The ground just to the left of the Pig exploded as a fresh barrage chased after them. Then came the rockets, a half dozen of them, launched off pods slung under the Hind's stubby wings. It was like driving through a sandstorm. The unguided missiles tore into the hills all around them. Linc swerved as best he could, zigging and zagging between each impact, hoping to buy a few seconds more. One rocket hit the rear bumper, rocking the Pig on its suspension but doing little damage beyond mangling the hardened steel.

Linc looked over at Murph. "Ready?"

"Do it!"

Linc cranked the wheel and slammed the brakes with every ounce of his considerable strength. The Pig whipped around, sliding on the shifting sands, its wide stance keeping it from flipping. The instant the nose was pointed back toward the Hind, Mark unleashed a pair of Javelins, trusting their heat seekers to find the target because he couldn't take the time to aim properly.

The Hind's pilot lost his target in the swirling maelstrom of dust and held his fire for a moment so the wind would blow the dust away. It was from this impenetrable curtain that the two missiles emerged. The cryonic cooling system of one of them had failed to reach the proper temperature, so it couldn't acquire the target against the still-warm desert floor. It augered into the ground and exploded well shy of the chopper.

Pointed nose-on at the incoming rockets, the Hind posed a small thermal cross section because its hull shielded the exhaust from its turbines. The pilot knew this and did nothing, hoping that playing possum could cause the missile to fly past. But the Javelin locked on anyway. To its computer brain, the four glowing tubes hanging below the helicopter's chin were enticing enough to commit to attack.

The heat seeker sent minute corrections to the missile's fins, aiming it straight for the still-hot barrels of the Hind's Gatling gun. The pilot tried to pull up at the last second, so the Javelin missed the gun but impacted directly under the cockpit. The explosion tore the helicopter in half, its front section nearly disintegrating, while the hull and tail boom reared up from the force of the blast. Because the main rotor was still fully engaged, the chopper lost all stability and began to spin, smoke pouring from the blackened hole that had been the cockpit. When the chopper canted over almost ninety degrees, the blades lost lift, and the ten-ton Hind crashed to earth. Its aluminum rotors tore furrows into the ground until they blasted apart, sending shrapnel careening at near-supersonic speeds. So much grit was sucked into the Isotov turbines that they flared out and seized.

The chopper's self-sealing fuel tanks had done their job. There were no secondary explosions, and the flames around the engines' exhausts quickly starved for gas.

Mark blew out a long breath.

"Nice shooting, Tex," Linc drawled. He then called back to Linda, "You okay back there?"

"I know what James Bond's martini feels like."

"Sorry about that."

She poked her head back into the cabin. "You guys took down the Hind, so it was an observation, not a complaint. What is this place? Some sort of border station?"

"Probably," Linc replied.

"Take us over to the Hind, will you?" Mark asked. He was studying the downed chopper through the FLIR.

"That isn't such a good idea. We should clear out while the clearing's good."

"I don't think this is a border station," Murph said. "I need a closer look at the helo to be sure. Also, we have to do a sweep for any communications gear left intact. If there are survivors out here, the last thing we need is them calling in reinforcements."

Linc dropped the transmission into gear and drove the quarter mile to the wreckage. The Pig wasn't even stopped before Mark threw open his door. Like a primitive hunter approaching a dangerous prey that he wasn't sure was dead, Mark crept closer to the downed Hind. Linda was back up in the hatch, watching the smoldering ruins of the camp over her machine gun's iron sights.

"What are you looking for?" she asked without looking down from her perch.

"Not *for*," Mark corrected. "At."

"Okay, then, at."

"The air intakes aren't normal. They're oversized. Also, the stubs of the rotor blades."

"And?" Linc prompted from the Pig's cab.

Mark turned to look at him. "This chopper's modified for high-altitude operations. I bet if I checked the fuel lines for their turbines, they'll be larger than normal, too. And this"—he slapped a hard-point mount under the gunship's wing—"is the launch rail for an AA-7 Apex missile."

"So?"

"The Apex isn't part of the typical load-out for a Hind. These are ground-attack choppers. The Apex is designed for air-to-air combat, specifically for the MiG-23 Flogger."

"How can you be so sure?" Linda asked.

"Weapons design is what I did before coming to the Corporation. I lived and breathed this stuff," he replied. "You guys have put two and two together, right?"

"Air-to-air missile, high-altitude chopper"—Linc made a motion like he was balancing these two elements in his hands—"it isn't exactly a mystery worthy of Sherlock Holmes. They used this bird to shoot down the Secretary's plane."

Linda asked, "So is this place Libyan or some terrorist compound?"

"That's the million-dollar question," Mark replied, stepping back into the Pig. "Let's check it out and see if we can come up with an answer."

They drove into the confines of the desert base. The tents were little more than ash, and the fronds had burned off all the palm trees. Linc braked next to the body of one of the Hind's mechanics, placing the Pig between the corpse and the open desert. Mark jumped down and turned the body over. In the wavering light of the nearby fires, he could see a chunk of metal, probably from the tank of the fuel truck, was embedded in the man's chest. What Mark didn't find were rank insignia on the uniform or any kind of identification in the man's pockets, not even dog tags.

He checked several more corpses, never venturing far from the protection of the Pig. No one showed any rank or carried ID. He poked around the ruined tents, finding a satellite phone, which he pocketed, and a big radio transceiver, which had been destroyed by the blast, but nothing to indicate who these men were or whom they served.

"Well?" Linda asked when he clambered into the cab of the Pig and closed the door for the last time.

"This place is a complete cipher." He raked his hand through his stringy hair in a gesture of frustration. "We know the how of the crash, but we still don't know the who or the why."

"I'm not worried," Linc said as he started them away from the camp and toward the Tunisian border. "I bet the Chairman had those two questions pegged five minutes after landing in that other helo."

SIXTEEN

As soon as the helicopter's clamshell doors opened and Juan's eyes adjusted to the bright light streaming in from outside, he knew he was into it. Deep.

Avoiding detection at a Libyan air base should have been relatively easy. There would be a thousand men stationed there, dozens of buildings to hide in, and the anonymity that came with the transient nature of military personnel who were shuffled from duty assignment to duty assignment.

But the Mi-8 hadn't landed at an Air Force facility. It had landed high in the mountains on a shielded plateau that still commanded views over several breathtaking valleys. Below the compacted-earth landing pad was a training camp. Exiting the rear of the helo with the others, he could see dozens of tents, a parade field, an obstacle course, and a shooting range.

Juan made sure not to jump to a conclusion. The fact that this appeared to be a terrorist camp didn't necessarily mean it wasn't government backed. He was still in Libya after all.

Off to one side of the compound was the mock-up of a three-story building constructed of metal scaffolding draped in burlap. The building it represented was large, like an office block, with a perimeter wall, a cantilevered porte cochere extending out over the circular drive, and a side wing that somehow made Juan think of a solarium, except the structure was too big for a private residence. The back of the building was an enclosed space, and while the men here hadn't landscaped it like the real place, they had erected burlap fences to represent hedges.

With the turbines winding down, Cabrillo heard generators chugging away below them and the cry of a muezzin calling the faithful to noontime prayers. Men were streaming across the camp, each carrying a prayer rug. They began assembling on the parade ground, orienting their mats to face east and the holy city of Mecca. He estimated there were at least two hundred men—a large number, to be sure, but not big enough for him to remain anonymous for long. Someone would eventually miss the real Mohammad, and a thorough search would be conducted.

As much as he needed to gather intelligence about this group, his only chance lay in ducking away early and hoping he could return for a nocturnal reconnaissance.

"Get moving," he was ordered from behind, and he shuffled off the chopper's rear ramp.

Off across the valley, Juan spied some sort of construction site or excavation. He tugged his headscarf tighter around his face and started for the footpath leading to the camp below. He stayed close to the man in front of him so no one could get a look at his eyes and made sure to walk in a slight stoop to hide the fact that he was taller than most of the others.

He didn't know if the men sent out to sabotage the downed airliner were stationed in the same barracks, but it stood to reason. He had watched them work, and while not as disciplined as professional soldiers they had a cohesiveness that came from working and training together in a tight group. Once they reached their billet, Juan knew his life would be measured in seconds.

The path wound along the edge of a steep ravine, its flank crisscrossed with countless intersecting gullies and wadis and covered with loose rock and sand. There was a shelf halfway down that sat atop a vertical cliff at least thirty feet high. Juan was judging the odds of his making it to the bottom alive as slim to nil when the team leader at the head of the little column turned around and started collecting their kaffiyehs.

The majority of the men knew this was coming and had already unwound their kaffiyehs from around their heads. Juan glanced down again at the camp to his left. No one had his head covered. It was a bonding tool, he knew. Only to outsiders would they be anonymous. Safe here at their camp and among their brothers, they showed themselves openly.

The odds no longer mattered.

He rammed the heels of his hands into the back of the man in front of him and snarled, "Watch yourself."

The man whirled, his eyes fierce. "What did you do that for?"

"You elbowed me in the stomach," Juan retorted. "I should kill you for the insult."

"What's going on back there?"

"This son of a pig pushed me," Juan shouted.

"Who is that?" the leader called. "Show yourself."

"Only when he apologizes."

"I will not. You hit me in the back first."

Juan swung at the Arab's face, a lazy roundhouse lacking a tenth of Juan's strength. The man saw it coming a mile away, ducked instinctively inside Juan's reach, and fired two quick punches into Juan's stomach. It was the excuse Juan needed. He yanked off the other man's headscarf, turning him so Juan's back was toward the rest of the men and no one could see his face.

"I don't know you!" Juan cried in mock surprise. "This man is an impostor, an infiltrator."

"Are you mad? I've been here for seven months."

"Liar." Cabrillo. seethed.

The man went to push Juan. Rather than resist, Cabrillo grabbed his wrists and stepped back off the trail. His feet immediately began to slide. The gradient was gradual at first but quickly steepened. They started gaining speed, and when they reached a tipping point Juan fell backward, flipping the hapless terrorist over his head without relinquishing his grip, so the momentum tumbled him onto the man's chest like an acrobat. It was now the terrorist's body grinding against the sharp rocks as they slid down the ravine with Juan lying on top.

They crashed into the first gully, and Cabrillo heard bones breaking against the hiss of gravel avalanching down the hill with them. The Libyan screamed in Juan's ear as their speed careened them into the gully. They went down like bobsledders, only the terrorist was the sled. All around them, more and more rocks were loosened by the pair's passage until, from above, the two must have been completely obscured by dust. Both of the man's legs were broken below the knee and flopped sickeningly as he and Juan whooshed down the defile, swaying up and down the sides according to the vagaries of the terrain.

Cabrillo used his artificial leg as a sort of rudder to keep them in the center of the gully as best he could. Each time he extended the limb, it was like a sledgehammer blow against his stump, but without Juan bracing them they would have started to tumble uncontrollably.

More gravel and sand was building up around them, and then suddenly they were on top of the avalanche they had created. The friction of the terrorist's battered body scratching against the ground vanished without warning, and their speed seemed to double. Juan could no longer control their slide. When the gully began to twist to the left, the sheer volume of material rocketing down the hillside could no longer be contained and burst from its banks like a river in flood, bearing Juan and the Arab with it. They caught air as the ground dropped sharply away. When they came down, the terrorist was no longer screaming, and they had gained a few precious yards on the wall of gravel now in pursuit.

This new valley was wider and deeper than the first but twisted more often. Again, the avalanche caught up to them and again Juan rode the man as though he were straddling a tree trunk in a logging flume. Just ahead, he could see the debris cascading off the shelf he'd spotted from the top. He chanced a look up the slope. Behind the shifting thrust of gravel and sand, boulders tumbled in the avalanche, succumbing to the forces of gravity and the weight of dirt from above. It was like looking into the grinding mouth of an industrial wood chipper. The boulders banged and rattled against one another, pulverizing themselves as they fell.

He looked back downslope. The avalanche arced ten feet through space beyond the cliff before cascading to earth. Had it been water, Juan would have gone over the falls and had a good chance of swimming away at the bottom. But not here.

Cabrillo dug his prosthesis into the gravel, forcing it down into the avalanche until he felt solid ground beneath. Seconds before he and the Arab were carried over the precipice, he pushed off with everything he had, launching himself off the terrorist's corpse in an awkward lurch that carried him right to the edge of the avalanche.

He scrambled onto all fours and started clawing his way upward, fighting the remorseless downward plummet of the gravel under him. It was like crawling against a treadmill set on maximum. There was no way he could gain any ground. The avalanche was much too fast. He only hoped to buy himself a few precious seconds as he angled himself farther up the side of the gully, driving himself to get out of the landslide's grasp before it carried him over the cliff.

With ten feet to go, he was still mired in the fringes of avalanche. His bloodied fingers dug into it with machinelike tenacity, and his legs pistoned, kicking up dirt with each thrust. But it wasn't enough. He was too far from the slide's boundary to haul himself clear.

It wasn't in him to give up, and he made one last supreme effort. The cascade of loose debris claimed the shattered remains of his companion at the same instant his fingers felt solid ground. Cabrillo groped to find purchase, and his hands clasped something hard and round. With no choice, he grasped it in his left hand and swung to find purchase with his right.

He knew the first rule of rock climbing was never to trust

vegetation. It could let go without a moment's notice. But with no other choice, he clung to the root of a gnarled tree left exposed to the sun.

Almost immediately, the root started to tear away from the earth as if he had yanked on the end of a rope that had been buried just beneath the surface. Though he had managed to drag all but his feet free of the landslide, he was relying entirely on the root, and the more its tangled subterranean connections snapped, the more he fell toward the edge of the cliff.

His legs went over the edge, and then his hips. He held on to the root with everything he had while less than a foot away a continuous torrent of sand and rock plummeted past his shoulder. His fall checked for an instant, he tried to pull himself upward, only to have more of the root break away. He slipped completely over the edge, dangling by his arms. Just before he went over, he saw that the wall of boulders and rocks was seconds away from cascading over the falls.

He forced himself to crab along the cliff face to his right, his head and shoulders pounded by the light rubble, lengthening the angle between himself and where the root was anchored on the side of the gulley. Then he raced back, running through the deluge seconds ahead of the boulders. He burst from the landslide, swinging like a pendulum. He reached out with his left hand and just managed to grasp a knuckle of rock in his fist.

His movements scraped the root against the razor-sharp edge of the cliff, like a length of string against a saw blade. Cabrillo had no time to gain a better purchase on the piece of sandstone in his hand when the root parted. His body crashed into the cliff. The tree root that had saved his life tumbled away, swallowed by the debris pouring down the mountainside.

Hanging by only one hand, he looked down in desperation. At first, the cliff appeared to be as smooth as a pane of glass and as perfectly vertical as the side of a skyscraper. But just a couple of inches below his feet was a shelf no wider than a paperback book.

The friable sandstone knuckle he was holding started to come apart in his grip.

Juan gathered a breath and let himself drop. There wasn't enough room to absorb the shock by bending his knees, and he could feel the void sucking at his heels. The satellite phone, which had stayed with him for his wild plummet, was dislodged by the impact, snaking down one pant leg and emerging from the cuff. There was nothing he could do when it clattered off the shelf and disappeared into the valley below.

He couldn't hear it land over the din of falling debris, but he knew it was a total loss. He clutched at the cliff face. The stone was warm on his cheek.

Next to him, curtains of dust rose from the rock and sand falling over the cliff, but already the landslide was slowing. With the steady wind swirling around the mountaintop, it wouldn't be long before the dust blew away, exposing Cabrillo to anyone observing from above. The vertical drop to the next part of the mountain slope was at least thirty feet, with an additional hundred of steep terrain to the valley floor.

He looked to his right. The avalanche was almost over. The largest of the boulders now littered the ground below while only a thin trickle of sand poured over the edge of the cliff.

The second rule of climbing was never descend a rock face unless you know the route.

Juan had no idea what lay below him, what handholds and toeholds he would find, but with twenty armed gunmen doubtless peering down the hill to see what had happened to their comrades, the rules of safe climbing weren't particularly relevant.

He bent down as far as he dared and lowered a leg off the shelf, feeling with his toes for some kind of hold. He also locked the ankle joint of his artificial leg. His foot found a slight depression, barely big enough for all his toes, but it was enough to take his weight. He lowered himself farther still, so that his elbows rested on the narrow shelf. He switched feet in the little niche and again poked blindly for another irregularity in the rock. There was nothing to be felt. The stone was featureless.

A thick tangle of rope suddenly shot past his face, uncoiling as it fell. Looking up, he saw that the cliff hid him from the terrorists above. They weren't throwing him a lifeline, he realized, they were going to send someone down to check on survivors. It was just his good luck that they had chosen to send the climber exactly where he was clinging to the stone.

Juan quickly climbed back onto his shelf and carefully pulled off his boot. He yanked free some buttons of his uniform shirt and stuffed the boot against his chest. Then he wrapped the rope around the smooth molded foot of his prosthesis, looping it twice around, almost like the artificial limb was a pulley. He started to feel the rope dance and jerk in time with the movements of the man who had volunteered to check on his fallen teammates. Cabrillo grasped a handful of the line dangling over the void and stepped into empty space. With his back against the rock face, he slowly paid out rope through his hands. Because of the loops of rope around his foot and his locked ankle, he lowered himself down the cliff hand over hand, so smoothly that the guy above never felt him on the line.

It took less than a minute to reach the base of the cliff. If not for the artificial foot, a traditional descent would have alerted the terrorist of his presence or torn the flesh from his limb until all that remained was bone and gristle. He scrambled across the slope and hurled himself over a defile a moment before the climber reached the edge of the cliff and peered over.

His voice echoed across the valley. "I don't see anything but a pile of rocks. I think they're both dead."

Juan chanced looking up at him. The soldier—or terrorist, depending on what Cabrillo discovered about this place— regarded the pile of rubble for a moment longer, then started climbing back up the rope. Juan collapsed, allowing the first waves of pain to wash over him. Nothing felt broken, but he knew his body was a sea of black-and-blue. He allowed himself only a ten-minute rest—any longer and he would have stiffened to the point of immobility.

Juan considered it a sign of good fortune when he found his kaffiyeh half buried in a mound of sand. He slipped it over his head and unlocked his prosthetic ankle. His plan was to find a safe place to hole up for the day and then make his way up over the mountain on the other side of the construction site that he'd spotted in the next valley. Given its proximity to the terrorist training camp, he had to assume the two facilities were connected.

Once there, he would have to trust on luck again to find out what it was, and hope that Secretary Katamora was being held in one camp or the other.

Deep in the pit of his stomach, he knew no one was that lucky.

SEVENTEEN

LINDA ROSS AND FRANKLIN LINCOLN APPROACHED the archaeological camp on foot an hour before dawn. Both were operating on too much adrenaline and too little sleep. Murph had taken the Pig off into the deep desert to rendezvous with George Adams, who was flying in the bladder of fuel they would need to complete their mission.

No one liked the idea of splitting up. Finding only the one body near the drill truck and no sign of the other two Americans at the helicopter service area meant they had been taken elsewhere. The guess was, wherever the Libyan cargo chopper had taken the Chairman. If that were the case, their interrogation would be swift, brutal, and more than likely successful. Even now, a team of terrorists could be headed toward the archaeological dig in the Mi-8 helicopter.

But time was ticking down. The summit was fast approaching, and, more important, the longer the Secretary was held, the more likely she would be tortured as well.

With the sun climbing the horizon, the camp began to stir. Linda and Linc noted the archaeologists were mostly grad students spending a summer doing fieldwork. There were a few older expedition members who they assumed were full professors and faculty advisors. The camp also supported a staff of roughly ten native Tunisians, one of whom was dressed in an ill-fitting suit and looked agitated and did very little, so they assumed he was the government minder.

They had to watch for nearly an hour before Dr. Emile Bumford emerged from his tent. For a man who had lost three-quarters of his team, the prissy doctor didn't appear overly upset. He yawned theatrically when he stepped into the sun, as if his sleep the night before had been untroubled. Wearing a ridiculous safari suit with a Panama hat, he ambled to the mess tent. Cooks worked over grills set behind the structure, and while the smell didn't carry to Linda or Linc, both imagined the scent of eggs and country-fried potatoes. Their breakfast had been cold MREs. The meal went long; no doubt there had been a staff meeting after everyone ate. The students left the mess first, returning to their tents briefly to grab packs and hand tools and heading over a low rise to the Roman ruins. The teachers were a bit more leisurely, but they, too, vanished over the hill separating the camp from the archaeological site.

Bumford returned to his quarters after all the others had gone to work. He was inside for only a minute before settling himself on a chair under a sunshade just outside his tent's entrance. The book he cracked open was easily as thick as an encyclopedia volume. Linc wanted to sneak into the camp and grab Bumford now, but native workers were moving about, gathering laundry and tidying the students' tents.

"I took an archaeology class my junior year in college," Linda whispered. "We went on a dig for a long weekend. We never had servants like this."

"You didn't have the State Department paying extra to let some of their people tag along."

"Good point. So what do you make of Bumford?"

"If I were to guess, I'd say he's making a healthy per diem being out here and is in no hurry to find out what happened to Alana Shepard and the others."

"Nice," Linda said sarcastically.

The Tunisian representative approached Bumford about an hour after he'd settled into his chair. They spoke for only a moment. Bumford made elaborate gestures with his arms and ended the conversation with a nonchalant shrug.

Linc whispered in a thick, faintly Arabic accent, "'Professor Bumford, have you heard from your people?'" He then made his voice pinched and nasally. "'I have no idea what happened to them . . . Surely you have contacted your university and reported them missing . . . That isn't my responsibility. I am only here as a consultant . . . But aren't you concerned? They are several days overdue . . . Not my problem.' And local guy exits stage right."

Linc's pantomime and prediction was spot-on. Bumford didn't give the conversation a second's thought before returning to his book.

They waited twenty more minutes for the camp to quiet down. The native staff was nowhere to be seen, so Linc crept from his hiding place and threaded his way to the back of Bumford's tent. He slipped a knife from a deep pocket of his coveralls. It was an Emerson CQC-7A. The blade was so sharp that when he slit the nylon, it made no more sound than a knife cutting butter.

Stepping silently into the tent, he crossed over to the entrance. Bumford's back was toward him, less than a foot away, and the man had no idea anyone was looking over his shoulder. Linc glanced across to where Linda crouched behind barrels used to keep the camp's generator fueled. She held up a slim hand for Linc to wait while one of the cooks crossed the compound headed toward the pit latrine. As soon as he vanished, Linda clenched her fist.

Linc reached out and grabbed Bumford under his arms and heaved him into the tent in a fluid motion that sent the Ottoman specialist sprawling onto the dirt floor. Lincoln was on him like a dark wraith, one hand clamped over Bumford's mouth, the other poised with the knife so the portly professor could see it.

A moment later, Linda stepped into the tent through the hole Linc had cut. "Damn, you made that look easy. He must weigh two-fifty."

"Closer to two-seventy. That was my variation on the clean and jerk. I call it heave the jerk."

Linda hunkered low next to Bumford's head. The doctor's eyes were as big as saucers, and sweat beaded his domed forehead. "My colleague is going to remove his hand. You are not going to move or cry out. Understand?"

Bumford lay there like a gutted fish.

"Nod if you understand."

When he still didn't move, Linc prompted him by yanking his chin up and down. Bumford's eyelids fluttered as the first wave of terror ebbed, and he nodded vigorously.

When Linc pulled his hand away, Bumford whimpered, "Who are you?"

"Keep your voice down," Linda said. "We're here about Alana Shepard, Mike Duncan, and Greg Chaffee."

"Who are you?" Bumford repeated. "I don't recognize you. You aren't part of this group."

When Linda reached across him, Bumford seemed to try to burrow into the ground. She straightened his glasses on the bridge of his nose and curled one of the spectacles's arms around his ear where it had dislodged. "We're friends. We need to talk to you about the other members of your team."

"They aren't here."

"What is this guy, an idiot savant?" Linc asked.

"Professor Bumford," Linda opened again, as smoothly as she could, "we're here to ask you a few questions. We're part of an American search-and-rescue team."

"Like the military?"

"Strictly contract civilians, but people in Washington thought your mission important enough to hire us."

"It's a waste of time," Bumford said, regaining a little of his equilibrium, and his arrogance.

"Why do you say that?"

"You do know who I am, yes?"

Linda knew he was fishing for a little recognition to prime his ego. "You're Emile Bumford, one of the world's foremost experts on the Ottoman Empire."

"Then you must know I needn't explain my opinions. You

may take them as fact. This expedition for the State Department is a complete waste of time."

"Then why in the hell did you come?" Linc asked.

Bumford didn't answer right away, and Linda saw the furtive look in his eye. "Don't lie," she cautioned.

With a sigh Bumford said, "I lost my tenure because of an affair with a student, and I'm now in the middle of a divorce. My soon-to-be-ex-wife's lawyer is treating my wallet like a piñata, and I didn't make that much teaching in the first place. Add that to the fact that I haven't published a book in ten years, and you figure it out."

"Money."

"The State Department is paying me five hundred dollars a day. I need it."

"That's why you're out here sitting on your butt even though the rest of your team is missing. You're just racking up your per diem." There was neither denial nor shame in Bumford's expression.

Linda wanted to slap his smug face but instead said as calmly as she could, "Well, it's time you start earning your money. Tell me exactly why you think this trip is a waste of time."

"Do you know the story of Suleiman Al-Jama we were told—about how he befriended an American sailor and had a change of heart concerning his jihad against the West?"

"We've heard it," Linda said.

"I don't believe it. Not for a second. I've studied everything Al-Jama ever wrote. It's almost as if I know the man. He wouldn't change. None of the Barbary corsairs would. They made too much money waging war against European shipping."

"I thought Al-Jama fought for ideological reasons, not monetary gain," Linc countered.

"Al-Jama was a man like any other. I'm certain he would've been tempted by the riches that raiding provided. He might have started off wanting to kill infidels for the sake of killing them, but in some of his later writings he talks about the 'rewards' he accumulated. His word, not mine."

"Reward doesn't necessarily mean treasure," Linda said, realizing that Bumford was interpreting Al-Jama through his own moneygrubbing prism.

"Young lady, I was brought out here because I am the expert. If you don't care to listen to my explanations, please leave me be."

"I'm curious," Linc said. "Just how lucrative was piracy for the Barbary pirates?"

"What do you really know of them?"

"I know the Marines kicked some butt like the song says—'to the shores of Tripoli.'"

"That was actually five hundred mercenaries under the command of ex–American consul William Eaton and a handful of Marines who sacked the city of Dema, a backwater in the Bashaw of Tripoli's holdings. True, their action may have hastened a peace treaty, but it was far from a legendary battle worthy of a hymn."

Linc had some Marine Corps friends who would have killed the man for such a remark.

"Between the fifteenth and nineteenth centuries," Bumford continued, "the Barbary pirates had a stranglehold on the most lucrative sea routes in the world—the Mediterranean and the North Atlantic coast of Europe. During that time, those nations that wouldn't or couldn't pay the exorbitant tributes had their shipping fall prey to the pirates. Their cargos were stolen and their crews either ransomed or sold into slavery. Nations like England, France, and Spain paid the pirates millions in gold to protect maritime commerce. For a time, even the United States was paying them. And by some accounts, more than a tenth of the federal revenue went to various Barbary Coast rulers. The pirates also went on raiding parties to kidnap people from seaside villages as far north as Ireland. By some estimates, more than a million and a half Europeans were taken from their homes and sold into slavery. Can you imagine?"

"Yeah," Linc said with a trace of irony.

Bumford had warmed to his subject and chose to ignore the African-American's gibe. "We're talking about one of the preeminent naval powers of their time. And Suleiman Al-

Jama was perhaps the most successful and by far the most ruthless pirate of them all. Though he had first studied to be an Imam, his family had a tradition of piracy that went back for generations. There are tales of his ancestors preying on ships returning from the Crusades. It was in Al-Jama's blood. I'm sorry, but from what I know of him, he would never renounce what he saw as a holy war against the Western powers any more than the modern terrorist of the same name would."

And Linda saw her mistake. His prism wasn't that of his own personal greed. He saw what they were trying to accomplish through the lens of the continuation of inevitable terrorism and the triumph of indefatigable Islamic dogma. She was speaking to a man defeated, a man who had never fired a shot in the war against extremists of a culture he professed to study but had never understood.

She went on anyway. "But this is when Thomas Jefferson decided the United States would no longer pay tribute. For the first time in their history, the pirates were facing a first-class navy that was willing to fight rather than hand over money. Surely Al-Jama must have understood their free rein was over. Jefferson's unilateral declaration of war against piracy was the beginning of the end for them. One nation had taken a stance against their form of savagery despite the rest of the world continuing to cower."

Even as she said it, the parallels to the present struggle against terrorism sent a chill down her spine. Europe had spent the latter part of the twentieth century living under the constant threat of terrorism. There'd been bombings in nightclubs, kidnappings, assassinations, and hijackings all across the continent, with very little response from the authorities.

The United States had taken a similar route following the first attack on the World Trade Center. The government had treated it as a criminal act rather than what it truly was: the opening salvo in a war. The perpetrators had been duly arrested and sent to prison, and the matter was largely forgotten until 9/11.

Rather than ignore the truth for a second time, the government had responded to the 2001 attack by taking the fight back to any and all who supported terrorism in its many forms. Like it had chosen two hundred years earlier, America had proclaimed to the world that it would rather fight than live in fear.

Bumford said, "Even if I grant the possibility that Al-Jama had a change of heart and found ways to reconcile the differences between Islam and Christianity, there is the practical matter of finding his ship, the *Saqr*. It is simply impossible that a vessel has remained hidden in the desert for two centuries. It would either have been destroyed by the elements or looted by nomads. Trust me, there is nothing left to find."

"For the sake of argument"—Linc cut in when he could tell Bumford's pessimism was about to make Linda snap—"if it somehow survived, would you have any clue where it might be?"

"From the letter I read back in Washington, I do believe it must be on the dry riverbed to the south of us, but Alana, Mike, and Greg have scoured it completely. They stopped only when they came to a waterfall that when the river was flowing would have been impassable. There is no Barbary pirate ship hidden out there."

"Was there any other clue in the letter? Something insignificant, even."

"Henry Lafayette said it was hidden in a large cavern that was accessible only through the use of, and I quote here, 'a clever device.' Please don't ask me what that means. Alana pestered me for weeks on end about it. The only other thing I have is a local legend that the ship is hidden beneath the black that burns."

"The what?" Linda asked.

"The black that burns. The tale comes from the journal of Al-Jama's second-in-command, Suleiman Karamanli. It survived because he happened to be the Bashaw of Tripoli's nephew, so it was housed with the Royal Archives. What it means, I'm afraid, is beyond me. I am sorry."

"So am I," Linda muttered.

If a trained archaeologist like Alana Shepard couldn't find Al-Jama's ship after spending weeks using sophisticated equipment, there was little hope she and Mark and Linc would discover it in the remaining days before the peace conference.

Linda glanced at her watch. They had an hour to hike back to where they were going to rendezvous with Mark and the Pig. After reporting that they'd struck out with Bumford, she was going to tell Max their best course of action now was to prestage the Pig to Juan's location in the hope that the Chairman had had better luck.

"Come on, Linc," she said. "Dr. Bumford, thank you for your time. And I don't think I need to remind you that we were never here."

"Yes, of course," the scholar said. "By the way, have you found any sign of the rest of my team?"

Linda bit back a barb about his concern for the others being an afterthought. "One of the men is dead. Either Greg Chaffee or Mike Duncan. Single gunshot to the head. The vultures didn't leave enough to make an ID. We don't know about the other two."

"Dear God. Is it safe for me to remain here? Maybe I should return to the States."

Linc grabbed her arm before she decked the Ottoman scholar. "Easy, girl. He ain't worth it. Let's go."

The two of them slipped out the back of the tent and made their way across the quiet camp. Neither noticed the small figure of a boy who'd listened to the conversation by crouching at the side of the tent. He waited until the pair disappeared over a sand embankment before scampering away to find the Tunisian representative. Twenty minutes later, the information was passed on to a contact in Tripoli for a healthy sum of money, and a further forty minutes after that the turbines of an Mi-8 helicopter at a remote mountaintop training camp began to shriek.

EIGHTEEN

WHEN AMBASSADOR MOON CAUGHT HIS FIRST glimpse of the debris field from the cabin of an executive helicopter, it took all his self-control not to throw up on the lap of his companion, Foreign Minister Ali Ghami. The devastation was nothing less than total. The remains of the State Department plane were strung out for almost a mile, and other than a fifty-foot section of the cabin and the engines there didn't appear to be any pieces larger than a suitcase.

"Allah, be merciful," Ghami said. It was his first time at the site as well.

Down on the ground, protected by a cordon of Libyan soldiers, men were examining the wreckage. This was the advance team from the NTSB as well as a couple of local aviation experts. They'd arrived only a short time before the American Ambassador, and their helicopter was parked a good mile from the wreckage.

"Mr. Minister," the pilot called over the intercom in the specially soundproofed cabin. "We will need to land near their chopper so our rotor wash doesn't disturb the site."

"That's fine," Ghami replied. "I think the walk and fresh air will do both the Ambassador and me some good."

"Understood, sir."

The Minister turned to Moon, resting a hand on the American's shoulder. "On behalf of my government, and myself, I am so sorry, Charles."

"Thank you, Ali. When you called with the news that the plane had been found, I held out hope." He gestured out the helo's Plexiglas window. "Now . . ." He let his voice trail off. There was nothing more to say.

The pilot settled the French-built EC155 executive chopper next to a utilitarian helicopter with military colors. Ghami's bodyguard, a tight-lipped, no-necked mountain of a man named Mansour, opened the helicopter's door while the blades still whirled overhead. Ignoring the blast of grit kicked up by the rotor wash, Ghami leapt down to the ground and paused while the more portly Moon followed.

They started walking toward the wreck. Moon was sweating after only a couple of paces, but neither the Libyan Minister nor his guard seemed affected by the heat and the blazing sun. The smell of charred plastic and aviation fuel carried over to them on the occasional slap of wind.

In Moon's estimation, approaching the debris on foot made it look worse than from the air. Everything was burned dark and warped by the fire that had consumed the plane. They paused at the cordon of soldiers and waited for the lead investigator from the NTSB. The investigator was moving slowly through the debris, snapping pictures with a digital camera, while a man with him was recording everything on a camcorder. When the investigator finally noted the dignitaries, he said a couple of words to his companion and trudged over. His face was long and gaunt, his mouth turned down at the corners.

"Ambassador Moon?" he called when he was within earshot.

"I'm Moon. This is Ali Ghami, Libya's Foreign Minister." They shook hands. "I'm David Jewison."

Moon saw Ghami shift position ever so slightly at hearing the name.

"Can you, ah, tell us anything?" Moon invited.

Jewison glanced back over his shoulder and then returned his gaze to the Ambassador. "We weren't the first people to come here. That much is certain."

"What are you saying?" Ghami asked sharply.

Moon knew that Libya's handling of this crisis would have an impact on their relations with the United States and the Western powers far beyond the Tripoli Accords. Jewison's revelation doubtless put both Ghami and his government in a difficult position. If there was any evidence of tampering, then an accusation of a cover-up wouldn't be too far behind.

"From what we can tell, a group of nomads has been over the site. They left behind hundreds of footprints, as well as cooking fires, camp detritus consistent with their lifestyle, and the body of a camel that had been shot in the head. Our local guide said the camel appeared to be near the end of its life, judging by the wear on its teeth, and was probably put down because it no longer had value.

"Parts of the wreckage have been disturbed, some possibly removed. The passengers' remains have also been moved. I believe Muslim custom is to bury people within twenty-four hours of their deaths. My Libyan counterpart here says it's likely the nomads did just that. I have no reason to doubt his assessment, but we won't know for sure until we get some cadaver dogs up here."

"Do you have any preliminary ideas what happened to the plane?"

"From what we can tell—and this is very, very early—the aircraft lost part of its tail section sometime during the flight. We don't know why, because it has not been recovered here at the scene. We're sending out our chopper in a few minutes to visually search what we know to be the flight path. This damage could have caused a loss of hydraulic fluid as well as the failure of its rudder and elevators. Without the hydraulic system, the flaps, ailerons, slats, and spoilers on the main wings would have also failed. Had this been the case, the plane would have been difficult, if not impossible, to control."

Ghami asked, "Is there any indication why part of the tail was lost?"

"Nothing yet," Jewison replied. "We'll get an idea once we find it."

"And if you don't?" This was from Moon. The question wasn't a deliberate provocation, but he was curious about Ghami's reaction. Just because he personally liked the man didn't mean he had forgotten his role here.

"Barring some other evidence, it would officially be classified as reasons unknown."

Ghami looked to the Ambassador. "Charles, I promise you that it will be located and the reason for this tragedy explained."

"No offense, Minister," Jewison interrupted, "but that may not be a promise you can keep. I've been a crash investigator for eighteen years. I've seen everything there is to see, including an airliner that exploded in midair and was pulled out of the ocean off Long Island. That was a relatively straightforward investigation compared to this. We can't tell what damage was done by the crash and what was done by your people." Ghami made to protest, and Jewison staved him off with a gesture. "I mean the nomads. They're Libyan so they're your people, is all I mean."

"The nomads are citizens of no country but the desert."

"Either way, they messed with this scene so badly I don't know if even finding the tail will give us a definitive answer."

Ghami held the aviation expert's stare. "Ambassador Moon and other representatives of your government have explained to me that you are the best in the world at what you do, Mr. Jewison. I have their assurance and thus their confidence that you will find an answer. I am certain that you treat each and every airline disaster with your utmost efforts, but you must surely know the gravity of this situation and the importance of what you find."

Jewison looked from one man to the other. His expression was even more dour as he came to understand that politics was going to play as large a part in his search as forensic science.

"How long until the conference?" he asked.

"Forty-eight hours," Moon answered.

He shook his head with weary resignation. "*If* we can find the tail and *if* it hasn't been further damaged by nomads, I might have a preliminary report for you by then."

Ghami held out his hand, which Jewison took. "That's all any of us ask for."

• • •

THE *OREGON* HAD BEEN rigged for ultraquiet. There was little that could be done about the sound of waves lapping against the hull except to keep her bow into the wind. Other than that, nothing about the ship's position was left to chance. Max Hanley had surrounded the vessel at a distance of thirty miles with passive buoys that collected incoming radar energy and relayed that information via secure burst transmitters to the onboard computer. This gave them ample warning if another ship was in the area without the use of their own active radar suite. If a target appeared to be headed in their direction, the ship's dynamic positioning system would move the *Oregon* using power supplied by her massed banks of silver-zinc deep-cycle batteries, so she crept along with the barest whisper of water forced through her pump jets. With her hull and superstructure doped with radar-absorbent material, a passing ship would almost need to be in visual range to detect her.

A passive-sonar array dangled from the moon pool down at her keel. Capable of listening three hundred and sixty degrees, the acoustical microphones covered any threats lurking below the surface. Other sensors were vacuuming up electronic data and radio chatter from shipping, aircraft, and shore-based facilities along Libya's coast. This ability of drift and lift, or as Murph called it "lurk and work," was the exact type of mission Juan had designed the *Oregon* to perform. Her stealth capabilities allowed the crew to station the ship off a hostile coast for days—or weeks, if necessary—gathering intelligence on fleet movements, electronics signaling, or anything else her clients demanded.

They had lain off the coast of Cuba for twenty-eight days during the time that Fidel Castro's illness made it necessary for him to transfer power to his brother, Raul, listening in on everything taking place behind the closed doors of the Communist dictator's private retreat. They had provided the American intelligence services unprecedented knowledge of the inner workings of the secretive regime and eliminated any uncertainty as to what was taking place.

Rigging the *Oregon* for ultraquiet also meant suspending all routine maintenance, which no one on the crew minded. However, the ship's fitness facility was closed to prevent weights from accidentally clanging together, and meals were reduced to prepackaged pouches boiled in a pot clamped to the stove in the galley. The culinary staff had outdone themselves in preparing the meals, but they remained a poor substitute for the gourmet dishes to which the men and women of the Corporation had grown accustomed. The normal silverware and fine china were replaced with paper plates and plastic knives and forks, and any television or radio had to be enjoyed with headphones.

Max Hanley was in his cabin working on a scratch-built model of a Swift boat, one of the fast riverine crafts he had commanded during Vietnam. Hanley wasn't a man who dwelled much on his past or gave in to the siren song of nostalgia. He stored the medals he'd won in a Los Angeles safe-deposit he hadn't visited in years and met up with former shipmates only at funerals. He was building the model simply because he could do it from memory and it kept his mind occupied with something other than his responsibilities.

Doc Huxley had suggested the hobby as a way of reducing stress and keeping his blood pressure in check. So far, he'd managed to stick to it longer than the yoga she'd prescribed before. He'd already built and presented a beautiful replica of the *Oregon* to Juan, which now sat under a plastic case in the executive conference room, and had plans for a Mississippi paddle wheeler when he was finished with the Swift boat.

The knock on his door was so soft that he knew it was Eric Stone taking the whole silent-rigging thing to the limit.

"Enter," Hanley called.

Eric stepped through the doorway, carrying a laptop computer and a large, flat portfolio. He looked like he hadn't slept in a week, which probably wasn't too far off the mark. Stone usually maintained a semblance of the military comportment drilled into him at Annapolis, but today his shirt was untucked, and his chinos were as wrinkled as a balled-up piece of aluminum foil.

While Max worried whenever they had people stuck out there in a hostile environment, Eric took it even further. Max had been Stoney's mentor when he'd first joined the Corporation, but since then he'd grown to idolize Juan Cabrillo, and Mark Murphy was like the brother he'd never had growing up. Fatigue lines etched his normally smooth face, and while he'd never had much of a beard it was obvious he hadn't shaved in a while.

"You have something?" Max asked without preamble.

He showed off the portfolio. "Detailed maps of Juan's location and a rundown of the place's history."

"I knew you could do it." Hanley cleared a wide space on his desk for Eric to lay out the map. He stood to give himself a better perspective. "Tell me what I'm looking at."

He could see a small training facility, built high in the mountains, roughly twenty miles from the coast. The camp was well hidden by the peaks, and, had it not been for its proximity to a large open pit of some kind, it would have been easy to overlook, even knowing its location because of Juan's implanted GPS transponder. There was a dark line snaking up from the shore to the pit that closely followed the contour of the land. Where the line met the coast were a couple of old buildings and a long jetty. There were other buildings along the rim of a valley where the earth had been excavated.

Eric pointed to the port area first. "This is what remains of a British-built coaling station dating back to the 1840s. It was updated with a bigger pier in 1914, possibly in anticipation of World War I. That pier was partially destroyed during Rommel's North Africa campaign, and the Germans rebuilt it to use as a staging area for their push toward Egypt. The dark line here is a railroad that linked the station to the coal mine here." His finger followed the railroad tracks to the buildings overlooking the open-pit mine. "There used to be a barge canal to transport the coal, but the aquifer dried up and the railroad was laid in."

"Looks to me like someone's reopening the place," Max remarked.

"Yes, sir. About five months ago. The rail line was refurbished to accommodate larger ore cars, with an eye toward extracting coal from the old mine."

"Did anyone ask if this makes sense in a country sitting on forty billion barrels of oil?"

"I did as soon as I figured out what this place was," Eric replied. "And, in a word, it doesn't. Especially in light of their government's attempts to go green with the tidal generating station farther down the coast."

"So what's going on here, really?"

"The CIA thinks it's a cover for a new subterranean nuclear-research program."

"I thought Uncle Muammar gave up his nuke ambitions," Max remarked. "Besides, the CIA was probably convinced my mother-in-law was pursuing a nuclear program when she had a new root cellar dug."

Eric chuckled. "Foreign intelligence services dismiss the CIA estimate. They think this is a legit enterprise. Problem is, I can't dig up any corporate entities charged with working there. Which isn't all that surprising. The Libyans aren't known for their transparency. There was one article in a trade publication that said Libya is interested in pursuing coal gasification as an alternative to oil, and claims they have a system that will be cleaner than natural gas."

"You don't sound convinced," Max said.

"It took some digging, but I found records from ships that had once used the station back in the day. Building up a picture over time, it appears vessels that regularly refueled there showed a fifty percent increase in maintenance and a twenty percent reduction in efficiency."

As an engineer, Max immediately grasped the implications of Eric's findings. "The coal is filthy, isn't it?"

"An archived log from the captain of a coastal freighter called *Hydra* says he'd rather fill his bunkers with sawdust than use the coal from the station."

"There's no way any current gasification technology can make it clean. So what is this place, really?"

"The facility to the north of the mine was once used by the Libyan military as a training base."

"This whole thing is government sanctioned after all," Max said, jumping ahead.

"Not necessarily," Eric countered. "They stopped using it a couple of years ago."

"Back to square zero," Max said bitterly.

"'Fraid so. In the past two days, there have been suspicious military maneuvers in Syria, so our satellite coverage has gone east to keep an eye on them. This picture here is two months old, and is the most current I could find."

"What about getting some shots from a commercial satellite company?"

"Already tried and struck out. Even offering double their normal fees, we can't get new shots until a week from now."

"Too late for Juan or Fiona Katamora."

"Yup," Eric agreed.

"And you've tried everything to pierce the corporate veil of the company working on the rail line?"

"Do onions have layers? They're better shielded than anything I've ever seen before. I've hit dead end after dead end trying to trace ownership. But the thing I learned about companies working in Libya is, they are generally partnered with the government in a sort of quasi-nationalized arrangement."

"So we come full circle, and it's Libya's government behind all this?"

"You're familiar with Cosco, aren't you?"

"It's a Chinese shipping company."

"Which many suspect is actually owned by the People's Liberation Army. I'm wondering if we don't have something similar going on here."

"You're saying it's not Libya's central government that's involved but a segment of it?" Max asked, and Eric nodded. "The military?"

"Or the JSO, the Jamahiriya Security Organization, their principal spy agency. Ever since Qaddafi started playing nice, the JSO has been marginalized. This could be a play for them to regain some of their lost prestige."

"One hell of a gamble, since we know these people are somehow connected to the downing of Katamora's plane," Max said. Stone didn't argue, so Hanley went on. "What about terrorists paying this rogue faction to look the other way? That worked for Bin Laden in the Sudan, and then Afghanistan, until we toppled the Taliban."

"That was my next thought," Eric said. "We know Libya's sheltered terrorists in the past. The mine and railroad could be a terrorist front for a training camp, with an eye toward using the proceeds to fund their activities. Al-Qaeda had done that in Africa, trafficking conflict diamonds."

Max took a moment to light his pipe, using the familiar distraction to organize his thoughts. When it was drawing evenly and a wreath of smoke began to form a haze along the ceiling, he said, "We're spinning our wheels. There's no sense in you and me trying to guess who's doing what. Juan will probably have the answer. So as I see it, our priority is to get him out of there and find out what he's learned."

"Agreed."

"Any suggestions?" Hanley invited.

"Not at this time. We need to wait until he makes contact."

Max Hanley was known by the crew as a man who kept his own counsel, so Eric was surprised when he suddenly blurted in frustration, "I hate this."

"I know what you mean."

"Juan shouldn't have taken off like that."

"He saw it as a tactical necessity. How else would we know where they staged from?"

"There are better ways. We could have tracked the chopper on radar."

"We never saw them flying to the accident site," Eric replied. "How would we have tracked them out? They were flying nap-of-the-earth the whole way. Completely invisible to us from this distance. And before you say it, there wasn't time to get satellite coverage again. Juan made the only decision open to him."

Max raked his hand through his thinning ginger hair. "You're right. I know. I just don't like it. There are so many variables at play here that I don't know if we're coming or going. Is this state-sponsored terrorism, a rogue faction within Libya's government, or some garden-variety terrorist group, most likely Suleiman Al-Jama's outfit? We have no idea who we're up against or what they want. We don't know if Katamora's alive or dead. Basically, we don't know squat. Linc, Linda, and Mark discover a chopper that looks like it was armed to take the Secretary's plane down, but, again, we don't know who's behind it. Then we've got a group of missing archaeologists who may or may not be involved, and some other academic weenie who says they've all been navel-gazing so he can pay off an ex-wife. Did I miss any other pieces to this jigsaw puzzle? Oh yeah, the most important peace conference since Camp David is in a couple of days. And with Juan incommunicado, I don't know what piece fits where."

And there it was, Eric thought. The crux of Max's problem. Hanley wasn't a natural leader, not the way Cabrillo was. Give Max a technical challenge and he will work it until he has a solution, or present him with a plan and he will see it carried out to the letter. But when it came to making the hard decisions, he agonized because it wasn't his forte. He wasn't a strategist or tactician, and he, more than anyone else, knew it.

"If it were up to me," Eric said diplomatically, "I would get Mark and the others to within striking distance of the mine–terrorist camp for when Juan calls."

"What about the archaeologists and the scrolls?"

"A distraction, for now. Our priorities are the Chairman and then Secretary Katamora."

Max's phone rang. He could tell from the display it was the communications duty officer. He hit the button to put the phone on speaker. "Hanley."

"Max, I just received a secure alert from Overholt."

"Now what?" he groused.

"A chopper fitting the description of the one Juan flew in earlier showed up at the Roman archaeology site across the border in Tunisia. Armed men kidnapped Professor Emile Bumford, the Tunisian government overseer, and one member of the camp staff, a local boy who may be related to him."

Max looked Eric in the eye, arching one of his bushy brows. "A distraction?" He then addressed the comm specialist. "Okay. Send an acknowledgment to Lang that we received his message." He snapped off the phone and leaned back into his padded chair. "Another damned piece that just won't fit."

Eric wisely didn't add that the piece might be part of an entirely different puzzle.

NINETEEN

H IS PRECIOUS FACE WAS A MIX OF DETERMINATION
and delight. His mouth was formed into a tiny O, and
his eyes were open despite the chlorine sting. Beads of water
clung to his impossibly long lashes like diamond chips. His
body wriggled with the almost rhythm of his kicking legs,
and the inflatable bands around his arms kept bumping into
his chin with each awkward stroke.

Alana felt like her heart was going to explode, as she stood
waist-deep in her condo's community pool, Josh striking out
for her as she retreated a slow pace at a time. He knew the
game, would complain bitterly if he tired out before reaching
her, or beam with pride if he made it to the sanctuary of her
waiting arms.

Her buttocks pressed against the pool's concrete side.
Josh was a few feet away, his mouth now spreading into a
triumphant grin. He knew he was going to make it. And then
his water wings suddenly vanished, and his face fell into the
water. Alana tried to push herself off the wall, but it was as

though her skin and swimsuit were adhered to the concrete and tile.

Josh came up, sputtering. His eyes were wide with panic as the first choking cough shook his little body. Water and saliva bubbled from his lips. He managed to cry out "Mommy!" before his head slipped under the surface again.

Alana stretched her arms, feeling like they were pulling from their sockets, but she couldn't reach him. Couldn't move. There were people all around the pool area, lounging on chairs or sitting at the water's edge with their feet dangling in the cool water. She tried to call to them but no sound escaped her lips. They were oblivious to her plight.

Josh's thrashing became less frantic, his longish hair spreading around his head, swaying in the eddies like some sea creature. His hands were balled into little fists, as if trying to hang on, but there was nothing Alana could do. The pool's filtration system was pushing him farther from her. Her arms screamed with the strain of trying to reach him, and her head pounded with an unholy ache—the punishment for being a bad mother, she knew.

Her baby was dying.

She was dying.

And she would have accepted such a fate, but reality was much more cruel.

She came back from the nightmare.

The pain in her head was from being clubbed and momentarily stunned by one of the guards. Her arms ached because she was being dragged from the serving line, where moments earlier she had been slopping a thin gruel onto the tin plates of the other prisoners. Her backside felt numb because the ground was rough gravel and the man dragging her set a strong pace.

Another of the guards shouted at the man who had hit her. He stopped midstride and let her fall to the dirt. She paid no attention to the rapid-fire Arabic the two shot at each other. She simply lay still, hoping against hope that they would forget about her.

The image of her son drowning, something her imagination conjured up to add more pain to her already brutal existence, was like a dull ache in her chest. Josh was eleven now, not the five-year-old she had seen, and he was an excellent swimmer.

The shouting match between the two guards grew more heated until a third man entered the fray. She knew he was one of the senior people at the work camp, and a quiet word from him ended the discussion instantly. The man who had hit Alana toed her in the ribs to get her on her feet and motioned for her to retake her place at the trestle table that served as the prisoners' buffet. The servers were all women, while the people they fed were mostly men, men who were wasting away in the heat until their ragged clothes hung off their thin frames and their cheeks were shadowed hollows.

Alana had been here less than a week and already knew that most of these poor souls had been here for months. They looked no better than the prisoners liberated from Nazi concentration camps.

When she retook her place behind the table, the woman next to her muttered something in Arabic.

"I'm sorry, I don't understand."

The woman, who had once been heavyset, judging by the slabs of flesh that hung from her neck, pointed to Alana's eyes and then pointed down to the table. Don't look at the guards, she was trying to say. Or that was Alana's interpretation. Maybe, keep your eye on your work. Either way, when the next prisoner shuffled up to her, she lifted her gaze just enough to see the plate he held in one trembling hand.

After getting their food and a cup filled with water that was hot enough to scald the tongue, the prisoners ate on the ground. A few were lucky enough to be able to rest their backs against one of the old buildings. The buildings were all two and three stories high, with badly rusted iron roofs. Their sides were powdery clapboards that the sun and heat had curled and split. On the other side of the buildings were rail sidings holding a few railcars as well as two locomotives, one not much larger than a truck. Unlike the buildings and railcars, the locomotives were newer, though still coated in dust. A little farther down the main line, which vanished around a curve in the mountains a half mile away, was an enormous rusted-steel structure with old conveyor belts and metal chutes that sagged from neglect.

It hadn't taken her long to realize this was an old mine, and that the prisoners were working to reopen it. Gangs of the strongest detainees went off every morning to labor on the tracks to the north, while others toiled in the massive open pit at the bottom of the valley. There was little heavy equipment being used, only a crane mounted on a rail flat-bed, to help lay track, and a couple of bulldozers. Everything else was done by hand under the watchful eye, and quick fists, of the guards.

A buzz of soft whispers suddenly swept through the prisoners while eating their meal, their eyes turned to the east, along the rim of the valley. A vehicle was approaching, coils of dust billowing from its tires as it negotiated the narrow trail.

The vehicle was identical to the one that had captured the two Americans, a desert-patrol truck with tall, knobby tires, and a machine gun mounted on its roof. As the truck drew closer, Alana could see a bundle of some kind roped to its hood. And closer still, she could tell it was the body of a man. His clothes were missing, and his once-dark skin was burned red and had begun to peel off in great sheets. She could tell an animal had gotten to the body, because there were bloody gouges all over his arms and chest. His face was a raw, pulpy mass.

The patrol had been sent out to track down an escaped prisoner.

The truck stopped just short of the trestle tables and the passenger's door flew open. The man who emerged spoke to the guard captain for a moment. He, in turn, made an announcement to the assembled prisoners. Alana didn't need to understand the language to know he was telling them that this is what happens to those who try to escape. He then drew a knife, cut the bindings holding the body to the truck, and strode away. The corpse hit the ground with a meaty sound, and the flies that were a constant swarm over the serving dishes suddenly found a more appetizing meal.

There wasn't enough food in Alana's stomach for her to

throw up. Instead, she bent at the waist, braced her hands against her knees, and dry-heaved until her stomach was a knotted lump. When she straightened, a guard she didn't recognize eyed her with some interest.

A half hour later, the meal finished, Alana and the other women were cleaning the tin serving dishes, using fistfuls of sand to scour the metal. Not that the prisoners back laboring in the mine and along the railroad had left much behind on their plates. One of the principal means for the guards to maintain control was to keep all the captives on the verge of starvation.

She was kneeling on the ground, swirling sand inside a bowl, when a shadow loomed over her. She looked up. The other women working with her kept their attention on their work. Alana was suddenly yanked to her feet and turned around violently. It was the guard who had slapped her earlier. He was close enough that she could smell the tobacco on his breath and see that he wasn't much older than twenty, and that there was a lifelessness in his eyes. He didn't see her as another human being. There wasn't enough behind his gaze to make her think he saw her as an animate object at all.

The other guards meant to watch over the dozen women were purposefully looking away. An arrangement had been made, a deal struck. For however long he wished, Alana Shepard belonged to this man.

She tried to ram a knee into his groin but must have telegraphed her intentions because he turned aside adroitly and took the glancing blow to his thigh. The leering expression on his face didn't change, even when he slapped her on the same cheek that was already swollen and beginning to bruise.

Alana refused to cry out or collapse. She swayed on her feet until the stinging subsided and her head cleared. The guard spun her again, and with a bony hand clamped on her shoulder so that his fingers dug into her flesh he maneuvered her away from the others.

A hundred yards off was an old shed. Half the roof was missing, and the sides were bowed like the swayed back of an old horse. The door hung askew on a single rusted hinge. Just at the threshold, the guard shoved Alana hard enough to send her sprawling. She knew what was coming, had suffered the ordeal once before in college, and had vowed never to let it happen again. When she turned to face him from her supine position, her arm swept the floor to scoop up some pebbles and dirt.

He came forward in a rush and kicked her wrist. Her fingers opened reflexively and her arm went numb. Her meager weapon was scattered back to the ground. He said something in Arabic and chuckled to himself.

Alana opened her mouth to scream, and he was suddenly on her, one filthy hand clamped over her nose and mouth—the other she refused to think about. She tried to thrash under his weight, to bite his fingers, to block out the horror of what was about to happen, but he held her pressed to the earth. She couldn't breathe. His lunge had knocked the air from her lungs and his hand shut off her airways. Her head began to swim, and after just a few seconds of a defense she thought she would never give up, her body betrayed her. Her motions became less frantic. Unconsciousness loomed like a black shadow.

Then came a loud crackle, like the staccato snap of a bunch of twigs, and she could turn away and draw breath. Above her, she saw the back of a man's hand and the back of her attacker's head. The guard was dragged off of her, and Alana could breathe more deeply, short, choppy gasps that nevertheless filled her lungs. The would-be rapist came to rest next to her, his face inches from hers. If it was possible, death brought a certain amount of life to his unblinking eyes.

Kneeling over her was the guard who had watched her dry-heave in the mess line. He had snapped the other man's neck with his bare hands.

He spoke in a soothing voice, and it took her a second to realize she recognized the words. He was speaking English. "You're okay now," he'd said. "His ardor has cooled. Permanently."

"Who? Who are you?" He'd pulled aside his kaffiyeh. He was older than all the other guards she had seen, his skin weathered by a lifetime of living outdoors. She noticed, too, that unlike any of the other people she'd seen recently, one of his eyes was brown and weepy while the other was a startling blue.

"My name is Juan Cabrillo, and if you want to live you and I have to get out of here right now."

"I don't understand."

Cabrillo got to his feet and extended a hand to Alana. "You don't need to. You just have to trust me."

● ● ●

AFTER A NIGHT OF moving by moonlight across the valley toward the construction site, gaining access to the facility had been simplicity itself. The guards had orders to keep people in. There was nothing about keeping men dressed like themselves out.

When Juan had been questioned about his presence, as he stood casually in line for breakfast with the other guards after sunrise prayer, he'd replied that he had been sent from the other camp as punishment for failing on the obstacle course. The young man who'd questioned him had judged the answer adequate and said nothing more.

Just like that, Cabrillo was part of the landscape—another Arab in desert fatigues, with half his face hidden by a checkered scarf. He had to be careful. During his tumble down the mountain, he had lost one of his brown contact lenses. The other he washed as best he could in his mouth, but it was ingrained with grit, and every time he blinked it felt like he was scratching his cornea with sandpaper. The eye streamed a constant flow of tears.

He spent the morning wandering the workings, staying close enough to other guards that he didn't attract anyone's attention. He quickly grasped that this was a forced-labor camp, and, judging by the prisoners' condition, it had either been here for a long time or they hadn't been in the best shape when they arrived. He believed more in the latter than the former, because it didn't look like a great amount of work had been accomplished.

And that was the point, he realized after a couple of hours. These people weren't meant to accomplish anything at all. The holes they had excavated at the bottom of the valley appeared random, with no oversight by a mining engineer. As best he could tell, reopening the facility was make-work, something to keep them tired and hungry and grateful for the meager meals they were given. But whoever sent them here didn't want them dead. At least not yet.

It made him think about Secretary Katamora and how she, too, currently existed in limbo. Neither dead nor alive, at least by any official designation.

By listening to the other guards, Juan built up a picture of the place, not what it was about—no one talked about that— but who staffed it. He heard Arabic in every accent imaginable, from the worst gutter talk of a Moroccan slum to the urbane polish of a university-educated Saudi. His belief that these were terrorists recruited from the far corners of the Middle East was confirmed by listening to the Babel of inflections and dialects.

At one point during the day, he'd gotten close enough to the command tent to hear who he believed to be the guard captain speaking into either a radio or, most likely, a satellite phone. Juan paused to tie his boot, watched by a guard stationed outside the tent's sealed flap, and was pretty sure he heard Suleiman Al-Jama's name. He knew better than to linger and moved away before the guard became suspicious.

It was during the noontime meal that he realized not all of the prisoners were Arabs. He spotted a fair-skinned man with thin blond hair among the detainees. The sun had burned him cruelly. And when one of the guards struck a serving woman, he saw that she, too, wasn't native to the region. She was petite, with closely cropped bangs peeking out from the headscarf she had been given, and her eyes were a brilliant green. She could have been Turkish, he guessed, but there was a girl-next-door, all-American wholesomeness to her that made him think otherwise.

He had kept an eye on her afterward and was in position when her attacker returned to avenge his humiliation at being dressed down by the guard captain in front of everyone.

Cabrillo was wearing what he dubbed his combat leg, a prosthetic crafted by Kevin Nixon in the Magic Shop with the help of the *Oregon*'s chief armorer. In its plastic-encased calf had been hidden a wire garrote, which he could have used but wanted to avoid the blood, as well as a compact Kel-Tec .380 pistol. The weapon didn't have a silencer, so it stayed in his pocket, and he'd resorted to snapping the man's neck.

• • •

"I GUESS I DON'T have a choice," Alana said as she took Juan's proffered hand.

The shed was far enough away from the rest of the compound that none of the guards could see it directly. They knew what was supposed to be taking place within, so none made an effort to watch it overtly. Juan was able to lead Alana from the building to a low ridge beyond. Once over the ridge, they lay flat against the hot stone and waited, Cabrillo watching the camp for any sign they'd been seen.

Everything appeared to be normal.

After a few minutes, Juan judged it safe to move, and he and his new charge slid down the face of the ridge and started for the open desert, moving away from the distant terrorist training camp and deeper into the barren wastes.

He estimated they had at least an hour before anyone thought to look for the missing guard, and when they performed a head count of male prisoners capable of breaking another man's neck they would discover everyone accounted for. The confusion would add to the delay if they chose to send out patrols. However, once clear of the camp, he wasn't worried about pursuit. He'd seen the performance with the escapee during lunch and understood that the guards let the desert do the work for them and waited for the buzzards to lead them to their quarry.

Most likely, they would send out a patrol car in a day or two to search for circling vultures.

By then, he fully expected to be lounging in the copper tub in his cabin aboard the *Oregon*, with a drink in one hand and a Cuban cigar in the other. And because he'd lost his sat phone, there would be a blood-soaked bandage on his leg.

TWENTY

A N UNFAMILIAR ALARM WOKE DR. JULIA HUXLEY. Her cabin was located next to her office, with the door perpetually open. The alarm was coming from her computer, and when she glanced over she could see the screen coming to life, a milky glow that spilled across her tidy desk and glinted off the stainless-steel arms of her rolling chair.

Julia threw aside her covers, her hands automatically bunching her hair into a ponytail and binding it with the elastic band sitting on her nightstand. In her one major, although secret, feminine conceit, she wore a hand-laced white satin nightgown that clung to her curves like a second skin. If she knew there would be a chance of a middle-of-the-night emergency, usually when the *Oregon* was gearing up for combat, she slept in an oversized T-shirt, but when things were quiet she had a whole closetful of clingy sleepwear. She'd nearly been found out a couple of times, but with a pair of clean scrubs folded at the foot of her bed she could change in seconds and no one was the wiser.

Julia padded in bare feet across her cabin and plopped

herself in front of her computer. By the time she'd flicked on the articulated light clamped to her desk, she knew what the alarm was. One of the biometric tracking chips implanted in all shore operators' legs had failed. There were several tones the computer generated, depending on the nature of the failure. Most commonly, it was a dying electric charge, but what she heard sent a chill down her spine. The sharp electronic wail meant that either the chip in question had been removed or the owner was dead.

The story was writ across her computer screen.

Juan Cabrillo's tracking chip was no longer transmitting its location to the constellation of orbiting GPS satellites. She scrolled back to check his movements over the past several hours and saw he had left the general area of the terrorist camp and old mine, striking out to the south at a steady four miles per hour. He'd covered almost twenty-five miles. He had then stopped ten minutes earlier, and, without warning, the chip had ceased functioning.

She reached for the phone to call Max when the alarm stopped. The chip was transmitting once again. Julia typed in a command to run a system diagnostic, noting the Chairman hadn't moved. The tracking chips were still a new technology, and while they hadn't had too many problems, she understood they weren't infallible. According to the system, Cabrillo had either been dead for thirty-eight seconds or the chip had been pulled from his body and then returned to it, recontacting with pumping, oxygenated blood, completing the circuit it needed to transmit.

Just as suddenly as the alarm went silent, it started up again, keening for thirty or so seconds. And then it started dropping in and out, seemingly random.

Blip, beep beep. Blip, beep. Beep, blip, beep. Blip.
Blip, blip, beep. Blip, beep beep, blip.

Through the chaos of tones, she thought she recognized a pattern. Making sure her computer was recording the telemetry from Juan's chip, she opened an Internet connection and checked her hunch. It took her nearly a minute to decipher the first series of sounds even as more came in.

Wake . . . up . . .

Blip, blip, blip, blip. Blip, blip, beep. Beep, blip, blip, beep.

Hux . . .

Juan was interrupting the signal from the chip somehow and was sending a message in old-fashioned Morse code.

"You crafty SOB," Julia muttered in admiration.

And then the alarm shrieked a continuous cry that went on and on.

Julia knocked over a cup of pens reaching for the phone.

● ● ●

AFTER TREKKING THE FIRST four miles from the terrorist camp, Cabrillo had found a sheltered spot out of the sun's brutal gaze to hole up. He and his new charge, Alana Shepard, would need to wait until nightfall in order to tackle the open desert. He told her to sleep while he backtracked a mile to make sure their spoor had been obliterated by the wind. He knew Muslims didn't keep dogs, even for tracking purposes, so he felt confident that no one would be on their trail, at least for a while.

When they started out again shortly after sunset, he wanted to put much distance between themselves and the camp, sensing that once they stopped he wouldn't be able to walk much farther afterward. If he and Alana were still alone in the desert come dawn, the vultures would start circling. With food so scarce in the desert, the vultures would loiter for days waiting for their prey to die. It would be the same as raising a sign that said ESCAPEES HERE. If the terrorists sent out a patrol, especially the chopper, they would be spotted quickly.

One more thing he had to consider was Alana's endurance. She appeared in better condition than the other prisoners he had seen, but she still suffered from deprivation. He had swiped a couple of canteens during his earlier meanderings and allowed her to drink as much as she could, yet she remained sorely dehydrated. And there was nothing he could do for the rumbling in her belly that she felt compelled to keep apologizing for.

CORSAIR 221

It was three in the morning when he could tell she was spent completely. She might make it another mile, but there was no real need. It was time now to rely on his people and not her stamina.

"So tell me more about the dig you were heading up," he invited to distract her, settling himself on the ground with his back against a rock. He had led her up a small outcrop of rock with a natural bowl at its summit that provided cover as well as a strong vantage point.

Because he had pushed the march so hard, they hadn't really spoken much beyond introductions.

"It's frustrating." She sipped from the canteen. Despite what must be a raging thirst, she had good survival instincts and drank sparingly. "The original source material strongly indicates the Suleiman Al-Jama's *Saqr* is still buried in a cave someplace, but I'll be darned if we could find any sign. For one thing, the geology is all wrong for caves or caverns."

"And for all you know, this guy Lafayette's bearings were off and you're searching the wrong riverbed," he said, finishing her thought. He rolled up his pant leg.

Alana stared at the molded titanium-and-plastic limb, saying nothing.

"Shaving cut," Juan said with a lopsided grin.

To her credit, she didn't miss a beat. "You should stick to depilatories. The third, and most likely, scenario is the Arab retainers Henry Lafayette mentioned in his journal returned to the cave after Al-Jama's death, looted what they could, and destroyed the rest."

"That's actually the least likely of the three," Juan countered. From his combat leg, he pulled a throwing knife, basically a flat piece of surgical steel that had been balanced and honed to a razor's edge. He went on: "If they were that loyal to Al-Jama in life, the respect would have continued after death. A devout Muslim would no more desecrate a grave than he'd have ham for Easter dinner."

"But Muslims don't eat . . . Oh, I get it."

"If that one generation of servants kept quiet about the entombed ship, then I'm pretty sure it's still buried out there."

"Not where we've been looking." In the moonlight, her eyes dimmed. "Are we going to be able to rescue Greg Chaffee?"

He looked at her. "I'm not going to BS you. My team and I have another priority that trumps his rescue. I'm sorry. As soon as we're done, I will go back. That I can promise."

"You're searching for Fiona Katamora's plane, aren't you?" She took Juan's silence as confirmation. "We saw it going down. That's why Greg, Mike, and I crossed the border into Libya. We were looking for it, too."

"That explains why you were taken prisoner."

"A patrol found us. They . . . they killed Mike Duncan. Shot him dead for trying to come to my aid."

He could see tears glinting on her cheeks in the moonlight. Juan knew some women would want him to take them in his arms and comfort them, but there remained a defiant lift to Alana Shepard's chin. She didn't need his sympathy, only his help. His respect for her went up another notch.

"There's an important peace conference coming up," he said softly. "Her presence there would have pretty much guaranteed success."

"I know. It was the State Department that hired me to find Al-Jama's ship in the first place. They believed that some writing he left behind would help her during the meeting."

"So this isn't just about archaeology?" She shook her head. "Tell me everything from the beginning."

It took only a few minutes for her to lay out the story, from her summons to Christie Valero's office at the State Department to meeting with her and St. Julian Perlmutter to her capture by what she thought had been a routine border patrol.

"I know Perlmutter by reputation," Juan mentioned when she finished. "He's perhaps the best maritime researcher in the world, and if he's convinced the *Saqr*'s still buried in the desert, that's good enough for me. I wonder why he didn't take this to NUMA. I thought he was some sort of consultant with them."

"I don't know. I'd never heard of him before. I did get the impression that because of the diplomatic angle he thought the State Department should handle it."

"Still, should have been NUMA," Juan said, thinking back to the professionalism he'd encountered with that agency over the years. "I've been meaning to ask, do you have any idea who the other detainees were back at the labor camp?"

"No," Alana admitted. "Greg might have. He speaks Arabic. Other than mealtimes, I was kept away from the men, and none of the women I tried to speak with understood English or the little bit of Spanish I know."

"Another mystery for another time," he mused. "Now it's time to call in the cavalry."

Cabrillo unbuckled his belt and lowered his pants to expose his upper thighs. He had been such an enigma to Alana since first rescuing her that nothing he did surprised her. There was an inch-long red scar on the thickest point of his quadriceps.

Without so much as a calming breath, Juan sliced open the scar with the throwing knife. Dark blood welled from the open lips of the wound.

"What are you doing?" she asked, now suddenly alarmed.

"There's a tracking device in my leg," he replied. "I can use it to signal my people to come get us."

He plunged two fingers into the gash, fishing around, his mouth tight and set against the pain. A moment later, he withdrew the device, a black plastic object the size and shape of a cheap digital watch. He wiped its underside against his uniform shirt, waited silently for about thirty seconds to elapse, and then pressed it into the blood trickling out of his leg. He repeated what he'd just done, and then started moving quicker, dabbing and wiping so his hands were in constant motion.

"U . . . P . . . H . . . U . . . X," he said, transmitting each letter.

Like a desert djinn rising up from the ground, a spectral figure leapt over the rock parapet sheltering Juan and Alana. It crashed into Juan, the impact sending the slippery transmitter skittering off into the dark. Bony fingers clawed for his neck, the sharp nails digging into his flesh.

With an oozing wound in his leg and his pants pulled

down to his knees, Cabrillo was at a complete disadvantage. The filthy creature made a guttural screech as it tried to ram its knees into Juan's chest while its feet raked across his legs like a cat trying to eviscerate its prey. Nails as tough as horns, ripped out trenches of Juan's skin.

The Kel-Tec pistol was buried inside the pocket of his bunched-up pants, and the knife was out of reach. Juan reared his head back as far as he could and smashed it into his attacker's nose. He didn't have the leverage to break bone, so he had to find satisfaction in the spurts of blood that began to patter across his face and the howl of pain his blow elicited.

He twisted onto his stomach under the figure, gathered his legs under him, and thrust upward with everything he had. The creature was thrown from his back, sailing across the bowl and smashing into the far side. Cabrillo had already crouched and rolled to grab the knife, and he had it in his hand and cocked by the time the monstrosity crumpled into an untidy heap.

His knife arm came down, the blade glinting, and it would have flown true had two things not occurred to Cabrillo at the last instant. His attacker had been unbelievably light, and the man was dressed in the same rags he'd seen the prisoners wearing. It was too late to stop the throw, but he managed to angle it ever so slightly. The blade embedded itself into the sandstone an inch from the man's head.

Five seconds had passed since Juan was first attacked. In that time, Alana had managed to raise her hands to her mouth in alarm and nothing more.

Juan blew out a breath.

"Oh my God." Alana gasped. "Greg told me two prisoners escaped a couple of days ago. They only brought back one."

Juan considered the odds that they would come across the only other human within twenty miles and guessed they were actually pretty good. He had put the camp directly behind him as he and Alana had struck out, and they had followed the easiest terrain to gain distance. It had been the most logical choice, and the prisoner had done the exact same thing.

They had obviously moved faster than the man, and, considering his wasted condition, it was no surprise. The miracle was that he had made it this far at all. He must have been using the hillock as an observation post, spotted Alana and Juan walking toward him, and remained hidden until Cabrillo was at his most vulnerable.

Juan shuffled over to the prisoner and reached out a hand for Alana to pass him the canteen.

"Drink," Juan said in Arabic. "We're not going to hurt you."

Under the dirt and grime and weeks of matted beard, he saw the guy was about his own age, with a strong nose and broad forehead. His cheeks were hollow from hunger and dehydration, and his eyes had a dull sheen. But he had had the strength to hike this far and launch a pretty well thought out assault. Cabrillo was impressed.

"You've done well, my friend," he said. "Our rescue is close at hand."

"You are Saudi," the man rasped after drinking half the canteen. "I recognize your accent."

"No, I learned Arabic in Riyadh. I'm actually American."

"Praise be to Allah."

"And to His Prophet, Muhammad," Juan added.

"Peace be upon him. We are saved."

"We?"

TWENTY-ONE

J UAN NEVER TRANSMITTED AGAIN AFTER THE SALU-
tation Julia had laboriously transcribed, so Max made
the decision to have Linc, Linda, and Mark head to his final
coordinates in the Pig.

It took the trio two hours of hard driving to reach the area.

Hanley was in the op center. The ship's computer was
maintaining their position so there was no need for anyone
other than a skeleton watch to be in the high-tech room, but
a dozen men and women sat in the chairs or leaned against
the walls. The only sounds were the rush of air through the
vents and the occasional slurp of coffee. Eric Stone was at
the helm, while next to him George Adams lolled in Mark
Murphy's weapons station. With his matinee-idol looks and
flight suit, the chopper pilot cut a dashing figure. He was one
of the best poker players on the ship, after the Chairman himself, and his only tell was that he toyed with his drooping
gunfighter mustache when he was really nervous. At the pace
he was going on this night, he would have twisted the hair off
his lip in another hour.

The main monitor over their heads showed a view of the predawn darkness outside the ship. There was the merest hint of color to the east. Not so much light but the absence of pitch-black. A smaller screen displayed the Pig's progress. The glowing dots representing the Pig and Juan's last position were millimeters apart.

When a phone rang, everyone startled. The tech sitting in Hali Kasim's communications center glanced at Max. Max nodded, and fitted a headset around his ears and adjusted the microphone.

"Hanley," he said, making sure to keep any concern out of his voice. He wouldn't give Juan the satisfaction of knowing how worried he'd been.

"Ah, Max. Langston Overholt."

Max grunted in irritation at the unexpected call. "You've caught us at a rather bad moment, Lang."

"Nothing serious, I hope."

"You know us. It's always serious. So are you at the tail end of a late night or just getting an early start?" It was midnight in Washington, D.C.

"To be honest, I don't even know anymore. It's all blended into one of the longest few days of my life."

"It's gotta be bad, then," Max said. "You were in the Company during the Cuban Missile Crisis."

"Back then, I was still so wet behind the ears they wouldn't give me the code for the executive washroom."

Max Hanley and Langston Overholt had come from opposite poles of the American experience. Max was blue-collar all the way. His father had been a union machinist at a California aircraft plant, his mother a teacher. His commands during Vietnam had come through merit and ability. Overholt, on the other hand, had been born into a family from such old money they still considered the Astors nouveau riche. He was the result of twelve years of prep school, four years of Harvard, and three more of Harvard Law. Yet the two men had a strong respect for each other.

"Now I think one of the stalls is named after you," Max quipped.

"Enjoy your normal prostate while it lasts, my friend."

"So, what's up?"

"Libyans are reporting that a fighter jockey on a night-time training exercise spotted something in the desert just inside their border with Tunisia. A patrol was sent out and discovered a secret base equipped with a Hind helicopter. The place had been hit hard. The gunship was destroyed, and there appeared to be no survivors."

"Yeah, I was meaning to tell you about that. Our people stumbled onto it. They took out the Hind and determined it had been modified to fire air-to-air missiles, specifically the"—he looked to Eric, who mouthed *Apex*—"Apex. It's Russkie-built."

"Damn it, Max, you should have told me about that when I told you Professor Bumford had been kidnapped."

"No offense, Lang, but you hired us to find the Secretary of State. I consider everything else to be collateral."

Max knew Overholt had to be calming himself, because he didn't say anything for almost thirty seconds. Max wasn't concerned. They hired the Corporation because they had no place else to turn. How missions were accomplished, the recent fiasco in Somalia notwithstanding, was up to his and Juan's discretion.

"You're right. Sorry. Sometimes I forget you guys get to operate with a level of autonomy I can only dream of."

"Don't worry about it. So what's this about the chopper?"

"The Libyans claim they found a computer buried under the command tent, or what was left of it."

Max opened his mouth to say that his people had gone over the site, but he knew their search was relatively cursory. Instead, he asked, "What was on the computer?"

"Links tying the chopper to Suleiman Al-Jama, for one thing, and indications that they've opened a terrorist training camp right under the Libyans' noses using a dummy company purportedly opening up an old coal mine."

Max and Eric Stone shared a significant look. This was exactly as they had discussed the night before.

"How are we getting this information?" Hanley asked.

"Through a deliberate leak to the CIA station chief in

Tripoli, a guy named Jim Kublicki. His contact is an opposite number in the JSO, the—"

"Jamahiriya Security Organization. We know who they are. How good is his source?"

"Given the level of cooperation we've gotten from the Libyans leading up to the summit and the help they provided trying to find Fiona Katamora's plane, I'd say pretty good."

"Or it could all be a trick. The damned Libyans could be into this up to their necks."

"Not according to the rest of my news."

"Max," the duty communications officer interrupted, "there's a call coming in from the Pig."

Max glanced at the overhead screen. The dot representing the Pig and the one for Cabrillo's last known location overlapped. "Wait one sec, Lang. Go ahead, patch through the new call. This is Hanley."

"Good morning, Max."

By the tone in Juan Cabrillo's voice, Hanley knew the Chairman was okay. "Hold the line, Juan." He flipped circuits back to Overholt. "Continue, Lang."

"What was that all about?"

"Nothing. Just Juan checking in. He can hold. What's the news that'll convince me this isn't the JSO or some other faction pulling a fast one?"

"Because the Libyans are going to hit the training camp in about two hours. Jim Kublicki is at one of their Air Force bases suiting up now to accompany them in a chopper for verification. If that's not enough, there's the possibility that Fiona Katamora is at the base as we speak. Also, the computer provided a clue to track down Al-Jama himself. The chopper and other equipment were funneled into the country with the help of a corrupt harbor pilot named Tariq Assad. They have a record that such a guy exists and has worked for the harbor authority for five years, but there's nothing in their system before then. No school records. No employment records. Nothing. They believe this Assad is actually a cover name for Al-Jama himself, and are already on their way to grab him."

The look Max and Eric exchanged this time was one of absolute horror.

Juan and the others were twenty-five miles from the terrorist training camp. They had more than enough time to find decent cover before the Libyan assault. The horror the two men shared stemmed from the fact that Eddie Seng and Hali Kasim had been shadowing Tariq Assad since the night the *Oregon* docked. With stakes as high as they were, Juan hadn't entirely trusted their Cypriot facilitator, *L'Enfant*, so he had ordered his best covert operative, Seng, and his only Arab, Kasim, to watch the man for any signs of treachery.

Other than the fact that Assad spent money like water on a string of mistresses all over Tripoli, they hadn't discovered anything suspicious. This was why the deadly shoot-out at the roadblock on the way out of the city that first night had been dismissed as a coincidence. Now Max realized Assad had set them up from the beginning.

Depending on how wide a net the JSO threw to capture him, Eddie and Hali were in real danger of being drawn into it.

Hanley finally found his voice. "Lang, what you've given me changes our tactical picture a hundred and eighty degrees. I need to coordinate with Juan or we're going to be in a world of hurt."

"Okay. Keep me pos—"

Max cut him off and switched phone lines. "Juan, you still there?"

"I don't know if I want to talk to you anymore," Cabrillo said, trying to sound sulky.

"We got trouble, my friend."

The gravity in Max's voice killed any of the playful relief Juan harbored from being rescued by Linc, Linda, and Mark. "What's happened?"

"The Libyans are two hours away from attacking the training camp where you just were. They think the Secretary might be there, so this is both a search-and-destroy mission and a rescue attempt. On top of that, they are going to arrest Tariq Assad because he's Suleiman Al-Jama."

"What about the mine?" Juan snapped.

"I'm not sure," Max admitted. "Why?"

Cabrillo didn't answer. Hanley could hear him breathing over the secure radio link. He understood the Chairman and knew he must be making a tough choice.

"Damn," Juan muttered, and then his voice firmed. "First thing is to get word to Eddie and Hali to watch themselves."

"Eric's on that now."

"There are more than two hundred tangos garrisoned at that training camp. If Fiona Katamora's there—which she may well be, for all I know—she is as good as dead. It'll take the Libyan strike force twenty or thirty minutes to secure the camp, plenty of time for someone to put a bullet in her head. We've got to even the odds."

"How?"

"I'm working on it. Where are you guys?"

"About eighty miles off the coast."

"And we've got two hours?"

"More or less."

"Okay, Max, I don't want to hear you grumble about your precious engines, but I need you on the coast as fast you can get here. Sound general quarters, and put Gomez Adams on fifteen-minute alert."

"Helm, give me emergency power," Max shouted. "All ahead flank. Get us to the coaling station dock. Don't worry, Juan. We'll get you out of there."

● ● ●

STRETCHED OUT on the back bench of the Pig, with Linc stitching up his leg under local anesthetic, Cabrillo looked across the front seat at the Libyan prisoner he and Alana had saved. Fodl was his name, and already the salt tablets and liter bottles of water he'd consumed had revived him tremendously.

"Yes, you will," Juan said to Fodl and Max. "All of us."

TWENTY-TWO

I N A COUNTRY THAT FOR ALL INTENTS AND PURPOSES was one hundred percent ethnically homogenous, Eddie Seng should have been at a disadvantage when the Chairman had given him and Hali Kasim the job of tailing their harbor pilot. He hadn't complained, though. Like Juan, he felt there was something suspicious about Assad, some quality that had made the hairs on the back of his neck stand erect.

Having a suspicion and proving it were two separate things, though, and there was no getting around the fact that every one of Eddie's relatives going back a couple hundred generations was Chinese and nearly all the people walking the streets of Tripoli were born in the Middle East.

But it wasn't quite all bad. There wasn't a city on the planet that didn't have an enclave of Chinese immigrants. And on that first night, while Hali trailed Tariq Assad, carrying a hand-lettered card proclaiming he was a mute to cover the fact that he spoke no Arabic, Eddie had gone off in search of Tripoli's Chinatown.

What he found came as a shock, though, upon reflection, it shouldn't have been. Buoyed by petrodollars, Libya, and especially Tripoli, was undergoing a building boom, and a number of the projects were being erected by construction firms out of Hong Kong and Shanghai. Apart from the workers brought in, there was also a large support system of restaurants, bars, shops, and brothels, catering strictly to a Chinese clientele, that was nearly indistinguishable from Eddie's New York Chinatown home.

And, like New York, there were both legitimate and illegitimate layers of society. It had taken him only a few minutes of wandering to find gang symbols that he recognized spray-painted on a couple of the storefronts. And a few minutes more to see the symbol he wanted. It was small, just a few inches tall, and was sprayed in red paint on an otherwise plain gray metal door. The door was set in a heavy-duty structure of a warehouse, with a row of windows running only along the second floor.

Eddie knocked, using a code he knew from home. No one answered the door, so he knocked again, this time as a civilian would, a few hard raps with his knuckles. Judging by the dull echo he heard, he guessed the door was solid steel.

The door creaked open after a few seconds, and a boy of about ten poked his head around the jamb. There would be three or four armed men just out of sight. The boy didn't say a word.

Neither did Eddie.

He pulled out the tails of his shirt and turned, exposing his back up to the shoulder blades.

The boy gasped aloud, and suddenly Eddie felt other eyes on him. He slowly lowered his shirt again and faced the door. He took it as a good sign that the two gang members now studying him had their pistols lowered.

"Who are you?" one asked.

"A friend," Eddie replied.

"Who gave you the tattoo?" asked the second.

Eddie glanced at him with as much disdain as he dared. "No one gave it to me. I earned it."

On his back was inked an elaborate, though now-faded, tattoo of a dragon fighting a griffin. It was an old gang symbol of the Green Dragon Tong, from when they had battled a rival gang for control of the Shanghai docks back in the 1930s. Only senior members of the Tong or especially brave foot soldiers were allowed it on their skin, and, given the global reach of the Chinese underworld, Eddie had known it would gain him entrée here.

He just hoped they didn't test it because Kevin Nixon had applied the stencil only a few hours earlier from a catalog of gang and prison tattoos he kept aboard the *Oregon*.

"What are you doing here?" the first thug asked.

"There's a man who works at the harbor. He owes people I represent a great deal of money. I want to hire some of your guys to help me keep an eye on him until it's time to collect."

"You have money?"

Eddie didn't bother to answer. No one in their right mind would make such a request without being able to pay for it. "Four or five days. Eight or ten guys. Ten thousand dollars."

"Too tough to exchange. Make it euros. Ten thousand."

With the currency rates the way they were, that was almost fifty percent more. Eddie nodded.

And, just like that, he had enough men to keep Tariq Assad under twenty-four-hour watch, while he and Hali waited in a fleabag hotel that the Tong controlled. The gang supplied updates on Assad's movements every six hours via disposable cell phones, so over the course of a few days they had a pretty good pattern of his movements.

Generally, Assad worked eight hours on the night shift at the dock, though he would usually take off for a couple if no ships were expected. On those nights, he went to an apartment not too far from the harbor where he kept a mistress. She wasn't the prettiest of the ones he frequented, but she was the most convenient.

After work he went home to be with his family, slept maybe six hours, and then went out to have coffee with coworkers before visiting other apartments dotted around Tripoli.

Eddie asked his new employees to put together a list of the women's names, and when he asked Eric Stone to cross-reference them using the *Oregon*'s computer it came back that Assad was bedding the wives of midlevel government employees. Even the plain girl near the harbor was the sister of the deputy director of the Energy Ministry.

Given that Assad wasn't particularly attractive by anyone's standards, his conquests were all the more impressive.

Eddie and Hali both concluded that Assad was nothing more than a mildly corrupt harbor pilot with an overactive libido and one hell of a pickup line. That was until Max Hanley called with his bombshell announcement. Assad's ingratiation into the bedrooms of Libya's government took on a whole new and darker aspect.

● ● ●

JUAN LISTENED OVER THE phone as Eric Stone described the route the old rail spur took through the mountains toward the coast, twenty-odd miles away. The satellite pictures didn't give the gradient of the line, but Juan's tracking chip had put him at nearly a thousand feet above sea level when he'd gotten off the helicopter at the terrorists' training camp.

From the outline of a plan that was forming in his mind even as Eric spoke, Cabrillo decided it was going to be one hell of a wild ride.

Worse, though, the timing was going to be incredibly tight, and he could think of no excuse he could have Overholt pass on to the Libyans to delay their assault without tipping his hand.

Adding to his problems, he hadn't slept more than six hours out of the past forty-eight, and, judging by the appearance of his three shipmates, they weren't faring much better.

"What is it?" Linc asked, his surgical gloves covered with blood as he finished the last of the tight stitches. He had sewn the cut in Juan's leg by layering three rows of catgut, moving from the deepest part of the wound out to the skin, so there was no way it would reopen. With a local anesthetic keeping the pain to a dull ache, Juan felt confidence in his body's abilities.

"What?"

"You just chuckled," Linc replied, snapping off the gloves and stuffing them into a red biohazard-containment box.

"Did I? I was just thinking that we are so deep over our heads right now I don't know if what I have in mind is going to work."

"Not another of your infamous plan C's?" Linda groaned. She stood just outside of the Pig, looking over Linc's massive shoulder.

"That's why I laughed. Gallows humor. We're well past C and into D, E, or F."

There were two options facing Cabrillo but no real choices. He was about to put them all into a shooting gallery, with the Pig playing the role of sitting duck.

Linc duct-taped a gauze pad over Juan's wound, and said, "If Doc Huxley has a problem with my work, tell her to take it up with your HMO."

Juan struggled back into his pants. They were ripped in a dozen places, and so crusted with sand that they crackled when he drew them over his hips, but the Pig didn't carry any spare uniforms. He did a couple of deep knee bends when he leapt to the ground. The cut was tight, but both the stitches and the anesthesia held.

The sun had yet to show itself over the distant mountains, so the stars blazed cold and implacable overhead. Cabrillo studied them for a second, wondering—and not for the first time—if he would live to see them again.

"Mount up," he called. "The show's gonna be mostly over by the time the *Oregon* arrives, and we've got a lot of grim work ahead of us."

"Just curious, Juan," Linc said casually. "Who are these people we're going to rescue? Political prisoners, common criminals, what?"

"I think maybe they're the key to this whole thing."

Linc gave a little nod. "All right."

"If you ask me," Mark said and started to add, "I've got a bad feeling about—"

Cabrillo cut him off with a look.

Forty-eight minutes, by Juan's watch, ticked by before he judged they were ready. Barely. He had seen the quality of the guards looking after the prisoners and knew they weren't a serious threat in small numbers, but there were forty or so of them, and if his timing was off the two hundred more he hoped to lure from the training camp would reach the mine before everyone had made good their escape.

On their approach to the mine, they had left Linc to make his way to higher ground overlooking the stockyard behind the old administration buildings. With a Barrett .50-caliber sniper rifle, the ex-SEAL could have accurately hit targets from well over a mile away. His effective range with the smaller REC7 assault rifle was still an impressive seven hundred yards, and for what Juan had planned, Linc would be taking significantly shorter shots than that. The Pig was just out of sight of the mining camp, atop the narrow trail where the day before the desert patrol had returned with the body of the escapee.

Dawn was a brushstroke in the distance, so darkness filled the hollows and gullies around them, and the air carried the chill of the distant sea.

Juan wished there was a way he could leave Alana and their new companion, Fodl, out of the fight, but he couldn't risk leaving them in the desert in case he and his team couldn't return. He had explained his plan to them, made sure they understood the dangers involved, and both were ready to do whatever he asked of them.

"Just so you fit in with all the other archaeologist-adventurers out there, I'll get you a fedora," he said, and smiled at Alana when she had told him she was game.

"And a whip?" she'd joked back.

"Kinky," he'd admonished with another grin.

"Comm check," Linc called over the tactical net.

"I've got you five by five, big man."

"I'm on top of the old ore-loading structure," the sniper reported. "The guards are starting to roust the prisoners for breakfast. It's now or never."

"Roger," Juan replied, and swallowed hard, his throat

suddenly as dry as the desert sand. He looked across the driver's seat to Mark Murphy. The success or failure of Juan's plan hinged on Murph's virtuosity with the Pig's weapons systems. "Ready?"

Mark nodded.

"Tallyho!" Juan said.

Mark keyed up the Pig's roof-mounted mortars. They had already been sighted in with Linc's help, using a laser range finder. They fired simultaneously, and the weapon's autoloader had a second round dropped into each of the four tubes before the first rounds had traveled a hundred yards on their high, arcing parabolas.

The second fusillade launched with a comically hollow sound, and Mark shouted, "Go!"

Juan already had the Pig's engine revved, so that when he dropped it into gear, all four tires spun. They roared over a ridge, and the camp came into view. As he'd planned, no one had heard the mortars fire. Ragged prisoners were lining up for their pitifully small breakfast while guards casually harassed them. He saw one guard use a baton on a man, crashing it into the man's kidneys so hard his back bent like a bow at full stretch and he collapsed in the dust.

The mortar rounds hit the apex of their flight and started barreling earthward, each packed with a kilo of high explosives. Mark had spent part of the drive to the camp removing most of the shrapnel from each round to minimize the chance of hitting any of the detainees.

Linc laid the crosshairs of his REC7 on the guard who'd just clubbed the prisoner, let out half a breath, and squeezed the trigger. "We have pink mist," he reported when the guard's head exploded.

He took out another pair of guards before the first ripple of concern passed through the security contingent. The captain of the guards appeared from a tent. His chest was bare, and he wore his uniform pants bloused into his combat boots. Linc noted the radio antennae sticking up through a hole in the tent's roof and moved his aim onto another target.

Four mortar rounds struck the ground at precisely the same instant. The path leading down to the floor of the open-pit mine erupted in geysers of dirt and greasy fire. A moment later, more rounds hit even closer to the camp.

Both guards and prisoners alike pulled back, moving toward the large wooden buildings, while Linc continued to thin the ranks of terrorists, one shot—one kill—at a time. He made the ones carrying weapons his priority.

Cabrillo raced the Pig down on the camp like a rally driver dashing for the finish line. Next to him, Murph fought to keep the aiming reticle of the Pig's onboard missiles locked on one of the terrorists' trucks. He got tone and fired.

The rocket screamed off the rails, carving an erratic path through the air, and exploded against the truck's cab, snapping its chassis in half so it rose up like a ship that had been torpedoed.

The blast further corralled the frightened prisoners closer to the building, while the guards were rushing back to their tents, where many had left their automatic weapons.

The Pig was a hundred yards from the camp when the freshly armed terrorists started running from the tents, brandishing their AKs and firing long strings of rounds in random directions. Up in the Pig's cupola, Linda watched them over the sights of her M60 machine gun. The weapon bucked in her arms, slamming into her shoulder like the business end of a jackhammer, but her aim never wavered.

The ground around the running gunmen came alive as rounds blew into their midst. Men fell, clutching at horrendous wounds, some struck by their own comrades who had whirled at this new threat and opened fire indiscriminately.

"He's had enough time," Juan yelled over the snarling engine. "Take out the command tent."

Cabrillo's plan had two goals. The first was to rescue as many of the prisoners as he could because he wasn't sure if the Libyan military would take the time to discern friend from foe. He wasn't even sure of their definition of those terms at this point. The second objective was to get as many terrorists as possible away from their training camp before the main attack. If Fiona Katamora was really there, then every gunman engaged at the mine was one less gunman trying to kill her before she was rescued.

This was why Linc had been told specifically to let the mine's garrison commander contact the training camp on the radio. They needed him to raise the alarm. But now that he had . . .

Mark put a missile through the command tent's front flap at just the right angle for it to hit the ground before it flew through the far side. The canvas rose up on a blossoming column of flame, and the piles of military gear stacked outside were blown flat by the concussion. The tent caught fire like flash paper and turned to ash that fell to the ground like dirty snow.

They were deep into the camp now. Above Juan and Murph, Linda continued to work the M60, taking out clusters of guards and using the tracer rounds to keep the prisoners moving toward the stockyard where the terrorists stored their railcars and train engines.

Cabrillo could tell that the guards' will had been broken by the sudden and furious assault. Many of them were running down into the mine or over the ridge and into the desert. Fifty or more prisoners were huddled against the side of the old mine office building. A gunman suddenly reared up from behind a bulldozer. He had a perfect bead on the defenseless men and women and an RPG-7 lifted to his shoulder.

Murph flipped the controls from missiles to gun, and the .30-cal under the Pig's snout chattered. The terrorist went down, but not before he fired his rocket-propelled grenade. The five-pound missile made it less than ten feet from the tube before it inexplicably exploded in midair.

"Damn, Linc," Juan said in awe, "was that you?"

"It's all a matter of knowing how to read them," Linc replied. He would later admit that he was shooting at the terrorist and the rocket flew into his bullet.

Juan whipped the Pig around the side of the building, braking hard so the big truck slid onto a set of tracks, its tail resting just a couple of feet from a boxcar with a handwheel on its roof for brakemen to mechanically slow the antique rolling stock. The track was a good foot narrower than the Pig's tires. Juan searched the dash for a second and found the control that could alter the vehicle's ground clearance by pulling in the wheels on articulated suspension joints.

He had to jockey the truck back and forth, as the wheels drew inward, until they were resting directly on the rails, and there was a full two feet of open space between the chassis and the crushed-rock ballast on the ground.

With another button, Juan deactivated the automatic tire-inflation system and then jumped from the cab. "Mark, Linda, get busy," he called over the tactical radio. "Linc, cover them. Fodl, with me."

He grabbed up a REC7 assault rifle, and had the FN Five-seveN pistol in his hand when he hit the ground. He fired at the left-side tires. The truck's weight made them go flat instantly, and, just like that, the steel rims were cradled around the rails, with the rubber acting as extra grip. He couldn't prevent a satisfied smile. Mating the Pig to the railroad tracks had been the cornerstone of his plan.

He ran for the corner of the building as his new Libyan friend clambered out of the Pig still wearing his prisoner's rags. Across the compound, he could see a few guards hunting for targets, but for the moment no one was paying the detainees any attention.

A couple of them who were pressed against the building looked at Juan fearfully when they saw his weapon. Then Fodl appeared at his side.

"Come with us," Fodl told them with an aura of command that didn't surprise the Chairman. "These people are here to help."

A few of the emaciated prisoners stared back at him uncertainly. "Go. That is an order."

Like a breached levee, the few heading toward the railcar that Linda held open turned into a flood. Cabrillo stood at the corner, sweeping the compound for any interested guards. If any looked their way, he put them down, while next to him Fodl waved in more of his people. A group of women appeared from under the overturned serving tables and raced for the building, only to have someone open fire at them from their flank. One of the women went down before Juan could counterfire, hammering home a steady burst into a pyramid of crates from where the shots had originated.

The other women helped the injured girl to her feet, supporting her under her arms and making her almost hopscotch to safety.

"Bless you," one of them said to Juan as they passed around the building and into protective cover.

Another prisoner paused at Juan's side. He gave the man a passing glance and then returned to scanning the compound. The prisoner touched Juan's sleeve, and he looked at him more carefully. He wasn't an Arab like all the others. His hair and face were pale, although his skin was burned raw by the sun.

"You Chaffee?" Juan asked.

"Yes. How did you know?"

"You've got Alana Shepard to thank for your rescue."

Chaffee sagged with relief. "Thank God. We were told last night she was shot for trying to escape."

"Are you in any condition to fight?"

The CIA agent tried to pull himself erect. "Give me a gun and watch me."

Juan pointed to where Mark Murphy was securing the old boxcar to the Pig's rear tow hooks. From this distance, the train car looked massive and the chain as thin as a silver necklace, but there was nothing he could do about it. "Report to that guy over there. He'll take care of you."

"Thank you."

Cabrillo looked at his watch. Eight minutes since the first shot fired. They had less than ten more before a horde of gunmen arrived from the training camp, and just an hour until the Libyan military arrived and opened fire on anything that moved.

Prisoners continued to stream toward the railcar, and no matter how Juan tried to urge them to hurry they just couldn't. They were so far gone from their ordeal that even the offer of freedom couldn't make their bodies move faster than a painful shuffle. He could almost hear his watch ticking.

Glancing over his shoulder, Juan watched them climb into

the train, each one pausing when he or she was inside to help the next in line.

It wasn't his watch Juan thought he heard. It was the rhythmic *whomp-whomp-whomp* of an approaching helicopter. George Adams was still twenty minutes out. It had to be the terrorists' Mi-8.

It didn't matter that the train car was full anyway, and only one old woman was struggling to make it to the railhead from across the compound, while behind her tents and equipment burned, sending columns of smoke into the pinking sky.

Time had run out.

TWENTY-THREE

WHEN BULLETS PEPPERED THE GROUND IN THE OLD woman's wake, Cabrillo was slapping home a fresh magazine into the underside of his assault rifle. He hadn't expended the first, so there was no need to cock the weapon.

To Juan, at this moment, the more than one hundred people crowded into the boxcar didn't matter. Only the old woman.

It was perhaps a fault in his logic, a synapse that fired a little off. He made no distinction between the needs of the many versus the needs of the few. At that moment, her life meant as much to him as all the others.

He broke cover and fired from the hip, laying down a blistering barrage that silenced the terrorist's gun. The woman had frozen in place. *Deer caught in headlights* flashed through Juan's mind.

He reached her in a dozen long strides, ducking as he approached so he could scoop her up over his left shoulder without pausing. She was a solid one hundred and eighty pounds, despite the starvation diet, and must have tipped the scales at two-fifty before her ordeal. Juan staggered under the weight, his wounded leg almost buckling. The woman gave a startled yelp but didn't struggle, as Cabrillo started back for the building, running awkwardly, half turning to watch their rear, his rifle held one-handed.

The woman suddenly screamed. Juan twisted back. A guard had appeared out of nowhere. He was armed only with a club, a suicide charge, but Cabrillo's rifle was still pointed in the wrong direction. As he spun, the old woman's feet missed the guard's head by inches, and when Juan came around to get his REC7 aimed, the woman used his momentum to fire a solid punch to the guard's chin an instant before the club crashed down on her exposed neck.

The terrorist staggered back and was starting forward again when a round from Linc in the loading tower drilled him to the ground.

"Lady," Juan panted in Arabic, "you've got a right cross like Muhammad Ali."

"I always thought George Foreman had a better punch," she replied.

He almost dropped her when he started to laugh. He dumped her into the boxcar and nodded to Linda to slam the rolling door closed. "Murph, you set?" he called over the radio.

The sound of the approaching chopper grew by the second.

"I'm good to go."

"Linc, get ready. We're rolling in thirty seconds."

On his way to the passenger's seat, Mark Murphy flattened the Pig's right-side tires. It took him two shots each despite the point-blank range. Linda had already helped Fodl into the rear cargo compartment, and Greg Chaffee stood with his head and torso thrust out of the open top hatch.

Juan threw himself into the driver's seat. Ahead of them loomed a diesel-electric locomotive, a huge machine capable of hauling strings of ore cars up and down the mountain. He would have been concerned about it following them, but its engines were cold and would take at least a half hour to get running at temperature.

Max Hanley had designed the Pig with a twenty-four-gear

transmission. Juan dropped it into low range and selected the lowest of the four reverse gears. Pressing his foot to the accelerator, he felt and heard the engine revs build while the twin turbos screamed. The railcar behind them weighed eighteen thousand pounds, according to the faded stencil on its side, and packed within was another five tons of humanity. From a dead stop, he had no idea if he could get such a load moving.

The truck shuddered as the deflated tires slipped against the slick steel rails.

Juan unclipped a safety device attached to the floor shifter and pushed down on a red knob. From the integrated NOS, nitrous oxide flowed into the engine's cylinders, breaking down in the extreme heat and releasing additional oxygen for combustion.

The Pig didn't have the torque, as Max had boasted, "to push the *Oregon* up Niagara Falls," but the two-hundred-horsepower boost provided by the nitrous oxide was the kick Juan needed to overcome the train's static inertia.

Starting out at barely a snail's pace, the Pig started pushing the laden railcar along the track, and each foot gained increased their speed fractionally. The digital speedometer on the dash ticked to one mile per hour, and had reached three when the train began to pass under the skeletal support frame of the old coal-loading station where Linc had made his sniper's nest.

When the Chairman had radioed they were ready to go, Linc had climbed down from the top of the rusted conveyor belt and stood poised over the open mouth of a coal chute straddling the tracks. The leading edge of the car rolled into view, and he dropped through space, landing and tumbling in one smooth motion. The coaling station had been designed for low-slung hopper cars, not the tall, boxy freight car, and as he pressed himself up to get to his feet he spotted the razor-sharp edge of another coal chute about to slice his head off.

He dropped flat, the chute passing an inch above his nose, and he remained perfectly still as they accelerated under a dozen more. Only when they had cleared the rusted bulk of the loading station did he dare draw a breath. "I'm aboard," he radioed.

"Good," Juan answered. "You've got more time behind the wheel of this thing. Get your butt down here and drive."

For the first mile out of the mine, the ground was dead level, and the Pig was accelerating smoothly, so Juan hit the cruise control and unlimbered himself from his seat. In the cargo bed, he stuffed extra magazines for his Barrett REC7 into his pant pocket. "How are you two holding up?" he asked Alana and Fodl without looking at them.

"You have given me hope for the first time in six months," the Libyan replied. "I have never felt better."

"Alana?" he asked, finally able to give her his attention. He'd strapped a double holster around his waist for a pair of FN Five-seveNs.

"I haven't done anything to deserve that fedora yet."

"You've done plenty."

"Ah, who's driving the train?" Linc asked as he lowered himself past Greg Chaffee and spotted Juan.

"First corner isn't for another half mile or more. We do this exactly like we talked about and we should make it. Oh, damn," Cabrillo said, suddenly remembering something. He ducked his head back into the Pig's cab. "Mark, the box-car weighs nine tons. Throw in another five for the people. Math it."

"I need its dimensions."

"Guess."

Mark looked at him, incredulous. "Guess? Are you kidding?"

"Nope."

" 'Math it,' he says," Mark griped to Juan's departing form. " 'Guess.' Jeesh!"

Juan climbed out onto the Pig's roof. He estimated they were up to fifteen miles per hour and continuing to accelerate. So far, so good, he thought briefly before looking up and seeing no sign of the helicopter.

He stepped aft and was bracing himself to leap up onto the boxcar's roof when Greg Chaffee opened up with the M60.

Cabrillo turned to see a camouflaged truck careen toward the stockyard. It was the first of the terrorists from the training camp. There were a dozen holding on to the rails of the truck's open bed. Their gun barrels bristled.

The road they were on clung to the side of a hill running a little above and parallel to the rail line. Chaffee had been quick with the machine gun, firing at the truck's tires before the driver had regained full control of the vehicle. Rounds peppered the area near the front tire until it exploded, shedding rubber like a Catherine wheel throws sparks.

The truck swerved when the mangled rim gouged into the soft gravel shoulder. The men in back started to scream as the vehicle tipped further. Still moving dangerously fast, the truck flipped onto its side, skidding down the hill. Some of the terrorists were thrown clear, others clutched the supports to keep themselves inside when it rolled onto its roof. The cab plowed a furrow into the earth before it flipped again, barrel-rolling violently, sheet metal and men peeling away in a cloud of dust.

A second desert-patrol vehicle appeared before the first had settled back on its ruined undercarriage. The driver of this one caught a break. Greg Chaffee had blown through the last of the ammunition in the belt and stood impotently as Linda showed him how to swap it out. The truck dashed down the hill and braked for cover behind the hulking shadow of the locomotive. The men in the bed opened fire at extreme range, and a few lucky hits were close enough to make Linda and Chaffee duck.

Cabrillo had lost precious seconds watching the spectacle and roused himself with an angry shudder. The boxcar's roof was four feet above his head, and he needed a running start to launch himself, so he hit the edge with his chest. Kicking at the smooth metal sides and straining with his arms, he hauled himself atop the car and looked forward. The first curve was a quarter mile away, and they had sped up to at least twenty miles an hour.

He knew from the map Eric had e-mailed from the *Oregon* that this was a long, sweeping corner taking the tracks around the very top of this mountain and that the grade started to fall away as soon as they entered it. Twenty miles an hour was okay going in, but if they continued to accelerate, eventually they would lose control of the boxcar.

Juan moved all the way to the front of the car where a rusted, four-spoked metal wheel gave him control over the car's mechanical brakes. In the days before George Westinghouse invented his fail-safe pneumatic-braking system, teams of brakemen would ride atop trains and turn devices like this one to squeeze the pads against the wheels in an uncoordinated and often deadly ballet. Cabrillo prayed as he grasped the wheel that it wasn't frozen solid by rust, and that after the decades the car had been used on the line there were any brake pads remaining.

Prepared to heave with all his strength, he cursed when the wheel spun freely in his hands. It felt like it wasn't connected to anything, but then he heard the squeal of metal on metal as the old brakes clamped over the top of the car's wheels. They worked after all and had been recently greased. Grinning at his luck, he cranked the wheel another half turn, and his elation turned to dismay. The added pressure should have tightened the brake pads further and changed the pitch of the screech coming from the wheels. It didn't happen.

They had brakes, yes. But not much.

The Pig pushed the freight car into the turn, and Juan lost sight of the ore-loading superstructure as it vanished around the hilltop. To his right, he had a commanding view over another valley and, as if to remind him of their predicament, a string of ore cars that had left the tracks a hundred years before at its bottom, looking like discarded toys. If he had to guess, the steam engine that had gone over with them probably had five times the Pig's horsepower.

"Linc, you there?" he radioed.

"Yes."

"What's our speed?"

"Twenty-eight."

"Okay, don't let it go past thirty. We don't have much braking left on the boxcar."

"Is that bad?" Linda asked over the net.

"It ain't good."

There were ladder rungs welded to the front of the car, so Cabrillo climbed over and down. Next to him was the shaft that linked the wheel above to a worm gear that activated the brakes. Juan hooked his legs around the forward coupling and braced one hand on a stanchion so he could peer under the edge of the car. Creosote-blackened railroad ties zipped by inches from where he dangled. A stone was lodged between the turning rod and the worm gear. When he twisted the wheel, the stone had kicked the gear's teeth out of alignment so it turned without activating the brakes. Redoubling his grip, he stretched until his chest was under the car. Weeds growing in the old railbed whipped his cheek and face.

His fingers sank into the grease that coated the gear, but no matter how he tried he couldn't get a grip on the tightly wedged stone chip.

"Screw this," he muttered, and reached behind his back for one of his automatic pistols.

His body swayed as he drew it, and for a moment he was looking up the tracks. A metal jerry can had fallen from an earlier train or been left between the rails by one of the work crews. Juan was hurtling toward it at more than thirty miles per hour and didn't have the time or leverage to pull himself clear. Hanging practically upside down, he aimed at the can and opened fire as fast as the gun would cycle. The high-velocity bullets from the FN Five-seveN punched through the can's thin sides without moving it. He was ten feet from having his face smashed into the container when a round caught on one of its corner seams and sent the can skittering harmlessly away.

He twisted back and fired the last round at the worm gear. The rock popped free and fell away.

"Now, that's what I'm talking about," he crowed, high on accomplishment and adrenaline.

"Repeat that, Chairman," Linc asked.

"Nothing. I think I've fixed the brakes." He straightened himself up and reached for the ladder. "What's our speed?"

"Thirty-four. I'm using the Pig's brakes, so that carbon-fiber dust is blowing off the pads something fierce."

"No problem. This is why we started in reverse. Throw her into first gear and start slowing us using the engine. I'll get on the brake up here, and between the two we should be okay."

Juan reached the top of the boxcar. They had dropped a hundred feet or so from the mountain's summit as they curled around its flank. Above them, the hillside was sparse scrub. Then he saw that there was a road that ran parallel to and slightly higher than the railbed. He only noticed it because of the dun-colored truck that emerged from around a bend and started pacing the train as it glided down the tracks.

A man with his head wrapped in a ubiquitous kaffiyeh stood bracing himself in the back of the truck. Cabrillo had left his REC7 on the boxcar's roof when he'd crawled down to fix the brakes. He lunged up and over the front of the car at the same instant the fanatic leapt from the speeding truck.

His defiant scream was lost in the wind as he arced through the air. Juan's fingers had closed around the rifle's barrel when the man crashed onto the roof close enough to send the weapon skidding toward the side. Jacked up on even more adrenaline than Cabrillo, the man shouted a battle cry and kicked Juan full in the face.

Cabrillo's world went dark in an instant, and only started returning in painfully slow increments. When Juan was somewhat conscious of what was happening, the terrorist had pulled his AK-47 from around his back and was just lining up. Juan rolled over and scissor-kicked his legs, twisting on the hot steel roof enough to catch the man in the shin. The AK stitched four holes into the roof next to Juan's head, and inside the car someone screamed out in pain.

Goaded beyond fury, Cabrillo reached up and grasped the weapon by its forward grip. As he pulled down, the gunman reared back and actually helped pull the Chairman to his feet. Juan fired two punches into the gunman's face. The Arab was so intent on keeping his weapon that he didn't defend himself. Juan landed two more solid blows, and over the terrorist's shoulder saw two more men preparing to leap for the train.

He rammed his elbow into his opponent's stomach as he rolled into him, turning them both so that when he grabbed at the guy's right hand and forced his finger onto the trigger the AK's barrel was pointed back at the truck. The spray of tracers caught one of the men just as he gathered himself to jump. He fell out of the side of the truck and vanished under its rear wheels, his body making the vehicle bounce slightly on its suspension.

The second man flew like a bird and landed on the roof with the agility of a cat.

Cabrillo continued to spin the first terrorist, and when he let go the guy staggered back one pace, two, and then there was no more train roof. He went cartwheeling into space, his headscarf coming unwound and fluttering after him like a distracted butterfly.

Juan threw his empty pistol at his new opponent and charged him before the man could pull his assault rifle across his body on its canvas sling. Juan hit the guy low and reared up, lifting him nearly five feet into the air before letting go. The gunman crashed onto the roof, his breath exploding from his body in a rancid gush. If his back wasn't broken, he was still out for the duration.

Unless Linda or Linc had noticed the first guy go over the side of the boxcar, they weren't at the right angle to see what was happening behind them, and with Juan's radio dislodged from his ear he had no way of warning them. The Pig was giving its all to slow the train, but without the addition of the car's brakes they continued to accelerate. Juan guessed they were nearing forty-five miles an hour. The grade remained at a constant downward slope and the curve was still gentle, but if they got going much faster he feared that they wouldn't be able to slow when they hit the first sharp corner.

Three more terrorists jumped for the boxcar. Two landed on the roof. A third smashed into its side, his fingers clawing at the edge of the roof to keep himself from falling off.

One of the gunmen caromed into Juan when he landed, grabbed him tight, and slammed a hardened fist deep into the Chairman's kidney. Cabrillo's grunt at the staggering pain drove the man into a frenzy. He fired two more punches, grinding his knuckles into Cabrillo's flesh with each impact. Juan then felt his second FN Five-seveN being pulled from its holster. He shifted violently just as the man fired at his spine. The bullet singed the cloth of Cabrillo's shirt and hit the second terrorist in the throat. Blood fountained from the wound in time to the man's wildly beating heart.

The sight of his comrade's life pumping from his body might have distracted the gunman, but it held no sway over Cabrillo. Juan yanked his pistol free from the man's slack grip, stepped back a pace, and put two through his heart.

Both bodies hit the roof at the same instant.

"Juan? Juan? Come in."

Cabrillo reset his earpiece and adjusted the mic so he could communicate. "Yeah."

"We need brakes," Linc was shouting. "Now."

Juan looked forward. They were coming out of the turn, and the tracks dipped for a hundred yards before another, sharper bend to the right. He ran for the brake wheel and was nearly there when the terrorist who he thought had a broken back threw out an arm and tripped him. Cabrillo went sprawling and didn't have time to recover before the guy was on him, throwing punches with abandon. There was no power behind the shots, but all Juan could do was defend himself while the train hurtled for the corner.

He felt the sudden dip in the line and knew he had seconds. He tucked his legs to his chest, managing to plant his feet on the terrorist's chest, and in a judo move threw him over his head. The guy crashed down onto the roof on his back. Juan spun and, using his right hand to power his left elbow, drove it into the man's throat. The crushing of cartilage, sinew, and tissue was nauseating.

The instant Juan's fingers grasped the metal wheel, he started spinning it with everything he had. They were doing fifty on a corner meant to be taken at thirty. The brakes screamed and threw off showers of sparks as they entered the turn. Too late, Juan knew. Way too late.

The centrifugal force made the boxcar light on its outside wheels, and despite its massive weight they started losing contact with the rails. Juan cranked the brake wheel until it was locked tight. Behind him, the Pig's engine roared with the flood of nitrous oxide Linc had dumped into the cylinders, and rubber smeared off the deflated tires when they spun against the steel tracks. The freight car's outside wheels bumped and lifted, bumped and lifted, gaining centimeters with each judder. He wished there was some way he could communicate to the men and women inside the car. Their weight could make all the difference.

Inspiration born of desperation made Juan snatch up one of the terrorist's AK-47s and step to the outside edge of the car. The valley stretched below him seemingly forever. He aimed along the length of the train and loosened a full magazine. The bullets hit the steel flank at such an angle that they all ricocheted off into space, but the din inside was enough to frighten the prisoners over to the opposite side of the car above the bouncing wheels.

Their weight cemented the train back to the tracks.

The boxcar shot out of the turn and onto another gentle stretch of line. Juan shook his head to clear it and was about to sit down to give his body a rest when Mark's panicked voice exploded in his ears. "Take off the brake! Hurry!"

Cabrillo started turning the wheel to take pressure off the pads and chanced a look behind them. The road was no longer visible, the truck loaded with flying terrorists out of the picture at least for now, but farther up the line, barreling down the tracks, was another truck that had been modified to run on the rails. Unburdened by fourteen tons of train car and people, it came toward them at breakneck speed. Over its cab, Juan could see more men eager for the fight, and even at this distance he could tell they were armed with rocket-propelled grenades.

The Pig's windshield was so badly cracked, it wouldn't hold up to autofire, so he had no illusions what an RPG would do.

Linc had the transmission back in reverse, forgoing the low-range gears for the higher ones in hopes that the truck's power and the rolling stock's momentum would be enough to buy them some time. So long as they continued to sway through the gentle bends, the terrorists couldn't take a shot.

"When's our next tight turn?" Juan asked. He knew Mark had a scrolling map going on his laptop slaved to the Pig's GPS tracker.

"Two miles."

"Missiles?"

"Only one."

"Keep it. I've got an idea."

Juan raced aft, leaping from the train car onto the Pig's roof. Linda had replaced Greg Chaffee on the M60. Chaffee was sitting down in the cargo area with Alana and Fodl. He looked spent. "The instructors at the Farm would be proud, especially . . ." Juan mentioned the name of a legendary staffer at the CIA's training center, a name known only to those who'd gone through it.

Chaffee's eyes widened. "You're . . . ?"

"Retired."

Juan popped the hinge pins from one of the cabinets built into the inside wall of the Pig. The door was three feet square and weighed about sixty pounds. He passed it up through the hatch with Linda's help and then crawled onto the Pig's cab. His timing didn't necessarily have to be that good, but his luck had to hold. The train-truck was a quarter mile distant, gaining fast. Someone on it spotted Cabrillo out in the open and fired with his AK. Juan hauled up the metal door, using it like a screen, and bullets pinged off it like lead rain, their kinetic energy like sledgehammer blows.

The Pig went into another shallow curve, just enough for their pursuers to lose sight of them. Juan slid the sheet steel down along the retreating truck's nearly vertical windshield and let go.

The metal plate hit the outside track with a ringing crash and slid for several long seconds before its lip caught a tie and it spun to a stop. It came to rest across one of the rails.

Thirty seconds later, the truck showed itself from around the corner. It had to be doing sixty miles an hour. This time the Pig was too tempting a target for the men with the RPGs, and several made ready to let fly.

TWENTY-FOUR

THE DRIVER OF THE HYBRID TRAIN-TRUCK HAD JUST seconds to react, and in saving his life he saved Cabrillo and the others. He spotted the piece of sheet steel sitting on the track and recognized immediately that hitting it would cause a derailment. Stomping the brakes, he yanked a lever on the floor next to his seat. Hydraulics raised the train wheels that sat just inside the truck's regular tires, and as the wheels tucked under the chassis the outside tires made contact with the railroad ties.

Between the brutal deceleration and the staccato impact of running over the raised ties, the gunmen leaning over the cab readying their RPGs had no chance to accurately fire. Rocket contrails arrowed away from the truck in every direction—skyward, where they corkscrewed like giant fireworks, or into the valley below, where they detonated harmlessly in the desert.

The truck bounced over the metal plate, and once they were clear the quick-thinking driver had to slow even further in order to mate the steel train wheels with the track once again.

Cabrillo's idea had gained them only a half mile or so, not the outcome he had hoped. The next tight corner was coming up, and he had to return to the brake wheel. He climbed over the back of the Pig, nearly gagging at the smell of burning rubber from the shredded tires. They were at forty miles an hour again, and the wind made leaping up to the boxcar a tricky maneuver. Below him, he could see the darkened ties blur by in the tight gap between the Pig and her ponderous charge.

The track rose slightly as they approached the turn, helping to slow the convoy, but it would quickly fall away again, and their speed was still too great to negotiate the bend. The uneven railbed had rattled the car so much that the bodies of the two terrorists had vanished over the side of the train. Only the corpse of the man whose throat Cabrillo had crushed lay where he'd left it.

The car crested the rise and, despite the Pig's awesome power, the train picked up more speed.

Juan stepped past the dead man's inert form and was reaching for the wheel when the terrorist lunged for him. Too late, Cabrillo remembered the man he had killed had been wearing a blue kaffiyeh, and this man's head was swathed in a red one. He remembered the three men leaping from the truck and how one hadn't seemed to make it. He had clambered aboard when Juan had been back in the Pig and had assumed the dead man's position.

Those thoughts flashed through his mind in less time than it takes to blink but time enough for his legs to be wrapped up and his body to be dragged down. He hit hard, unable to cushion the impact. It was when the terrorist pressed his weight against Juan's thighs that another realization hit him. His attacker was huge, easily outweighing him by fifty pounds.

Juan went for his remaining pistol. The fanatic saw him move and clamped a hand over Cabrillo's. Juan tore his hand free and tried to twist away. Ahead of the boxcar, the turn loomed closer and closer.

"If you don't let me go," he cried in desperation, "we both die."

"Then we both die," the man snarled, crashing an elbow into the back of Juan's leg. He seemed to have grasped the situation and was content to keep Cabrillo pinned on his stomach until the out-of-control train finished them both.

Juan torqued his body around so the tendons in his back screamed in protest, and he put everything he had into a punch that connected with his attacker's jaw at the point it attached to his skull. There was a sickening pop as his jaw dislocated, and for a fleeting moment Juan had the other guy dazed. Wriggling and kicking, Juan threw off the man's deadweight and landed another blow in the exact same spot. The Arab roared at the pain. Juan scrambled to his feet and grabbed the brake wheel, spinning it furiously.

He managed only a couple of revolutions before the guy had him in a choke hold. Juan bent his knees as soon as he felt the thick arm over his neck and then kicked upward, planting a foot on the wheel and kicking again. He went up and over the terrorist's back, breaking the grip and landing behind him. The giant towered a head taller than Cabrillo, so when the man turned Juan had to punch up to deliver a third blow to the jaw. This time, the bone snapped.

Blinded by pain, the man tried to get Cabrillo into a bear hug. Juan ducked below the outstretched arms, pounded the back of his fist into the man's groin, and went back to the wheel, knowing he had no time. He gained two more turns, forcing the overheated pads tighter against the wheels.

He sensed more than heard the next attack and had his pistol out before he turned. As his hand extended, his attacker clamped it under his arm, wrenching it up so that Juan was suddenly on his toes. The colossus brought an elbow down on Juan's shoulder, trying to break his collarbone. Juan shrugged before the blow hit and he took the impact on the socket joint rather than the vulnerable clavicle.

His attacker leered, knowing even the glancing blow was agonizing. Juan sagged in the man's grip, kicking up a leg and knee while fumbling behind his back. There were two straps that he used to keep his leg in place when he was going into combat, and his fingers deftly unhooked them. He pulled the prosthesis off his stump and swung it like a club. The steel toe of his boot glanced off the corner of the man's eye, tearing open enough skin to fill the socket with blood. The blow wasn't all that powerful, but coming from such an unexpected quarter it had the element of surprise.

Cabrillo's backhand follow-through hit him in the face again, loosening teeth, and also loosening his viselike grip on Juan's arm. When he tried to yank his arm free, his pistol was stripped from his fingers and clattered onto the roof, so he swung the leg again. The blow staggered his opponent, and Juan didn't waste a second. After so many years of having only one leg, his superior balance allowed him to hop after the man, swinging the artificial limb like a logger would an ax.

Left, right, left, right, reversing his grip with each blow. He bought himself just enough distance to release two safeties built into the leg and to press a trigger integrated into the ankle. There was a stubby .44-caliber single-shot pistol—little more than a barrel and firing pin—that fired through the prosthesis's heel. The Magic Shop's last refinement to Juan's combat leg had saved him on more than one occasion, and when it discharged he knew it had saved him again. The heavy bullet hit the terrorist's center mass and blew him over the side of the car as limp as a rag doll.

The train was just entering the turn by the time the Chairman applied the full brakes, and as before the timing had been cut so finely that the car's outside wheels started to skip off the rail. Someone inside the compartment must have understood the situation, because suddenly the wheels smacked down again and stayed there. They had used their mass as a counterweight to keep the rolling stock stable.

Cabrillo looked back to see the terrorists' train-truck crest the rise they had flashed over moments earlier. Smoke puffed from under the Pig's cab, and the sound of autofire reached the Chairman an instant later. Mark Murphy had locked the Pig's targeting computer on the rise and waited for their hunters to show themselves.

A stream of 7.62mm rounds raked the unarmored front of the pursuit vehicle. The windshield dissolved, flaying open the skin as shards were blown into the cab. The radiator was punctured a half dozen times. An eruption of steam from the grille enveloped the truck in a scalding cloud, and bullets found their way into the engine compartment. The vulnerable distributor was shredded, killing power to the engine, and one round severed the hydraulic line that kept the train wheels in the extended position.

The truck came down off its second set of wheels so hard and so fast that the driver couldn't react. The tires slammed into a railroad tie, lifting the rear of the vehicle high enough to throw two of the men in the cargo bed over the roof of the cab and onto the rail line. They vanished under the truck.

With its front suspension broken, the cab settled heavily into the ballast stones, and the oddball vehicle came to a complete stop in a haze of steam and dust.

Cabrillo whooped at the sight of their vanquished foe splayed across the tracks.

A deep blast echoed off the valley walls.

Air horn blaring, the diesel-electric locomotive that Juan was certain wouldn't be able to follow them came over the small rise like a rampaging monster. It towered fifteen feet above the railbed and tipped the scales at more than a hundred tons. The smoke blowing from its exhaust was a greasy black, testimony to its poor maintenance, but the engine was more than up to the challenge of chasing down the fleeing prisoners.

A couple of the luckier men in the back of the train-truck leapt free before the locomotive smashed into the rear of the disabled vehicle. It came apart as if it had been packed with explosives. Sheet metal, engine parts, and the chassis burst from the collision, winging away as though they weighed nothing. The ruptured gas tank splashed flaming fuel into the mix so it looked like the train was charging through an inferno.

And then it was clear. The truck had been reduced to scrap metal and contemptuously shoved aside.

Juan spat a four-letter expletive, and started easing off the brake, deadly corner or no deadly corner.

From the side of the Pig, an arrow lanced out riding a fiery tail. Mark had fired their last missile in a snap shot. Juan held his breath as it ate the distance to the locomotive. The rocket connected an instant later. The resulting explosion was many times that of the impact with the truck. The engine was wreathed in fire, and the blast shook the very air. The locomotive looked like a meteor hurtling down the tracks, with flame and smoke boiling off its hide.

But for all its fury, the missile made no difference on the two-hundred-thousand-pound behemoth. It shook off the blast like a battle tank hit with a pellet gun and kept charging after the Pig.

Their little caravan was once again picking up speed, yet it was no match for the diesel-electric engine. It was bearing down on them at twice their velocity. For a fleeting second, Cabrillo considered jumping clear. But the idea was dismissed before it had fully formed. He would never abandon his shipmates to save his own skin.

The locomotive was fifty yards from the Pig, the flames all but blown out. There was a smoldering crater low on the engine cover and some blackened paint. Other than that, there was no visible evidence the four-pound shaped charge from their surface-to-surface missile had done anything at all.

However, what Juan couldn't see under the front of the locomotive, where the leading wheel truck was secured to the steel frame, was that the mounting pins had taken a direct hit from the jet of searing plasma produced by the warhead. The train hit one more jarring bump in the old rails and the pins failed entirely. The lead truck for the four front wheels derailed, the hardened wheels splintering the thick ties and peeling sections of track off their supports.

With its front end no longer held in by the rails, the locomotive broke free entirely, tipping in slow motion until it crashed onto its side. The added friction from plowing up ballast stones and yanking dozens of ties from the earth weren't enough to check its awesome momentum. Even in its death throes, it was going to collide with the Pig.

It was twenty feet from them, coming on as strong as ever. Linc had to have had his foot to the floor in a last-ditch effort to set them free. The Pig and boxcar continued to sweep through the turn, barely clinging to the tracks as they curved around the mountain.

Without the tracks to guide it, the locomotive kept going straight, driven by its massive weight and the speed it had built chasing its quarry. It passed no more than a yard in front of the Pig as it careened toward the edge of the steep valley. There were no guardrails, nothing to keep it on the man-made rail line. Its nose tore a wedge out of the ground when it reached the lip of the precipice and sent a shower of gravel pattering down the hillside, and then it barrel-rolled over.

Low down in the Pig's cab, Linc and Mark could no longer see it. But from his vantage high on the boxcar's roof, where he was already tightening the brakes again, Cabrillo watched the locomotive tumble down the hill, gaining speed with each revolution. Its huge belly tank split open, and fuel ignited off the hot manifolds. The resulting explosion and pall of dust obscured its final moments before it crashed into the rocky valley floor.

The freight car went around the last of the corner on its outside wheels only, at such an angle that Juan thought it would never recover. But somehow the plucky old antique finished the curve and flopped back onto the rails. Juan sagged against the brake wheel, catching his breath for a moment before strapping his artificial limb back on his stump.

He estimated there were only another ten or so miles to the coaling station and the dock where the *Oregon* would be waiting, and they were home free.

The only thing he didn't know, and couldn't understand, was what had happened to the Mi-8 helicopter that he was certain he'd heard before they'd escaped the mine depot. The tangos hadn't tried coming after them with it, which to Cabrillo made no sense. True, a cargo chopper wasn't the most stable platform to mount an assault, but considering the lengths the terrorists had gone to in order to stop them he would have thought they'd have launched the helo at them, too.

For the next five minutes, the train eased around several smooth turns, each so gentle that Juan barely had to work the brakes. He was just switching comm frequencies to patch through to Max aboard ship when they rounded another bend that had hidden his view of the tracks ahead.

His blood went cold.

The rail line left the relative safety of the mountain's flank and angled off over the valley across a bridge straight out of the Old West. It resembled a section of a wooden roller coaster and towered a hundred or more feet off the valley floor, an intricate lattice of timber beams bleached white by decades of sun and wind. And at its base, its rotors still turning at idle, sat the Mi-8.

Juan didn't need to see exactly what the men moving gingerly along the framework were doing to know they were planting explosives to blow the bridge to hell.

TWENTY-FIVE

WHEN THE PHONE WAS FINALLY ANSWERED, Abdullah, the commander of the terror camp they irreverently referred to as East Gitmo, wasn't sure if he should be afraid or relieved.

"Go," a voice answered, a voice that in just one word conveyed a malevolence that was dredged up from a dank well which contained normal men's souls.

There was no need for Abdullah to identify himself. Only a handful of people had the number to this particular satellite phone. He hated to think the equipment was made by the cursed Israelis, but the phones were one hundred percent secure. "I need to speak with him."

"He is busy. Speak to me."

"This is urgent," Abdullah insisted but vowed he wouldn't press further if he was rebuffed. In the background, he could hear a ship's horn and the merry clanging of a buoy's bell. Other than those noises, his response was silence. He honored his promise to himself. "Very well. Tell the Imam that the prisoners are attempting to escape."

Abdullah didn't know the details himself, so he kept his briefing vague. "It appears they overpowered the guards and stole one of the small trucks designed to ride on the old rail line as well as a boxcar." Again, the man on the other end of the call said nothing. Abdullah plowed on. "Attempts to stop them at the mine failed, and a few trainees from the camp haven't been able to stop them either. I dispatched some of our elite forces in the helicopter. They are going to blow up the trestle bridge. That way, we are certain to get them all."

The terrorist commander swallowed audibly. "I, er, thought that with the information we learned from the American archaeologist our presence here is no longer necessary. We now know that our belief that the original Suleiman Al-Jama's hidden base was in this valley, to the south of the "black that burns," as the legend goes, is wrong. Al-Jama and the *Saqr* based out of another old riverbed in Tunisia. The men we sent there should find it anytime now."

Again, all he could hear was the buoy clanging and an occasional blast of an air horn.

"Where are you?" Abdullah asked impetuously.

"None of your concern. Continue."

"Well, since we no longer need the pretext of reopening the coal mine, the burning black we mistook for the legendary sign, I figured blowing up the bridge was the best course of action. Two for the price of one, as it were. We kill all of the escapees and begin to dismantle our operation here."

"How many of our elite forces remain there?"

"About fifty," Abdullah answered at once.

"Do not risk those fighters on something as trivial as prisoners. Send more of the less trained men, if you must. Tell them that to martyr themselves on this mission will find them in Allah's special graces in Paradise. The Imam so decrees."

Abdullah thought better of explaining that there wasn't time to withdraw their crack troops from the bridge. Instead, he asked, "What about the woman Secretary?"

"Helicopters should be arriving there in about thirty minutes. One of them has orders to take charge of her. Your primary concern is the prisoners' deaths and making certain that our forces in Tripoli are at full strength. There will be legitimate security personnel at the gathering who they will have to overcome to gain entrance to the main hall. Once inside, of course, the targeted government officials aren't armed. It will be a glorious bloodletting, and the end of this foolish bid for peace."

That was the longest Abdullah had ever heard the other man speak. He believed in their cause as much as any of them, as much as Imam Al-Jama himself. But even he had to admit there were levels of fanaticism on which he wouldn't dwell.

He'd often listen to the boys they had recruited chatting among themselves, youths from slum and privilege alike. They made almost a game of thinking up sadistic tortures for the enemies of Islam as a way to bolster one another's confidence. He'd done the same years earlier, during the Lebanese civil war, when he had come of age. But secretly each knew, though never admitted, that it was only a diversion, a way to boast of your dedication and hatred. In the end, most were too petrified to even hold a pistol properly, and suicide vests had to be made as idiotproof as possible.

But not so the man on the other end of the phone. Abdullah knew he reveled in slicing off Westerners' heads with a scimitar that reportedly dated back to the Crusades. He had roasted alive Russian soldiers in the desolate mountains of Chechnya and helped string up the mutilated bodies of American soldiers in Baghdad. He had recruited his own nephew, a teenager with the mind of a two-year-old who liked nothing more than to separate grains of sand into precise piles of one hundred, to walk into a Sunni laundromat in Basra carrying forty pounds of explosives and nails in order to flame sectarian violence. Fifty women and girls perished in the blast, and the reprisal and counterreprisals claimed hundreds more.

Abdullah would do his duty, as he saw it, for Allah. His contact within the Imam's inner circle, Al-Jama's personal bodyguard, killed and maimed because he enjoyed it. The open secret within Al-Jama's organization was that the man didn't even practice Islam. Though born a Muslim, he never prayed, never fasted during Ramadan, and ignored all the faith's dietary laws.

Why the Imam allowed such an abomination had been the subject of debate among senior commanders like Abdullah, until word of such discussions reached Al-Jama's ear. Two days later, the four who had questioned the Imam's choice of top lieutenant had their tongues cut out, their eyes plucked from their heads, their noses and fingertips removed, and their eardrums punctured.

The meaning had been clear. By talking about the man behind his back, they had shown they had no sense, so they would forevermore have no senses either.

"The Imam's will be done, peace be upon him," Abdullah said hastily when he realized he should have replied. The line was already dead.

● ● ●

"LINDA, GET YOUR BUTT up here with the M60," Juan shouted over the radio. "And as much ammo as you can carry. Mark, I need you to separate the Pig from the boxcar."

"What?" cried Murphy. "Why?"

"You can't go fast enough backward."

Linc came over the tactical net. "I thought our problem was slowing down this crazy caravan."

"Not anymore."

Seconds later, the .30-caliber machine gun from the Pig's roof cupola landed with a thud on the railcar's tarry roof. Cabrillo rushed back to give Linda a hand with the unwieldy weapon. Behind her Alana Shepard stood with an ammo belt slung around her neck like some deadly piece of jewelry. At her feet were two more boxes of rounds. She handed up the boxes, and he helped boost her up.

"Trying to earn that fedora, I see." Juan smiled.

Spying the bridge for the first time, Linda Ross understood why the Chairman needed the heavy firepower. As soon as she reached the front of the car, she extended the M60's stumpy bipod legs and was lying behind the weapon, ready for him to feed the first belt into the gun. With Alana pulling a second hundred-round belt from one of the boxes, Juan loaded the M60 and slammed the receiver closed. Linda racked back on the bolt and let fly.

The bridge was well beyond the weapon's effective range, but even random shots pattering against the wooden trestle would force the terrorists to find cover and hopefully buy them the time they needed.

Her whole body shook as if she were holding on to a live electric cable, and a tongue of flame jetted a foot from the muzzle. Watching the string of tracers arcing across the distance, she raised the barrel until the bead of phosphorus-tipped rounds found their mark. At this range, all Juan could see were small explosions of dust kicked off the blanched timbers when the rounds bored in. It took nearly a third of the first belt before the men working under the railbed realized what was happening. None had been hit, as far as they could tell, but soon they were all scrambling to hide themselves in the tangle of crossbeams.

Using controlled bursts to keep the barrel from overheating, Linda kept the men pinned, getting one lucky shot that yanked a terrorist off the delicate trestle. His body plummeted from the bridge, falling soundlessly and seemingly in slow motion, until he slammed into a beam and cartwheeled earthward. He hit the ground in a silent puff of dust that drifted lazily on the breeze.

Mark Murphy could hear the chattering .30-cal but had no idea what they were firing at. He had unhooked himself from his safety straps, climbed up and out of the Pig, and was now crouched over the rear bumper, trying not to notice the ties blurring under his feet.

He had woven a tow cable back and forth around the bumper and the railcar's coupling to keep them attached. Linc was accelerating slightly faster than the car was rolling down the tracks, so there was no tension on the line. Using a large pair of bolt cutters, he attacked the braided steel, snipping at it as fast as he could. If the car started pulling away from the Pig, the tension would snap the cable, and Mark's legs would most likely be taken off at the knees.

They started going through a curve. Murph noticed Linda's machine gun had gone silent and realized the hills were blocking her aim. The car also started picking up speed. The thin cable stretched taut, and braids began to part, curling off the line like silver smoke.

"Linc, goose it a little," Mark called, and Lincoln gave the Pig more gas.

As soon as the tension was off, Mark worked at it again, heaving on the big cutters with everything he had.

"When you're through the last cable," Juan shouted into the radio, "jump onto the coupling so we don't lose the time it'll take you to climb aboard the Pig."

Mark swallowed hard, not sure what he liked less—the prospect of clinging to the rusted coupling or the thought of what the Chairman knew about their situation to ask him to do it in the first place.

"You hear that, Linc," Cabrillo continued. "As soon as Mark's done, turn the Pig around and shove this boxcar with everything you've got. Hear me?"

"I'm through," Mark announced before the SEAL could respond.

In the Pig, Linc stood on the brakes, blowing off clouds of carbon dust from the nearly spent pads. He cranked the wheel as soon as he felt it safe enough. The tires hit the railroad ties with bone-jarring regularity, and the heavy truck grew light on one side. He rammed it into first before he'd come to a complete stop, kicking up twin sprays of ballast stones. The truck leapt after the runaway freight car, Linc aiming to put the wheels atop the rails once again. His vision blurred, and it felt like his molars were going to come loose from his jaw before he could center the Pig on the tracks.

Once the wheels were aligned, he chased down the car until the reinforced bumper kissed its coupling. He watched, amazed, as Mark Murphy planted one foot on the bumper and bent to strip off coils of towline from the Pig's forward winch and started to wrap it around the coupling to secure the two vehicles together. Linc had never doubted the kid's courage, but even he would have thought twice about the dangerous maneuver.

"Chairman," he called, "I'm around and pushing hard. Murph's tying us to the train car with the winch."

"Mark, have you run your calculations?" Cabrillo asked. He stood over the young weapons expert and watched him work.

Murph snapped the winch's hook around a couple of loops of cable and climbed up the Pig's windshield before turning to the Chairman and answering. "Yeah, just like you asked, I mathed it. The freight car's got enough buoyancy to hold us on the surface. The unknown is how fast water is going to fill it up."

"Max will just have to be quick with the *Oregon*'s derrick crane."

"Tell him he should switch from a lifting hook to the magnetic grapple."

Juan instantly saw the logic to Murph's suggestion. The big electromagnet wouldn't require crewmen to secure the crane to the freight car.

Behind him, the train must have cleared another hill because Linda opened up again with the M60. He caught whiffs of cordite smoke in the air as the railcar continued to accelerate. He turned. The bridge was still some distance away and looked as delicate as a railroad hobbyist's model. Under the hail of tracers arcing in toward the structure, the men setting the explosives hid behind the trestle supports again. At the speed the Pig was pushing the old freight car, they would be sweeping through another turn in seconds, and the terrorists would be free to finish their work.

Cabrillo went ashen under his tan. He knew with certainty that they weren't going to make it. The Pig snarled as it pushed the boxcar, but they were just too far away, and without a direct line of fire to keep the sappers pinned they would be ready to blow the bridge at about the same time the train hit the trestle.

He was just about to order Linc to stand on the brakes in the vain hope that they could unload the passengers and

272   CLIVE CUSSLER

make some sort of stand when movement on the far side of the bridge caught his eye. At first, he couldn't tell what he was seeing because the heavy timber supports obscured his view.

And then without warning the Corporation's glossy black McDonnell Douglas MD-520N helicopter roared over the bridge. With its ducted exhaust eliminating the need for a rear rotor, and by using every scrap of cover he could find, George "Gomez" Adams had achieved complete surprise.

The sound of the rotors and Adams's rebel yell filled Cabrillo's earpiece. The noise was quickly drowned out by the hammering of a heavy machine gun. A figure silhouetted in the chopper's open rear door had opened fire at near-point-blank range. The thick timber supports had stood for more than a century, baking and curing in the relentless desert heat until they were as hard as iron. And yet chunks of wood exploded off the bridge under the relentless fire, leaving behind raw white wounds and a steady rain of dust and sand. Where the bullets met flesh, the damage was much, much worse.

"About time you showed up," Juan radioed.

"Sorry about the dramatic entrance," Gomez Adams replied. "Headwind the whole way here."

"Keep them pinned on the bridge until we cross, then fly cover for us until we hit the dock." Juan changed frequencies. "Max, you there?"

"Sure am," Max said breezily as if he didn't have a care in the world, which showed how worried he really was.

"What's your ETA?"

"We'll be alongside the dock about two minutes before you get here. Just so you know, it's a floating pier, and at the speed you're doing, you're going to hit the rail bumpers at the end—you're going to kill everyone in the boxcar."

"That's your idea of an FYI? You have a plan?"

"Of course. We've got it handled."

"All right," Juan said, trusting his second-in-command implicitly. With so much happening on and around the train, he would leave the details to Hanley.

They were barreling through the turn now. The engineers who'd built the line had carved a narrow shelf into the side of the hill, barely wide enough for the freight car. He imagined that when they normally took the big locomotive through the tight curve, they did so at a snail's pace. Living rock whizzed by the edge of the car with less than a hand span's clearance.

The tight tolerances saved their lives.

The train's outside wheels lifted off the track, and the top edge of the car slammed into the blasted-stone wall, gouging out a deep rent in the rock and showering Cabrillo with chips as sharp as glass shards. The impact forced the car's wheels back onto the rail, and for a moment they held before the incredible centrifugal forces acting on them lifted them up again. Again, the top edge of the car tore into the rock, but this time Juan turned so it was his back and not his exposed face blasted by debris.

"Chairman?" There was something in Franklin Lincoln's voice that Cabrillo had never heard. Fear.

"Don't you dare slow down now!" Juan said. Below him he could hear their passengers' screams of panic. As bad as it was riding on top of the car, he couldn't imagine what they were experiencing in the pitch-darkness inside.

Twice more, they hit the rock, before the turn started to lose its tight radius and the wheels stayed firmly planted on the hot iron rails. That was the last curve before they hit the bridge. Before them was a straight shot down a gentle defile, then across the trestle. A flash of light blazed off the binoculars of an observer in the valley below the bridge. Juan could almost sense the man's thoughts despite the distance. Seconds later, an order had to have been given, because the men rigging the bridge with explosives started swarming down the trestle, ignoring the blistering fire from Gomez Adams in the MD-520N.

Cabrillo moved to the leading edge next to where Linda and Alana crouched behind the M60.

"I know I'm dating myself," Linda said, her face a little pale under its dusting of freckles, "but that's what I call an E-ticket ride. Makes the Matterhorn feel tame."

She no longer had an angle to fire at the men, but Adams was making their retreat hell.

"There's nothing more we can do," Juan shouted over the roar of wind filling his ears. They were pushing sixty miles per hour, and the rush of wind over the carriage threatened to blow them off if they rose above a crouch. "Let's get back to the Pig."

He hefted the big gun, with its necklace of shining brass shells dangling from the receiver, so Linda and Alana could crawl back to the rear of the car together. They lowered themselves down onto the Pig's cab and then vanished through the open hatch. Cabrillo paused for a moment, forcing his eyes to slits to look up the tracks. Adams ducked and weaved in the chopper, dancing away from enemy fire, while his door gunner—Cabrillo thought he recognized the beefy form of Jerry Pulaski—peppered the bridge supports whenever the helo was steady enough to shoot.

The tone of wheel against rail suddenly changed. They were on the first section of the bridge. A quick glance over the side of the car confirmed that the ground was beginning to recede from under them.

The explosion came farther along the bridge's length, on the valley floor near one of the trestle supports. Smoke and flame climbed the wooden members, mushrooming outward and upward like a deadly bloom. Cabrillo threw himself flat as the train barreled through the pulsing surge of fire and emerged on the other side with no more damage than some singed paint.

Behind them the blast had weakened the bridge's lattice framework, but Linda's and then Adams's sniping had prevented the terrorists from properly rigging the structure. The supports stood firm for a solid ten seconds after the train had rushed past, allowing them to get nearly to the end of the long span before the structure started to collapse. The great timbers fell in on themselves, the valley choking with dust thick enough to obscure the waiting Mi-8 helicopter and the tiny figures of running terrorists.

The bridge fell like dominoes, the steel rails sagging as though they had no more strength than piano wire. Linc had to have seen what was happening behind the Pig in the wing mirrors, because the engine beat changed when he flooded the cylinders with nitrous oxide.

Wood and iron tumbled in a rolling avalanche that chased after the fleeing boxcar. Cabrillo watched awestruck as the bridge vanished in their wake. He should have felt fear, but his fate wasn't in his hands, so he saw the spectacle with almost clinical detachment. And even as the Pig gained more speed, so, too, did the structure's incredible failure. A hundred feet behind their rear bumper, the rails quivered and then vanished into the boiling maelstrom of dust.

He didn't dare look ahead to see how much farther they had to travel. It was better, he thought fleetingly, not to know.

Just as the rails started to dip under them, the hollow sound of air rushing below the carriage changed once again and thick wooden ties appeared under the line. They had made it just as the last of the bridge crumpled into the valley, rending itself apart so that nothing showed above the billowing debris.

Cabrillo pumped his fist, shouting at the top of his lungs, and nearly lost his footing in his excitement. "That was a hell of a piece of driving," he called to Linc. "Is everyone okay?"

"We're all good," Lincoln replied.

There was something in his voice, something Cabrillo didn't like. "What is it, big man?"

"I tore the guts out of the transmission the last time I hit the nitro. I'm looking down the tracks in the mirror and see we're laying one hell of an oil slick."

It was only after it was reported that Juan noticed he couldn't hear the motor's aggressive growl. Without gears, there was no reason to leave the engine running.

"Mark says the rest of the line is pretty gentle, but . . ." He let his voice trail off.

"And let me guess," Juan added, "our brakes are shot, too."

"I've got my foot pressed to the floorboards, for whatever good it'll do us."

Juan looked in the direction they were heading. The ocean was a slag-gray shimmer in the distance. The train tracks' terminus was hidden in a fold of land, though he estimated they had only a few more miles to go. He also agreed with Mark Murphy's assertion that the rest of the way was a gentle glide down to the sea. He could only hope that whatever reception Max had planned would work because when he clamped on the boxcar's brakes he could tell they, like the Pig's, were worn down to nothing.

"Max, do you read me?" he said into his mic.

"Loud and clear."

"Where are you?"

"We're in position and ready to pick you up."

"Any word on the choppers of the Libyan strike team?"

"No. I suspect they'll come in from the south, so we'll never see them. And more important, they'll never see us."

"As soon as you have us with the magnet, I want Eric to make best possible speed into international waters."

"Relax, Juan. Everything's ready. Doc Huxley and her people have set up the forward hold with cots, blankets, and plenty of IV drips. The cooking staff's been whipping up enough food to feed the people you've found, and I've got every weapons system on the ship locked and loaded in case someone wants to take them back."

"Okay. Okay, I get it. We'll be there in about three minutes."

The last section of the rail line came out of the mountains through a valley that ran right to the sea. The Corporation people, along with Alana, Greg Chaffee, and their new Libyan charge, Fodl, were strapped into the Pig, while the rest of the refugees in the boxcar had been given a shouted warning to brace themselves.

The old coaling station was a run-down ruin, little more than the metal framework of a couple of buildings with bits of wood still somehow clinging to their sides. The cranes that once filled freighters with coal were long gone, and the desert had hidden where the anthracite had once been mounded in the lee of a cliff.

The *Oregon* loomed over the newly installed floating dock. Her main cargo derrick was swung over into position, and the large electromagnet dangled less than twenty feet over the pier.

Juan's pride usually swelled a bit whenever he saw his creation, but this time his mind was on the speed the train was making as it raced for the station. He fought the urge to glance at the speedometer but guessed they were pushing seventy. He'd expected Max would have laid down some sort of barrier foam to slow the train, but he saw nothing on the tracks. Then he realized the dock was much lower in the water than he'd first thought. In fact, the far end of it was completely submerged.

He laughed aloud when the hurtling train left its old railbed and started along the pier. Max had holed the large interlocked plastic pods that made up the dock, most likely with the *Oregon*'s Gatling gun. The pier's own weight started it sinking, and as the boxcar pressed down the pier dipped deeper.

Two curling sheets of water peeled off the car's leading edge, and the ocean absorbed the train's momentum so smoothly that no one in the Pig felt their seat-belt tensioners react. Two-thirds the way down the pier, the Pig was down to twenty miles per hour, and the water was well above its lugged tires.

The boxcar was barely moving when it tipped off the edge of the pier, dragging the truck with it. The car bobbed in the water for only a few seconds before the magnet swooped over them, and when current was applied it stuck fast. Moments later, the old railcar, with the Pig dangling from its rear coupling, was pulled from the sea. Juan knew Max Hanley himself had to be at the controls because the operator had estimated the train's center of gravity perfectly.

With water pouring from the car, they were swung over the *Oregon*'s rail and set onto the deck. Juan threw open his door the instant the tires touched the deck plate. A crewman was standing by with an oxyacetylene cutting torch and was already slicing through the cables that bound the Pig to the boxcar. Juan rushed past him and nearly collided with Dr. Huxley in his haste to open the train's sliding door. With her were several teams of orderlies with gurneys at the ready.

"Looks like you don't think I've been earning my pay keeping your rogues patched up, eh?" she said. "You had to bring a train car full of patients for me."

Deep below his feet, Juan could feel the magnetohydrodynamics ramping up. "What else do you give a doctor as a gift after a little relaxing shore leave?"

Juan pulled back on the sliding door and a fresh cascade of water poured onto the deck. Then from the gloomy interior emerged the first skeletal prisoner, owl-eyed and soaking wet.

"You're safe now," Juan said in Arabic. "You are all safe. But you must hurry, understand?"

Fodl joined him and Dr. Huxley an instant later, and together they cajoled the shell-shocked men and women out of the car. There were a few injuries, sprains mostly, but a couple of broken limbs as well. And one man who'd caught a bullet in the wrist from one of the terrorists Cabrillo had fought on the car's roof. As was his custom, Juan would more regret hurting these people further than take satisfaction in saving their lives.

He spotted Mark Murphy. The lanky weapons expert had his kit bag slung over one shoulder and a waterproof laptop case in his hand. He was heading for a hatchway that would lead him to his cabin. "Forget it, Mr. Murphy. As of this second, you and Mr. Stone are on a priority research job."

"Can't it wait until after I shower?"

"No. Now. I want to know everything there is to know about something called the Jewel of Jerusalem. Alana Shepard mentioned it may be buried with Suleiman Al-Jama but isn't really sure what it is."

"Sounds like a legend out of a trashy novel."

"It might just be. Find out. I want a report in an hour."

"Yes, boss," Mark said dejectedly, and shuffled away.

"Who are all these people?" Julia Huxley asked, passing a woman down to the waiting arms of an orderly.

"They were all in the upper levels of Libya's Foreign Ministry," Juan told her. "One of these poor souls should be the Minister himself."

"I don't understand. Why are they all prisoners?"

"Because unless I messed up my reasoning, the new Foreign Minister, the esteemed Ali Ghami, is Suleiman Al-Jama."

TWENTY-SIX

T HE HELICOPTERS PAINTED WITH LIBYAN MILITARY colors swarmed out of the empty wastes of the southern desert like enraged wasps. Four of the five Russian-made choppers were done in mottled earth-toned camouflage, while the other wore the drab gray of the Libyan Navy.

In his fifteen years with the CIA, Jim Kublicki never thought he would be an observer on a Libyan helo assault of a terrorist base camp. Ambassador Moon had arranged his presence on the attack with Minister Ghami personally. On the surface, the new level of cooperation out of Tripoli was amazing, but both Moon and Kublicki harbored their doubts. The chief among them was the result of the eyes-only report that had been delivered from Langley. Kublicki had no idea how operatives had penetrated Libyan airspace during the height of the search for the Secretary of State's plane, but somehow they had. The evidence they found led to the only conclusion possible: Her plane had been forced down before the crash—presumably, to remove the Secretary herself. Then the Boeing was intentionally slammed into a mountaintop.

The report also documented how a team of men in a chopper had landed at the crash site and deliberately tampered with the scene. The exact words from the document were "they tore through the wreckage like a twister through a trailer park."

The team from the National Transportation Safety Board had issued a secret and still-preliminary report backing up what Langley had said. Despite the best efforts of the terrorists, there were inconsistencies in the wreckage that could not be easily explained. When Moon had met with David Jewison of the NTSB and outlined the CIA report, he'd nodded, and said it was quite possible the plane had landed briefly before the crash.

When Kublicki had arrived at a remote air base outside of Tripoli where they were staging the assault, he'd met with the operation's leader, a Special Forces colonel named Hassad. He'd explained that the Libyan desert was dotted with hundreds of old training bases left over from the days when his government had allowed them sanctuary. In the few years since the government renounced terrorism, he and his men had destroyed most of the ones they knew of, but he admitted there were dozens more they did not.

Hassad sat in the right-hand seat next to their pilot, while Kublicki crammed his six-feet-six-inch frame into a folding jump seat immediately behind the cockpit. There was only a handful of men in the rear section of the utility chopper. The bulk of the assault force was in the other helicopters.

The Libyan colonel clamped a hand over his helmet's boom mic and leaned back. He had to raise his voice over the whopping thrum of the rotor blades. "We're landing in about a minute."

Kublicki was a little taken aback. "What? I thought we were going in after the assault."

"I don't know about you, Mr. Kublicki, but I want a piece of these people for myself." Hassad shot him a wolfish grin.

"I'm with you there, Colonel, but the uniform you lent me didn't come with a weapon."

The Libyan officer unsnapped the pistol at his waist and

handed it over butt first. "Just make sure that me giving you a sidearm doesn't make it into your report."

Kublicki smiled conspiratorially and popped the pistol's magazine to assure himself it was loaded. The narrow slit along the mag's length showed thirteen shiny brass cartridges. He rammed the clip home but wouldn't cock the pistol until they were on the ground.

From his low vantage strapped in behind the cockpit, Kublicki couldn't see through the windshield but knew they were about to land when his view of the sky was blocked by dust kicked up by the helicopter's powerful rotor wash. He hadn't been in a combat situation since the first Gulf War, but the combination of fear and exhilaration was a sensation he would never forget.

The craft settled on the ground, and Kublicki whipped off his safety belts. When he stood to peer over Hassad's shoulder, he saw the terrorist camp a good hundred yards away. Men in checkered kaffiyehs, brandishing AK-47s, were running toward them with abandon. He saw no sign of the soldiers from the other choppers in pursuit.

Fear began to wash away the exhilaration.

Hassad threw open his door and swung to the ground. He vanished from sight for a moment, and then the chopper's side door slammed back on its roller stop.

Kublicki blinked at the bright light flooding the hold.

The two men stared at each other for what to Kublicki felt like a long time but was only a few seconds. A current of understanding passed between them. The veteran CIA agent cocked the pistol and aimed it at the Libyan in one smooth motion. What had sounded like cries of fear from the gathering terrorists was actually exaltation, and it rose from a hundred throats.

Kublicki pulled the trigger four times before he realized the weapon hadn't fired. A gun barrel was jammed into his spine, and he sat frozen as Hassad reached across and yanked the pistol from his hand. "No firing pin." He repeated the phrase in Arabic, and the group of terrorists laughed in approval.

In the last seconds of life Jim Kublicki had remaining, he

promised himself he wouldn't go down without a fight. Ignoring the assault rifle pressed to his back, he launched himself out of the chopper, his hands going for Hassad's throat. To his credit, he got within a few inches of his target before the gunman behind him opened fire. A one-second-long burst from the AK stitched his back from kidney to shoulder blade. The kinetic energy drove him to the ground at Hassad's feet. The Libyan stood over him in the stunned silence that followed the attack. Rather than salute a valiant foe who'd fallen into an impossible ambush, Hassad spat on the corpse, turned on his heel, and walked away.

He found the camp commander, Abdullah, outside his tent. The two men greeted each other warmly. Hassad cut through the polite period of small talk that was so much a part of Muslim life and struck to the heart of the matter.

"Tell me of the escapees."

The two men were of similar rank within Al-Jama's terror cell, but Hassad had the more forceful personality.

"We got them."

"All of them? Ah, yes, I heard you were going to blow up the bridge. It worked, eh?"

"No," Abdullah said. "They got past. But they were going so fast when they hit the end of the dock that they sailed off the end."

"Someone saw this happen?"

"No, but it was only fifteen or so minutes after they cleared the bridge that our chopper reached the old coaling station. There was no sign of the prisoners on the quay, so they didn't get off, and they spotted the boxcar about two hundred yards from shore. Only the roof was above water, and it sank completely as they watched."

"Excellent." Hassad clapped him on the shoulder. "The Imam, peace be upon him, won't be pleased he couldn't witness our former Foreign Minister's death, but he will be relieved the escape was foiled."

"There is one thing," Abdullah said. "The reports from my men aren't precise, but it appears the prisoners might have had help."

"Help?"

"A single truck, carrying several men and perhaps a woman, attacked the camp at the same time the prisoners were starting to make their break."

"Who were these people?"

"No idea."

"Their vehicle?"

"Presumably, it sank with the boxcar. Like I said, the eye-witness accounts come from some of our rawest recruits, and it's possible they mistook one of our own trucks for another in their enthusiasm."

Hassad chuckled humorlessly. "I'm sure some of these kids see Mossad agents behind every rock and hill."

"After tomorrow's attack, when we move from here to our new base in the Sudan, at least half of them are going to be left behind. Those who show promise will come with us. The rest aren't worth the effort."

"Recruiting numbers has never been our problem. Recruiting quality, well, that is something else. Speaking of . . ."

"Ah, yes."

Abdullah said a few words to a hovering aide. A moment later, the subaltern came back with another of their men. Gone were the dust-caked and tattered camouflage utilities and sweaty headscarf. The man wore a new black uniform, with the cuffs of his pants bloused into glossy boots. His hair was neatly barbered and his face was carefully shaved. The leatherwork of his pistol belt shone brightly from hours of careful cleaning, and the rank pips on his shoulders glinted like gold.

While the recruits trained with AK-47s that had knocked around the terrorist world since before many of them had been born, the weapon this man carried at port arms was brand-new. There wasn't a scratch on the receiver or a nick in the polished wooden stock.

"Your credentials," Hassad barked.

The man shouldered his rifle smartly, and from a pocket on his upper arm produced a leather billfold. He snapped it open for inspection. Hassad looked at it carefully. The military identification had been made in the same office that produced the real ones by a sympathizer to the cause. Libya's military was riddled with them at every level, which was how they'd gotten the helicopters for today's operation and the Hind gunship they had used to disable Fiona Katamora's aircraft.

Opposite the ID was a pass authorizing the bearer to work the security detail for tomorrow's peace summit. It had been deemed too risky to try to get them from the issuing office, so these had been forged here at the camp. Hassad had friends in the Army who would be at the conference as part of the massive security force, and he'd studied their passes. What he saw before him was a flawless copy.

He handed back the papers, and asked, "What do you expect tomorrow?"

"To be martyred in the name of Islam and Suleiman Al-Jama."

"Do you believe you are worthy of such an honor?"

The answer was a moment in coming. "It is enough for me that the Imam believes I am worthy."

"Well said," Hassad remarked. "You and your compatriots are going to strike a blow against the West that will take them years to recover from, if ever. Imam Al-Jama has decreed they will no longer be allowed to dictate to us how we should live our lives. The corruption they spread with their television and movies, their music, and their democracy, will no longer be allowed. Soon we will see the beginning of the end for them. They will finally understand their way of life is not for us, and that it is Islam that will take over the world. This is the honor of which Al-Jama believes you are worthy."

"I will not let him down," the terrorist said, his voice firm, his eyes steady.

"You are dismissed," Hassad said, and turned back to Abdullah. "Very well done, my old friend."

"The military training was relatively easy," the commander said. "Keeping them true to the cause without making them appear like wild-eyed fanatics was the difficult part."

Both men knew that countless suicide attacks had been thwarted because the perpetrators looked so nervous and out of place that even untrained civilians knew what was about to occur. And the fifty men they were sending to Tripoli today would be surrounded by legitimate security forces on full alert for the very type of attack they were attempting. They had culled through hundreds of recruits from training camps and madrasas all over the Middle East to find the right men.

Hassad glanced at his watch. "In eighteen hours, it will be over. The American Secretary of State will be dead, and the palace hall will be awash in blood. The tide of peace will once again be pushed back, and in its absence we will continue to spread our way of life."

"As the original Suleiman Al-Jama wrote, 'When in the struggle to keep our faith from corruption we find our will slacking, our resolve waning, our strength ebbing, we must, at that moment, make the supreme effort, and the supreme sacrifice if necessary, to show our enemies that we will never be defeated.' "

"I prefer another line: 'They who do not submit to Islam are an affront to Allah and worthy only of our bullets.' "

"Soon they shall have them."

"Now, why don't you introduce me to the American woman. I have a little time before she needs to board the frigate for her date with destiny, but I would like to gaze upon her."

TWENTY-SEVEN

CABRILLO'S HOPE FOR A LONG BATH FOLLOWING HIS return to the *Oregon* was not meant to be. He allowed himself a quick shower only after all the prisoners had been made as comfortable as possible in the hold. He had been introduced to Libya's ex–Foreign Minister by Fodl, who'd been his deputy. As it was nearing noon, Juan had shown him in which direction Mecca lay relative to the ship so they could all pray for the first time since their incarceration.

He was dressing when Max Hanley knocked on his cabin door and entered without waiting. In tow were Eric Stone and Mark Murphy, who still wore his filthy uniform.

On seeing Cabrillo, he said, "Man, that is totally not fair."

"Privilege of rank," Juan replied airily, and finished tying a pair of black combat boots. "What do you have for me?"

"They apparently bought the trick with the sinking rail-car," Max said. "They sent out a chopper to investigate about fifteen minutes after you boarded. Mark's time estimation of it sinking was spot-on. They must have seen it seconds before it went under."

Eric cut in. "Then I swung the UAV back over the terrorist camp. Because of the altitude I had to maintain so they wouldn't hear it, the camera's resolution wasn't the best, but we have a pretty good idea of what was happening."

"And?"

"You were right," Max replied. "The flight of Libyan military choppers landed with no opposition. It looks like there were only a few men aboard any of them."

"Sounds like transport back out to me," Juan guessed.

"That's our read, too," Eric replied. "They're going to be moving more men than they can carry in that old Mi-8 you flew on from the crash scene."

"What's the capacity of the choppers?"

"Fifty at least."

"Hell of an assault force."

Mark said, "The target has to be the peace conference."

Eric Stone shook his head. "Never happen. The security is impenetrable. There is no way a terrorist is going to get within a mile of a single dignitary."

"They would if the Libyan government's in on it," Max countered.

"That's the million-dollar question. If Minister Ghami is Suleiman Al-Jama, does Qaddafi know it?"

"How could he not? He appointed him."

"Okay, say he does, Max. That still doesn't mean he knows what Al-Jama is planning."

"What difference does it make?" Hanley asked.

"Maybe none, but it's something we need to know."

"And how do we find out?"

"I'll get to that in a minute. Mark, is there any chance we can take out those choppers?"

"We'd need to launch another UAV," Eric said before Mark could answer. "The first drone's out of fuel, and I had to ditch it. Though not before taking this."

He handed Juan a grainy still photograph from the drone's video camera. Details were murky to say the least, but it looked like two armed men escorting a third person toward one of the helicopters.

"Is that Secretary Katamora?"

"Possibly. Factoring the height of a typical Libyan male and comparing the middle figure to them, the height is right, and the build certainly fits. The person's head is covered so we can't see hair, which would have been a dead giveaway—hers flows to the middle of her back."

"Best guess?"

"It's her, and by the time we turn around she's going to be long gone."

Juan frowned. He'd made a conscious decision to save the Libyan prisoners rather than wait out the terrorists. The balance of one life versus one hundred tipped the same way no matter who sat on the scales. But being so close and not getting her irked. "Okay, what about taking out the other choppers?" he said to get the meeting back on course, his eyes lingering on the picture.

"We could laze them from the second UAV so I can guarantee a missile hit, but we have to consider collateral damage if Secretary Katamora's there."

"Options?"

"Nail the choppers in flight if they come out over the ocean. But, again, we risk her life if she's a hostage aboard one of them."

"They'll stick to the desert anyway," Eric said.

Max cleared his throat. "Listen, why not pass on what we know to Overholt and let him tell the other delegates about the possibility of a massive attack?"

"We'll tell Lang," Juan replied, "but I don't want that information disseminated."

"Why the hell not?"

"Two reasons. One, if they know the attack is coming, they will call off the conference, and the chance to get these people in a room talking peace again is zilch. The conference has to proceed. Second, we have nothing concrete linking Ghami to Al-Jama. This is our one and only chance to expose him and his entire operation."

"You're risking a lot of important lives."

"Mine, for one," Mark said.

"I admit it's the biggest toss of the dice we've ever attempted, but I know it's worth it. Overholt will agree. He understands that if we can nail Al-Jama on the eve of the peace conference, it will give it such a boost that the delegates are certain to hammer out a comprehensive and lasting treaty. In one blow, we take out the second-most-wanted terrorist on the planet and guarantee lasting peace."

"Boy, Juan. I'm not sure. The prize is awesome, yes. But the price, you know . . ."

"Trust me."

Still uncertain, but never one to doubt the Chairman, Max asked, "So how is this going to work?"

"In a minute." He turned his attention to Murph and Stoney. "What did you two come up with?"

"There's not a whole lot out there that doesn't fall into the realm of fantasy."

"Hold it," Max interrupted. "What did you have them research?"

"Alana said there might be something called the Jewel of Jerusalem stashed in the original Suleiman Al-Jama's tomb. She was told about it by St. Julian Perlmutter. Even he wasn't sure what it was. What did you guys find?"

"You haven't given us much time on this, so our report is sketchy at best. There are two schools of thought. Well, three, if you include the vast majority of scholars who think the whole thing is baloney. Anyway, one school says the jewel is a cabochon ruby about the size of a softball with some words carved into it. People believe it may be Sura 115 from the Koran, a final chapter to the Muslim holy book that appears nowhere else because Muhammad believed it so perfect and so special that it could only be written on a flawless jewel."

"Any idea what it says?" Juan asked.

"Depends on which side of the radical line you stand. The nut jobs think it says they should kill infidels all the livelong day. Moderates ascribe to the idea that it promotes peace between Islam and Christianity."

"So no one knows."

"Exactly," Mark said skeptically. "Take any object, give it the ability to bring special knowledge or power, and, voilà, you've got yourself a legend that'll last for generations. Kinda like the Ark of the Covenant. Total bunko, but people still look for it today."

"Skip the commentary and stick to the story."

"Okay. They say that Saladin first brought the jewel to Jerusalem following his siege of the city in 1187 and that the stone was kept in a cedar box in a cave beneath the Dome of the Rock. The legend says that any man who dared gaze upon the stone went blind or mad, or both. Convenient, eh?

"So the stone sits in its underground vault until the Sixth Crusade in 1228. During this one, Frederick II of the Holy Roman Empire made a treaty with the ruler of Egypt that turned over control of all Jerusalem to the Christians, except the Dome of the Rock and the nearby Al-Aqsa Mosque. It was during this period that German mercenaries working for the Knights Templar stormed the Dome and stole the jewel."

"Why would Christian knights want an Islamic relic?"

"Because they thought it was something else. Remember, I said there were two schools of thought. This is where their paths cross. You see, the Templars believed the Jewel of Jerusalem wasn't a ruby at all. They thought it was a pendant fashioned a thousand years earlier for a man named Didymus, or Judas Tau'ma."

"Never heard of him," Max grumbled.

Eric said, "You know him better as Doubting Thomas, one of Christ's twelve Apostles."

"And this pendant?" Juan prompted.

"As you know, in the Bible story Thomas didn't believe Christ's resurrection and demanded to touch the wound. The Bible doesn't say whether he did or didn't touch Him, but the Templars were convinced that he did. They believed the Jewel of Jerusalem was a crystal into which an alchemist called Jho'acabe had encapsulated the traces of blood left on Thomas's fingers. The crystal was then hung from a necklace that fell into Muslim control when Saladin took the city."

"If that were true wouldn't the Muslims have destroyed it?" Hanley asked.

"Actually, no," Eric replied. "By all accounts, Saladin treated the city's Christians and their churches respectfully. He might not have given back the pendant, but I doubt he would have intentionally destroyed it either."

"So now the jewel, either a ruby or a necklace, is in the hands of the Templars. How does it end up entombed with Suleiman Al-Jama?"

"Because the ship carrying them back to Malta—"

"—is attacked by Barbary pirates." Juan answered his own question.

"One of Al-Jama's ancestors, in fact," Eric said. "The cedar chest with the jewel inside gets passed from father to son until Al-Jama's death. Henry Lafayette left it in the tomb, and so it sits today."

"It's all crap," Mark spat. "Chairman, if you saw some of the websites where we found this stuff you'd know there's nothing to it. It's a myth like the Loch Ness Monster, or Bigfoot or the Lost Dutchman Mine."

"There was a kernel of truth behind the myth of Noah's Ark, if you recall from our little adventure a few months ago." The Chairman went quiet for a moment. "We know for a fact from Lafayette that in his later years Al-Jama saw there was hope of peace between Christians and Muslims. This has only recently come to light, right? It isn't something conspiracy buffs are privy to. Here's a little speculation. What if the first version of the story's right, about the jewel being an inscribed ruby, and Al-Jama read Muhammad's last words and that led to his change of heart. It does lend a little credence, yes?"

"Possibly. But come on. What are the chances it ends up in Al-Jama's possession?"

"Why not? He was a noted Imam from a family with a long history of piracy. Even if one of his ancestors wasn't part of the attack on the Templar ship, it's still possible the jewel was given to them as a tribute."

"Gentlemen, let's get back on course," Max suggested.

"At this stage in the game, it doesn't really matter what the jewel is, or even where it is. Our focus should be on saving the Secretary and stopping Al-Jama's attack."

"Max, you said something about how the Libyans are claiming our old buddy at the harbor, Tariq Assad, is Al-Jama."

"Obviously a smoke screen, if we're right."

"Has Eddie reported anything that makes you think Assad's involved with Al-Jama's faction?"

"No, but this morning they noted Assad's house and his office are surrounded by covert agents. The Libyans are making good on their promise to nab him."

"And when the dust settles, they'll have their scapegoat," Eric remarked. "They'll put on a quick show trial and execute him for the attack."

"The Libyans have to be targeting him for a reason. There must be something to this guy, right? Max, get on the horn and tell Eddie to pick up Assad. We need to question him."

Cabrillo studied Mark Murphy for a moment. Murph's jaw was blurred with stubble, and he slouched in his chair as if he were melted into it, but his eyes were still bright. In the past few months, after a lot of ribbing from the crew, he had embarked on the first exercise program of his life. He'd been through a lot in the past forty-eight hours, yet Juan suspected he was ready for more. "You up for another op?"

"I still want that shower first, but yeah."

"I want you and Eric over the border into Tunisia to find Al-Jama's tomb." Cabrillo didn't like losing his best helmsman at a time like this, but Murph and Stone worked together on such a deep, intuitive level that he felt it necessary to send both.

"Better take along a couple of gundogs," Max suggested. "Don't forget the tangos kidnapped the fourth member of Alana Shepard's team."

"Bumford," Mark said. "Emile Bumford. Linda and Linc say he's a tool."

"Just so you know what you're up against," Hanley

continued, "the other archaeologists report that there were at least a dozen terrorists who snatched him."

"Gomez can chopper you over and be back in a couple of hours."

"We still have fuel left in the cache we set up in the desert when we first talked to Bumford."

"Good. I want you guys in the air in two hours. For now, all I want you to do is find the tomb. If they've beaten you there, stick close and watch. No matter what, don't engage them. Greg Chaffee's volunteered to fully debrief the prisoners, but from what I've been able to gather from them so far Al-Jama wants that tomb as badly as we do. His entire operation out in the desert was an attempt to find it. Be ready for anything."

"Ready is my middle name."

"Herbert's your middle name," Eric teased.

"It's better than Boniface."

Cabrillo's phone rang. It was the duty officer in the op center. "Chairman, I thought you'd want to know, radar picked up a low-flying aircraft parallel to the coast near the approximate position of the terrorist training camp."

"Could you track it?"

"Not really. It popped up only for a second and then vanished again. My guess is it's flying at wave-top height."

"Did you get its speed or bearing?"

"Nothing. Just the blip, and then it was gone."

"Okay. Thanks." He set the Bakelite handset back on its cradle. "Al-Jama's men are bugging out."

Max glanced at his watch. "Didn't take them long."

"I'd like to think our little fracas pushed their deadline," Juan said, "but I doubt that's the case." He went quiet for a moment. "What the hell were they doing near the coast?"

"Hmm?"

"The chopper. Why risk getting close to the coast where they could be spotted? Eric's right. They should stick to the empty desert. Max, I want you to do a search on Libya's naval forces. I want to know where every ship capable of landing a helicopter is right now."

Hanley asked, "What about you?"

"I'm going to call Langston and convince him to stick to my script. Then I want Doc Huxley to look at where I gouged out my subdermal transmitter and give me another dose of local. I have a feeling I'm going to need it."

TWENTY-EIGHT

Eddie Seng gently closed his cell phone and thought he'd contained a sigh, but from across the sweltering hotel room Hali Kasim asked, "What's up?"

Max had already briefed the pair about what had been happening, so the call had lasted for less than five seconds, but from the look on Seng's face the news couldn't be good.

"The Chairman wants us to grab Tariq Assad."

"When? Tonight?"

"Now."

"Why?"

"Didn't ask."

Because the dingy room they rented from the Chinese gang lacked air-conditioning or even running water, both men were stripped down to their boxer shorts. Both their bodies ran with sweat, although Hali seemed to be suffering the worst. His chest and upper shoulders were a matted pelt of hair, a legacy of his Lebanese heritage.

Eddie had been leaning against one of the single bed's headboards when his cell had chimed. He stood and started getting on his clothes. He shook out the cockroaches before legging into his pants. A trickle of aromatic steam from the restaurant below the room rose from a seam in the old wooden floors.

"Are we really doing this?" Hali asked, a fresh wash of perspiration slicking his face.

"Juan says that Assad's the key, so, yeah, we're doing this."

"The key? Assad's the key? The guy's nothing more than a two-bit, two-timing corrupt official."

Seng looked across at the Corporation's communications specialist. "All the more reason to wonder why they've staked out his house, and his office at the dock. Max said yesterday that their government thinks he's tied in with Al-Jama's crew, even though that makes no sense. Assad's lifestyle is too conspicuous for him to be a terrorist. Real tangos don't carry on a half dozen romantic liaisons and draw potential police interest by taking bribes."

Hali thought for a moment. "Okay, I'll buy that. So if he's not with Al-Jama, why do the Libyans want him so badly?"

"For the same reason Juan does. He knows something about this whole mess, only no one knows what."

Kasim was on his feet, securing a compact Glock 19 to an ankle holster before slipping on his pants. "This is why I stay on the ship. There my job is easy. Radio call comes in, I answer it. Someone wants to talk to a guy on the other side of the world, I make it happen. Shore Operations need encrypted phones that look like cigarette packs, I can get 'em. Skulking around in broad daylight trying to abduct a man wanted by the Libyan secret police isn't exactly my cup of tea."

Putting on the accent of an elderly Chinese sage, Eddie said, "Broaden your appetites, grasshopper, and the world will feed your soul."

Seng was not noted for his sense of humor. It wasn't that he didn't enjoy a good joke but that he was rarely the source, so Hali's laugh was disproportionately loud and long. Telling it had been Eddie's way of reassuring Hali that he knew what he was doing.

"Don't worry. Our last report puts Assad at the house of

girlfriend number three. The Libyan authorities are nowhere near there. By now, he has to know he's a wanted man, so anyone offering him a lifeline is going to seem like a godsend. We're just going to stroll up, explain to him he's out of options, and bring him back here. Piece of cake."

Assad's third mistress, the Rubenesque wife of a judge, lived with her husband in a neighborhood of four- and five-story buildings built of stone covered with stucco and dating back more than a hundred years. The windows and balconies were protected by wrought-iron grilles, and the flat roofs were seas of satellite dishes. The ground floors of most of the buildings were shops and boutiques that catered to the upscale residents.

The sidewalks were wide and generous, while the roads were narrow and twisting, a leftover from when the neighborhood was serviced by horses rather than cars. The meandering nature of the streets gave the neighborhood a feeling of exclusivity, a quiet little enclave in the otherwise bustling city.

The Chinese gang members they had hired to track Tariq Assad hid in plain sight with a broken-down delivery van. They were parked opposite the mistress's building, with the hood up and engine parts spread across a tarp on the nearby sidewalk. Men and women, some dressed in robes, others in Western fashion, moved around them without a glance.

Eddie found a spot for their rental car in front of a small grocery store down the street from the van. The smell of oranges from bins flanking the door filled the air.

He fumbled in the glove compartment while focusing on the street, searching for anything out of the ordinary. Nothing seemed out of place, and his instincts, which had served him well over the years, told him the area was clear. The two old men playing backgammon at an outdoor café were what they appeared to be. The stock boy dusting a table in the front window of a furniture store kept his eyes on his job and not on passing traffic. No one was just sitting in his car as the afternoon sun beat down mercilessly. Other than the gang members, there were no vans for an observation team to use as a base.

At the end of the block was a large construction site with a crawler crane, hoisting material up the ten-story, steel-and-concrete framework of what would soon be luxury condominiums. Again, Eddie saw nothing suspicious about the parade of cement mixers and trucks moving through the gates.

"Ready?" he asked Hali.

Kasim blew out a breath so his cheeks puffed like a horn player's. "How do you and Juan and the others keep so calm?"

"Juan, for one, thinks out every possible scenario and makes sure he has a contingency plan for whatever crops up. Me? I don't think about it at all. I just clear my mind and react as needed. Don't worry, Hali. We'll be fine."

"Let's do this, then."

They opened their doors. Eddie adjusted his hat and dark glasses, the only form of disguise he was using to hide his Asian features. Both men wore baggy tan slacks and open-necked shirts, which was about as anonymous as one could get in many quarters of the Middle East.

As they strolled past the van, Eddie palmed a disposable cell phone off on one of the gang members. He whispered, "Push back your perimeter, and watch that red Fiat we drove here. Speed-dial one is my phone."

The Chinese youth gave no indication he heard anything other than the slam of the van's hood. Eddie and Hali walked on without breaking stride.

The front door to their target building wasn't locked, but there was a watchman in a dark uniform sitting on a sofa in the lobby, reading a newspaper. The pair had walked in as if one of them had just told a joke. Both were laughing, and they ignored the guard when he set aside his paper and asked something in Arabic that neither man understood.

Hali never saw the move. He didn't believe they were even close enough.

Eddie had lunged like a fencer, the fingers of his right hand held stiff and ridged. He connected with the hollow of the guard's throat just below the Adam's apple. He could have killed the man had he wanted, but the strike was measured.

The Libyan started to gag, and Eddie threw another blow, the edge of his hand connecting on the side of the man's neck. The watchman's eyes rolled up until only the whites showed, and he crumpled back onto the couch.

Seng glanced out the glass door to see if anyone was paying attention, and then with Hali's help he dragged the unconscious watchman into a back room, where one wall was lined with mail cubbies.

"How long will he be out?"

"An hour or so." Eddie rifled the man's pocket, looking for ID. It said the guard's name was Ali. "Come on. Assad's on the fourth floor, front-side corner."

Both men drew their pistols as they climbed an interior stairwell. They weren't concerned about running into anyone. People who lived in buildings like this invariably used the elevator.

Eddie cautiously opened the door on the fourth-floor landing. The hallway beyond was carpeted and lit with wall sconces. The six apartment doors were solid, made of heavy carved wood—left over from a time of superior craftsmanship. He was relieved the doors didn't have peepholes.

He approached the door to the mistress's apartment and rapped respectfully. A moment later, he heard a muffled woman's voice. He assumed she was asking who it was, so he said, "Ali, *sayyidah.*"

She spoke again, most likely asking what he wanted, so Eddie said the first thing that popped into his head, and prayed his pronunciation was close. *"Al-Zajal, sayyidah."* Federal Express, ma'am. He'd seen their distinctively colored trucks all over the city.

Eddie mouthed *Stay back* to Hali, while inside the apartment a chain rattled and a pair of locks disengaged. He slammed his shoulder into the door, meeting more resistance than he'd expected but managing to shove the woman aside. He dove low, and a bullet from a silenced pistol cut the air inches over his shoulder.

The woman screamed. Seng rolled once, coming to his knees behind a couch. "Tariq, don't shoot." He kept his voice as calm as the adrenaline dose would allow. "Please. We're here to help."

The woman's cry turned into slow blubbering, as a few seconds ticked away on the grandfather clock pressed up against one plaster wall.

"Who are you?" Tariq Assad asked.

"A couple of nights ago, you made arrangements for us to unload a large truck in the harbor."

"The Canadians?"

"Yes."

"Who was I contacted through?"

"L'Enfant."

"You may stand," Assad said.

Eddie got to his feet slowly, making certain Assad could see his finger was nowhere near his pistol's trigger. "We're here to help you get out."

Hali entered the room cautiously. Assad watched him for a moment, then turned his attention back to Eddie. Seng had removed his hat and glasses so the harbor pilot could see his features. "I recognize you from that night. You acted as helmsman. You know, since then I thought I was going insane. I've had the feeling of being watched, and everywhere I turn I see young Chinamen acting strangely. I guess you are the explanation."

"I hired some local boys to keep tabs on you," Eddie said, slipping his pistol into the waistband of his pants.

Assad crossed to the crying woman, helping her up onto her piano legs. She wiped at her nose with the back of her hand, smearing a wet trail through her fine mustache. Eddie guessed she tipped the scales above two hundred, and standing at a little over five feet she looked like a basketball in her burnt orange robe.

Tariq Assad was no Adonis, with his graying hair and single dense eyebrow, but he had a good personality and Eddie thought he could have done better than this rather bovine woman. If not love or lust, he guessed information. She was the wife of a judge, after all.

As the Libyan muttered reassurances into her cauliflower

ear, Eddie surveyed the apartment. The judge's home was well furnished, with a new leather sofa and chairs and a marble-topped coffee table with a neatly arranged fan of glossy magazines. There was an impressive oriental rug on the hardwood floor, and shelves for matching leather-bound books. The walls were adorned with intricate needlework of geometric design framed under glass. Her handiwork, he assumed. A breeze worked the gauzy curtains near the balcony, and the apartment was high enough that the traffic below was a low-register thrum.

Assad patted his mistress on her ample rump to send her back to the bedroom.

"She's a good girl," he remarked before she was out of earshot. "Not too bright, and a little rough on the eyes, yes, but a veritable tiger where it counts."

Eddie and Hali shuddered.

"May I get you gentlemen a drink?" Assad offered when the bedroom door closed. "The judge favors gin, but I brought Scotch whiskey. Oh, and I am sorry for firing at you. It was reflex. I thought it was him."

"I think you can drop the act, Mr. Assad."

No one spoke for a few seconds. Eddie could read Assad's face. He'd been out in the cold, in spy parlance, for a while, and was debating if the two strangers represented a way out.

His shoulders sagged slightly. "Okay. No more act." Though he still spoke English with an accent, it was subtly different. "I'm pretty screwed no matter what happens now, so it doesn't really matter anymore. Who are you people? I figured CIA, when I met with you on your ship."

"Near enough," Eddie replied. "That's Hali Kasim. My name's Eddie Seng."

"You're in Libya to find out what happened to your Secretary of State?"

"Yeah. But the mission's also morphed into a hunt for Suleiman Al-Jama."

"As I figured it would. His organization is like an octopus with its tentacles wrapped all through the Libyan government. They work in the shadows, infiltrating one high-ranking office after another."

"Who are you and what's your deal here?"

"My name's Lev Goldman."

Understanding hit Eddie like a punch to the gut. "My God, Mossad. We have information that says you've been here five years."

"No. My cover goes back that far. I arrived in Tripoli eighteen months ago. Tel Aviv suspected Al-Jama was going to take over a North African country through slow subterfuge. They sent deep-cover agents into Morocco, Algeria, Tunisia, and here to keep an eye on the government. When it became clear that Libya was the target, the other agents were pulled and I remained."

"So these women?"

Goldman lowered his voice even further. "Lonely housewives of powerful men. Oldest trick in the book."

"And your work at the harbor?"

"Nothing goes in or out that I don't know about. Arms, supplies, everything Al-Jama's brought here. Including a modified Hind gunship they bought from the Pakistanis. It was used in the high mountains of Kashmir, and can reach elevations unheard of for a regular helicopter. I had no idea why they wanted it until Fiona Katamora's plane crashed."

"Members of our team took it out," Eddie told him. "They also rescued about a hundred people who used to work in Libya's Foreign Ministry."

"There were rumors of a purge when Ali Ghami was named Minister despite the press reports that everyone who left had retired or been transferred to other branches of the government. This is still a police state, so everyone knew not to question the official word."

"Listen, we can get into all of this later. We need to get you out of here. The secret police have staked out your home and office."

"Why do you think I was hiding here?"

"What's your exit strategy?"

"I have a couple, but I thought I'd have a little warning from some of my contacts. I'm flying by the seat of my pants now. I had planned to ambush the judge when he got home from work and steal his car. I have an electronic device that will broadcast my location to an Israeli satellite. My orders are to get out into the southern desert as far as I can and await extraction by an Army helicopter disguised as a relief agency helo doing charity work for Darfur refugees in Chad."

"We can get you out quicker and safer, but we have to leave now."

No sooner had Eddie spoken the words than his phone rang. He answered without speaking, listened for a few seconds, and cut the connection. "Too late. Our guys just reported a police van moving into the area. They also hear an approaching helicopter. They'll be establishing a wide perimeter before closing in."

"I have a secret exit from this building but it won't get us far enough away. I had it in case the judge ever came home early."

Eddie made a snap decision. "We're going to split up. Hali, stay with Lev. Get yourselves to an embassy, but not ours. Try Switzerland, or some other unallied country. You'll be safe there until this all blows over."

"What about you?"

"I'm the distraction. Lev, where's the master bathroom?"

"Through there." He pointed to the closed bedroom door.

All three men strode into the room. Lev and the judge's wife spoke for a few moments, he trying to reassure her, she accusing him of God knows what. Eddie ignored them and flipped on the bathroom light. He searched through several drawers until he found the items he wanted.

First, he moussed his hair to give it Goldman's curls and then sprinkled it with talcum powder so it matched his salt-and-pepper. He filled in the space between his eyebrows with a cosmetic pencil, and used a wad of toilet paper and the contents of a mascara bottle to give his face Goldman's heavy five o'clock shadow.

Goldman saw what Eddie was doing and had his harbor pilot shirt off and ready to swap. Eddie tossed Goldman his shirt and slipped on Goldman's.

The Israeli agent led them out of the bathroom and into the woman's closet. He pushed aside a section of the hanging clothes, ignoring the increasing whine of her pleading questions. He moved a rather odorous shoe rack to reveal a piece of wood pressed up against the stucco wall. When he pulled it away, there was an open void about two feet across that ran the depth of the building. Opposite, they could see the back-side of the laths for the next apartment. Budging plaster filled the gaps between the boards. Above, light filtered into the void from a pair of dusty skylights.

"This was left over from when the building was converted from offices," Lev explained. "I found it on the old blueprints. At the bottom, I cut another hole that leads to the garage."

"Okay, you two go down. Hali, get our car and pick up Lev in the garage. The cordon shouldn't be too tight yet, and with any luck the police will be focusing on me."

"If it is the police," Goldman said. "Remember, Al-Jama is running a shadow government inside Qaddafi's."

"Does it really matter?" Hali pointed out, thrusting a leg into the opening.

He braced a foot on each wall and slowly started making his way down. His motion kicked up a thick cloud of fine white dust, and his weight caused the old laths to bow. Chunks of plaster broke away and fell into the darkness below.

Goldman had to disentangle himself from his distraught mistress. Her eye makeup ran in dark smudges down her apple cheeks, and her heavy bosom heaved with each sob.

"Women," he remarked when he was finally free and crawling after Hali.

Eddie followed him, but rather than descend he moved laterally for a few feet, so any plaster he dislodged wouldn't hit the men below, and started climbing. It was only a single story, so it took just a few minutes before he was pressed up under one of the skylights. The heat in the shaft was stifling, a weight that pulled at him as surely as gravity.

He could hear the rotor beat of the police helicopter and judged he had a few more seconds. The glazing holding the panes of glass to the metal frame had dried rock hard and came away with just a little pressure.

A shadow passed over the skylight. The chopper.

Eddie swallowed hard and popped one of the large panes

free. The sound of the helicopter doubled, and even though he was exposed to the noonday sun it felt like he was moving into air-conditioning.

He rolled onto the flat, tarry roof and got to his feet. The chopper was a couple blocks away, hovering a few hundred feet above the rooftops. Eddie had to wait almost a minute before he was spotted. The big machine twisted in the air and thundered toward him. Its side door was open, and a police sniper stood braced with a scoped rifle cradled against his shoulder.

Eddie ran for the wall separating this building from the next, his feet sinking slightly into the warm tar. The wall was built to chest height and topped with jagged bits of embedded glass to prevent people from doing what Seng was attempting. But unlike barbed wire, which never loses its keen edge, the glass had been scoured by wind for decades and was almost smooth. Pieces snapped flat when he vaulted over the wall. He landed on the other side.

This building's roof was virtually identical to the first, a wide area of a tar-gravel mix punctured by the elevator housing and dozens of satellite dishes and defunct antennae.

The chopper swooped low over the roof, and Eddie made certain the sniper saw his face and hoped it was a close enough match to Tariq Assad's. He got his answer a second later when a three-round burst from an automatic weapon pounded the roof at his feet.

Now that the police believed their suspect was on the roof, Hali and Goldman should be able to slip away undetected.

Eddie raced for the back of the building, cutting a serpentine path to throw off the sharpshooter, and almost threw himself from the edge before realizing that, unlike the mistress's apartment house, this one didn't have a proper fire escape. There was just a simple metal ladder bolted to the side of the structure, a death trap if he committed himself to it with the sniper hovering so close overhead.

He glanced back the way he came. He'd be running right for the circling chopper if he retreated, so instead he ran for the next building, vaulting the wall and opening a gash in his palm for the effort. Not all the glass had weathered the same.

More bullets pounded into the roof, kicking up hot clots of tar that burned against his cheek. He pulled his pistol and returned fire. The wide misses were still enough to force the pilot to retreat for a moment.

Sprinting flat out, he raced for the next building, throwing himself over the wall and almost dropping down. The next building was a story lower than the previous ones, and beyond that was the open expanse of the construction site. Dangling from his fingertips, he looked quickly to see if there was any evidence of a fire escape and saw none, not even a cable house for an elevator.

He made the decision to pull himself back over the wall and find some other route when the sniper zeroed in on his hands. Bullets tore into the brick and mortar, forcing Eddie to drop free. He rolled when he landed to absorb the impact, but surviving the ten-foot drop didn't mean he was any less trapped.

TWENTY-NINE

B Y THE TIME HALI KASIM REACHED THE BOTTOM OF the air shaft, he was covered in dust, and his shoulders and knees ached mercilessly. He promised himself that when he returned to the *Oregon*, he'd spend more time in the ship's fitness center. He'd seen how effortlessly Eddie had climbed, and the former CIA agent was nearly a decade older.

The floor here was littered with fragments of plaster and dried layers of pigeon guano. Lev Goldman lowered himself the last few feet. Sweat had cut channels through the dirt caked on his face, and the dust coating his beard aged him twenty years.

"You okay?" Hali panted, resting his hands on his knees.

"Perhaps I should have thought up a better escape route," the Israeli admitted, fighting not to cough in the mote-filled air. "Come. This way."

He led Kasim toward the rear of the building and an area where the lath had been cut way low to the ground. Together they kicked at the two-foot-square spot. At first, the blows merely cracked the plaster. But then bits of it broke away.

Goldman used his hands to tear out inch-thick chunks until the hole was big enough to crawl through.

They emerged into an underground garage. The lot was mostly vacant, with only a few cars, usually driven by the stay-at-home wives, sitting in their assigned spots. Had any of them been older models, Hali would have considered hotwiring one of them, but they were all fairly new and would be equipped with alarms.

"Meet me at the exit and stay out of sight," he said. "Our car is right around the corner."

Hali dusted himself off as best he could as he jogged up the ramp and into the blazing sunshine. The street was a scene of pandemonium. The shots fired from the helicopter had forced everyone to find cover. Oranges from the grocer's littered the sidewalk where someone had run into the display. The chairs where the old men had played backgammon were overturned. Police vans were just now arriving.

It didn't take much acting for Hali to pretend to be just another frightened Libyan. He reached their rental car and opened the door. Sirens filled the air, drowning out even the heavy throb of the chopper's blades.

The Fiat's engine fired on the first try. Hali's hands were so slick that the wheel got away from him, and he clipped the rear bumper of the car parked in front of him, its alarm adding to the keening police sirens.

The first of the officers, outfitted in black tactical gear, began to emerge from a van. They would have the block surrounded in seconds. Yet none of them seemed interested in anything except the building's front door. Eddie's distraction was working. They thought they had their man cornered and ignored proper procedure.

Hali drove around the corner, slowed, but didn't stop for Lev Goldman, who threw himself into the passenger's seat, and eased into traffic on the next side street.

Every block they drove exponentially increased the area the police had to cover in order to find them. After eight stoplights, Goldman felt safe enough to pop his head up above the dashboard.

"Pull over into that gas station," he ordered.

"Can't you hold it?"

"Not for that. We need to switch seats. It is obvious you don't know the roads or how to drive like a local. No one here obeys the traffic rules."

Hali cranked the wheel into the gas station's lot and threw the car into park. Lev sat still for a moment, expecting Hali to jump out so he could slide over. Instead, he was forced out of the car, and Kasim took the passenger's seat.

He chuckled humorlessly when he engaged the transmission. "In a situation like that, Mossad training says driver should exit the vehicle."

Kasim looked at him skeptically. "Really? Doing it your way means there is no one at the wheel for several seconds longer. You should talk to your instructors."

"No matter." Lev grinned, this time with genuine amusement. "We made it."

He asked as they made random turns away from his mistress's neighborhood, "I am sorry, what is your name again?"

"Kasim. Hali Kasim."

"That is an Arab name. Where are you from?"

"Washington, D.C."

"No. I mean your family. Where were they from?"

They took what Hali assumed was a shortcut in an alley between two large, featureless buildings. "My grandfather emigrated from Lebanon when he was a boy."

"So are you Muslim or Christian?"

"What difference does that make?"

"If you are Christian, I wouldn't feel so bad about this."

The report was just a sharp spit in the confines of the Fiat's cramped interior. A fine mist of blood splattered the passenger's window when the bullet burst from Hali's rib cage. Goldman fired his silenced pistol again at the same instant the car hit a pothole. His aim was off, so the round missed entirely, blowing out the side window in a cascade of minuscule chips.

Hali had been so stunned in the first instant of the attack, he had done nothing to stop the second shot. His chest felt like a molten poker had been rammed through it from side to side, and he could feel hot wetness trickling past his belt line.

He grabbed for the gun as it recoiled up, forcing Goldman to let go of the wheel and throw an awkward body shot that still hit directly on the entrance wound. Hali screamed at the unimaginable agony of it, and he lost his grip on the handgun's warm barrel.

Rather than fight a battle he had no chance of winning, he used his elbow to push open the door release and let himself fall from the car. They were doing perhaps twenty-five miles per hour, and he landed right on his butt, so he didn't tumble but rather slid along the pavement, until skin smeared from his body.

The Fiat's brake lights lit up immediately, but by the time the car had come to a stop Hali had pulled his pistol from his ankle holster. He fired as soon as he saw Goldman's head emerge from the car. Hali missed, so he fired again, this time aiming through the car. Glass splintering sounded like tiny bells. The pistol's recoil made him feel like he was being kicked, but he kept at it. Three more rounds hit the car, other rounds shot masonry off the building beyond. The man Hali thought was an Israeli agent decided killing him wasn't worth it.

"If you'd only gotten out at that gas station, I would have simply driven away," he said. The Fiat's door slammed, and the car sped off with a chirp of its tires.

Hali collapsed onto his back, his chest heaving as his blood pumped from both entrance and exit wounds. He yanked up his shirt to see the damage. There were tiny bubbles foaming from the right-side bullet hole. He didn't need Doc Huxley to tell him he had been shot in the lung, or that if he didn't get to a hospital soon he was a dead man.

The alley where he'd been both duped and dumped was long, and he couldn't see traffic crossing either entrance. This had been a perfect setup, he thought fleetingly, gritting his teeth against a fresh wave of pain when he levered himself to his feet. Whoever Goldman was, he had played them like a maestro.

Hali made it no more than a couple of paces before he collapsed against the building and dropped to the ground amid the broken bottles, thorny weeds, and trash.

His last thought before succumbing to oblivion was relief that Eddie would most likely make it out. Nothing could stop the wiry ex-agent.

● ● ●

EDDIE SENG COULD ONLY HOPE that Hali and Goldman were safe, because he was in serious trouble. The police helicopter roared into view overhead, and he put two bullets into its underside before it swept out of pistol range. The sniper wasn't so limited by his weapon and blazed away. Bullets pounded the wall behind Eddie, forcing him to run again. The marksman adjusted, leading Eddie ever so slightly, and put a round through the roof less than an inch from his right toe.

Eddie felt as exposed as an actor on an empty stage. Without any cover, it was only a matter of time before the bullets found their mark. Ahead of him, the roof ended in a low decorative cornice, and beyond was the skeletal framework of the new high-rise under construction. An Olympic long jumper would still miss the building by fifty feet from here. The boom of the crane that he and Hali had seen was closer, but there would be nothing to grab onto if he made it.

It was swinging across the sky and Eddie could see its cable reeling upward, but he had no idea what was being maneuvered to one of the building's upper floors.

At this point, it didn't matter.

Putting on a burst of speed, he raced for the horizon, running flat out without any deviation. The sniper high above zeroed in, laying down a rain of fire that chased Eddie's heels. Just before reaching the cornice, he saw down below that the crane was lifting a pallet of Sheetrock. He altered his speed slightly, put one foot on the cornice, and launched himself into space, leaping through a stinging cloud of exploding masonry.

He flew out and down, a forty-foot drop sucking at his body, his stomach lurching at the rapid earthward acceleration. The pallet of Sheetrock was twelve feet below him and rising when he leapt, so when he crashed into it the impact turned his ankle and he almost slid off the far side.

Before he could grab one of the cables, his weight unbalanced the load. It tipped, and he had to scramble on his bad leg. Sheets of gypsum board began to slide against one another as the angle increased. He lunged for the cable as the entire two tons slipped free. The sheets separated as they fell, spreading out as though a giant had tossed a deck of playing cards into the air.

Eddie's fingers clutched at the cable, his body jerking spasmodically because the cable was bouncing to adjust to losing the load. He managed to change his grip and loop a leg around the cable.

To his credit, the crane's operator was quick-thinking. He had been watching the lift from the cab, had seen the figure leap from the adjacent building, and understood why the heavy sheets had fallen. Rather than take the time to slowly lower the dangling figure to the ground, he locked the cable spool and continued to swing the boom toward the unfinished building.

The heavy hook at the end of the cable had enough weight to pendulum Eddie through the building's open side, and he let go, tumbling onto a concrete floor. The workers who'd seen his stunt were several floors above him. It would take them a few moments to come down the ladders leaning inside what would become a stairwell.

Favoring his sprained ankle, Eddie loped to the edge of the building, where a debris chute had been attached. He peered over the edge. The chute was a metal tube about twenty-four inches in diameter that ended just above a large green Dumpster sitting atop a flatbed truck. He stepped in, wedged his good foot against the wall, and braced his hands behind him. His descent was measured and controlled. His only real concern was that someone higher up might toss something in the Dumpster after him.

He landed lightly on chunks of concrete and rebar torn out

from a cement pour gone wrong. Seconds later, he was over the side of the Dumpster and striding across the construction site. Everyone still assumed he was up on the third floor, so no one paid him the slightest attention. Most important, the hovering sniper was watching the building and not the lone figure crossing the construction yard.

Parked near a pump truck designed to force concrete up armored hoses to the upper stories was a cement mixer, its rear chute extended with cement flowing into the pump's hopper. Eddie leapt onto its front bumper, stepped onto its driver's-side fender, and grabbed the big wing-mirror support before the driver was aware of Eddie's presence. Eddie swung himself through the open window, caught the man on the jaw with his good foot, and dropped into the seat as the man collapsed sideways.

The whole truck vibrated with the power of the huge cement drum turning just behind the cab. Eddie kicked the unconscious man down into the passenger's footwell, yanked the gearshift into first, and started forward. He couldn't hear the shouts of the surprised workers, but he could see them running after the cement mixer in his wing mirrors.

He drove the truck across the site on the dedicated dirt road. In his wake, wet cement continued to fall from the chute like the mixer was some diarrheal mechanical monster. The chopper had to have alerted the ground forces that their man had leapt for the construction site, because a half dozen cops were rushing for the chain-link gate when Eddie smashed through, scattering men like bowling pins.

When he cranked the wheel over, the steel chute pivoted outward like a baseball bat at full swing, knocking over two more men and smashing out the windshield of a parked sedan. A police car charged after him, its siren wailing. When it pulled alongside, Eddie braked hard and turned the wheel. The cement mixer rode up onto the cruiser's hood. The massive weight of the truck and its load of concrete blew out the front tires and burst the radiator. The truck's rear wheels skidded into the patrol car so it blocked both the road's narrow lanes.

The move sent the chute flinging the other way and it tore

through the glass of another car. It ricocheted back and forth like a metal tail, smashing into automobiles and keeping the pursuing police well back.

Eddie could see them pause to fire at the truck, but their shots were deflected by the enormous revolving drum, and he was increasing the range with every second. The problem wasn't them. It was the helicopter circling overhead. Eddie couldn't make his escape with them watching his every move and radioing his position

The street straightened and widened as he left the neighborhood. In the distance, approaching at nearly seventy miles per hour, were three more police cars, their lights winking rhythmically. Charging along with them was some sort of wheeled armored vehicle. Eddie assumed it would have a mounted heavy machine gun.

He pressed the accelerator to the floor, short-shifting the transmission to build up his speed as quickly as possible. With a hundred feet separating him and the cruisers, Eddie slammed on the brakes and spun the wheel over hard. The front fender caught the rear corner of a big delivery truck, and it was enough to unbalance the cement mixer. It went up onto its outside wheels, even as it continued to careen sideways, and then it smashed over onto its side.

Eddie held on to the wheel to stop himself from tumbling onto the passenger's door, covering his face with his elbow to protect it from the flying glass of the shattered windshield. The truck's regular operator was sufficiently jammed into place that he was okay as glass rained down on him.

The collision with the ground was hard enough to snap the pins holding the cement drum in place and break the links of its chain drive. Momentum did the rest.

Eleven tons of steel and concrete began rolling down the street, wobbling slightly as the cement sloshed in the huge barrel. Two of the police cars had the good sense to peel out of the way and jump onto the curb, one smashing into a utility pole, the other coming to rest with its front end embedded in a wall. The armored car and the other cruiser were closer and didn't stand a chance. The barrel rolled up the armored car's front glacis and tore its small turret from its mount. The gunner would have been sliced in half had he not ducked at the last second.

The drum smashed back onto the road, cracking the asphalt before hitting the police cruiser in a glancing blow that was still enough to flatten it from the rear seat back. The barrel came to rest against the side of a building, with cement as stiff as toothpaste oozing from its open mouth.

Eddie grabbed a spare work shirt that had been hanging from a peg at the back of the cab and stepped through the shattered windshield. He was hidden from the view of the chopper by the truck, so he took a few seconds to wipe the cosmetics from his face and don the denim shirt. The pain radiating from his ankle was something he could contain and compartmentalize, so when he moved away from the truck he walked without a limp. He went no more than a few feet and stopped to stare with the people who'd poured out of shops and homes to see the accident. As simply as that, he was just another rubbernecker.

When the police arrived and began questioning witnesses, he was virtually ignored. They were looking for a Libyan, not an Asian man who spoke no Arabic. He slowly drifted away from the scene, and no one stopped him. Five minutes after calling their hired gang members, he was in the van headed away from the neighborhood entirely.

• • •

FIVE MILES AWAY IN the rented Fiat, Tariq Assad was on his cell phone.

"It's me. There was a raid today. The police almost got me. First, find out why I wasn't warned. This should have never happened. As it was, I had a little help in escaping from those people off that damned ship. I was pumping them for information when the police arrived."

He listened for a moment, and replied. "Watch your tone! You arranged the ambush on the coast road, and those were your handpicked men. We've both seen a copy of the investigation report, thanks to our mole in the police. Rather than let vehicles pass unmolested, your supposedly well-trained men were shaking down motorists for bribe money. I don't know how these American mercenaries managed to kill them all, but they did. Then they proceeded to blow up our Hind, free most of our prisoners, and generally disrupt what had been a perfectly executed plan . . . What? Yes, I said free. Their cargo ship must have been berthed at the coaling station dock. Our men saw an empty train car sinking . . . How should I know? Maybe the vessel is faster than it looks or the men in the chopper were bigger fools than the ones you sent to stop their truck in the first place.

"I have to get out of the city now," he went on. "Actually, out of the country. I know a pilot who is sympathetic to our cause. I will ask him to fly me in his helicopter to where the men are searching for Suleiman Al-Jama's tomb, and I will take control personally. Despite the setbacks, it appears you have everything controlled from this end. Fiona Katamora should be in her execution chamber by now, and Colonel Hassad phoned to tell me our martyr force is en route.

"I won't speak to you again until it's over. So let me say that Allah's blessings be upon us all."

He killed the connection and tossed the encrypted phone on the seat next to him. He was a man who had always been able to keep a grip on his emotions. He wouldn't have lasted as long as he had if he couldn't. Today's close call enraged him. He hadn't been lying when he said they had spies and sympathizers in every level of the Libyan government. He'd had ample warning that the police were staking out his office and apartment, so he should have been told about the raid.

It seemed the supreme leader, Muammar Qaddafi, needed reminding that his autonomy remained limited.

THIRTY

Moving as slowly as he could, Eric Stone reached under his chest and carefully turned the rock that had been digging into his ribs for the past fifteen minutes. He could feel the disapproval that he'd moved radiating off Franklin Lincoln, who was lying prone next to him. On his other side was Mark Murphy, and beside him was Linda Ross. Next to her was Alana Shepard.

Despite everything she'd been through and the dangers now presented by the terrorists, she had insisted on coming with them. Dr. Huxley had given her a brief medical exam and cleared her for the mission.

Because of her rank within the Corporation, Linda was in charge of the group, so it was her call. She'd figured Cabrillo would nix the idea, so she hadn't bothered asking when she'd agreed to let Alana come with them.

They were on a ridge overlooking the dry river valley where Alana and her team had spent so many weeks searching for Suleiman Al-Jama's lost tomb. Below them were a dozen terrorists from the training camp. They might have been proficient at killing and maiming, but they were useless when it came to archaeology. The squad leader had no idea what he was doing, so he had the men scrambling all over the wadi, moving random stones and climbing the steep banks looking for any clue as to the tomb's location. At their current pace, they'd reach the old waterfall Alana's team had found in four or five hours.

With them was Professor Emile Bumford. It was difficult to tell without binoculars, which they couldn't use for fear the sun would flash off the lens, but he didn't look the worse for wear. He was searching like the others, and while he moved slowly, he wasn't limping or favoring any injury. There was no sign of the representative from the Tunisian Antiquities Ministry or his son. He'd been paid for betraying the Americans and was probably back in Tunis.

There was no sign of the old Mi-8 helicopter the terrorists were using as a base, so the team assumed it was farther down the river and would leapfrog the searchers when they reached a predetermined distance away.

Linc tapped Eric's leg, the signal for them to retreat off the ridge. He slithered back as carefully as he could, followed by Linda, Mark, and Alana. The former SEAL stayed in position for a couple more minutes, making certain no one below saw any movement.

He led them southward for twenty minutes before he judged it safe enough to talk, albeit in whispers.

"What do you think?" Mark asked.

"I guess we have to ask ourselves WWJD?"

Mark looked at him strangely. "What would Jesus do?"

"No. What would Juan do?"

"That's easy," Eric said. "Take out the bad guys, find the tomb, and somehow manage to bed a local Bedouin girl."

Alana had to cover her mouth to stifle a laugh.

"Seriously," Linc went on. "Now that we know where the bad guys are, we've only got a few hours before they reach the falls. Do you two geniuses have any idea how to find the tomb?"

"We need to see the falls to be sure, but, yeah, we've got some ideas."

This was the first Alana had heard of their plans, and she said, "Hold on a second. I've seen the old waterfall for myself. There's no way a sailing ship could have negotiated them. They're too steep. The top one is practically a vertical wall."

"You're not giving credit where it's due," Eric said mildly.

"Here's the plan." Linda made eye contact with each member of her team. "We're going to try to find the tomb. Linc, I want you to stay behind and keep an eye on these guys. Radio when you think there's an hour left before they reach the falls so we can bug out. Any questions?"

There were none.

Having already marched to the wadi from their chopper's distant landing zone, the two men and two women still made good time hiking the six miles to the first set of cataracts that blocked the unnamed river. They had stayed on top of the bluff overlooking the bed so when they reached the falls they had a bird's-eye view. Linda ordered Alana to stay with the men while she scouted the area. Mark and Eric took up a position overlooking the cliffs and scanned them methodically with binoculars.

It was only from above, a vantage Alana and her partners had never enjoyed, that the odd nature of the riverbed became apparent. Upstream from the first cataract, there was a natural bowl that spanned the full width of the river, a basin formed of living rock that had resisted the efforts of erosion for aeons. It was roughly a hundred feet long, and its upstream side was yet another cliff face, only this one was just four feet higher than its predecessor. A man-made wall constructed of dressed and mortared stone ran its length. Unlike the streambed, which had been scoured clean by the powerful currents that once washed between the banks, the basin floor was littered with water-rounded boulders.

Also from above, she could see the footings of another ancient wall that had long since vanished, stretching from the base of the first falls and extending another hundred or so feet downstream.

She borrowed a pair of binoculars from Eric when she first spied the boulders and spent several minutes observing them, as if she expected them to move. Nothing changed, and yet they were telling her a story about what was happening farther into the mountains.

"Those are basalt," she said, handing back the glasses. "Same with that wall."

"So?"

"It's the first indication of anything other than sandstone in this whole godforsaken country. It means there was volcanic activity someplace around here."

"And that means?" Mark prompted.

"The possibility of caves."

"Of that there is no doubt."

Her tone turned to disappointment. "But it doesn't make any difference. Al-Jama couldn't have gotten his ship above the falls. Period."

"You're looking at this place like a geologist, not an engineer." He turned his head to talk to Eric. "Where do you think?"

"They'd need them on both banks. The river's too wide for just one." He pointed to a flat ledge just above the riverbank. "There for our side, and that promontory twenty feet higher on the other side."

"Agreed."

"What are you talking about?" Alana asked. Her only experience with the Corporation was witnessing them as soldiers. She didn't know what to make of Eric Stone and Mark Murphy. To her they were techno-geeks, not mercenaries, and they seemed to speak in a private code only they understood.

"Derricks," they said simultaneously. Eric added, "We'll show you."

They made their way down to the ledge. It would have remained a few feet above the water level even at the height of the spring runoff. It was almost dead even with the first cliff spanning the river, and was large enough to accommodate a city bus. The two men scanned the ground intently.

When something caught their eye, one would bend to brush at the dirt covering the sandstone.

"Got it," Mark cried softly. He was on his haunches, excavating sand from a perfectly round twelve-inch-wide hole that had been drilled into the rock. He didn't hit bottom even when lying on the ground and burying his arm to the shoulder.

"What is that?" Alana asked.

"This is where they stepped the mast for the derrick," Murph replied. "Most likely the dressed trunk of a tree. Attached to it would have been an angled boom that could reach halfway across the river. As you can see by the hole, the boom was massive and would have been capable of supporting several tons. There would have been another on the opposite bank."

"I don't get it. What are they for?"

"Using these they could lower stones into the river—"

"Not stones," Eric countered quickly. "We talked about this. They would have used woven baskets, or possibly bags made of sailcloth, that were filled with sand. This way they would eventually dissolve in the current and wash away."

"Fine," Mark said with a tinge of irritation. Alana might be a dozen years older, but she was attractive, and Murph's only real hope with women was showing off his intellect. "Large bags of sand were lowered onto the wall they'd constructed below the first fall to divide the river channel. That way they could dam up the downstream end on one side and not stop the river entirely. Their earthworks would never have withstood the full force of the current.

"With the *Saqr* tucked into what was essentially a shipping lock, they allowed a controlled amount of water into the chamber, building the walls higher as it filled until they could haul the boat forward into the second lock, the one nature had created and which most likely inspired old Suleiman's engineer in the first place."

"They would repeat the process again," Eric added, "and draw the *Saqr* onto the upper river."

"You guys figured this out without ever visiting this place?" There was respect in Alana's voice.

Mark opened his mouth to brag, but Eric beat him to the explanation, saying with his trademark earnestness, "A lock is the only thing that could possibly explain what Henry Lafayette had meant by 'clever device.' Knowing that, we studied satellite imagery to verify our hypothesis."

"I am impressed," Alana told them. "And a little mad at myself. I stared at this stupid pile of rocks for hours but never saw it."

Mark was about to use this as another opening to brag when Linda Ross approached so silently no one heard her until she was right behind them. "You boys need to be a little more aware of your surroundings. I wasn't even trying to be quiet. What have you found?"

"Just as we suspected," Mark said, giving Eric a look. "During a particularly dry spell, when the river stopped flowing entirely, Al-Jama's people converted the waterfall into a lock system so they could hide their ship where no one would ever think to look."

"So the cave is farther upstream?"

"Gotta be."

"Then let's start hiking," Linda said.

She radioed Linc to tell him what was happening and inform him they might lose radio contact because of the distance and topography. He must have been close enough to the terrorists not to risk replying. Her acknowledgment was two quick clicks in her earpiece.

They started southward, marching three-quarters of the way up the bank so as not to silhouette themselves against the distant horizon, as well as to shield themselves from the worst of the wind that had started to kick up. This region of the desert was enough to make anyone feel insignificant. The brassy sky towered over the party, and the relentless sun beat down on them as they trudged along. They each carried enough water for a day so that wasn't a concern, but three of the four were operating on minimal sleep and the effects of a punishing few days.

For the members of the Corporation, they pushed themselves because they saw it as their duty. For Alana, she marched with them because, if she didn't, she would never lose the image of Mike Duncan's lifeless eyes, as the petroleum geologist lay on the desert floor with blood leaking from the hole in his forehead. She was an archaeologist and mother, and her place was as far from here as possible, but she wouldn't be able to live with herself if she'd not come. The decision certainly wasn't rational. However, she'd never been more certain.

Her life was dictated by rules that the men who killed Mike and kidnapped her had broken, and, simply put, she wanted revenge.

Two miles above the falls, the riverbed changed dramatically. The sandstone banks gave way to a lighter gray rock that had been part of a saltwater reef millions of years ago but was now limestone.

"This has got to be it," Alana said when she recognized the geology. "Limestone is notorious for caves and caverns."

Mark tapped Eric on the arm and pointed to a spot across the dry wash. "What do you think?"

It was an area where a landslide had torn away some of the bank and dumped untold tons of rubble into the riverbed. The slide stretched for a hundred and fifty feet, and behind it the riverbank was significantly taller than anywhere else they had seen.

"Bingo," Stone said, and high-fived Murph. "The cave's riverine entrance was blasted and the cavern sealed. Behind that mess is Suleiman Al-Jama's corsair, the *Saqr*, his tomb, and just possibly the Jewel of Jerusalem."

The initial excitement of finding the tomb's location faded quickly.

Alana voiced the concern. "There's no way we can move that much debris without heavy construction equipment and several weeks' time."

"Don't you get us yet?" Mark asked her seriously.

"What do you mean?"

"Back door," Stone and Murphy said in perfect sync.

It took ten minutes to climb down to the riverbed and

cross the river before they were standing atop the crushed section of bank. The back side of the hill facing the western desert was a folded warren of gullies and ravines that had been eroded when the Sahara had been a lush, subtropical jungle. They found the first cave entrance only moments after splitting up into pairs and starting their systematic search.

Eric pulled a small halogen flashlight from a pocket on his upper sleeve and stepped into the man-sized aperture. Ten feet in, the cave turned ninety degrees and petered out into a solid wall of rock.

Linda and Alana found a second cave that went a little deeper before it, too, came to an abrupt end. The third cave was smaller than the others, forcing Eric and Mark to crawl on their hands and knees. It ran deep into the hillside, twisting with the vagaries of the matrix stone. At times, they could stand and walk upright, and then the next moment they were forced to slither through the dust on their bellies. Stone used a piece of chalk to mark the walls when the cave began to branch off.

"What do you think?" Eric asked after they'd been underground for fifteen minutes. He was pointing to a carving on one wall. It was crude, done with a knifepoint or awl, and neither man could read it, but they recognized the looping Arabic script. "Al-Jama's version of 'Kilroy was here'?"

"This has got to be it," Murph replied. "We're going to need help exploring all these side tunnels." He tried radioing Linda but couldn't get reception this deep into the earth. "Rock, paper, scissors?"

The two men made their choices, paper covered rock, so Mark turned himself around for the laborious climb back to the surface, his echoing grumbles diminishing as he retreated.

Eric Stone shut off his light to conserve batteries, but when the weight of darkness pressed in on him like a palpable sensation he quickly flicked it back on. He took a few calming breaths to steel himself, shut his eyes, and killed the light again.

It was a long thirty-minute wait until he heard the others crawling down the tunnel.

When Mark's light swept Eric's face, Murph chuckled. "Man, you are as white as a ghost."

"I've never been fond of tight spaces," Stone admitted. "It's okay with the lights on. Not so much in the dark."

Normally, Mark would have ribbed him more, but considering their situation all he said was, "Don't sweat it, dude."

Linda quickly drew up a plan of attack to survey the subterranean warren of interconnected tunnels and caves. Whenever they came to a fork, one team would check the left tunnel, the other would head right. They would meet back at the branch after ten minutes no matter what. Whichever option looked the most promising was the way they would all go.

Another hour passed as they laboriously checked each section. It was all the more difficult because of the weapons and extra ammunition the three Corporation people carried. Knees and palms were scraped raw from contact with the rough stone, and without proper equipment each one of them had struck his or her head at least once. Eric had a piece of gauze taped near his hairline where he'd gashed his skin. Blood had dried coppery brown in the furrows of his forehead.

The four of them were together walking down a long gallery with heaps of shattered stones on the floor when Eric happened to play his flashlight on the ceiling ten feet over their heads. At first he thought the hundreds of projections hanging down were stalactites formed from mineral-rich water seeping into the cavern, but then he saw one was wearing pants.

Horror crept up his spine. "Oh my God."

Alana looked up and gasped.

Hanging from the ceiling were dozens of pairs of mummified legs, some showing just the foot from the ankle down, others hanging from the upper thighs as if materializing from the living rock. One person was suspended on his side, half of the corpse contained within the matrix stone while the other half dangled grotesquely. The neck was bent at such an angle that the back of the skull was hidden, and the cadaverous face leered down at them through sightless eye sockets.

There were animal legs, too, long, awkward camel legs ending in big skeletal feet and horses' limbs with their distinctive fused hoofs. The dry air had retarded putrefaction, so skin hung from the bones as brittle as parchment and clothing remained intact.

Mark studied the uneven floor, stooped, and came back up holding a leather sandal that began to crumble almost immediately.

Linda asked, "What happened to them? How did they get fused in the rock?"

Over his initial shock, Eric studied the ceiling more carefully. Unlike the rest of the cave system, the ceiling here was black and glossy under a coat of dust.

"Everyone cover your ears," he said, and brought his assault rifle to his shoulder. The crack of the shot was especially brutal in the tight confines.

The bullet had knocked free a splinter of the ceiling. He retrieved it, looked at it for only a moment, and tossed it to Mark Murphy.

"Completely solidified," he commented. "When the cave below the pit collapsed, it left them hanging."

"Of course," Alana said, examining the material.

"Little help for the nonscience types." Linda didn't bother looking at the rock sample. Her only exposure to geology was a "rocks for jocks" class back in college.

"Above us is the bottom of a tar pit," Eric answered, "like La Brea in L.A., only smaller and obviously dormant."

"It's actually asphaltic sand," Alana corrected.

"During the summer months, it warmed enough to get sticky and entrap the animals. My guess is, the people were thrown in as a form of execution. Then, at some point over the past two hundred years, the bottom of the pit collapsed—that's all this rubble on the floor—and exposed the victims at the very deepest part of the pit."

"There was something I was told by St. Julian Perlmutter a couple of days after our initial meeting," Alana said, suddenly remembering. "He'd come across one additional scrap of information. It comes from a local belief about Al-Jama's tomb. It is said he was buried beneath the 'black that burns.' That's why they had us digging in an abandoned coal mine. The terrorists thought the black was coal, but it was this."

Eric took the shard of hardened tar from her and held the flame of a disposable lighter to the thumb-sized lump. In seconds, it caught fire, and he dropped it to the ground. The four of them watched it burn silently.

Linda snuffed it out with her foot. "I would say we're getting close."

But another hour of exploration still hadn't revealed the hidden tomb.

Eric and Mark had separated from the women at yet another juncture. They approached the dead end of a particularly straight and easy section of tunnel deep under the river's original water level. Eric paused to take a sip from his canteen before they retreated to the rendezvous. The end of the tunnel sloped up in a perfectly flat ramp that met the ceiling. Something about it intrigued him, and he climbed up the incline until his face was inches from where it joined the roof.

Rather than solid rock, he saw a jagged line, a crack barely a millimeter wide, that ran the full width of the tunnel. He fumbled in his pocket for the disposable lighter, and called over his shoulder, "Kill your light."

"What? Why?"

"Just do it already."

He thumbed the lighter and held the flame close to the crack. There wasn't much of a flicker, but it was enough to convince him that there was an open space on the other side of the ramp and a slight breeze was getting through. He turned on his light again, examining every square inch of the incline. It was a neatly fitted piece of work. The cracks along the walls were almost invisible.

"This is man-made," he announced. "I think it's like a giant teeter-totter. Give me a hand."

They stood, stooped, as far up the ramp as they could go, with their backs braced against the ceiling.

"On three," Eric said. "One . . . two . . . three."

They pushed with everything they had. At first, nothing happened, and the sounds of their straining bodies filled the tunnel. Then, imperceptibly, the floor under them gave way slightly, pushed down by their combined strength. When they relaxed, it snapped back into position.

"Again. Harder."

Their second attempt pushed the big stone lever down about an inch, enough for Eric to see there was a large chamber beyond. He jammed the lighter into the crack just before they let go, but the weight of stone was too great and the plastic case was crushed.

"Good idea, though. I think the four of us should be able to do it. There's enough room to stand side by side."

They found Linda and Alana a few minutes later, sitting with their backs against a wall sharing a protein bar.

"Not to keep repeating myself," Linda said around a monstrous bite, "but we hit another dead end."

"Eric and I think we found something."

Moments later, Eric explained how the rock incline was a pivoting device, balanced in the middle, halfway up the ten-foot-high slope. The four got into position at the top of the ramp, standing side by side, their upper shoulders pressed to the ceiling.

"And go," Linda ordered.

Their combined strength made stone grate against stone, and the incline began to flatten out. What had been a tiny crack yawned into the entrance of another chamber, one they could see was partially lined with mud bricks. Harder they pushed, groaning at the effort. The lever dipped on its fulcrum, so the ramp became perfectly flat.

"You know once we're through, there's no going back," Linda grunted, fresh perspiration flushing her pixie face.

"I know," Mark replied. "Push."

The rock platform began to slope down into the bricked chamber beyond the tunnel, and they were able to shuffle back so they stood at its very lip, muscles quivering. They were only a couple feet above the sand-covered floor.

Linda judged they had enough clearance. "Ready? Go!"

The four leapt off the stone slab, tumbling into the dirt. Behind them the rock-slab lever crashed back to the ground with an echoing boom. There was a space under it like the nook beneath a flight of stairs. They could see the actual fulcrum was a thick length of log resting on notched-stone blocks. In the crease where the rock met the floor was another small wooden contraption whose purpose was unknown.

No sooner had the echoes died away than there came a new sound, a deep, rumbling hiss from someplace above them. Eric flashed his light to the ceiling twenty feet over their heads just as sand began to pour out of dozens of man-hole-sized openings.

"You've got to be kidding me," Mark said.

The wooden device was the trigger for a booby trap that activated when the pivot returned to its original position.

They cast their lights around the room. It was about ten feet square. Three of the walls were natural rock, part of the limestone cavern—one had the alcove for the lever device. The fourth wall was mud bricks laid with mortar between the joints. They ignored the rock and concentrated their attention on the brick. There were no holes or openings of any type, no handles or other kind of mechanism for getting out of the room.

In the five minutes they spent searching the wall, two feet of sand had built up on the floor in uneven piles that shifted and spread, with more dropping down from above. Linda pulled her knife from its sheath and pried at the mortar near one brick. It crumbled under the blade, and she was able to loosen the brick enough to work it out of the wall. Behind it was an identical layer. And, for all she knew, there were a half dozen more.

"We'll have to try to move the lever from underneath," Linda said. She accidentally backed into the stream of fine sand cascading from the ceiling and had to shake her head like a dog to dislodge the grit.

There were three holes directly in front of the alcove, and already it was half full of sand.

Eric countered, "With that much sand right in front we'll be buried before we can push it open."

"We're trapped," Alana said, panic making her voice crack. "What are we going to do?"

Stoney looked at Mark Murphy, and for the first time neither man had an answer.

THIRTY-ONE

Tariq Assad thanked his pilot friend and stepped from the helicopter. He closed the flimsy door, gave it a tap, and scurried from under the whirling blades. The small service chopper lifted off the desert floor in a dust storm of its own creation. Assad had to turn his back to it and keep his eyes tightly closed.

As soon as the helo had lifted clear, he strode toward the team commander. The seething anger he had felt in the wake of the police raid back in Tripoli had been replaced with unmitigated joy. He embraced the terrorist leader, kissing him on both cheeks effusively.

"Ali, this is going to be a great day." Assad grinned.

He'd radioed ahead that he was coming and saw with satisfaction that his orders had been carried out. The men were waiting at the rear cargo ramp of their Mi-8. When Assad waved, they gave him a rousing cheer. Their prisoner was bound to one of the bench seats, a rag tied over his mouth.

Ali noticed Assad's look. "When we do not gag him, he shrieks like a woman. If he wasn't such a supposed expert on

Suleiman Al-Jama, blessings be upon him, I would put a bullet through that fat lout's head and be done with it."

"What a remarkable turn of events," Assad said, Emile Bumford's treatment all but forgotten. "A few hours ago, I was moments from being grabbed by the police, and now we will shortly discover the lost tomb."

"Tell me again how you found it," Ali invited. They strode to the waiting chopper, whose blades started to beat the superheated air.

"Coming in on the helicopter, I had the pilot swing south when we crossed the border into Tunisia, and as we came down the old riverbed, flying just above it, I spotted an area where it appeared that a section of the bank had been blasted into the river. Had I known about the waterfall a little farther downstream, I wouldn't have paid it any attention, for surely a sailing ship couldn't have navigated it. But I didn't know, so I had the pilot set down so I could investigate."

"When was this?"

"Moments before I radioed you. What, a half hour ago? And when we landed, I saw evidence that people had been there recently. There were four distinct sets of shoe prints. Two are women, or maybe small men, but I think one might be the American archaeologist who worked with our guest there." He pointed across the cargo bay to Bumford.

The turbines' whine made it so Assad had to shout to be heard by the man sitting to his left. "The prints all disappeared into a cave located behind a hill along the river. They must all still be inside. We have them, Ali, the Americans who have disrupted our plans for the last time, and Suleiman's tomb."

● ● ●

JUAN ACCEPTED A CUP of coffee from Maurice, the *Oregon*'s chief steward.

"How are you feeling, Captain?" the dour Englishman asked.

"I think the expression is 'rode hard and put away wet,'" Juan said, taking a sip of the strong brew.

"An equine reference, I believe. Filthy creatures, only good for glue factories and betting at Ascot."

Cabrillo chuckled. "Dr. Huxley juiced my leg so it's feeling pretty good, and the handful of ibuprofen I scarfed down are kicking in. All in all, I'm not doing too badly."

The one secret about pain Juan had never shared with anyone other than Julia Huxley, as medical officer, was that he felt it constantly. Doctors call it phantom pain, but to him it was real enough. His missing leg, the one shot off by a Chinese gunboat all those years ago, ached every minute of every day. And on the good days it only ached. Sometimes he'd be hit with lances of agony that took all his self-control not to react to.

So when it came to dealing with the discomfort from where he'd cut out his tracking chip, it wasn't bravado that made him ignore it. It was practice.

Around them, the op center buzzed with activity. Max Hanley and a pair of technicians had an access panel removed under one of the consoles to replace a faulty computer monitor. The duty weapons officer was talking with teams working throughout the ship to make certain her suite of armaments was operating exactly to standards, while the helmsman maintained a steady course well beyond Libya's twelve-mile territorial limit.

The ship and crew were ready, only, for the time being, Cabrillo had nothing for them to do.

They still hadn't received an updated list of Libyan naval assets capable of landing a helicopter, and until they did there was nothing for the *Oregon* to do but wait.

Juan hated to wait. Especially when he had people on the ground. His feelings toward them made it as though everything they went through exacted a physical price on him, too.

"Call coming through," the radio operator said over her shoulder.

Juan hit a switch on the arm of his chair, and from hidden speakers came the sound of heavy breathing, almost panting.

"You've picked a bad time for an obscene phone call," he said to the unknown person.

"Chairman, it's Linc." Franklin gasped. "We got trouble."

"What's happened?"

"You can forget your theories about Ali Ghami being Al-Jama." Lincoln continued to wheeze. It was obvious he was running. "Our old buddy Tariq Assad just showed up, and after a little Arab-style kissy face with the leader of the group searching for the tomb they beat it southward in that old Mi-8 of theirs. He's Al-Jama, Juan. I tried calling Linda but they're still underground. I'm now hightailing it after them, but I figure I got four or five miles to go."

"That confirms it." Agitated, Juan stood and began pacing the deck. "A couple hours ago, we got suspicious because Hali Kasim hadn't checked in, and his GPS chip hadn't moved in a while. I sent Eddie to find him. Hali'd been shot at such close range, there was GSR all over him. The last person with him was none other than Tariq Assad."

"Jesus, is Hali okay?"

"We don't know yet. Eddie said it was bad. All he could do was stabilize him and call for an ambulance. He stuck around long enough to follow it to a hospital, but he can't exactly barge in and start demanding answers."

A fax machine built into the communications center started whirring.

"For Assad to bug out like he did," Linc panted, "he must have seen something he liked in the same area as Linda and the others."

"I can get a backup team to you by chopper, but it's going to take a couple of hours," Juan offered lamely, for he knew it would be over long before then.

The communications officer handed him the fax. He glanced at it quickly. It was the report on Libya's Navy he'd been expecting for hours now.

"Nah. I'll be okay. I'm doing eight-minute miles so I'll have something in the tank when I get there. A dozen tangos in a cave when I have the element of surprise shouldn't be too difficult."

Juan was barely paying attention. He crossed to the navigation computer to punch in the GPS numbers and plot the vessels' coordinates and recent movements.

One leapt out at him immediately. His instincts screamed at him that they had found it. The ship would have been within helicopter range of the terrorist training camp, and, while all the others were converging on Tripoli for a military review as part of the peace conference, this particular vessel was loitering near the Tunisian border.

"Linc, call me back when you reach the cave. I've got to go."

"Roger that."

"Helm, plot me a course for that ship." He pointed at the blinking light on the overhead display. The edge in his voice caused those around him to stop their work and look. A wave of expectant energy swept the op-center crew.

"Course laid in, Chairman."

"What's our ETA at best possible speed?"

"A little over three hours."

"Okay, hit it."

An alarm the crew was all too familiar with began to wail. When the ship was pushing near her maximum speed, the ride was usually rough, and every loose item from the saucers in the galley to the makeup pots in Kevin Nixon's Magic Shop had to be secured.

The acceleration was smooth as the *Oregon*'s revolutionary engines came online, the cryopumps whining a high-pitched tone that became inaudible to humans but would have sent a dog into paroxysms.

Juan returned to his central seat and called up the specifications for the Libyan vessel. She was a modified Russian frigate, purchased in 1999, weighing in at fourteen hundred tons. She was two-thirds the length of the *Oregon*—three hundred and thirteen feet—and the Corporation's ship outclassed the Libyan when it came to weapons systems. But the frigate *Khalij Surt* still packed a powerful punch, with four three-inch deck guns, multiple launchers for the SS-N-2c Styx ship-to-ship missiles, as well as an umbrella of Gecko rockets and rapid-fire 30mm cannons to ward off an air assault. The *Khalij Surt*, or *Gulf of Sidra*, could also fire torpedoes from deck launchers and lay mines from her stern.

Juan studied a picture of the vessel from *Jane's Defence Review*'s website. She was a lethal-looking craft, with a tall, flaring bow, and a radio mast festooned with antennae for her upgraded sensor systems behind her single funnel. The big cannons were paired in armored turrets fore and aft, and just behind the lead gun sat her antiship missile launchers.

Cabrillo had no doubt he could take her in an engagement. The *Oregon*'s ship-to-ship missiles had twice the range of the *Sidra*'s Styx system, but blowing the Libyan frigate out of the water with a missile shot from over the horizon wasn't the point.

He needed to board the *Sidra*, rescue Fiona Katamora if his hunch was right, and get her to safety.

"That her?" Max asked. He'd moved to Juan's side silently and was pointing at the computer monitor.

"Yup. What do you think?"

"Judging by the radar specs, they'll see a chopper coming fifty miles off. And it looks like she's loaded for bear, with triple-A and SAMs."

"Which means we're going to have to lay in alongside her and do this old-school."

"You mean go toe-to-toe with her, don't you?"

"We'll need a distraction to get in close, but, yeah, that's what I'm thinking."

Max was silent for a moment. Naval war-fighting doctrine had changed dramatically in the years since missiles had been perfected. No longer did heavily armored battleships pound at each other with their big guns, hoping for a hit. Sea battles now oftentimes were fought with the combatants hundreds of miles apart. The power of high-explosive-tipped missiles made thick plates of protective steel superfluous, so modern navies rarely bothered.

The *Oregon* had built-in protection, but not against the *Sidra*'s three-inch cannons, and certainly not if she managed to slam a couple of Styx missiles into the *Oregon*'s side. Juan was proposing to get close enough to the Libyan frigate to send across a boarding party under the full onslaught of the *Sidra*'s guns and missiles.

"When was the last time two capital ships dueled it out like this?" Hanley finally asked.

"I'm thinking March 9, 1862, at Hampton Roads, Virginia."

"The *Monitor* and the *Merrimack*?" Juan nodded. Max added, "They fought to a draw. We don't have that option. And you do realize that unless we sink her as soon as we have the Secretary, we're going to have just as tough a time getting clear again. We might get lucky sneaking up on their ship, but don't think the Libyans are gonna let us just sail away, you know?"

"Already thought about that."

"You have an idea?"

"No," Juan said airily. "But I *have* thought about it."

"And your distraction? Any ideas on that front?"

"Don't have the foggiest. But since we'll attack under the cover of darkness, we've got until dusk to come up with one. One thing, though . . ."

"Yeah?"

"A ship the size of the *Sidra* is going to take twenty minutes or more to sink, no matter how we do it. That's more than enough time to give the *Oregon* a missile enema."

Max put on a long-suffering expression. "Oh, you are just full of cheery news, aren't you?"

"I'll add insult to injury. Before we face the *Sidra*, we're loading our new Libyan friends into our lifeboats. I don't want them aboard when we go into battle. So if something goes wrong, we've got no way off the *Oregon*."

"Why did I ever take that first phone call from you all those years ago?" Max cried theatrically to the ceiling.

"Chairman," the comm officer said, "you have another call coming through."

"Linc?"

"No, sir. Langston Overholt."

"Thanks, Monica." Juan donned a headset and keyed his computer to accept the call. "Lang, it's Cabrillo."

"How are you feeling?"

"Good. Tired, but good."

"And your guests?"

"Grateful and ravenous. They've gone through half our stores in a single day."

"I'm calling for an update and to give you some news."

"Tariq Assad just showed up near where my people are looking for Suleiman's tomb."

"He's the official who Qaddafi's government said is Al-Jama?"

"And it would appear they were right, and we helped him escape and nearly lost a man doing so."

"Lost someone. Who?"

"Hali Kasim, my head communications officer, was shot in the chest. Eddie Seng got him to a hospital, but we have no idea yet on his condition."

"I'll get word to Ambassador Moon so he'll look into it."

"I'd appreciate that, thank you."

"Does this clear Minister Ghami from your list of suspects?"

"Not in the slightest. Terrorists might have taken down the Secretary's plane without government help, but there was a cover-up afterward. It could have easily been orchestrated from the top or manipulated from the shadows. If Al-Jama's people have infiltrated the Libyan government the way we suspect, then the tangos could have been tipped off early enough to put the cover-up in place."

"Or Ghami is high in Al-Jama's organization, and he ordered the destruction of the plane's wreckage as well as the convenient timing of its discovery."

"Exactly. And let's not forget that the person who Ghami replaced, plus most of his senior staff, were arrested and left to rot. That could have come from Ghami, or Qaddafi himself could have ordered a purge."

"What a mess." The CIA veteran sighed. "Despite our warnings, the Vice President is insisting on going to a scheduled reception tonight at Ghami's home for many of the conference's senior attendees."

"Bad idea," Juan snapped.

"I concur, but there isn't anything I can do about it. The

Secret Service detail has been informed there may be an assault, but the VP is adamant he attend."

"The guy's a moron."

"I concur with that, too. However, it doesn't change the facts. On the plus side, Ghami's house is totally isolated, and the security personnel are the same people being used for the conference in Tripoli tomorrow morning. They've all been vetted. Even if Ghami is somehow connected to the terrorists, I think this dinner should be okay."

"Really? Why?"

"Would you stage a massive attack on your own home? Especially when you'll have the same people gathered together the next day with the world's press watching every move they make. You must remember the impact of Anwar Sadat's assassination being broadcast nearly live. If there's going to be an attack—"

"Not *if*, Lang," Juan said.

"*If* there's going to be an attack," Overholt persisted, "it'll be tomorrow, or sometime during the conference."

"I don't like this."

"Nobody does, but there isn't any other way. All of these leaders know they're putting their lives at risk by attending the conference, either there in Tripoli or back home when their own fundamentalists rouse themselves into a frenzy. In these troubled times, being the President of a Middle Eastern country is a dangerous occupation, especially for those willing to work on a peace deal. They all know it and are still willing to go ahead. That says something." Overholt then changed tack as his way of saying that was the end of the discussion, and he asked, "How are you coming with finding Secretary Katamora?"

"I think we have a lead." Juan had already explained to Overholt about the radar blip they'd seen and his theory that she was being taken to a ship offshore. "She may be on a frigate called the *Gulf of Sidra*, or *Khalij Surt*, and we're on our way to her now."

"What are you planning to do?"

"Board her, rescue the Secretary, and put the *Sidra* on the bottom."

"Absolutely not!" Overholt roared. Juan winced. "You will not sink a naval vessel belonging to a sovereign nation. I can't even condone you boarding her."

"I'm not asking for permission, Lang," Juan retorted hotly.

"Juan, as God is my witness, if you sink that ship I will see to it that you are charged for piracy. I can authorize you to discover if she is aboard. After that, it falls on our diplomats, and possibly our military, to resolve the situation."

"Diplomats?" Juan scoffed. "These are terrorists. Murderers. You can't negotiate with them."

"Then our Navy will handle an assault, if it comes to that. Am I clear?"

"Might as well pack it in now, Lang, because if you follow that plan she's as good as dead."

"You don't think I know what's at stake?" Overholt shouted. "I know her life is probably forfeit, but I also have rules, and when *I* have them so do you. You were hired to find her, and if she's on the *Gulf of Sidra* you've done your job. Take your money and go."

"Damn it." Juan's anger spilled into his voice. He had no idea why the conversation had veered in this direction, but he wasn't going to take an insult. "This isn't about money, and you know it."

"Christ. I'm sorry," Lang replied contritely. "That was a low blow. It's just this whole situation."

"I understand. Marquess of Queensberry."

"What's that?"

"Just something Max said a while back. Don't worry. I won't destroy their ship, you have my promise. But if there's a chance I can get her back, I'm going for it. Okay?"

"All right. It's just that we can't handle another diplomatic incident with Libya right now. On the heels of the plane crash, they'll see the destruction of one of their frigates as retaliation no matter who was responsible, and they'll treat it as an act of war. You'll scuttle the conference before it even starts."

"We're on the same page, Lang. Relax, and I'll call you

later." Juan killed the connection and turned to Max. "Good thing that wasn't a video call."

"Why's that?"

"He would have seen my fingers crossed."

THIRTY-TWO

WITH SO MUCH SAND POURING THROUGH THE CEIL-
ing, the air in the subterranean chamber was becom-
ing unbreathable, even though they had rags tied across their
mouths. Their lights cast meager, murky beams through the
choking pall. The glow was closer to burnt umber than the
halogen's normal silver.

Doggedly, Linda, Alana, Eric, and Mark dug their way
upward to stay atop the growing pile. The sand was coming
so fast that even a few seconds' rest would see a limb buried.
They moved on pure survival instinct, buying themselves a
little more time before they were buried alive under the hiss-
ing onslaught. The mound was so deep now that they could
no longer stand upright but had to stoop slightly against the
ceiling.

Whoever had designed the trap those hundreds of years
ago would find comfort in heaven or hell that it still worked
after centuries.

The women were faring better than the men because their

bodies were lighter, and they helped Eric and Mark dig themselves free whenever they got into trouble.

Alana had just yanked Stoney's foot clear when a realization hit him. He shouted over to Murph, "Are you sure this room's below the old river level?"

"Pretty sure. Why?"

"We're idiots. One-point-six."

"One-point-six?"

"One-point-six," Eric confirmed. "And figure a fifty percent overengineering factor."

"Of course. Why didn't I see that?"

"Do you mind explaining what's so important about one-point-six," Linda called over the sound of falling sand.

"Because this part of the tunnel is below the river, the trap was most likely designed to fill with water and drown its victims. Over the years, sand filled the reservoir."

"So?"

"Sand is one-point-six times heavier than water by volume."

Linda didn't see his point, and made an impatient gesture for him to continue.

"The brick wall was constructed to withstand the pressure of a certain amount of water. But now that this room is filling with sand, it's holding back one-point-six times more weight than its builders intended. Any good engineer will factor in an additional fifty percent safety margin to be certain. Even if they overbuilt the wall, the sand is still ten percent heavier than it can withstand. It's only a matter of time before it fails."

Skeptically, Linda looked from Eric to Mark. Both still struggled to stay ahead of the rising tide of sand, but the grim fatalism that had been etched on their faces moments before was gone. The two of them were certain they were getting out of the trap alive. That was good enough for her.

Moments later, the wall still hadn't collapsed, and the four were forced to their hands and knees. It was much more difficult to keep ahead of the sand in this position. Linda and Alana struggled right along with the men now. With their backs pressed to the ceiling, there were only twenty inches of space remaining before the chamber was completely full. Those last seconds would go fast.

Linda's brief elation that they were going to survive ebbed, though she would fight until the bitter end. Mark and Eric contorted themselves, digging frantically to keep above the rising tide of sand, but Alana Shepard had given up. They could hear her sobs over the cascade's din.

"Damn," was all Eric said. His cheek was mashed to the roof, and he had created a tiny air pocket around his mouth a moment before a wave of dirt buried his face.

Twenty feet below them, the multiple courses of brick at the wall's base bowed under the hundreds of tons of sand, the mortar cracked in places, and wispy trickles of grit dribbled through the crevasses.

All at once the entire ten-foot width of the wall gave way. The wall failed completely, collapsing and falling outward into another chamber beyond like a burst dam. A tidal wave of sand swept through the breach, pushing the wall's remnants like so much flotsam.

The four people who moments earlier were muttering their final prayers were borne along the tsunami and deposited unceremoniously in a tangle of limbs, the very sand that had been seconds from killing them cushioning their wild ride.

Mark was the first to recover, his booming whoop of joy bouncing from wall to wall in the large chamber. He reached across and held out a fist to Eric so they could tap knuckles. "Good call, my friend. Damned good call."

Eric was a little pale. "I wasn't so sure at the end."

"Never a doubt." Mark hoisted Stone to his feet, and they then helped Alana and Linda to theirs.

Alana threw her arms around Eric's neck and kissed him as if predicting the wall's collapse had made it happen. "Thank you," she breathed into his ear.

"You're welcome," he replied awkwardly.

It took a few minutes to find their weapons and clean the sand from the barrels and receivers. The assault rifles weren't designed to take this kind of punishment, so they had to be thorough.

They found themselves in another cave, still part of the same complex of limestone caverns riddling the hill above them. There was only one exit, a narrow cleft ten feet up the far wall and accessible by steps carved into the living rock.

"Now that we know this place is booby-trapped," Linda said at the base of the stairs, "I'm taking point. Eric, you're behind me, then Alana, then Mark. And from now on, we stick together, no exploring on your own. Everyone stay on your toes, and look for anything unusual—an odd rock, writing on the walls, anything."

They climbed into the tight cave. Headroom wasn't a problem, but the tunnel was so narrow it was difficult to walk without scraping their shoulders. The cave climbed steeply, and, with space so tight, their footing was uneven. A wrong step could twist an ankle. Linda was concentrating on her movements yet still aware of danger, and she spotted the trip wire well before she was going to trigger it.

It was a thin filament of copper that stretched across the tunnel at the level of her shins, with one end secured to the wall with an iron screw and the other vanishing up into the gloom ahead. She pointed it out to the others and cautiously stepped over it.

The sharply ascending tunnel ended another hundred feet from the trip wire in a small room with a low ceiling. They had to crawl under a wooden trestle built at the tunnel's exit. The wire wrapped around a metal lever built into a device that would fall back when it was tripped. This in turn would release a carved-stone ball sitting on the angled cradle. The ball was about three feet around and weighed in at half a ton. A direct hit, after rolling and bouncing down the shaft, would crush a man flat, while a glancing blow would surely break bone.

"We should trigger it," Mark said, mostly because the kid in him wanted to watch the stone hurtle down the tunnel.

"Leave it," Alana said. The archaeologist in her hated the idea of disturbing what was the find of her career.

"We'll compromise," Linda said. She plucked a stone from the ground and wedged it under the boulder. Even if someone hit the trip wire and the lever were released, the rock would prevent it from moving.

There were a few other man-made items in the room—a battered wooden chest missing its lid, an empty sword scabbard for one of the Barbary pirates' wicked scimitars made of beaten brass, a couple lengths of rope, and a half dozen thin metal shafts Mark identified as ramrods. They took the opportunity to change out their flashlight batteries, and started exploring further.

Three different tunnels branched off from what they called "the boulder room." They explored one tunnel without incident and were halfway down the second one when Linda placed a foot on a hidden trigger. There was just the tiniest give under her foot, but she knew they were in trouble.

Just under the surface of the sandy passage, a wooden board had been buried and cleverly concealed. Her weight rasped a piece of steel against flint under the plank to produce enough sparks to ignite a fuse. The cask of gunpowder was secreted farther in the hole, and contained enough explosive to kill all four of them.

Linda jumped back instantly and, in a tackle that would have done a pro football player proud, pushed her three companions back until the whole pile of them went down. But the blast never came. Instead, the powder ignited and burned unevenly, a flaring, sputtering cauldron of fire that filled the tunnel with noxious white smoke. In the two hundred years since the trap had been set, the powder's acidity had eaten through the wooden cask, so when it lit there was nothing to contain the fire and cause an explosive detonation.

"Everybody all right?" Linda asked when the last of the powder had burned itself out.

"I think so," Alana answered, stifling a cough.

"I feel like I just went three rounds with Eddie in his dojo," Eric replied, rubbing his ribs where Linda's shoulder had hit him. "I never knew someone so small could hit so hard."

"Amazing what a little adrenaline can do." She stood and brushed herself off. "The fact that this tunnel's boobytrapped tells me we're on the right path."

They kept going, and the tunnel started climbing. There was no way of knowing how deep they had gone or where they were in relation to the riverbank, but all of them felt they had to be getting close.

There was more evidence that people had spent a greater amount of time in this part of the cavern. There were marks in the sand coating the ground where men had walked, men who had constructed the elaborate traps they had already passed. Twice more, Linda stopped the party to check the ground, but they found no additional hidden bombs.

The tunnel turned sharply. Linda peered around the corner before committing herself and came up short. Around the bend stood an iron door embedded in the rock. The metal had a reddish hue, a tracery of rust having formed from exposure to damp air when the river still flowed. There was no lock or keyhole. The door was a featureless slab of metal, so they knew the hinges must be on the other side.

Linda dropped to one knee to dig through her pack.

Mark moved until he was directly in front of the door, spread his arms wide in a theatrical pose. "Open sesame," he intoned. The door didn't budge. He glanced over at Alana. "You know, I kind of thought that would work."

"This will." Linda straightened, holding a block of plastic explosives.

She used a piece of cardboard torn from a box in her first-aid kit to slip between the door and jamb to determine which side it hinged from and set her charges over the hinges. She selected a pair of two-minute timing pencils and rammed them home.

"Coming?" she called sweetly, and the four of them retreated fifty yards back down the tunnel. The distance muted the blast, but the pressure wave hit with enough force to ripple their clothes.

When they returned, the door had been blown from its hinges and tossed ten feet into the next section of the tunnel.

Unlike the claustrophobic nature of much of the cave, the chamber they found themselves standing in was vast. It was longer than the reach of their flashlights and equally broad.

The ceiling lofted forty or more feet over their heads. Much of the cave was limestone like they'd been seeing since entering the earth, but the wall to their right was a vast mound of rubble, the debris blasted over the cave's entrance when Henry Lafayette started his long journey home.

On the left side of the cavern ran an elevated platform that looked like it had once served as Suleiman Al-Jama's pier. And tied to it, canted slightly because its keel rested on the ground and wasn't floating as it should, was the infamous pirate's ship, the *Saqr*.

Her mast had been lowered and her rigging stowed in order to enter the cave, but otherwise she looked fully capable of sailing once again. The dry air had perfectly preserved her wooden hull. She was facing away from them, so the mouths of her stern long guns looked like enormous black holes.

On closer inspection, as they peered down on her from the quay, they could see where she had sustained damage during her running battle with the American ketch *Siren*.

Chunks of her bulwarks had been blown apart by cannon shot, and there were a dozen places where fire had scorched the deck. One of her guns was missing, and, judging from the damage around its emplacement, it had exploded at some point during the battle and was lost over the side.

"This is absolutely amazing," Alana said breathlessly. "It's a piece of living history."

"I can almost hear the battle," Mark agreed.

There was so much more to explore, but for several minutes the four of them stared down on the corsair.

A flicker of movement to his right caught Eric's attention and broke him from his reverie. He cast the beam of his light back to the remnants of the mangled doorframe just as a figure slipped through. He was about to shout a challenge when an assault rifle opened up ten feet from the first man's position, its juddering flame winking in the darkness.

In the half second before he reacted, he saw several more gunmen in the uneven light. Bullets filled the air around them when more weapons opened up.

The four had no idea how Al-Jama's people had found

them so quickly, but the fact was clear. They had arrived with almost three-to-one superiority, and more ammunition because they were prepared for a fight, and now they controlled the only way out of the cave.

THIRTY-THREE

JUAN TOOK A SECOND TO LOOK ACROSS THE SEA. IT was a view he would never tire of. To him, the ocean was mystery and majesty and the promise of what lay over the horizon. It could be the still, sultry waters of a tropical lagoon or the raging fury of an Asian cyclone tearing away the surface in sheets that stretched for miles. The sea was both siren and adversary, the duality making his love for it all the stronger.

When he'd conceived the Corporation, basing it aboard a ship had been the logical choice. It gave them mobility and anonymity. But he had been secretly pleased by the fact that they would need a vessel like the *Oregon* so he could indulge in moments like this.

There was a bare whisper of wind, and the waves were gently lapping against the hull as though the ship were a babe rocked in a cradle. This far from shore the air was fresh, tinged with a salt tang that reminded Juan of his childhood on the beaches of southern California.

"Captain, excuse me," a voice said. "I do not wish to disturb you, but I wanted to thank you again before we leave."

Juan turned. Standing before him in a suit provided by the Magic Shop was Libya's former Foreign Minister. He had his hand out.

Cabrillo shook it with genuine warmth. "Not necessary."

Juan wanted to make sure the escaped prisoners left the *Oregon* during daylight. He had full confidence in his ship and crew, but no captain ever likes to put people into lifeboats, and doing so at night only compounded the risks. He looked down from the bridge wing at the mass of humanity standing on the deck in the shadow of one of the boats.

They hadn't been able to provide everyone with new clothes, so many of them sported the rags they'd been wearing since their incarceration. At least they'd had the chance to eat and bathe. A few noted him looking down and waved. It quickly turned into a rousing cheer.

"They would all be dead without you," the Minister said.

Juan turned back to the diplomat. "Then their lives are thanks enough. We will be in contact with the crewmen I'm sending with you so you'll know exactly what's happening. And we should be able to pick you up at first light. If something goes wrong, my men will take you to Tunisia. From there, it'll be up to you where you go."

"I will return home," the Libyan said forcefully, "and somehow take back my job."

"How was it you were arrested? Was it Ghami who ordered it?"

"No. The Minister of Justice. A political rival of mine. One day I'm Foreign Minister, and the next I'm being shoved into a van and Ghami has my job."

"When was this?"

"February seventh."

"And what was Ghami before? He worked for your ministry, right?"

"That is something he wants people to believe. I don't know what he did before taking my office, but he didn't work in the Foreign Ministry. What I have been able to piece together is that he managed to get a meeting with President

Qaddafi, which is difficult to say the least. The next day it was announced that I had been arrested and Ghami had been named my replacement."

"Could he have something on Qaddafi, some sort of leverage?"

"You cannot blackmail a man who is President for Life."

"Hold on one second." Juan stepped onto the bridge and keyed the wall-mounted microphone. The duty officer in the op center answered straightaway. "Do me a favor," Juan said. "Check international press reports of any crime involving Libyan nationals going back a month prior to February seventh of this year."

"What is it you suspect?" the diplomat asked when Juan stepped back outside.

"You don't give a job like yours to a complete unknown without a reason." Juan wanted to call Overholt and at the very least demand that the Vice President not attend this evening's dinner. "I still don't know if Ghami's tied to Suleiman Al-Jama, but I don't trust this guy one whit. He's put on a hell of a show in diplomatic circles, and orchestrating the summit is the achievement of a lifetime . . ." Juan's voice drifted off.

"What is it?"

"The timing and the fact you are who you are." His tone sharpened. "It isn't coincidence that you were in a terrorist camp run by Al-Jama. There is a link between him and Ghami. I'm certain of it."

"Captain, you must understand something about my country that I am not proud of. We have harbored many fighters so they may train on our soil, and allowing them use of our political prisoners is quite common."

"I thought your government had renounced terrorism."

"It has, but there are many who don't agree with that policy. Our own Justice Minister is one of them. I know for a fact that he has provided aid to Al-Jama in the past."

"So you're saying Ghami's legit?"

"As much as it pains me to say, it is possible. And I have more reason than you to think ill of him. The man took my job and even now lives in my house."

The intercom on the bridge squawked. Juan stepped through and punched the button. "Anything?"

"Nothing earth-shattering, if that's what you're looking for. A quick search shows a couple of Libyans arrested for smuggling heroin into Amsterdam, one killed in a traffic pileup that claimed four other people in Switzerland. A Libyan national living in Hungary was arrested for domestic abuse, and another for attempted murder stemming from a dispute with a shopkeeper just across the border in Tunisia."

"Okay. Thanks." Juan turned to the Minister. "Dead end."

"What were you thinking?"

"Truthfully, I don't know."

Below them the forty-seat lifeboat was lowered from its davits so the refugees could step through a gate built into the ship's rail. They would need to overload the boats to get all the people off the *Oregon*. The boats were fully enclosed and could weather a hurricane because of their self-righting hull design, so at worst the former prisoners would be cramped but not in any real danger.

Juan shook the diplomat's hand a second time. "Good luck."

Cabrillo watched until the last of the Libyans was safely aboard. He nodded to Greg Chaffee, who wasn't happy about being exiled with them. But, then again, Juan wasn't happy that Alana Shepard had snuck off with Linda and the others behind his back.

He waved to the general operations technician who would command the craft before the man ducked through the Plexiglas hatch and secured it behind him. The winches took up the strain and lowered the boat down the side of the *Oregon*'s hull. A moment later, the lines were disengaged from inside the boat and its motor fired. It started puttering away from the big freighter.

The second boat, lowered from the port side, met up with the first. The two would stay together throughout the night and hopefully would be back in their cradles in time for breakfast.

Juan took the secret elevator at the back of the pilothouse

to the op center and settled into his seat. He still didn't have a plan for how they were going to make their final approach on the *Sidra* or how they were going to avoid sinking her after they had rescued the Secretary. One corner of the main view screen showed the radar plot. Because of the *Oregon*'s vastly superior sensor suite, the Libyans had no idea they were being watched as they cruised only about a mile off the coast, tracking eastward at a lazy eight knots. The only other ship on the plot was a supertanker heading on a parallel track, most likely making for the oil terminal at Az-Zāwiya.

He glanced at his watch. The diplomatic reception at Ali Ghami's house was scheduled to start in a little more than an hour. The guests were probably already en route. Full darkness would follow two hours later. There was a quarter moon tonight that wouldn't rise until well after midnight, which severely tightened their window of opportunity.

To distract himself, and hopefully free his mind so inspiration would hit, Cabrillo checked the Internet for those police reports concerning Libyans. The car accident had been particularly brutal. Three of the victims were burned beyond recognition and had to be identified through dental records. The Libyan, a student, was IDed because he was driving a rental car.

He scanned a couple more reports, thinking about his conversation moments ago on deck. He called up a photograph of Libya's Justice Minister, and cringed. He was an ugly man, with a bulbous, misshapen nose, narrow eyes, and a skin condition of some sort that made his face appear pebbled.

On top of that, he'd been injured. Half his lower jaw was missing, and the grafts to cover the hole were taut, shiny cicatrices. The official bio said the wound came from the American bombing of Tripoli in 1986, but a little further digging in a CIA database Cabrillo still had access to told him that the Minister had been beaten to within an inch of his life by a cuckolded husband.

Cabrillo smirked. He compared this information to his impression of the ousted Foreign Minister. Now, that guy was a class act, he thought. He had lost his job, been imprisoned and forced to do hard labor, and yet wouldn't accuse Ghami of orchestrating the whole thing. He seemed more upset that Ghami was living in his house.

"Must be a hell of a place," Juan muttered to himself.

It took him a few minutes searching the Internet to find an article about Ghami's home that listed an address. He then found the GPS coordinates off a mapping site and keyed them into Google Earth. As the computer zoomed in on the precise location, pixels blurred for a moment. When they resolved, Cabrillo leapt from his chair so fast he startled the rest of the op-center crew.

He mashed the intercom on his chair's arm. "Max, get up here now. We've got trouble."

Cabrillo looked again at the satellite image. The house sat alone in the desert, miles from any other building, and was ringed with a perimeter wall. The driveway ran up to the home before looping back on itself under a cantilevered porte cochere. There was a glass-enclosed solarium attached to one side, and the back lawns were a veritable maze of box hedges. On the roof was a satellite-uplink antenna.

He'd seen this exact layout for the first time as a mock-up less than forty-eight hours earlier.

He understood everything at that moment. The attack was planned for tonight. Al-Jama wanted to do it before the conference to show symbolically that peace never stood a chance. Knowing the terrorist mastermind's sense of the dramatic and penchant for beheadings, he was pretty sure what would start the attack. He envisioned Fiona Katamora's graceful neck bent and a man standing over her with a sword.

When he closed his eyes, the sword came down in a shining blur.

THIRTY-FOUR

THE EXECUTIONER EXAMINED THE ROOM CRITICALLY. He was alone for now, but there was plenty of space for witnesses, though they had been forced to use a lottery system to choose the lucky ones. The black backdrop, a piece of thick cloth hung from a pipe, was in place. The camera sat on its tripod and had already been tested. The uplink worked perfectly. There was thick plastic sheeting on the floor to make cleanup afterward a bit easier.

He recalled the first time he'd used a sword to decapitate a man. His victim's heart had been racing and his blood pressure dangerously high, so when the head came free it was like a fountain. So much blood erupted from the stump that they opted to abandon the safe house in Baghdad they had used rather than clean the mess.

Tonight would be his eleventh, and for him the most satisfying. He'd never killed a woman before—at least, not with a sword. Since taking up arms he'd killed dozens of women in bombings from Indonesia to Morocco. And in firefights with Americans in Afghanistan and Iraq, stray rounds had certainly hit others.

He gave them little thought. Al-Jama had issued orders and he had carried them out. There was no more weight on his conscience than had he been told to shake his victims' hands rather than blow them up.

Of course the irony, and open secret within the organization, was that he wasn't a practicing Muslim. He'd been born into the faith, but his parents hadn't been devout followers so he'd visited mosques only on holy days. He'd only come to Al-Jama after a hitch with the French Foreign Legion had given him a taste for combat that he had yet to slake. He fought and killed and maimed for himself, not for some insane religious conviction that slaughter was somehow Allah's will.

He didn't try to understand the motivations of those who fought with him so long as they followed orders. He did admit, however, that the fear of missing out on Paradise kept the fighters motivated to a degree only the best-trained armies could achieve. And the ability to talk people into blowing themselves up was a weapon unlike any other in the arsenals of the world. It went so against the West's precepts for the preservation of life that the effects rippled from the blast's epicenter to the very hearts of any who learned of it.

A subaltern knocked softly at the doorframe behind him. "Does everything meet your needs, Mansour?"

"Yes," he said absently. "This will be fine."

"When should we get the American whore?"

"Not until just before her execution. It's been my experience that they are most terrified in those first moments when they realize their death is upon them."

"As you wish. If you need anything further, I am just outside."

The executioner didn't bother to reply, and the man stepped out of view again.

He doubted there would be any pleas for mercy from the woman. He'd observed her only briefly but had a strong sense of her defiance. He actually preferred it that way. The men loved the crying and wailing, but he found it . . . bothersome. Yes, that was the word, bothersome. Better to accept fate, he believed, than to demean yourself in worthless begging. He wondered if they actually believed carrying on would stop their execution. By the time they met him, their death was an inevitability, and pleading was as useless as trying to stave off an avalanche by raising your arms protectively.

No, the woman would not beg.

• • •

"WATCH THE RIGHT FLANK," Linda said, and fired a controlled burst over the *Saqr*'s rail. "They're trying to get around us by crawling along the rubble wall."

The muzzle flash drew counterfire from four different points.

Eric had been ready for it, crouched twenty feet farther along the deck. He raked the spot where one of the terrorists was hiding, but in the cavern's absolute darkness he had no idea if he'd hit anything.

In the first furious seconds of the gunfight, both sides scrambled to organize themselves after the surprise encounter. Linda quickly ordered her people onto the *Saqr*, which offered the best cover on short notice, while the terrorist leader shouted at his men to conserve ammunition and prepare for an all-out assault.

They came swiftly, flicking their flashlights on and off like lightning bugs in order to see the terrain but not overly expose themselves. The Corporation team concentrated their fire on the men with the lights before realizing their mistake. The men carrying torches only turned them on when they were behind cover. The beams were meant for others scouting ahead.

"Come on, come on," Mark chided himself as he tore through his pack, tossing aside gear with abandon. "I know it's in here."

Bullets stitched the side of the ship, several winging through a gunport and splintering wood inches from where he crouched.

Linda called to Eric, "On my mark. Go!"

They both popped up and let loose. In their scramble to

find cover, a terrorist accidentally stepped into the beam of his partner's light. He was climbing the old riverbank to gain access to the pier. Had he reached it, he would have been able to hose the deck and end the battle single-handedly.

The beam barely caressed his leg, but it was enough. Linda adjusted her aim, approximated where his torso would be, and fired again. She was rewarded with a scream that echoed over the rattling assault rifles.

She and Eric both ducked down when rounds filled the air around them.

"This is crazy," Eric panted.

He couldn't see her saucy grin but heard it in her voice when she said, "I've never been in a firefight that wasn't."

Something heavy rattled against the *Saqr*'s stern.

"Down," Linda shouted.

An instant later, a grenade exploded. The shrapnel flew over the prone figures, tearing away more of the ship's woodwork.

Linda's ears rang, but she didn't let it distract her. The grenade was meant to keep them pinned for seconds only, and she was determined not to give them even that.

She peered over the rail. Lights flickered from one side of the cavern entrance to the other. Linda fought the raw fear running through her veins. It was really two against a dozen, since Alana didn't have a weapon, and Mark Murphy couldn't shoot to save his life.

She searched an ammo pouch hanging from her combat harness and pinched off a wad of plastique. By feel, she selected a sixty-second timing pencil, rammed it home, and tossed it over the side. She laid down another three-round burst and ducked back again.

"We've got to stop them flanking us," she called across to Eric. "I tossed some plastique. When it blows, find some targets."

She took the opportunity to change out her magazine, uncertain how many rounds she'd fired. If they had time, she would have Alana consolidate the spare ammunition in fresh clips.

The blast came a moment later. The concussion was like a kick to the chest, and she'd been ready for it. The fireball crashed against the ceiling, bathing the cavern in demonic light.

Linda and Eric opened up. Terrorists who were caught in the open raced for cover, rounds screaming past them before the pair could zero in and put the men down.

Return fire came from eight different directions. Linda's chin was bloodied by a shard of wood torn from the rail, and as much as she didn't want to lose the last of the light she had to stay under cover from such a deadly barrage.

When it lessened, she fired blind at the riverbank below the quay in case anyone was trying to climb it again. Then, over the sharp stench of cordite, she smelled a familiar odor: wood smoke.

She looked aft just as the smoldering decking that had been hit by the grenade caught fire. The flame was low and smoky, but every second saw it grow. If it got out of control, they were as good as dead. The *Saqr* would become their funeral pyre.

"Mark, get that. We'll cover you."

Alana crawled from his side and approached Linda. "He's working on something. I've got it."

"Stay low," Linda cautioned, impressed with the archaeologist's courage.

The flames rose higher, first illuminating only the ship's stern. But, like a rising sun, the light's reach expanded rapidly. The terrorists used this to their advantage. They could see the vessel more clearly, and their accuracy improved.

Thirty feet from Linda, Alana slithered right to the edge of the burning section. She saw it wasn't the deck afire, but a bench for the helmsman. She swung onto her back, braced her feet under the burning seat, and heaved. Rather than fly over the side of the ship, the bench broke in two, showering her with embers.

Alana beat out the ashes where they seared her skin, ripped her T-shirt over her head, and with nothing to protect her skin but the thin cotton, she worked on snuffing out the fire by hand. All the while, Linda and the gunmen traded shots over her head.

By the time Alana extinguished the last of the stubborn

flames, her shirt had all but burned up, and most the skin on her palms was gone, leaving behind nothing but raw red meat that hurt like nothing she'd ever experienced in her life.

The pain was so intense, she couldn't crawl on her hands and knees, but rather had to slither like a snake to return to the others.

Linda shined a penlight on Alana's injuries and gasped.

"I'll be all right," Alana managed to say.

"Cover your ears," Mark Murphy whispered urgently.

He waited a beat, studying the array of winking flashlights over the touchhole of one of the Saqr's great cannons. When he thought the time right, he slipped a timer pencil into the gun's touchhole, where it sank into the plastic explosives he'd rammed down the barrel. Between it and the muzzle was a cannonball made up of dozens of small metal spheres fused lightly together.

The timer went off, detonating the plastique, and the gun belched the grapeshot in a ten-foot tongue of flame. The ropes secured to the cannon to prevent the recoil from pushing it across the deck failed at full stretch, and the two tons of bronze rocketed through the opposite rail and plowed into the steep riverbank below the pier.

The impact of the grape was lost in the gun's mighty roar, but when Murphy looked out to where he'd aimed, two of the three flashlights were no longer there.

It was as if the cannon's blast had signaled the end of round one and the beginning of the second. The gunmen opened up with renewed fury, rounds chewing at the Saqr as if to tear it apart piece by piece. The three Corporation operatives fired back, but the weight of the onslaught kept them pinned.

The cry of the terrorists' charge carried above the din. They were coming with everything they had.

Eric took a glancing bullet to the shoulder when he tried to shoot back and stem the tide. Unable to hold his rifle against the wound to aim, he flicked to full auto and raked the ground thirty feet from the Saqr's side, creating a curtain of lead the terrorists couldn't penetrate.

When the rifle bolt snapped back on an empty magazine, Murphy took up the duty, blasting away in a desperate bid to break the charge. His gun, too, fell empty. Linda screamed like a Valkyrie as she hosed the dirt. It didn't matter if she hit anyone. The intention was just to keep the terrorists back long enough that their courage would fail and they'd retreat for cover.

Bullets whizzed all around her, but to her absolute relief she saw the muzzle flashes were coming from farther and farther away. The charge had broken. They had stopped them.

She slipped down below the bulwarks, her entire body vibrating as an aftereffect of her rifle's recoil, and she was covered in oily sweat. "You guys okay?" she called to her people as the gunmen's fire slowed.

"I took one to the shoulder," Eric reported from the darkness.

"I'm still pissed at myself for not grabbing the night vision goggles from Linc," Mark said bitterly. "We go spelunking, and I forget the most important piece of gear we would need."

"Alana?"

"I'm here," she called softly, her voice pinched with pain.

"Mark, give her something from your med kit." The sound of gunfire that had risen and fallen erratically over the past ten minutes dribbled away to silence.

Everyone's ears rang, but not badly enough to miss a man's voice calling out from the cavern entrance. "I will give you this one chance to give yourselves up."

"Holy crap," Eric exclaimed. "I know that voice."

"What? Who is it?"

"I listened in when he and the Chairman were talking aboard the *Oregon*. That's the harbor pilot, Hassad or Assad or something."

"That explains the ambush on the coast road," Murph surmised.

"Doesn't change anything for us, though." Linda thought for a moment, then shouted back, "I think General Austin McAuliffe said it best when he was asked to surrender during the Battle of the Bulge. In a word: nuts."

Murph grumbled sarcastically, "Oh, that'll go well for us."

Round three started in earnest.

THIRTY-FIVE

THE FIRST PIECE OF GOOD NEWS CABRILLO HAD heard in a while was that he was familiar with the supertanker slowly overtaking the Libyan frigate. She was the Petromax Oil ULCC *Aggie Johnston*, and several months earlier the *Oregon* had saved her from being hit by a couple of Iranian torpedoes by firing one of their own at the sub that had launched them.

They were close enough now that he had to assume all communications could be monitored by the *Gulf of Sidra*. To get around that, he found the ship's e-mail address on the Petromax website and sent its captain a note. It was far from convenient, and their exchanges went back and forth for nearly ten minutes before he could convince the captain that he was the commander of the freighter now shadowing them from a thousand yards away and not some lunatic kid e-mailing from his parents' basement in Anytown, USA.

As Juan waited for each reply, he lamented that Mark and Eric weren't aboard. Those two could have hacked the parent company's mainframe to issue the orders directly, and he wouldn't have to explain what he wanted from the floating behemoth and why.

A fresh e-mail appeared in his inbox:

Captain Cabrillo, It goes against my better instincts and my years of training, but I will agree to do what you've asked, provided we don't come within a half mile of that frigate and you provide the same sort of protection you did in the Straits of Hormuz if they fire on us.

As much as I want to do more, I must place the well-being of my ship and crew above my desire to help you unreservedly. I've spent the better part of my career operating out of Middle Eastern ports and hate what these terrorists have done to the region, but I can't allow anything to happen to my vessel. And as you can well imagine, if we were loaded with oil rather than running in ballast the answer would have been an unequivocal no.

All the best,

James McCullough

PS: Give 'em one on the chin for me. Good hunting.

"Hot damn," Juan cried, "he'll do it."

Max Hanley was standing across the pilothouse chart table, the stem of his pipe clamped between his tobacco-stained teeth. "I wouldn't get that excited when you're contemplating playing chicken with a fully armed frigate."

"This will be perfect," Juan countered. "We'll be inside his defenses before they know what we're up to. We worked the vectors as we narrowed the gap and kept the tanker between us and the *Sidra* the whole time. As far as they know, there's only the one ship that's going to pass them. They have no idea we're here, and won't until the *Johnston* breaks off."

He typed a reply on a wireless-connected laptop as he spoke:

Captain McCullough, You are the key to saving the Secretary's life, and I can't thank you or your crew enough. I only wish that afterward you'd receive the accolades you so richly deserve, but this incident must remain secret. We will flash your bridge with our Aldis lamp when we want you to begin. That should be in about ten minutes.

Again, my sincerest thanks,

Juan Cabrillo

Spread across the table was a detailed schematic of the Russian-built Koni-class frigate, showing all her interior passages. Also there were Mike Trono and Jerry Pulaski, who would be leading the assault teams. They were well-trained fire-eaters who'd seen more than their share of combat, but Juan wished Eddie Seng and Franklin Lincoln would be in on the attack with him. Behind Trono and Pulaski were the ten other men who would be boarding the Libyan ship.

Outside the starboard windows lurked the thousand-foot slab of steel that was the *Aggie Johnston*'s hull. With the *Oregon* ballasted down to lower her profile and the supertanker nearly empty, the *Johnston* seemed to loom over them even at this distance. The accommodation block at her stern was the size of an office building, and her squat funnel resembled an upended railroad tank car.

"Okay, back to this. Do we all agree the most likely place for the execution is the crew's mess?"

"It's the biggest open space on the ship," Mike Trono said. He was a slender man with fine brown hair who'd come to the Corporation after working as a pararescue jumper.

"Makes sense to me," Ski remarked. The big Pole was a former Marine who towered half a head over the others. Rather than wear combat clothing, the men had donned sailors' uniforms that Kevin Nixon's staff had modified to resemble the utilities worn by Libyan sailors. An instant of confusion on an opponent's part on seeing a familiar uniform but an unfamiliar face could mean the difference between life and death.

"Why a ship?" Mike asked suddenly.

"Sorry?"

"Why carry out the execution on a ship?"

"It'll be next to impossible to triangulate where the broadcast signal originates," Max replied. "And even if you can, the vessel's long gone by the time anyone comes out to investigate."

"We're going to enter the *Sidra* here," Juan said, pointing to an amidships hatch on the main deck. "We then move two doors down on the right to the first staircase. We take it down one flight, then it's left, right, left. The mess will be right in front of us."

"There's gonna be a lot of sailors in there to watch," Jerry predicted.

"I'd agree, normally," Juan said. "But as soon as we make our move, they'll go to general quarters. The hallways will be deserted, and anyone left in the mess is going to be a terrorist. The legitimate crew will be at their battle stations. We take out the tangos, grab Miss Katamora, and get off that tub before they know we were even there."

"There's still one problem with your plan," Max said, relighting his pipe. "You haven't explained our exit strategy. As soon as we pull away, *Sidra*'s going to nail us. I've been thinking about it, and I want to suggest that another team board her, carrying satchel charges. The *Oregon* can disable some of her armaments during the attack, and they can blow up what gets missed."

Hanley wasn't known for his tactical insights, so Juan was genuinely impressed. "Why, Max, what a well-reasoned and carefully considered plan."

"I thought so, too," he preened.

"Only thing is those men would get cut down long before they could approach the *Sidra*'s primary weapons systems." Juan pointed to the schematic again. "They've got emplacements for .30-caliber machine guns on all four corners of the superstructure. We can knock out the ones we can see, but the two on the far side are protected by the ship itself. Our boys would be cut to ribbons."

"Send Gomez up in the chopper and hit them with a

missile," Hanley said, defensive that his plan was being questioned.

"SAM coverage is too tight. He'd never get close enough."

Max looked crestfallen, and his voice was a little sulky when he asked, "All right, smart guy, what's your idea?"

Juan peeled back the naval drawings. Beneath them was a chart of the Libyan coastline due south of their current position. Juan tapped his finger on a spot ten miles west of them. "This."

Max looked from Juan down to where he pointed and back up again. His smile was positively demonic. "Brilliant."

"Thought you'd like that. It's the reason we're delaying the attack for a few minutes. We need them close enough for this to work." Cabrillo added, "If there isn't anything else, we should all get into position."

"Let's do this," Mike Trono said.

The men descended the outside stairs to get to the main deck. Juan and Max lingered a moment.

"You still look a bit peevish," Cabrillo said to his best friend.

"You're going into the lion's den, Juan. This isn't like when we sneak into some warehouse in the middle of the night by knocking out a couple of rent-a-cops. There are some real bad apples on that ship, and I'm afraid as soon as they realize something's up they're going to kill her straightaway, and this'll all be for nothing."

A glib reply died on the Chairman's lips. He said somberly, "I know, but if we don't try they've already won. In a way, this war started in these waters two hundred years ago. We as a nation stood up back then for our core principles and said enough is enough. Wouldn't it be something if we end it here, too, fighting for the very same things?"

"If nothing more, it would be rather poetic justice."

Juan slapped him on the back, grinning. "That's the spirit. Now, get down to the op center, and don't hurt my ship when I'm gone."

Max shook his head like an old bloodhound. "That's one promise you know I can't keep."

Once they gave Captain McCullough the signal, the massive tanker altered her course southward toward the Libyan frigate. It was done subtly and without warning, but inexorably the distance between the two vessels shrank. On her original course, the *Aggie Johnston* would have passed the *Sidra* with a five-mile separation, but as the trailing distance closed so, too, did the range. Staying tight to her flank, the *Oregon*, too, closed in on its prey.

The radios stayed quiet until the tanker was a mile astern and two miles north of the frigate. Juan had a portable handset as he waited in the shadow of the gunwales with his men. With the sun beginning to set behind them, the worst of the day's heat had abated, and yet the deck was still too hot to touch comfortably.

"Tanker approaching on my stern, this is the *Khalij Surt* of the Libyan Navy. You are straying too close for safe passage. Please alter your course and increase your separation before coming abeam."

"*Khalij Surt*, this is James McCullough of ULCC *Aggie Johnston*." McCullough had a smooth, cultured voice. Juan pictured him standing around six-two and, for some reason, bald as an egg. "We're experiencing a rogue ebb tide right now. I have the rudder over, and she's starting to respond. We will comply with your directive in time, I assure you."

"Very good," came the curt reply from the *Sidra*. "Please advise if you continue to have difficulties."

McCullough had stuck to Juan's script, and the first act of the play had gone perfectly. Of course, the tanker's captain would maintain his heading and, in the process, buy the *Oregon* more time.

Ten minutes went by, and the speeds of the ships relative to each other had narrowed the gap by another half mile. Juan thought the Libyans would have called much earlier. He considered it a good omen that there didn't seem to be any alarm.

"*Aggie Johnston, Aggie Johnston*, this is the *Khalij Surt*." The man's tone was still cool and professional. "Are you still experiencing difficulties?"

"A moment, please," McCullough radioed back as if

pressed for time. When he didn't respond for two minutes, the Libyans repeated their request. This time, a bit more forcefully.

"Yes, sorry about that. The ebb intensified. We're coming out of it now."

"We did not experience this tidal action you seem to be facing."

"That's because our keel is forty feet down and stretches for three football fields."

Easy, Jimmy boy, Juan thought.

Juan and the captain had worked it out so the next call originated from McCullough. Two minutes after the last comment, he was on the horn again. "*Khalij Surt*, this is the *Aggie Johnston*. Please be advised our steering gear just failed. I have ordered an emergency stop, but at our current speed it will take us several miles. I calculate I will pass down your port beam with a half-mile clearance. May I suggest you alter your speed and heading."

Rather than slowing, the tanker began a steady acceleration, her single prop churning the water into a maelstrom at her fantail. This wasn't in the script, and Juan knew that McCullough was ignoring his own preset conditions in order to get the *Oregon* in as tight as he possibly could. Cabrillo vowed to find the man and buy him a drink when this was over.

The *Sidra* had begun to turn away and gain speed, but she was still going slow enough that her maneuvers were sluggish. The tanker dwarfed the warship as she started to cruise past, moving at eighteen knots only a third of a mile off the Libyans' rail.

Juan felt the *Oregon*'s deck shiver ever so slightly. Her big pumps were rapidly draining seawater from her saddle ballast tanks. They were going in.

In the op center, Max Hanley sat at the fore helm. Like Juan, he'd listened to the entire exchange, but unlike the Chairman he'd been able to at least watch some of the action. Next to him was the weapons tech. Every exterior door was folded back and every gun run out. The ship literally bristled.

He killed power to the pump jets, then reversed the flow.

Water exploded in a churning wave from the bow tubes, and the ship slowed so quickly her stern lifted slightly out of the water. As soon as she was clear of the *Aggie Johnston*, he cut reverse and applied forward pressure through the tubes. The cryopumps keeping the magnetohydrodynamics chilled to a hundred degrees below zero began to sing as the jets demanded more and more energy.

The *Oregon* accelerated like a racehorse, carving a graceful curve around the back of the tanker. In front of him was the low gray silhouette of the Libyan frigate.

He could imagine the consternation on the *Sidra*'s bridge when a ship twice its size suddenly appeared without warning from around the supertanker. After what had to have been a stunned thirty seconds, the airways came alive with expletives, demands, and threats.

Max nimbly tucked the *Oregon* between the two vessels even as McCullough turned sharply northward to gain sea room and safety.

"Identify yourself or we will open fire."

That was the second time Max had heard the challenge, and he doubted there would be a third. There was still a big enough gap for the *Sidra* to rake the *Oregon* with her three-inch cannons. He resisted the strong impulse to snatch up the handset and identify themselves as the USS *Siren*.

Watching on the monitor, he saw a cloud like a big cotton ball bloom in front of the *Sidra*'s forward gun. The shell shrieked by the bow and exploded in the sea fifty feet off her beam an instant before the concussion of the shot rumbled across the *Oregon*.

"Warning shot's free, my friend," Max said tightly. "Next one and the gloves come off."

The rear gun discharged this time, and an explosive shell slammed into the wing bridge, blowing it completely away.

Max could barely keep himself in his chair. "That's it. Fire at will."

The narrowing gulf between the two combatants came alive as the *Oregon*'s 30mm Gatling guns and bigger Bofors autocannon spewed out continuous streams of fire. The

Sidra's own antiaircraft guns added to the thunder of her main batteries, which were firing at a four-shot-a-minute clip.

The *Oregon* rang like a bell with each staggering impact. The rounds from the AAA penetrated her hull but were stopped by the next bulkhead. The deck guns' rounds burst through.

Already three cabins were in ruins, and slabs of marble had been ripped from the walls of the ballast tank that doubled as a swimming pool. Every impact saw more destruction. The boardroom where the senior staff met took a direct hit. The five-hundred-pound table was upended, and the leather chairs turned to kindling.

The automated fire-suppression system was battling a half dozen simultaneous blazes. Fire teams had been told to stay on the opposite side of the ship with the rest of the crew rather than risk themselves during the duel.

But the *Oregon* was giving as good as she got. All the *Sidra*'s bridge windows had been shot out, and enough tungsten rounds poured through the openings to mangle all the navigation and steering equipment. Rounds sparked off her armored hide. Her lifeboat shook like a rat in the jaws of a terrier when the Gatling hosed it. When it moved on, the craft was riddled with holes and hung drunkenly from one set of pulleys.

None of their smaller-caliber weapons could penetrate the armor protecting the turrets, so the weapons officer loosened the bow-mounted 120mm cannon. Because it used the same stability control system as an M1A2 main battle tank, this main gun had unbelievable accuracy. Its first round hit where the turret met the *Sidra*'s deck, and the entire mass jumped five feet into the air before smashing back again, greasy smoke billowing from the guns' barrels.

The two ships continued to pound on each other, each capable of absorbing tremendous punishment, as the gap grew narrower still. At point-blank range, there was no need to aim. Rounds impacted almost the instant they left the guns.

Nothing like this had been seen in the annals of naval

warfare for a century, and despite the danger Max Hanley wouldn't have wanted to be anyplace else in the world.

Not so for the Chairman and the men on deck. They were hunkered behind a section of rail that had been triple reinforced, but when a 30mm autocannon raked the bulwark they all felt naked and exposed.

Juan couldn't imagine fighting this way as a normal course of events. Technology had sanitized warfare, made it cold and distant. The press of a button was all that was needed to vanquish your enemy. This was something else entirely. He could feel their hatred. It was as if each shot they took was an expression of personal loathing.

They wanted him dead. And not just dead but blown out of existence, as if he had never been born at all.

Another shell slammed into the armor plate, and for a moment it felt to Juan like his insides had liquefied. For a terrifying moment, he thought he had made a huge mistake.

Then he thought no, these people would not stop until someone stood up to them. If they wouldn't listen to reason, they would have to face the consequences of their own barbarity.

There came a brutal shudder. The *Oregon* was alongside the *Sidra*. Max had known to ballast their ship so the two railings were even. Juan snatched up his compact machine pistol and threw himself over the side.

The shimmering trail of an RPG launched from a concealed redoubt astern of the *Sidra*'s rear turret passed inches over his head and hit the armored plate just as the rest of his twelve-man team was following. The hit couldn't have been luckier or worse. Ten of the men were blown back by the blast, bloodied and suffering concussions, and two were tossed forward just as a wave separated the ships slightly. They plummeted down into the tight space and hit the water simultaneously.

Max had seen the disaster on the closed-circuit television system and immediately hauled the *Oregon* away from the *Sidra* so the hulls wouldn't slam together and smear the men into paste. He didn't know if they were alive or dead, but he ordered the rescue team standing by in the boat garage to immediately launch a Zodiac.

A tech moved a joystick to swivel the camera and scan the *Sidra*'s deck.

"There," Max shouted.

Cabrillo stood alone on the Libyan ship, his Heckler & Koch machine pistol smoking after taking out the gunman who was reloading his rocket launcher. It was almost as if he knew the camera was on him. He looked directly at it with the most savage expression Max had ever seen and then vanished alone through the frigate's hatchway.

THIRTY-SIX

Ambassador Charles Moon was failing one of his principal tasks for the evening. He'd been expressly directed by the President to make sure the VP didn't drink too much during the reception at Minister Ghami's home.

The VP had an alcoholic's lack of self-control but not the tolerance, and he'd downed four crystal flutes of champagne during the half hour they'd been here. It might have been understandable, had he known the house was the likely target of a terrorist attack, but the administration felt that the Vice President couldn't be trusted with that information if their plan was going to work.

Moon set his own untouched champagne on a marble-topped table to wipe his sweaty palms on the legs of his tuxedo. Next to him, Vice President Donner got to the punch line of an off-color joke. The group of ten guests who were within earshot waited a beat before giving him a smattering of polite laughter. His press secretary, who was filling the role as his date for the evening, pulled him slightly aside before he could launch into another.

Moon took the opportunity to look around the elegant reception hall. Minister Ghami's isolated home was stunning. Built of stone and stucco, it had the feel of a Moorish castle, massive and secure. The main entrance off the porte cochere opened all the way to the roof three stories up. Elegant wrought-iron balusters ringed the upper stories, and the staircase that spilled onto the ground floor was easily twenty feet wide. An orchestra was set up on the midpoint landing, where the steps divided left and right. They played classical music with an Arabic flair.

As impressive as the house was, it paled in comparison to the importance of the guests. Moon counted no fewer than ten heads of state among the elegantly dressed throng. In one corner, under a dramatically backlit potted palm, the Israeli Prime Minister was sharing some private words with Lebanon's President, and on the other side of the room Iraq's PM was conversing with Iran's Foreign Minister.

Moon expected these people to speak cordially at a reception such as this—these were politicians and diplomats, after all—but he had a feeling this went a little deeper. There was true optimism in the room that the Tripoli Accords would be a success.

Then the voice of gloom in his head overshadowed his brief moment of confidence. First, they needed to survive the night.

By far the biggest group of people stood around Ali Ghami as he held court near a bubbling mosaic-tiled fountain. The two men's eyes met for a moment. Ghami raised his glass slightly, a solemn gesture that told Moon he acknowledged the most important guest to him was the one who wasn't here.

Fiona Katamora was the topic of most conversations this night. Moon had been told that Qaddafi, wearing a civilian suit rather than a uniform, would make a speech about her loss.

Moon's bodyguard for the night, wearing a borrowed ill-fitting tux, tapped him on the arm and nodded in the direction of the open entrance to the adjoining living room. Tucked away unobtrusively near the ceiling was a video camera.

"I've counted five so far," the man said.

"For security?"

"Or posterity. You can best believe those are switched on right now and ready to record tonight's attack. I also noticed that the plasma television in the living room is a temporary setup. The wires are taped down to the floor rather than run under the Persian rug. This way, everyone here will be able to witness the beheading. It'll also bunch the crowd together nicely for the attack. I think this is going to be a two-way performance because I saw a small webcam sitting next to the TV."

"It's really going to happen, isn't it?"

"That's their plan, but don't worry. We know what we're doing."

"Have you been able to tell which are the legitimate security guards and which are the terrorists?" Moon asked.

"The tangos are still outside. The planners of this attack know they wouldn't be able to hold their cover for long if they were in here now." The bodyguard felt confident, but he carefully watched the few Libyan agents mingling with the guests.

Muammar Qaddafi climbed a couple steps to get above the crowd, a wireless microphone in his hand. The orchestra fell silent, and the men and women turned expectantly for his tribute to Fiona Katamora.

The Libyan leader was known to be almost as long-winded as Castro. After five rambling minutes, Moon tuned him out.

He'd wiped his hands twice during that brief period of time and knew that if he took off his jacket the stains under his arms would reach his belt line.

Amazingly, the guard at his side looked totally relaxed.

• • •

IN THE CAVERN'S DARKNESS, Eric changed out his ammo magazine by feel. Only two clips remained in the pouch strapped to his harness. His shoulder throbbed in time with his racing heart, and he hadn't had a chance to tend to it. Blood ran hot and sticky all the way to his fingertips.

Another grenade thrown blindly hit just below the *Saqr*'s

gunwale and dropped to the dirt. The explosion was muffled by the hull, but it rocked the ship toward the pier, and they remained at a ten-degree list. This time, the desiccated wood caught fire immediately, and with the flames spreading outside the ship there was nothing they could do to stop it.

"As soon as it gets light enough, we're toast," Mark said grimly.

Already, Linda Ross could see his dim outline growing from the gloom. She knew he was right. The darkness had saved them until now, but when the fire reached a certain size and its light filled the cavern the advantage would shift to the terrorists. The question for her was whether they should wait it out and hope to somehow beat back the attack or retreat and find another way out of this trap.

She made her decision the moment she acknowledged her limited options. "Okay, we'll lay down a short burst of cover fire. Mark, Eric, take Alana, jump for the pier, and head away from the entrance. Try to find some defensible position. I'll give you a thirty-second head start. Hose 'em again, and I will be right behind you."

They quickly lined the *Saqr*'s rail. The fire burning aft of them wasn't yet big enough to illuminate the entire cave, but they could see ten or fifteen feet out. The body of a terrorist lay sprawled on the ground at the limit of their vision, a black stain pooled under his chest slowly soaking into the dirt.

"Fire," Linda ordered, and they loosened a blistering fusillade, raking the rubble that had been blasted to seal the cave from the river.

As soon as their guns emptied, Eric and Mark lifted Alana from the deck by her forearms. Linda was still shooting behind them, sniping into the darkness to keep the gunmen down. The three stepped up onto the *Saqr*'s rail and jumped the gap to the pier. Alana almost fell, and had Eric not grabbed her quickly she would have caught herself on her badly blistered hands.

Keeping as low as he could, Mark led them forward, his arms out in front of him. When he touched the cave's back wall, he turned right and groped his way along the uneven surface. Alana couldn't keep a hand on the rock, but behind her Eric laid one hand on her shoulder to keep her oriented.

They walked blindly for seventy-five feet, the staggering wall of sound from the renewed gun battle behind them never seeming to grow distant because of the confined acoustics.

Mark chanced flicking on his light. They were at the end of the pier. There was nautical gear piled just ahead of them, coils of rope mostly, but there was also some chain nestled in reed baskets as well as lengths of wood for spars. But what most caught his attention was the mouth of a side cave off the main cavern. A metal bar had been attached to the rock above it, and from it hung the tatters of what had once been a pair of tapestries that when closed would have afforded privacy inside.

"We might be okay," he said, and they all stepped into the new chamber.

Eric quickly drew the shades closed and changed out his magazine to stand guard while Mark played the flashlight around the room, keeping his fingers over the lens to diffuse the harsh halogen light.

"This is incredible," Alana whispered reverently. For the moment, she forgot the pain radiating from her hands and the noise of the firefight raging outside.

The cave floor was covered with several layers of intricate oriental carpets to prevent cold from seeping through the rock. More tapestries covered much of the walls and gave the chamber the cheery feel of a tent. There were two rope beds on one side of the room, one of them neatly made, the other rumpled. Other furniture included several chests and a large writing table, complete with ink pots and feather quills, which had grown limp over the centuries and wilted over the sides of their solid gold stand. The desktop was inlaid with complex geometric patterns done in mother-of-pearl. Books were stacked on the floor around it and filled an adjacent set of shelves. An ornate Koran had the place of honor next to a tattered, dog-eared Bible.

There was an alcove next to the shelves. It was stacked floor to ceiling with chests. The lid for one of them was sprung, and when Mark shone the light in the crack the unmistakable flash of gold dazzled back at him.

He tried to see if there was an opening behind the chests, but with them so tightly packed it was impossible to tell without moving them. He shoved at the topmost trunk to dislodge it. The trunk wouldn't budge. If it was full of gold like the lower one, it would easily weigh a thousand pounds.

He gave the light to Alana, who tucked it under her arm because she couldn't trust her hands to hold it properly.

"There's no way out," Mark said, returning to Eric's side. Stoney had reloaded Murph's rifle and handed it across. "On the bright side, we're going to die rich. Must be a hundred million in gold shoved in a closet back there."

The firing outside remained relentless, although Linda had to be on the move because they couldn't hear her weapon over the sharp whip-cracks of the terrorists' AKs. The stern of the *Saqr* was a pyre now, with flames almost reaching the cave's ceiling and quickly filling the cave with smoke.

Eric kept whispering "Marco" into the gloom and was rewarded with a return call of "Polo."

Linda reached the entrance and ducked through long before the gunmen were aware she had moved. "Tell me the good news."

"We're rich," Mark offered. "But trapped."

• • •

THE TWO SHIPS WERE so close to each other that it was impossible to get off a shot, so they had fallen on a deadly stalemate, although the *Oregon* was using her superior size and power to start herding the Libyan frigate closer to shore. Whenever the hulls came together, the smaller naval vessel was forced to cut starboard to avoid being crushed under the freighter. Occasionally, a brave, or suicidal, terrorist would pop on deck and try to launch another RPG at the freighter, but the antiboarding .30-calibers were deployed and aimed before he could take an accurate shot. The two RPGs they managed to fire at the *Oregon* flew right over the ship, and the gunmen were cut down for their efforts.

The corridors inside the frigate were a scene of bedlam, with damage-control teams running in every direction. The air was smoky from a fire in the forward part of the ship, although the antiquated scrubbers were working to clear it. Alarms wailed, and men shouted orders over the strident cry.

It was all music to Fiona Katamora's ears as she lay shackled to a bed frame in an officer's cabin. She had no idea what was happening around her other than that the men who'd kidnapped her were in trouble.

She knew she had been taken aboard a ship after the helicopter flight from the jihadists' training camp. She could tell from the salty air that wafted through the bag they had placed over her head and from the engine's thrum and the action of waves against the hull. She hadn't known which type of vessel until the cannons started firing.

It came as no surprise that Suleiman Al-Jama had been able to co-opt a Libyan warship. More likely, the entire crew were members of his organization.

Explosions wracked the frigate, and with each blast her sense of well-being grew. They would still kill her before it was over, she wasn't fooling herself about that, but the United States Navy would ensure they wouldn't have the chance to enjoy their victory.

A particularly loud explosion hit the ship, which seemed to stagger under the blow. When Fiona no longer heard the forward cannon firing, she knew the American warship had blown off one of the Libyan's main gun turrets.

The door to the cabin was hastily thrown open. Her jailors wore headscarves to mask their features and had AK-47s slung over their backs. Fiona's moment of well-being vanished as her cuffs were rearranged so her hands were bound behind her. Wordlessly, they yanked her from the room.

Uniformed sailors barely threw them a glance. They were too preoccupied with saving their ship to gloat over their prize. Fiona fell against a bulkhead when another fury of rounds slammed into the ship's side. The ferocity of the battle so distracted her for the walk down to another, larger room that she forgot to pray.

But when she saw the black cloth hanging across the back

wall, the video camera, and the man holding a massive scimitar, the words fell from her lips. There were others in the room, terrorists, not Libyan sailors. One was standing behind the camera, another near him fiddled with the satellite-uplink controls. The rest of the masked men were here as witnesses. She recognized their khaki utilities from the desert base. The man with the sword wore all black.

The alarm loudspeaker in the mess hall had been disabled, though it was still audible from other parts of the vessel.

"Far from saving you," the executioner said in Arabic, "that ship out there has pushed up our timeline by a few minutes." He stared hard at the Secretary, and she returned his defiance. "Are you ready to die?"

"For the sake of peace," Fiona replied, her voice as steady as she could keep it, "I was ready to die from the moment I understood the concept."

They secured her to a chair set before the drape. Plastic sheeting had been placed on the deck at her feet. A gag was tied across her mouth to deny her any parting words.

The executioner nodded to the cameraman and he began to film. The lens stayed focused on Fiona for a moment, to make sure the target audience knew exactly who was about to die. Then the swordsman stepped in front of her, holding the ornate scimitar so it was plainly visible.

"We, the servants of Suleiman Al-Jama, come before you today to rid the world of another infidel." He was reading from a typewritten script. "This is our answer to the Crusaders' efforts to thrust their decadence upon us. From this unholy woman has come the worst of their lies, and for that she must die."

Fiona willed herself to ignore the rant so in her head all she heard was "Our Father who art in heaven . . ."

• • •

SEEING HIS MEN HIT sent a lance of concern through Cabrillo's heart, but there was no chance to go back now. Rather than consider retreat, he went on single-handedly. None of the Libyan sailors paid him the slightest attention. With a handful of Al-Jama's terrorists using the ship as their base for Fiona Katamora's execution, an unfamiliar face in their midst wasn't cause for alarm. The few men moving around inside the ship were too focused on their jobs. When a fire-control team rushed toward him, Juan stopped running and flattened himself to a wall as any sailor would be trained to do.

"Come with us," the fire team leader shouted without breaking stride.

"Captain's orders," Juan replied over his shoulder, and raced away in the opposite direction.

He found the staircase and rushed down three at a time, bowling over a seaman clawing his way topside. On the next deck, he ran unerringly for the crew's mess. There were two armed guards posted outside the door. One was looking into the room, the other glanced at Cabrillo but dismissed him as part of the crew because of the uniform.

If Juan had needed confirmation he'd been right about a terrorist presence, it was these two, with their kaffiyehs and AKs.

Ten paces from them, Juan could hear a voice inside the mess saying ". . . killed our women and children in their homes, bombed our villages, and defied the very word of Allah."

It was enough for him. With a cold fury born of fighting for too long—for his entire life, it seemed—he whipped the compact machine pistol into view. The one terrorist's eyes widened, but that was the only reaction the Chairman allowed him. Cabrillo's weapon chattered in his hands, stitching both men across their torsos. One round blew off the top of a man's shoulder, the resulting blood splatter like obscene graffiti on the wall behind him.

Juan was moving so fast he had to push aside the collapsing bodies to get into the mess. Six armed men stood to his right beyond the sweep of a tripod-mounted camera. Two more were near the video equipment and another stood in front of it, a piece of paper in one hand, a curved sword in the other.

Fiona Katamora sat behind him, her mouth gagged but her eyes bright.

Cabrillo took in this tableau in the first half of a second and made his threat evaluation in the next. The executioner would need to move to make his killing stroke, and the men working the camera had left their weapons on the deck.

Juan skidded to his knees for a more stable firing position and then cut into the six terrorists. Two went down before they knew he was in the room. A third died as he tried to sweep his rifle into his hands. Because of the H&K's notorious barrel rise on full automatic, number five was a double-tap headshot that sent brain tissue spinning through the air.

Cabrillo had to release the trigger for an instant to adjust. Number six opened fire before he'd drawn a bead. Rounds pinked off the wall to Juan's right, chipping white paint off the metal and throwing ricochets in every direction.

The Chairman got his sight picture and let fly, drilling the gunman with a steady burst that threw him bodily into a bulkhead. He turned to the swordsman. The guy had the fastest reaction reflex Juan had ever seen. Four seconds had elapsed since he'd fired the first shots. Any normal human would have spent half that processing what his senses were telling him.

But not the swordsman.

He was moving the instant Juan's eyes had first swept past him. He drew back the sword, pirouetting in a graceful display, and had the blade arcing toward Fiona Katamora's exposed neck even before the sixth gunman went down.

Hyped on adrenaline, Juan watched it happen like it was slow motion. He began swinging the H&K's stubby barrel, knowing it was too late. He fired anyway, and from across the room the videographer pulled a pistol from a holster Cabrillo hadn't seen.

A line of raging pain creased the side of Juan's head and his vision went black.

THIRTY-SEVEN

A LI GHAMI GLANCED AT HIS WATCH FOR ABOUT THE
dozenth time since Qaddafi had started speaking. And
he kept looking over at an assistant, who hovered near the
front door, a radio bud in his ear. Every time he met the man's
eyes, the aide would shake his head imperceptibly.

Charles Moon's bodyguard had pointed out the behavior
to him, and as he studied the Libyan Minister more closely he
saw other signs of his disquiet. Ghami was constantly shifting
from foot to foot, or thrusting his hands into his jacket pocket
only to remove them an instant later. Many guests were growing tired of the long speech, which was now closing in on a
half hour, but Ghami seemed more agitated than bored.

He looked again at his aide. The suited man was turned
slightly away, his hand to his ear to listen better over Qaddafi's droning voice. He turned back a moment later and nodded at Ghami, a smile of triumph spread across his face.

"Showtime," Moon's guard said nonchalantly.

Ghami climbed one of the steps to get the Libyan President's attention. When Qaddafi cut off his rambling praises

of Fiona Katamora, the Minister climbed higher and whispered into his ear.

Qaddafi visibly paled. "Ladies and gentlemen," he said, his voice, which had been so compassionate and clear moments earlier, quavering. "I have just been given the worst news possible."

Moon translated for his companion's sake.

"It appears that the beloved American Secretary of State managed to survive the horrific airplane crash." This was met with a collective gasp, and conversations sprang up spontaneously all around the room. "Please, ladies and gentlemen, your attention, please. This is not what it seems. Following the crash, she was abducted by forces loyal to Suleiman Al-Jama. I have just been given word that they are about to carry out her execution. Minister Ghami also tells me they have a way of communicating with us in this house."

Qaddafi followed his Foreign Minister into the next room, and soon many of the more sangfroid of the guests were crammed into every corner. The guard had Moon hold back so they were still in the entry hall, peering over the shoulders of others. The television had been turned on, its pale glow making the people look like the blood had been drained from their bodies. Several women were crying.

An image suddenly sprang up on the monitor. Sitting in front of a black background was Secretary Katamora. Her hair was a tangled mess after her ordeal, and her wide dark eyes were red-rimmed. The gag tied across her mouth pulled her cheeks back in an ugly rictus, but still she looked beautiful.

The weeping intensified.

A man hiding his features with a checked kaffiyeh stepped into view. He carried a sword with a small nick in its blade. "We, the servants of Suleiman Al-Jama, come before you tonight to rid the world of another infidel," he said. "This is our answer to the Crusaders' efforts to thrust their decadence upon us. From this unholy woman has come the worst of their lies, and for that she must die."

Moon's guard watched Ghami's reaction closely. Something about what was playing out on the television had him off-kilter.

Qaddafi picked up the small camera from the television stand and held it at arm's length. "My brother," he said. "My Muslim brother who basks in the light of Allah, peace be upon him. This is no longer the way. Peace is the natural order of the world. Bloodshed only begets bloodshed. Can you not see that taking her life will accomplish nothing? It will not end the suffering in the Muslim world. Only discourse can do that. Only when we sit facing our enemies and discussing what brought us to such a state can we ever hope to live in harmony.

"The Koran tells us there can be no harmony with the infidel.

"The Koran also tells us to love all life. Allah has given us this contradiction as a choice for each man to make. The time for choosing hatred is over. Our governments are meeting now so we make this same choice for all our people. I beg you to lay down your sword. Spare her life."

No one could see the swordsman's features because of the headscarf, but his body language was easy enough to read. His shoulders slumped, and he let the heavy scimitar fall from view.

Then, from the back of the reception hall, came the sound of running feet, dozens of them pounding across the marble floor.

The plan was falling apart.

Ali Ghami yanked the camera from Qaddafi's hand. "Mansour," he screamed at his bodyguard, "what are you doing? Our gunmen are here. Kill her! Do it now!"

Rather than take up his sword again to slice off her head, the figure on the television helped pull the gag from Secretary Katamora's mouth.

"Mansour," Ghami cried again. "No!"

Someone yanked the camera away from the Minister at the same time he felt the barrel of a pistol crammed into his spine. He looked over to see an Asian man, Charles Moon's bodyguard, standing behind him.

"Game's up, Suleiman," Eddie Seng said. "Take a look."

On the monitor, the man Ghami thought was his most trusted confidant pulled the kaffiyeh from around his head.

"How'd it go?" Chairman Cabrillo asked, half his head swaddled in bandages.

"I think the term is *red-handed*."

The squad of President Qaddafi's personal bodyguards came to a halt in the entrance to report that they had overwhelmed the security personnel outside without needing to fire a shot.

Qaddafi, who'd been briefed on the operation by Charles Moon earlier in the afternoon, rounded on his Minister. "The charade is over. After receiving an anonymous tip this afternoon, members of the Swiss military raided the house where you've been holding my grandson after faking his death in an automobile accident. He is safe, so you can no longer sit like an asp at my breast threatening to strike if I don't allow you free rein.

"I truly did not know you were Al-Jama. I thought you blackmailed me to attain your current position for selfish gains of power. But now you have exposed yourself to the world. Your guilt is without question, and your execution will be swift. And I will work tirelessly to rid my government of anyone who even spoke of you highly."

Qaddafi spread his arms to encompass the important people in the room. "We stand united in rejecting your ways, and the failure of your plot to kill leaders from other Muslim nations will serve as notice to others who stand in the way of peace. Take this piece of garbage from my sight."

A burly Libyan soldier grabbed Ghami by the scruff of the neck and frog-marched him through the stunned crowd.

From the television came a woman's voice.

"Mr. President, I couldn't have said that better myself." Fiona Katamora was standing at Juan's side. "And I want to assure all the conference's attendees that I will be at the bargaining table tomorrow morning at nine o'clock sharp so together we can all usher in a new era."

• • •

THE BULLET THAT GRAZED the Chairman's head in the frigate's mess had knocked him out for only a second while the single round he'd managed to fire had done something far more remarkable. It had hit the sword as it swung, throwing off the executioner's aim. The blade had struck the metal back of the chair, knocking it sideways and tumbling Fiona to the deck.

Lying on the floor, Juan triggered off a pair of three-round bursts, killing the cameraman and his assistant. The swordsman had lost his weapon, and he backed away from Fiona, holding his hands over his head.

"Please," he begged. "I am unarmed."

"Uncuff her," Juan ordered. "And remove her gag."

Before he could comply, the man who'd been threatening her life moments ago wet himself.

"It's a little tougher facing armed men in combat than blowing up innocents, eh?" Juan mocked. When the gag came off, he asked the Secretary, "Are you okay?"

"Yes. I think so. Who are you?"

"Let's just say I'm the spirit of Lieutenant Henry Lafayette and leave it at that." Juan pulled the hand radio from his pant pocket. "Max, do you copy?"

"About damned time you called in," Max said so gruffly that Cabrillo knew he was beside himself with concern.

"I've got her and we're on our way out."

"Make it quick. The *Sidra*'s accelerating, and we've only got about two minutes for your extraction plan to work."

Fiona got to her feet, massaging her wrists where the cuffs had dug into her skin. She kept a wary distance from the swordsman but did the most astonishing thing Juan could imagine. She said, "I forgive you, and someday I pray you will come to see me not as your enemy but as your friend." She turned to Juan. "Do not kill this man."

Cabrillo was incredulous. "With all due respect, are you nuts?"

Without a backward glance, she strode from the room. Juan made to follow, turned back on the swordsman, and fired a single shot. He grabbed the script from the deck where it had fallen and noted the frequency the television camera was going to broadcast on, the final piece of his plan. When he caught up to her, he said, "I couldn't have him follow us, so I put one through his knee."

He took her hand, and together they raced for the main deck. The smoke, he noticed, was much thinner. A pair of sailors was on the top landing of the stairs. They didn't react until they recognized the Japanese-American Secretary of State. As if choreographed, they jumped at her simultaneously. Juan shot one as he flew, and the bullet's impact was enough to alter his trajectory. The second slammed into Juan's chest with enough force to blow the air from his lungs. Choking to refill them, Juan was defenseless for several moments, an opening the sailor took to throw a quick series of punches.

Fiona tried to wrestle him off her rescuer, and had she not been through the ordeal of the past few days she would have succeeded, but she was exhausted beyond her body's limit. The sailor shoved her aside contemptuously and threw a kick that caught Cabrillo on the chin.

From outside the confines of the ship came a roar that rattled the stairwell.

A missile had streaked off a hidden launch tube buried on the *Oregon*'s deck. It lifted into the growing darkness on a fiery column that seemed to split the sky. The explosive-tipped rocket began to topple almost immediately on its short projected flight.

The sound galvanized the Chairman, and he found a berserker's fury. The kick had rattled his brain, so he fought on instinct alone. He ducked as the next blow came at him and smashed his elbow down on the sailor's exposed shin with enough force to snap the bone.

The man screamed when he put weight on it and the shattered ends grated against one another. Juan gained his feet, rammed a knee into the sailor's groin, and pushed him down the rest of the steps. He grabbed Fiona's hand, and they rushed for the exit.

The hatch he had used to gain entry into the *Sidra*'s superstructure was closed, and when he opened it, expecting to see the *Oregon* hard against the frigate's side, he saw instead that his ship was a good thirty feet away. In her wake, the rocket's contrail hung in the air, a twisting snake that corkscrewed into the night.

From the far side of the frigate came an explosion much more powerful than anything felt since the battle had begun. The ship-to-shore rocket had impacted on the inside of the main sluice gates for the Zonzur Bay Tidal Power Station.

• • •

EIGHT ASSAULT RIFLES POURED their deadly fire into the mouth of the side cave. Stone chips and ricochets filled the air like a swarm of angry hornets. All four Americans were bleeding from multiple hits, though no one had as serious an injury as Eric Stone's shoulder.

There was so much coming in at them that there was no way they could return fire, so they hunkered near the entrance as the terrorists advanced behind a wall of lead.

One gunman suddenly burst into the cave, shouting wildly. He fired from the hip, raking the walls, tearing apart the bed, and blowing books off the shelves. Linda hit him with a three-round burst to the chest before he could aim at any of them, blowing his body back out into the main cavern.

It had been dumb luck that she had killed him before he got any of them, and she knew that wouldn't happen again. Next time, the entire team would rush them, and it would be over.

Linda checked her ammo. She had no spare magazines in her harness, and the clip jammed into her rifle's receiver was only half full. Eric was out of rounds and held his weapon like a club, ready to defend himself hand to hand. Mark Murphy couldn't have very many bullets left either, she knew.

A lifetime of defending her country had come down to this last stand in a dark cave far from home, fighting a bunch of fanatics who wanted nothing more than the right to keep on killing.

The firing outside the cave slackened slightly. They were preparing for the final push.

A grenade flew out of the smoke-filled passage and landed in the alcove loaded with chests. The wood absorbed half of the blast, belching splinters and glittering gold coins while the spray of shrapnel peppered the cave walls. Again, no one had been hit, but the concussion left them reeling. Bits of burning wood had landed on the beds and caught the linens on fire. In seconds, the air was choked with smoke.

Eric screamed something to Linda, but she couldn't hear him with her ringing ears. They would come now, she was certain. In the wake of the grenade's detonation, the terrorists had to know they had them. Filthy, aching, emotionally raw, she tightened her finger around the REC7's trigger.

But nothing happened for long seconds. Of the seven surviving terrorists, only one or two were firing into the cave now. They were waiting us out, Linda thought, knowing the smoke will force us to them, or hoping we die in the fire.

Lying prone to get out of the worst of it, Linda took tiny sips of the fouled air, but each breath seared her lungs. Assad's men were going to get their wish, she thought grimly. They couldn't stay here much longer. She looked over at Eric and Mark, her eyes questioning. They seemed to read her mind and both nodded their assent. Linda scrambled to her knees and launched herself onto her feet, her shipmates at her side.

"Let's go, Sundance," Mark shouted as they charged into the mouths of the waiting guns.

They sprinted past the burning drapery over the cave's entrance and made a good five feet and still hadn't drawn fire. Linda searched for a target in the wavering light of the ship burning in the distance but spotted no one standing to face them. There was a terrorist sprawled on the ground a few paces from her, a neatly drilled hole between his shoulder blades. Then she saw others they had somehow managed to hit. The cavern floor was littered with them. Her headlong rush slackened until she stood stock-still with a total of eight bodies at her feet.

She felt a superstitious tingle run the length of her spine.

One of the men moved weakly, clawing at the sand and gasping for air. Like the first, he'd been hit in the back. Mark kicked the AK out of the man's reach and rolled him over. Frothy blood from his ruptured lung bubbled from his lips. Linda had never seen Tariq Assad, so she didn't recognize his distinctive unibrow.

"How?" he gasped.

"Your guess is as good as ours, pal," Mark told him.

And then over the crackling of the burning *Saqr* and through the ringing in their ears came a rich melodious baritone singing, "From the Halls of Montezuma / To the shores of Tripoli; / We fight our country's battles / In the air, on land and sea."

"Linc?" Linda cried.

"How you doing, sweet stuff?" He emerged from his cover position with his rifle cocked on his hip and a pair of night vision goggles pulled down around his neck. "Got here as fast as I could, but this bod wasn't made for running across the damned desert."

Linda threw her arms around the big man, sobbing into his chest, the depth of determination to face her enemies in a suicidal charge dissolving into profound relief at being alive. Mark and Eric pounded his back, laughing and choking on the smoke at the same time.

"Looks like you guys made a good show for yourselves." Which, from Linc, was his greatest sign of respect.

Alana staggered from the cave, her torso bare and once-white bra blackened with soot. She was holding a couple of books as gingerly as she could. Their pages smoldered. When one started burning, Mark took it from her, dropped it on the ground, and kicked sand over it to snuff the flames.

"I wanted to save more," she managed between coughs, "but the smoke. I couldn't. I did get this, though."

"What's that?" Linc asked.

Dangling from a crudely fashioned chain of silver was a small crystal nestled in a rudimentary setting. The piece of jewelry wasn't particularly attractive; in fact, it looked almost like a child's attempt at making a Mother's Day present out of pipe cleaners and paste. But there was something compelling about it beyond its obvious antiquity, an aura as if it were a presence there in the cave with them.

A bullet had shattered the stone, so it lay in its cradle in tiny shards no bigger than grains of sugar, and from it oozed a single claret drop.

"Holy God," Mark said, dropping to his knees to scoop up

the soaked spot of sand. From a shirt pocket, he pulled out a power bar and ripped away its wrapping. He threw the food aside and carefully placed the tiny bit of mud on the paper and twisted it closed. There was a red streak on his palm that mingled with the blood from a deep cut he'd received at some point during the battle.

"When the covers burned away," Alana explained, "I realized there was a mummy on the bed, placed on his side facing Mecca as a good Muslim should. This was around his neck. Henry Lafayette must have placed Al-Jama like that when the old man died and left him with his greatest treasure. That is the Jewel of Jerusalem, isn't it? And that was His blood, preserved for two thousand years in a vacuum within that crystal."

"His blood?" Linc asked. "Who His?"

"Stuffed in that candy wrapper in Mark's hands may be the blood of Jesus Christ."

● ● ●

THE TIDAL STATION'S MASSIVE steel gate stretched for more than a hundred feet above the generating plant set in the desert depression. When the facility was operating at full capacity, the gate could be lowered more than thirty feet to allow water to flow into large-diameter pipes down into the long turbine room more than a hundred feet below sea level. With the sun setting rapidly to the west, the gate had been closed and the turbines idled so crews could remove excess salt left over by the sun's evaporation, the key to the zero-emissions facility.

The missile off the *Oregon* hit the exposed machinery that operated the gate dead center, blowing apart the hydraulic systems and smashing the gears that acted as a mechanical brake. Even the pressure of the ocean it was designed to withstand couldn't keep the heavy door pinned in place, and it started to lower on its own accord into a recess built into the artificial dike.

Water spilled over the top of the gate, first in thin erratic sheets tossed by waves lapping against the structure, and then in a solid curtain when it fell below the surface. With less surface exposed to the titanic forces holding back the Mediterranean, the gate accelerated downward. The curtain turned into a gush, and then into a torrent more powerful than the worst levee break on the Mississippi River. Millions of tons of seawater poured through the gap. The pipes to carry the water into the powerhouse were closed, saving the delicate turbines, so the deluge flowed wild and uncontained down the dike into the desert.

Even when the plant wasn't active, there was a two-mile exclusion zone around the facility for all shipping. It was a rule Max Hanley had gladly ignored. He'd been shepherding the *Gulf of Sidra* into the exact right position for when the missile hit. Up on the main view screen, he watched the ocean disappearing into the gap on the far side of the frigate, but, more important, he could feel the pull of the current in the way his beloved ship responded to his controls.

The *Sidra* had sheered away from the *Oregon* as soon as they were in the gravity-induced vortex, sucked toward the opening as surely as if she'd been aimed at it. Max goosed the directional thrusters and closed the gap, keeping one eye on the camera feed showing where Juan would appear.

"Come on, buddy. We don't have all day."

The Chairman suddenly burst through the frigate's hatchway, holding the hand of Secretary Katamora. Max steepened his angle and closed the gap, so the two ships brushed just enough to scrape a little paint off her hull. Juan was on the *Sidra*'s railing at that exact moment. He lifted Fiona off the deck and hurled her onto the *Oregon*, where she fell into the waiting arms of a still-woozy Mike Trono.

As soon as Juan's boots hit the deck, Max pulled the big freighter away from the stricken frigate and opened the throttles as far as they would go. The warship was also desperately trying to get clear of the maelstrom. Smoke belched from her stack and her props beat the water frantically, and yet she lost more ground with every passing moment.

The *Oregon*'s revolutionary engines gave her ten times

the power, and once water was humming through the tubes her lateral motion checked and she started to pull away. Max even eased back on the controls a touch, never wanting to push his babies harder than he had to.

The *Sidra*'s hull slammed into the open sluice intake at a perfect broadside. Water continued to rush under her keel, but half the floodwaters were suddenly contained once again. Balanced precariously, with the sea pressing in on the hull so her steel moaned at the strain, the crew could do nothing as the ship that had foiled their perfect plan steamed serenely away.

On the *Oregon*'s deck, the Corporation operators who'd been blown back by the RPG clustered around the Chairman and his guest. So little time had elapsed since that fateful moment that medical staff hadn't even arrived, but it looked as if Doc Huxley and her team weren't going to be busy after all. The injuries appeared minor.

Juan stuck out a hand to formally introduce himself to Fiona. "I want to say it is an honor to meet you. My name's Cabrillo, Juan Cabrillo. Welcome aboard the *Oregon*."

She brushed aside his hands and hugged him tightly, repeating her thanks into his ear over and over again. The thing about adrenaline heightening one's senses was that it had that effect on *all* of them, so before Fiona realized how much Juan was enjoying the contact he gently untangled himself from her willowy arms.

"I know you're a woman of many accomplishments, but I wonder if acting is among them?"

She looked at him askance. "Acting? After what we just went through you're talking about acting. You call *me* nuts."

He slipped an arm around her waist to lead her into the ship's interior. "Don't worry, you get to play yourself, and we just practiced the scene I want to reproduce for Ali Ghami."

"You know?"

"I even know how he got leverage on Qaddafi. His grandson was in Switzerland on vacation when he was killed in a car crash. The crash was staged and the boy kidnapped. If Qaddafi ever wanted to see the kid alive again, he had to make Ghami Foreign Minister, not knowing that he had just

made one of the worst terrorists in the world a senior government official and given him access to everything he needed
to pull off his little caper."

"And you?" Fiona asked. "How do you fit in with all of
this?"

He gave her a squeeze. "Just lucky, I guess."

EPILOGUE

THE SENIOR STAFF WAS ASSEMBLED ON THE AFT
helicopter pad when George Adams brought Hali Kasim
back to the ship from a Tripoli hospital. Hux had a wheelchair standing by, and she turned away from the chopper as
it flared in over the *Oregon*'s fantail.

The skids kissed dead center. Gomez killed the turbines.
Everyone rushed forward under the spinning blades to pound
on the rear door glass, laughing and aping for Hali as he sat
strapped in, a johnny pulled loosely over his heavily ban-
daged chest. He'd undergone five hours of surgery to repair
the damage Assad's bullet had done to his internal organs
and endured a week of hospital food before his doctors would
allow him to leave.

But he was the last of them home after what had been
perhaps the toughest mission the Corporation had ever
undertaken. At dawn, they had rendezvoused with their two
wandering lifeboats full of ex-prisoners. The Foreign Minister already had his old job back and was at the conference.
Adams had picked up Linda and the others from the desert

cave not long afterward. When they had emerged from the cavern, they discovered Professor Emile Bumford bound and gagged at the entrance. The two gundogs who'd gone into the drink during the attack on the *Sidra* had been picked up, half drowned, by the rescue Zodiac with nothing worse than flash burns on their hands and faces. Hux and her staff had patched them up, tended Alana's hands and Eric's shoulder, and removed what seemed like a pound of stone shrapnel from the group Mark dubbed the "Fantastic Four."

Alana had remained on the *Oregon* for just a night. She was anxious to return to Arizona and her son. Unfortunately, without any kind of provenance and with its crystal ruined, no one would risk their career by saying definitively if the necklace she'd found was indeed the fabled Jewel of Jerusalem. The real team of archaeologists who'd been excavating the Roman villa had been sent into the caverns after the pall of smoke had been extracted. The *Saqr* had been reduced to ashes, and only the gold remained in the side chamber. But it in itself was a numismatist's wildest dream come true. The gold was mostly in the form of coins from every nation of Europe and every corner of the old Ottoman Empire, stretching back hundreds of years. It was the accumulated hoard of generations of the Al-Jama family, and even the most conservative estimate put the coins' worth ten times higher than the value of the gold alone.

The delegates at the Tripoli Accords had already declared that the proceeds of the sale of so many perfectly preserved and diverse coins would help fund antipoverty programs across the Muslim world. And that was only the beginning of the sweeping reforms the leaders had on the table.

A half dozen helping hands eased Hali Kasim out of the chopper and into the waiting wheelchair.

"You don't look so bad to me," Max said, wiping at his eyes.

"I'm still on pain meds, so I don't feel so bad either," Hali replied with a grin.

"Welcome back." Juan shook his hand. "You sure took one for the team this time."

"I'll tell you, Chairman, I don't know what was worse:

getting shot or getting so completely bamboozled. Mossad agent, my brown butt. I just hope he suffered in the end."

"Don't you worry about that," Linc said. "Lung shot's about the worst way to go."

The bright note about the archaeological finds from the tomb were the three books Alana had managed to save. One was Henry Lafayette's Bible, which he'd left with his mentor, and another was Suleiman Al-Jama's personal Koran. The third was a detailed treatise on ways the two great religions could and should coexist if all of the faithful were strong enough to live up to the moral standards set down in the sacred texts. The writing had already been authenticated, and while some of the diehards called it a forgery and a Western trick, others—many, many others—were heeding the Imam turned pirate turned peacenik's words.

No one kidded themselves, least of all Juan Cabrillo, that terrorism was about to end, but he was optimistic that it was on the wane. He'd have no problem with that, even if it meant that the *Oregon* would head for the breaker's yard and he would light out for a tropical retirement.

Everyone followed Hali as he was wheeled into the ship except for Max and Juan. They lingered over the fantail next to the Iranian flag their ship sported. Water churned in the big freighter's wake as she started to get under way again.

Max took out his pipe and jammed it between his teeth. The fantail was too windy and exposed to light it. "Couple pieces of good news for you. A team of NATO commandoes raided the new base Ghami's people were building in the Sudan. With their leader imprisoned, they put up only token resistance. Not so, however, the ones still in Libya. The last of them tried to storm the prison where he's being held."

"And . . ." Juan prompted.

"Shot dead, to a man. A single guard was killed by a suicide blast when he tried to take one of them prisoner. Oh, hey," Max exclaimed, suddenly remembering something, "I read your final report this morning about this whole fur ball. Question for you."

"Shoot."

"On the *Sidra*, when you went back after the Secretary told you not to shoot Ghami's bodyguard . . ."

"Mansour."

"Right, him. You wrote you kneecapped him. Is that true?"

"Absolutely," Juan said without taking his eyes off the horizon. "Marquess of Queensberry rules, remember? Those are the restrictions we've placed on ourselves. Come to think of it, actually, I could have been a little more detailed in the report. I didn't mention that Mansour was bent over one of his men trying to get his weapon in such a way that his head was on the other side of the knee I blew out. I don't believe the good Marquess ever said anything about bullets overpenetrating."

Max chuckled. "I think that's true. Say, what was it Hux told you just before Hali arrived?"

"I'm not sure if you want to know." There was an odd undercurrent in Juan's voice. "I'm still trying to get my mind around it."

"Go ahead, I can take it," Max said in a way to lighten the suddenly somber mood.

"She managed to analyze the fluid that leaked out of the jewel. It was pretty degraded, and there was only a minute amount, so she can't verify her findings. Her official report states 'inconclusive.'"

"But . . . ?"

"It was human blood."

"Could be anybody's. Al-Jama might've made that jewel himself and used his own."

"Carbon dating puts the sample between fifty B.C. and eighty A.D. The real kicker is, she only found female DNA."

"It's a woman's blood?"

"No, the chromosomes proved the blood came from a man, only he had one hundred percent mitochondrial DNA, even outside the mitochondria, and please don't ask me to explain. Hux tried and just gave me a headache. Bottom line is, the mitochondrial DNA is only passed on to us through our mothers."

Max felt a chill despite the balmy weather. "What does it mean?"

"It means that the mother of whoever that blood belonged to provided all his DNA. One hundred percent. The father made zero contribution. It was almost as if he didn't exist."

"What are you saying?"

"Her words were something like if she were to imagine the blood work of a person who was of virgin birth, what we found was it."

"Jesus."

Max said it as a blasphemous expression of awe, but Juan responded to his comment anyway. "Apparently."